Human Capital

GRAHAM CUTMORE

Part One

Chapter One

"Don't get me wrong," said Terry, weighing the change in his hand and vacantly staring at the coins before slipping them into the front pocket of his trousers. "I liked the bloke."

David nodded and held out his glass in preparation for the usual ceremony.

"Cheers!" Terry banged his glass forcefully against his companion's, causing some of the froth to overflow and run down David's hand.

"Cheers," David replied. He brought the glass up to his mouth and took two uncertain sips. The beer had the same sour smell that pervaded the whole pub; he could never understand why the place was so popular.

"No," Terry went on, though it wasn't clear what, if anything, he was disagreeing with. He stopped again; he now wore a foam moustache and had his lips drawn back in a way that suggested the beer's after-taste was every bit as bad as its odour, but that this somehow gave him satisfaction. "No. Pleasant enough fella. But you know, not being funny..." Terry gazed round the bar and then looked intently at his companion with a pained expression on his face. "Well, you know," he continued, gesticulating widely with his free hand, "a lot of people were surprised at the time when he got the job. Great guy, maybe, but he was never really up to it, was he? At that level?" Terry suddenly became aware that David was not responding. "Was he?" he persisted.

David shrugged and nodded at the same time. "I suppose not," he began. "I don't know, I mean I never really worked with the guy. Met him a few times, seemed nice enough."

"Nice?" Terry pretended to choke on his beer, and then coughed exaggeratedly into his hand. "Nice? But this market isn't about nice, is it?"

"So what version of the story have you heard?" David asked quickly. He didn't want to get into a debate and was hoping to set Terry off on a long speech that he wouldn't necessarily have to listen to.

"Shall we get away from the bar?" Terry responded, turning away as he did so. David made an awkward about-turn and excused his way through a tight group of a dozen people standing immediately behind him. A few seconds later he exited into a clearer area where a number of elevated round wooden tables grew out of the floor. One of them appeared to have free space to one side and David headed towards it.

"This do?" he asked.

Terry wordlessly deposited his glass on the varnished surface. David did the same.

"Christ," Terry exclaimed, "it's like Piccadilly Circus in here today. Doesn't anyone do any work any more?"

"Just you and me, Terry," David replied with a smile.

"Too right."

"So anyway."

"So anyway what?"

"You were telling me about Ray Hudson?"

"Oh yeah, right."

Terry wasn't about to be rushed. He picked up his glass, took a long draught from it and then put it back down again. "The way I heard it," he began with perceptible relish, "- and this is a reliable source pretty close to the ground - is this. Right up until almost the end the company thought he was doing the bizzo, except he wasn't. Hadn't been for years! Must have been kosher at first or he wouldn't have got anywhere, but then they keep promoting him and he gets out of his depth, and when he can't meet his targets he panics and starts altering the paperwork so it looks like he has. And when no-one ever notices he starts thinking to himself that just changing the numbers is a lot less hassle than actually getting the biz, so he keeps going."

"How long did that go on for?" David asked.

Terry didn't welcome the interruption; he tried to wave the question away. "Best part of ten years, I think. Anyway.."

"I didn't think he was there that long."

"Well, whatever," Terry replied shortly. "He was at it for a long time, anyway. I couldn't tell you whether he started at half past four on a Tuesday!"

David was tiring of the conversation already; he doubted that Terry was going to tell him anything that he didn't already know. On the other hand it was just about preferable to going back to the office. "How did he get away with it?" he asked, trying to sound interested.

"Dunno. I guess nobody checked." Terry laughed. "If we knew how he got away with it we'd all be trying it, wouldn't we?"

David laughed as well. "Maybe. How much was involved?"

Terry picked up his glass, downed half a pint in two mouthfuls and then wiped his lips with the back of his hand. "Quite a lot. A few mill."

"Jesus! That much?"

Terry nodded seriously. "Sure. He had a hell of a lifestyle. Did you ever go to his place?"

David shook his head.

Terry feigned amazement. "Never? Oh, I thought everyone had. Huge pile in Virginia Water. Swimming pool, games room, stables for the kids' horses, the lot."

"Alright for some."

"Yeah. Three kids all at expensive public schools. Ferrari 460 in the drive, and a Range Rover for the wife."

"Wow," said David, who was pretty sure that Ferrari had never made a 460. "So what happened?"

3

"In what way?"

"Well, how did he get caught?"

"He didn't."

David waited but Terry said nothing more. He looked at David and then around the bar at the other drinkers. David considered whether to drink up and go back to work; it wouldn't be difficult to find out the facts of the story from someone else: half of the market was talking about it. But finally laziness and a curiosity made more acute by the alcohol that was starting to course through his veins got the better of him.

"Right, OK," David said with a small sigh. "So why isn't he still in his job?"

"Why?" Terry asked with exactly the display of feigned incredulity that David had been expecting. "Why do you think?"

David wasn't playing any more. He blinked and looked expressionlessly into space.

"Why?" Terry continued once it became clear that David wasn't going to speak. "Because he completely lost it. Started hitting the sauce. Was turning up at the office at ten, wearing yesterday's shirt, unshaven, smelling of booze."

"At ten o'clock?"

Terry leaned back against the table and nodded with satisfaction. "Yep. And then he was off to lunch by twelve. Coming back later and later. Completely rat-arsed when he did, and sometimes not making it back at all. I saw him myself a few months back, in here, about four o'clock on a Friday afternoon, pint in his hand, obviously as pissed as a fart."

"On his own?"

Terry closed his eyes and shook his head. "Not quite. With two or three young kids from the market, little chancers he shouldn't have been bothering himself giving the time of day to, except there wasn't anyone else to play to. Fucking embarrassing it was. Shouting about how clever he was and his

4

boss was a useless cunt and all that. Obviously thinking he was impressing these kids, but you could see them looking at each other and trying not to laugh."

"And wasn't one of his company's directors in the pub?" David thought he'd already heard something along these lines.

"Yes - well no, not when I saw him," Terry's said uncertainly. He cleared his throat. "What you're thinking about," he continued with renewed authority, "is when it all blew up a week back, in *Kimono's*."

"Wasn't it the CEO or something?" David asked.

"The CFO" Terry corrected him. "Nigel Chapman. Very switched-on guy, as you know."

David shrugged. "I've never met him."

"Really? No, he's good, very sharp. You don't want to cross him though."

"So what happened next?"

"In *Kimono's*?"

"Yes," David nodded patiently. The large wooden clock on the wall behind the bar was showing twenty to three. Allowing for all landlords' habit of setting their clocks fast to ensure that the pub was cleared as soon as possible after closing time, David figured that it must be half past two. He couldn't look at his watch without offending Terry. His glass was almost empty, as was Terry's, which meant that he had only a couple of minutes to decide whether or not to go back to work. He'd had three pints already, but that was hardly exceptional; and from experience David was fairly sure it wasn't enough to affect his judgment or visibly to alter his behaviour. He could suck an extra-strong mint on the way back to the office so that his breath didn't carry the vinegary reek of stale bitter. But another pint was a different matter: showing up at half three after four beers wouldn't be at all clever. He'd done it in the past and thought he'd got away with it, but you couldn't necessarily be sure: people noticed things and didn't always tell you what they thought; sometimes they saved information up for future use.

Perhaps he wouldn't go back at all. He hadn't done that recently. You only had to look round the pub to see how many people were in no hurry at all to get back to work, so there was nothing to feel guilty about. And he did do business with Terry, so if push came to shove then he could say that Terry had wanted him to stay, and it wasn't in the company's interest to upset him. Lastly it was Friday: the weekend beckoned. David put his hand inside his jacket and started to bring out his wallet.

"You know what the layout is like in *Kimono's*," Terry was saying. What else, if anything, Terry had been saying in the last few seconds, David wasn't sure.

David shook his head. "Never been there."

Terry was wide-eyed. "What? Never?" He looked over to the door and then back at David. "Not being funny, do you fucking know anywhere?" he asked loudly. "Or anyone?"

David instantly changed his mind. He looked at his watch.

"Oh God," he said with what he hoped sounded like genuine surprise, "I need to get back. I've got a client meeting at three." He smiled half-apologetically at Terry as he pushed his empty glass away. "Sorry. I'll have to owe you one."

Although he'd almost run out of the pub, once out of sight David slowed down and took a leisurely stroll back towards his office, stopping at a newsagent's kiosk on the way to buy some mints and taking the opportunity to flick through some of the men's 'lifestyle' magazines for a couple of minutes. He wondered if anyone really did live like that.

He felt very relaxed. In addition to the growing effect of the alcohol in his bloodstream it was a warm, sunny, summer's day and the weekend was within his grasp. A lot of young people in shirtsleeves and impossibly cool sunglasses were standing outside wine bars in a lazy hum of laid-back conversation, broken here and there by a sudden explosion of laughter.

David's pace slowed again as his company's building came into view. In the sunshine it resembled more than ever the plastic ice-cube tray from a home freezer, turned on its side and painted silver. As he turned into the familiar entrance, with its large 'TLO' logo etched into the ground-floor glass, David puzzled over his relationship with Terry. During David's marriage to Sonia they had often socialised with Terry and his wife at weekends. Barbecues, all that sort of thing. A few corporate days out as well. They'd even been away on holiday once, a week in Terry's place in Marbella. David couldn't remember why. In retrospect it seemed a strange thing to have done.

"Hi," said a female voice as David came through the door. Jill's face was ghoulishly illuminated for a brief moment by the light from the photocopier that she habitually used without lowering the lid. "We were just about to send out a search party for you," she said with a smile that accentuated the ring of lip gloss around her mouth. "Simon's been asking where you are for the past half hour."

"Has he?" David felt the muscles in his stomach begin to tighten. "What for?"

"Your three o'clock?"

"With?"

Jill looked down at one of the pieces of paper that she had been photocopying. "First Denver? Ring any bells?"

"Oh yes," David replied, "I think they're very big in Colorado." He listened to his own voice for signs of slurring and was relieved to find none.

Jill nodded seriously then thrust her sheaf of papers into David's chest. "Simon wanted these for the meeting," she announced briskly, "so you might as well take them with you. Room 12."

"Thanks." David made his way along the corridor, trying to remember what he knew about First Denver. A couple of faces came into his mind, but no names. That was always the difficult part.

He entered the room, which to his surprise was in half-light, offered a timid English apology for his lateness and stumbled across to an empty chair between two that were already occupied. Simon gave him a well-practised see-me-afterwards glare.

"No problem," said a deep, slow, heavily-accented American voice that belonged to a middle-aged thickset man standing by a screen at the far end of the room. "Great to see you again, David."

The man moved towards him and David awkwardly stood up again just as he was easing himself into the seat, taking the stranger's outstretched hand and maintaining his balance only by using his free arm to prop himself up against the table.

"Likewise," was all he could find to say.

The visitor smiled and lumbered back towards the screen. It was a gait that denoted a leg problem, David thought, or excess weight; or maybe a bit of both. Or gout.

The person on David's left pushed a business card towards him through the gloom. Someone on the other side of the wide table stood up and tried to skim his own card across. It spun in the wrong direction and stopped in the middle of the table. The two men tried to retrieve it from an area that they could both barely reach until David, with one foot off the floor, finally succeeded.

He sat down and once more met the cold stare of Simon, and an almost identical expression on the face of Guy who, he noticed for the first time, was sitting to his boss's left. David stared back at Guy until the latter was forced to look away.

"I was just sharing with these folks the great news about the year we just had at First Denver," the American, who had resumed his position at the far end of the room, was saying. To illustrate his point he pointed at the screen. It was displaying some sort of chart with two y-axes and a confusing mixture of lines and bars. But everything on the right was generally higher than everything on the left, which led the viewer to suppose that on the whole things were improving. The slide was finished off, in the lower right-hand corner, with the words *'First Denver'* and then some sort of logo in the form of a short, coiled-up rope ending in an arrow pointing skyward. There were several more exhibits, in rapid succession, in the same vein. Sales were up, profits were up, profits per unit of sales were up. Costs were down. David nodded in a show of approval.

"Best of all," the slim, dark-haired man on David's left interjected, leaning back in his chair and pointing towards the screen. "Look at headcount. Down twelve percent in one year. Down over twenty-three percent since Mr Sorensen took over as CEO in 2000. That's a truly amazing achievement."

"Unless," David heard himself say very quietly, "you're one of the heads that is no longer being counted."

"Excuse me?"

"That's a truly amazing achievement," David agreed with a smile.

The slim man now looked in turn to Simon and Guy in the clear expectation of receiving their congratulations. David noted the man's collar-length hair with its near-centre parting and decided it must have been worn like that for the past twenty years.

"That's really great," said Simon.

"Fantastic," added Guy, who had been careful not to speak first.

The thickset man's face showed his appreciation of the sincerity of his hosts' compliments. His facial muscles tensed and his eyes moistened behind his heavy, square-framed glasses. "And don't think we don't appreciate all the help we have had from our business partners, especially you folks at TLO here in Great Britain."

"We certainly do," concurred a voice to David's right.

"It's a privilege for us to do business with you guys too," said Simon in an accent that wasn't quite English, and seemed to have picked up a number of American inflexions in the few minutes since the meeting had started.

"Well I guess it's good for both of us!" replied the thickset man, removing his glasses and wiping the lenses on the sleeve of his shirt.

Everyone laughed.

"That just about wraps it up," the American continued, "unless you have any questions?"

Simon would have, David thought. Simon always did.

"Thanks, Bob," Simon said on cue. "Can you just briefly give us a heads-up on how the Street views your forthcoming IPO?"

"Sure," said Bob. "Say, why don't you take that one, Tom?"

"My pleasure," replied the man to David's right. "Thanks, Bob. That's a great question, Simon. You know, we spend a lot of time with the analysts, but we still can't always figure out where these guys are coming from."

David turned politely to watch his neighbour speak. The man was small and muscle-less and, despite a few incipient frown-lines on his forehead, had the fresh-faced demeanour of an earnest schoolboy, an impression he had evidently attempted to dispel by growing a moustache. Unfortunately for him the two clumps of facial hair drooped at almost forty-five degrees on each side of his mouth and stubbornly refused to meet up in the middle.

"In the year or so since I became CFO…" he began.

People said that it was a sign of age when policemen started to look young. What, David wondered, did it mean if Chief Financial Officers were beginning to look like adolescents? He looked around the room. He guessed that Bob was in his early fifties, but otherwise he himself, at thirty-nine, appeared to be the oldest person present. He watched his neighbour's moustache twitch up and down while he tried to calculate in his head how many days remained before his fortieth birthday. He worked it out twice but came up with different numbers. It didn't help that he couldn't remember exactly what today's date was and he didn't like to look at his watch. He gave up; he could do the sum on the train home in a couple of hours time.

But now David became aware that the child prodigy had stopped talking and was shifting uncomfortably in his seat, asking himself why the guy who arrived late was still staring at him. Simon would no doubt be wondering the same thing. David knew that he would have to come up with an intelligent question, quickly.

"That's very interesting," he heard himself say. "Do you see First Denver's future growth being mainly organic or acquisition-led?"

A lazy, clichéd question, but the pubescent finance director seemed to appreciate it.

"That's another good question," he said, smiling enthusiastically.

Bob interrupted him. "Maybe I'll take that one, Tom. If that's OK, with you, David?"

David nodded enthusiastically. He didn't care who took it, so long as it killed some time and brought the weekend a few minutes closer. David's instincts told him that about forty minutes had already elapsed, so twenty to go, and Bob from First Denver clearly didn't go in for one-word answers. Once he had finished, Guy would feel an overwhelming need to ask something, which would set at least one of the guests off for a couple more minutes. And then Simon would want the thick end of a quarter of an hour to turn the tables and tell the First Denver people about all the great things that had been happening at TLO since their last visit, whenever that had been. Simon would be sure to have that information to hand.

"...but only if the board believes that it would be genuinely earnings-accretive," Bob concluded. Does that answer your question, David?"

David smiled warmly. "Yes. Perfectly. Thanks."

Now Guy, having glanced briefly at Simon and received no discernible discouragement, was going to have his moment: "Do you think that the fact that the Street may undervalue your stock makes you potentially vulnerable to a takeover after the IPO?" he asked earnestly.

Bob's friendly smile instantly evaporated. Bad mistake, thought David. You feed their egos by telling them they may be the predator, not the prey. Don't remind them that there are much bigger fish out there, companies who have inexplicably grown much more quickly than they have. But you need experience to know that. And you, Mr Fast-Track with your sharp suit and your mobile phone almost permanently clamped to your ear, don't have it.

"No, Sir," said Bob gravely, his chin cupped in his right hand. "We have been an independent company since 1873. In our country that's a lot of history, and we're very proud of that. With Mr Sorensen and the team he has put in place, and our aggressive new business plan, we don't believe that anybody else could run our business better."

"I didn't mean...," Guy started to protest.

"In any case," the thin man to David's left chimed in, "the IPO is only for twenty-five percent of preferred stock, so no-one could acquire us."

And Guy ought to have known that as well, thought David, if he had done his homework properly. Simon wasn't going to be at all impressed. David hoped that *schadenfreude* wasn't written too plainly on his face.

Simon decided it was necessary to take control of the situation. "No, of course not," he said with a vigorous shake of the head. "It's a non-issue. Well, thanks for an excellent, informative presentation. We are delighted at your continued success, and hope that we at TLO have played at least some small part in contributing to it. We look forward to continuing our successful business partnership for many more years. Now, if there are a few minutes left I'd like to share with you some of the exciting recent developments here at TLO."

"Sure," Bob replied with renewed enthusiasm, "we'd like to hear that." He found a chair at the end of the table nearest to the screen and sat down.

David settled back and prepared to half-listen to Simon's spiel for the umpteenth time.

"Well, as I was saying," Simon began, bending down and, in a curious, familiar mannerism, pulling his socks up, one after the other, "TLO has had a great year too. New records for both top and bottom line, earnings per share, growth in book value and at January 1 our surplus had grown to…"

David looked around him and saw three weary jet-lagged men at the end of what had probably been a long week for them, nodding politely while the tenth identical limey tried to make his company sound in some way different from the other nine. The only person who appeared excited by the story was Guy, the enthusiastic, tail-thumping, yappy dog by Simon's side, trying to re-ingratiate himself by nodding vigorously at every new statistic and smiling at each of the Americans in turn. David was sure that Guy slept in pyjamas patterned with TLO logos. He knew Simon "didn't do cynical", but even so he found it hard to believe that Simon really appreciated Guy's wholesale, unreserved, anus-invading sycophancy.

"And none of our guys gets a raise unless…"

It grated on David to hear someone who naturally had a polite, slightly clipped, minor-public-school accent trying to speak American. And ending up by adopting a soporific lilt that made sleep so inviting for the listeners, not only those whose body clock was telling them they'd been working all night, but also one who'd had three pints on a drowsy summer afternoon and just wanted the weekend to start.

David took deep breaths and forced his eyes open. It appeared that the young, moustachioed CFO had fought a similar battle and lost it. Bob was nodding politely, but his eyes were staying shut longer each time he blinked.

"... proactively adding value throughout the market cycle," Simon was concluding. "So I guess these are exciting times for us all." He banged the flat of his hand against the table to emphasise his point. Bob sat up in surprise and momentarily looked at Simon as if he had never seen him before. Tom shuffled in his seat, cleared his throat and started to arrange the papers in front of him into a concentric stack.

"You bet!" he said.

Chapter Two

Terry was on the seven twenty from London Bridge, in what was roughly his usual seat on whatever train he took, trying to focus on the *Evening Standard*. It was OK if he only used one eye, but he knew that must look pretty odd and he wasn't quite pissed enough not to care what the other people in the carriage thought of him. Appearances mattered in business, and particularly now that he had started travelling first class – probably later than he should have in rights - he didn't want to do anything that would show himself up. He'd even stopped buying *The Sun* and now read the *Mail* on the way to work instead, though he often got bored quite quickly and went directly to the sport at the back. He recalled that David Kelsey, an old associate from the market who, as it happened, he'd met for a lunchtime drink that day, said that the *Mail* was just *The Sun* with net curtains, whatever that meant, but other people in the first-class carriage seemed to read it as well, so Kelsey was just talking bollocks. Admittedly there was also one bloke most mornings who actually did read *The Sun*, but he had untidy facial stubble and shovelfuls of gold jewellery and Terry thought he was just making a deliberate show of his oikdom. Fair play to him if that's what he wanted - it was still a free country the last time anyone had checked, despite the best efforts of Tony bloody Blair and his lot - but Terry also believed that if you'd managed to make something of yourself in the world then there was no harm in letting it show from time to time. As it happened people had always described him as a class act, even before he'd actually had any money.

Right now Terry was doing his best to keep calm. Almost as soon as he had got on and begun unwrapping the burger and fries he'd just bought at the station (from a *Megaburger* concession staffed by a Chinese girl who he'd tried without success to have a joke with - something about not wanting any chopsticks. Orientals, like most ethnics, never seemed to have much sense of humour) the guy across the way, a real toffee-nosed pinstripe effort with a joke-shop major-general moustache, had started tutting. Terry ignored him and concentrated on finding his way into the little sachet of tomato sauce and then pouring it onto his chips. What was Lord Snooty's problem exactly? It wasn't as if Terry was throwing his meal around the carriage. He was minding his own business; he wasn't looking for any trouble. He was hungry, he needed food. He had a wife who, despite the large amount of money he gave her every month, provided sustenance more and more sporadically – some crap about never knowing when he was coming home. It was this or starvation.

The snobby guy was lucky that Terry had mellowed as he had got older. In his younger days, back in Hackney, Terry would have chinned the bloke by now. Even a couple of years ago he would have given him a mouthful and let him know what was what; but now he was forty-three, and he was a divisional director of a successful City firm. Even with a few beers inside him - he wasn't sure exactly how many, but he'd got to the pub at twelve thirty and left at seven, and he could still drink quicker than most - he knew he couldn't afford to get involved in a ruck on a train.

With almost exaggerated calmness he finished eating, wiped his mouth on the paper serviette, licked the salt and chip grease off his fingers and carefully put all the empty containers back inside the brown paper bag they'd come in. He quickly looked around for a bin, but couldn't immediately see one; he screwed up the bag and neatly deposited it through his legs and under the seat. He flashed a look at Sir Rupert to see if he had any sort of problem with that, but the man had sensibly hidden himself, all bar his hands and lower arms, behind a copy of the *Telegraph*. Christ, now that *was* a boring paper.

The train had been moving annoyingly slowly for a few minutes, and now it had come to a complete halt. There was no way of telling how long it might be stuck here: it could be seconds, minutes or hours. The service in first class didn't seem to be any more reliable than it was in cattle class.

Terry became aware of the noise from the headphones that the young guy opposite was wearing. To be fair he was nothing like as bad as some of the rubbish that got on, particularly late at night, in second class - some of them had so-called music you could hear from one end of the carriage to the other, and the only consolation was that you knew the selfish fuckers were permanently damaging their own hearing - but you didn't expect to pay over three grand a year (over five grand you had to earn, because the bastards wouldn't give you tax relief on fares, as if going to work was a luxury) to sit marooned at some red signal being forced to listen to a lot of moronic bongo bongo hissing coming out of some fuckwit's headphones. It wasn't as if you could even make out the tune, because there wasn't one: it was the same jungle thump that had started to come out of Terry's eldest boy's bedroom after Serena had bought him his own computer. Terry had quickly put a stop to that, at least when he was in the house.

Terry now made eye contact with the young man, who blinked and looked in the other direction, through the window. Terry decided that polite diplomacy wasn't going to work. He leaned forward with every intention of marking the youngster's card, but then paused. At closer quarters the bloke definitely looked a bit ethnic, which meant there was a very good chance that he might make a scene, and call Terry a racist (which he wasn't: it was the number of them that he objected to, not the individuals), and he could do without that. On the other hand the racket was beginning to do his head in.

"Excuse me, mate" Terry began.

"Yes?"

"Down a bit," said Terry, using his hand held out straight and flat to illustrate a downward movement. "Too loud."

The young man shrugged in a surly sort of way, but he did make some sort of adjustment to the machine before slipping his headphones back on and turning his whole body to face the window.

Terry sat back with a feeling of satisfaction. Occasionally, he thought, you could still successfully push back against the little things that were gradually eroding the quality of life in Britain.

The train still wasn't moving though. Terry looked at his watch. It was a Cartier, one of the newer ones where the face was wider than it was tall. The first time he'd seen it in the jeweller's window Terry had thought that it looked like one of those hall of mirrors distortions, but he'd noticed a few top people in the market starting to wear them, and it had grown on him.

Quarter to eight. It was difficult to say where he was: the narrow landscape he could see through the window - some Victorian terraces and a deserted, desolate children's play area - might be anywhere in South London, but he guessed the train hadn't progressed more than a couple of miles since the journey began. Perhaps he should call Serena, and tell her what was what. As if she cared as long as all her bills got paid. Still, it would pass a bit of time.

Terry took his mobile out of his inside pocket and called Serena's number. It was a while before she answered, and when she did all Terry could hear for the first few seconds was static hiss and a whooshing sound in the background.

"Hello?" Serena said finally.

"Hiya," replied Terry. "It's me."

"Where are you?"

"I'm on the train."

Lord Snooty looked disapprovingly in Terry's direction. Terry stared back until he averted his gaze.

"But it looks like we're stuck."

"Right."

"Could be fucking ages. No-one's bothering to tell us anything. Where are you?"

"I'm in the X5. I'm dropping the boys off round at Rob and Christine's for a sleepover."

Terry couldn't remember who Rob and Christine were and didn't want to know. "Just you and me tonight, then, babe," he said quietly into the phone.

There was a loud banging at the other end of the line and then a couple of shorter thumps and four or five seconds of intermittent booming and screeching before Serena eventually came back on the line.

"What the fuck was that?" Terry asked impatiently. "For a second I thought you'd crashed the car."

"Sorry, love." Serena laughed nervously. "I dropped the phone. Had to fish around under the seat for it. Almost had a head-on with a Transit."

"Careful," said Terry. "That's forty grand's worth of my motor there."

"No harm done."

"Anyway," Terry said insistently. "Listen. Just you and me, then."

Serena didn't seem to be taking the hint. "Just a second while I get out of this junction," she replied in a disappointingly matter-of-fact tone. "Same to you, you stuck-up cow. The bitch is giving me the finger now. Charming. Well, I suppose we could go and see a film. Dunno what's on, but there's bound to be something. Or go out for a Chinese or Indian. Depends on how long you're going to be stuck on that train."

Terry rolled his eyes; he didn't know why he bothered.

Serena was still talking. "Or... I dunno, you normally decide everything. I suppose we could get a Chinese in, open a bottle of wine and watch a DVD."

Terry thought about it; it wasn't totally unappealing. Could he manage a Chinese after the burger and fries he'd just had? Yes, he probably could. He still wouldn't want chopsticks though. "And then for afters..." he whispered into the mouthpiece.

"Do what? It's not a very good line."

"Never mind." Terry slowly shook his head. He knew what he would be asking for later; he didn't need to spell it out now.

"Have you...?" Serena gingerly began to ask.

"Have I what?" Terry was beginning to wish he hadn't made the call at all. He wondered whether he could pretend he'd gone into a tunnel where there was no signal.

"You know. Been drinking. I don't mind, it's just that..."

"Look, I've told you a hundred times before, sweetheart," Terry snapped, "this isn't the sort of job where you get anywhere sitting quietly in the corner drinking tea. I have to go out there and get the biz. I meet people, I get an intro, the deal gets done. It's a social market. It pays for everything you want and the kids and nice cars and all that."

Terry momentarily enjoyed the silence at the other end of the line. "Today I just had a quiet drink with David Kelsey, as it goes," he added more calmly.

"Oh, I've always liked him," Serena said with what sounded like genuine affection. "How is he, poor old thing?"

There was something about the way Serena always talked about Kelsey that Terry didn't quite like. It was almost certainly just a mother-hen sort of thing, because she felt sorry for him after his wife upped and left him, but even so.

"He's OK." Terry said with affected boredom. "Still needs to sort himself out though. Drifts along. I told him, people are overtaking him."

"Bless him. Is there a new woman in his life?"

"Not as far as I know," Terry replied. "As I say, it was a business lunch; I didn't get the chance to quiz him about his sex life. He had to go back early for a meeting."

"So you've been in the office all afternoon?"

"Of course." Terry thought his voice struck just the right note of indignation. "Does that meet with your ladyship's approval?"

"I didn't mean it like that."

Terry enjoyed hearing the defensive and apologetic tone in his wife's voice. He knew if he exploited it correctly there could be something in it for him tonight. That something might just possibly have lipstick around it and be clamped around his gentleman's area.

In fact Terry hadn't been anywhere near the office. Once Kelsey had gone off - he'd become a bit of a lightweight on the alcohol front of late - Terry had had no trouble in a crowded pub finding people he knew and could have a drink with. For the first hour or so he'd hooked up with a crowd of the up-and-coming guys from Carsons, four or five of them, who knew who he was in the market, though he didn't know them. He'd done most of the talking - and more than his share of the drink-buying now he thought about it – and filled them in on the way the market had operated in the old days, when most of them had still been in short trousers.

At some point, though he couldn't remember exactly when, he'd gone across the road to the new wine bar, whatever it was called, Zucchini's or something, where he'd had to endure half an hour of Ted McClelland, by some margin the market's most boring drunk and drunkest bore, prattling on about how under-appreciated he was by his employers. As if he was ever sober enough to do any work or produce any business! After that Ted must have found someone else to drive to suicide - he wouldn't have gone home before chucking-out time - and Terry had been quite content to drink on his own for a while – he didn't know exactly how long - and to watch the basketball game showing on the small TV above the bar, though it hadn't always been easy to follow the score with the sound turned down.

Terry woke up with a start. Where was he? He was on a train and it had stopped and people appeared to be getting off. He looked out of the window. He couldn't see a sign but the layout of the platforms, the uneven patches of yellow lighting, the little café just across the way, seemed familiar, and suggested that this was probably his stop. He got up quickly, pulled his jacket down from the rack and struggled into it. He then bent to retrieve the *Standard* from the floor, but changed his mind half way down. From his half-stooped position he noticed a rectangular black object next to the newspaper, which on closer inspection turned out to be his phone. He picked it up, dusted it down and put it into his pocket. The ethnic kid wasn't there any more. With any luck he'd got off at a different stop; it was a wonder the phone hadn't gone with him. The snooty guy was still there, though, looking directly at Terry as if there was a bad smell in the air. Terry couldn't let that go.

"Self-made, pal. Sheer hard work. You should try it some day," he shouted in the man's direction. But he had no time to enjoy the reaction his words produced: the doors were starting to close. Terry turned quickly and scuttled out of the carriage; the rubber seal on one of the doors bruised his arm. With a sense of unfinished business he followed up with a V-sign as the train pulled out.

It was still warm and humid with almost no breeze. Terry headed towards the car park, fumbling in his pocket for the keys as he went. On days like today he didn't mind having the SLK, with its folding roof, though it was a bit girlie, and it was a worrying development that Serena seemed to think she could dictate more and more who had what car when. He needed to be more assertive about that. But not tonight. Not unless she started giving him grief about his having suddenly nodded off on the train while she was still talking to him.

Chapter Three

As soon as the weekend actually came round, David couldn't remember why he spent so much of the working week looking forward to it.

On Saturday morning he would wake up naturally around nine, and what happened then depended on whether he was seeing his daughter. If it was a non-Amy week (and two out of three were), he would have a protracted breakfast and unhurriedly read the paper until it would occur to him, some time after eleven, that anyone who came to the door and found him still in his dressing-gown, and with the curtains drawn, might think living alone was making him a bit odd. Then he would immediately take steps to admit daylight to the flat and quickly shower before driving along the familiar route to Tesco's, where he would pick up the few items that even a single person in full time work who didn't entertain very often couldn't do without.

An Amy weekend, which theoretically his daughter was supposed to spend with him, was altogether more fraught. It filled David with guilt that he didn't look forward to them. The fact that he loved his daughter didn't mean that he always, or even usually, enjoyed her company. She was a teenage girl, and for a fortyish man there was nothing very likeable about that species. And while David was always on the lookout for things they might have in common, Amy always seemed to seek the opposite: further proof of how out-of-touch, old-fashioned, insensitive and boring her father was. The problem wasn't helped by the fact that he saw her so infrequently; his reference points when he collected her from her mother could be up to three weeks old and that, in the life of a teenager, with its sudden group-inspired shifts in fashions and attitudes, might as well have been an eternity.

24

On this particular disappointingly overcast Saturday morning David drove over to the house with no aural accompaniment beyond the thrash of the car's underpowered engine. He did not exceed any of the speed limits he encountered despite being aware more than once that he was holding up the traffic. They would have to wait; he was in no hurry to arrive at his destination before he had come up with some sort of plan to keep his daughter entertained for the day. He was relieved that she was now too old for the wretched old cliché of the zoo visit, but what was there instead?

David parked the SEAT outside the house and walked up the path. It was now two years since he had left, and he had lived there for only four, but it still seemed odd to him to approach the building as a stranger. He resented having to squeeze past John's Audi to get to the front door, and at each visit he looked out for signs of change, a bush removed or a gutter repainted, things that were gradually lessening his imprint on the place.

He rang the bell. He did still have a key - Sonia had never asked him to give it up and he had not volunteered to - but he thought it would be needlessly provocative to use it. Presumably Sonia had not had the locks changed for the same reason.

Sonia opened the door. "Hi," she said cheerily, with a broad if not wholly convincing smile. She put one hand gently on his shoulder and gave him a small peck on the cheek, as she always did now. It was like being kissed by an aunt rather than the mother of his child.

"Are you ready yet, darling?" Sonia called up the stairs with mock impatience. "Your dad's here."

David couldn't make out the words in the reply, which managed to sound angry and bored at the same time. Sonia smiled and shook her head. A few moments later there was a rumble of heavy footsteps on the staircase and then Amy appeared, carrying a large plastic bag and looking down at the floor through a curtain of hair.

"Hi, beautiful," David said chirpily. He wasn't sure himself whether his cheerfulness was intended to be ironic.

"About eight o'clock tomorrow evening OK?" Sonia asked slightly diffidently. "John and I are going away overnight, bit of a break sort of thing."

"Fine," said David, hoping that his voice didn't betray the trepidation he felt at having to spend a couple of hours more with his daughter than he had already braced himself for. "Where are you going? Anywhere nice?"

"St Neots," replied Sonia. "Nothing fancy, just a break. Just call my mobile if you…"

"I'm sure we'll be fine," David said with an optimism that he didn't feel. He smiled at Amy, who looked at her mother. "You have a good time," David continued. "You deserve a break."

Sonia scanned her ex-husband's face for evidence of sarcasm, but quickly seemed to satisfy herself that there was none to find.

"Thanks," she said. "We will."

"Are we going to stand here the *whole* day?" Amy asked.

Amy listened to music on her iPod all the way over to David's flat, which struck him as rude, and possibly deliberately so, but at least saved him from attempting what would undoubtedly be stilted conversation. It also gave him more time to think what they might do for the next thirty-three hours, less the twelve or so that, mercifully, Amy habitually slept on a Saturday night.

David had noticed that getting into the SEAT still seemed to embarrass Amy. He had owned it for three months now, and was getting to like it. It was a few years old, but one-owner and low mileage, and when clean, with its bright red paintwork, in David's opinion it could have passed for new. It wasn't a patch on the Alfa 156 they had had as a family car, but that had had to go to fund the divorce settlement. And it *was* a considerable improvement on the rusting hulk of an old Escort David had driven in the meantime, the interior smell of which had reminded him of the changing room in his school gym. He had tried to interest Amy in the SEAT when he had first bought it, but she had looked bored and then told him about John's Audi.

"This car's very similar to the Audi A3," David had told her. "Mechanically it's almost identical."

"John's is an A4," Amy had replied definitively.

They now drew up outside David's flat and got out of the car. Amy still showed no inclination to remove her earphones. A couple of years earlier her father would not have thought twice about telling her to take them off, but in the intervening period not only had a certain amount of intimacy between them been lost, but David had come to feel that as a result of the divorce (ignoring whose 'fault' it might have been) he had to a large degree forfeited any moral authority. He suspected that Amy knew it too.

David turned the key in the lock and opened the outside door, gesturing to Amy to enter ahead of him. He followed her along the corridor and then opened the door to his own flat.

It was only when Amy came to visit that he became aware of just how middle-aged and male the atmosphere of the flat was. It wasn't so much the decoration which, with its predilection for pink and yellow and floral patterns, was actually more feminine than the family home had ever been - David rented the place so couldn't do anything about that - but there were certain other things that Sonia had brought to the communal nest that David now found impossible to replicate. The kitchen was never quite clear or quite clean: however hard David tried, surfaces remained sticky; crumbs were ever underfoot despite repeated sweeping; and the bin smelt bad, spontaneously overflowed and attracted mould. The main room was too TV-centred, cushions lay scattered and squashed, last week's papers and magazines had not been cleared away. It seemed OK when he was alone, but as soon as Amy came through the door into an environment where the smell of toilet-cleaner hung in the air like the afterthought that it was, everything seemed wrong.

Amy threw her bag through the open doorway of the second bedroom then walked into the main room and hurled herself onto the sofa. She lay down almost horizontally with her trainers against the leg of the coffee-table. David followed her and sat on the upright office chair next to the computer. Amy looked up at him, languidly paused the music she was listening to but still did not remove her earphones.

"So," David began. "Is there anything special you'd like to do this weekend?"

Amy shrugged. "Whatever."

"I mean," David persevered quietly, "I've told you before, this is your home as much as Mum's is. So we don't necessarily have to go out. And you're quite welcome to invite your friends round here if you want. That's no problem at all."

Amy looked around the room then back at her father. Her expression seemed to imply that bringing her friends here would be social suicide.

"Or we can go out," David suggested brightly, wondering how long he could keep this up. "Get some food. Perhaps go and see a film together."

"Maybe."

From past experience David concluded that 'maybe' was as good as it was going to get. He moved closer to Amy. "OK. Let's do that, then. Where can we eat?"

"McDonald's?"

David laughed nervously. "We can probably do better than that. How about…"

"Whatever. We can stay here."

David dreaded trying to cook for Amy. "OK, no, fine. I didn't think you were serious. If the lady wants McDonald's, that's what the lady gets."

Amy smiled for the first time since David had picked her up. In the teenager's smile David could still see the little girl he used to rush home to see. He wanted to hug her but didn't dare.

"Cool," she said simply.

David was feeling very proud of himself considering that he had done no more than queue up for two or three minutes to buy some large hamburgers, two portions of large fries and a couple of large colas, without forgetting to bring either the paper napkins or the straws to the table which Amy had gone to reserve for them. As he approached she was texting, the phone held in one hand while her thumb flew dexterously across the keys. David wondered what she was saying. He hoped it wasn't "I'm with my Dad again - how boring is that?" or something similar. He tried not to see.

Amy did not look up but she at least turned to face the table as her father arrived and deposited the overladen tray onto the formica.

"There you go," David said encouragingly. "Tuck in."

For the next couple of minutes they hardly exchanged a word, but David was content that Amy had at last put her phone down and was obviously enjoying her food, and they shared a laugh at her strained cross-eyed expression as she tried unsuccessfully to prise open her ketchup sachet. Even better, David was then able to do it for her with a little effort, just enough for it not to appear patronising. Then, for reasons that he couldn't even begin to explain, he was absolutely delighted when his daughter quickly finished her own fries and began to eat his.

The best part of it was that Sonia didn't approve of McDonald's. So this could be something that Amy and her father could share as a guilty secret, something that Sonia had no part in. He suspected Amy might enter a vegetarian phase at some time in the next year or two, but he could enjoy these moments until then.

They had both finished their food. Amy was slurping noisily at her drink, trying to extract the last vestiges of cola from between the ice cubes. She looked happy. It seemed as though this might be the best opportunity in ages to try to talk to her. David could see that there were an increasing number of people with trays of food anxiously scanning the area, trying to find somewhere to sit. Too bad; they'd have to wait. There wouldn't be much opportunity to talk at the cinema, and by the time they were in the car again or back at the flat the atmosphere would be different, the moment lost.

"I'd say you enjoyed that," David began, with a half-wink.

"I'd say you were right," Amy replied, her eyes wide and her teeth gritted in an artificial smile. If it was teenage sarcasm, David decided, it was best to let it pass. He cleared his throat.

"So how is everything?"

"Alright."

"Anything you want to talk about?"

"Such as?"

"I don't know. School. Friends. Your mum. John. I don't know - boys?"

"Fine."

"Just fine?"

"Yep. Wicked."

"Anything I can help with?"

Amy thought about it for a moment. "Naah."

"You sure? Because I'd like to if I can."

Amy screwed her face up. "John can be a bit arsey sometimes."

David sat up. "In what way?"

"He wants Mum, he doesn't really want me."

"I see." David looked at Amy's face to see whether he was being played, but she avoided his gaze and stared at her lap. "That's quite a big statement, love," he said sympathetically.

"You asked."

David desperately wanted to avoid Amy clamming up on him. "I mean," he persisted, "what does he say? Does he do anything?"

"No, he doesn't 'do' anything," Amy replied abruptly, momentarily looking directly at her father. "It's not exactly what he says. He doesn't say anything, to me, anyway. That's it. It's as if I wasn't there."

"I'm sorry to hear that, darling," David said quietly. He felt a rising indignation at John's behaviour, together with a huge sense of relief that Amy wasn't beginning to see John as a substitute father. "You know you can call me any time you like."

Amy shrugged and looked down at the drinking straw that she had removed from her cup and was folding over on itself. "It's not the same," she mumbled.

"As what?"

"You've never told me why you left," Amy said suddenly, looking directly at David from across the table. He recognised the expression on her face; it was as though his own eyes were looking accusingly at him.

David became aware of the presence of people at the adjoining tables. "Can we talk about this back home later?" he asked emolliently. He felt confused; he thought Amy knew the story. But she had been only twelve when he had left, so maybe nobody had ever thought to explain it properly to her.

Amy shrugged again. "If you don't care," she muttered under her breath, just loudly enough for her father to hear.

"That's not fair, is it?" David replied, trying unsuccessfully to conceal the emotion in his voice.

Amy ignored him. She reached for her phone, but before he knew what he was doing David had leaned across, taken it as gently as he could out of her hand and put it into his pocket. Amy looked surprised and squirmed uncomfortably in her seat. Then she went back to studying her straw.

"That's not fair, now is it?" David insisted.

Amy's eyes were downcast and her face had flushed. It was unlikely that she was going to concede anything now, but she wasn't running away and she seemed to be listening.

"Look," David said. "You know, perhaps I wasn't the greatest husband to your mother, and I'm sure I wasn't the greatest father in the world, either, though I really was doing my best."

He knew he should stop now; he sounded as though he wanted pity, and all he would get from a fourteen-year-old would be contempt.

"I didn't want to leave. It was your mother who met John at work," he blurted out, knowing that he was breaking the pact he had made with Sonia that they would not blame each other in front of their daughter, "and now I have to see him in our old house. With your mum. And particularly with you. How do you imagine I feel?"

David stopped. He could feel a lump in his throat.

Amy just looked embarrassed and bewildered. "I don't want to talk about this," she said, her eyes darting around the restaurant to ensure that no-one was eavesdropping.

"I thought you did..."

They sat in silence.

"OK," David said softly. "Perhaps I shouldn't have... Here. Sorry." He handed over the phone.

Amy took it. "Chill, Dad," she said.

David smiled. "Yeah, I'll do that." He looked around. A man he'd previously noticed, with long, lank grey hair, was still haplessly trying to find somewhere to sit.

"I think that guy would like our table," David told Amy. "And if we don't get off we're going to miss the start of the film."

Chapter Four

Terry stood on the first tee and slowly swung his three-wood around his head. The professional had told him several times that his practice swing was textbook. The only problem was when he had a ball in front of him; his natural aggression made him want to thrash the thing into the middle of next week. He breathed deeply and recalled the words of the professional: slow, rhythmic, keep your head down; the ball really would go further.

There was a queue building up behind. Some of them were looking at Terry as if they thought he should play. They obviously hadn't seen his drives: if he made proper contact there was every possibility that he would do some serious damage to the comedians up ahead. Not something that they would take kindly to at this posh club, where it had taken years to get in, still longer to get seven-day membership.

It occurred to Terry that as the years went by his weekends were becoming more and more like his weekdays. He was working today. Not that they would pay him any overtime for it – though he accepted that he was much too senior for that. The market was about people. It was his job to know who the right people were, what made them tick, what they needed. Better still: what they wanted, whether or not they actually needed it. In Terry's experience what they wanted came down to four things: piss-ups, good food, sport and fanny. Not everyone wanted all four, and knowing who liked what was part of the knack. For instance, today he was playing golf with Simon Stevens and young Guy from TLO. Stevens was strictly food and sport. You wouldn't impress him with a titty bar. Terry didn't know Guy that well, but suspected he'd be a more promising prospect on the fanny front, with a little encouragement. Terry would make it his business to find out if it looked like the kid was going places. The lad certainly seemed single-minded and determined, which was pretty well all you needed. It wouldn't be long before he eclipsed Serena's mate, 'poor David'. Kelsey had really lost it over the last couple of years, since he'd let his marriage get out of control. Terry had invited David today, though he'd always been a lousy golfer, but he'd come out with some crap about seeing his brat of a daughter. Well, his loss.

The green ahead was clear at last. Terry addressed the ball, looked towards the hole, tightened his grip, swayed slightly at the hips; addressed the ball again, jerked the club back and forth an inch or so, stretched his shoulder muscles, looked into the distance, breathed in deeply; addressed the ball for a third time, swung the club powerfully back, went just beyond the point of equilibrium, tottered slightly on the follow-through, forgot to look down. He made contact with the top of the ball and sent it skimming along the ground a hundred yards forward and ten to the right, where its spasmodic momentum was finally halted by a patch of semi-rough.

"Bad luck," Simon drawled.

Terry said nothing. He wasn't going to be patronised by someone like Stevens. Did Simon think he couldn't do better than that? Shit was shit.

Guy almost moved to put his ball down first, but thought better of it at the last moment. He'd suddenly, and in the nick of time, realised that although some bosses might respect that sort of self-confidence, Simon wasn't one of them.

Simon silently teed up his ball. He addressed it with his club, shuffled slightly, snapped the club back in what was not much more than a half swing, followed through smartly and hit the ball sweetly in the middle. It flew high and straight, but stopped well short of the green.

'Workmanlike' was the word for that, thought Terry: OK for the local course, safe but not pretty. You wouldn't get your handicap down below the high teens like that.

"Shot!" said Guy.

Simon ignored him.

Guy put his ball down, stepped back and looked quickly in the direction of the flag. There was, Terry thought, a certain natural litheness about the young man. His clothes, though they had all the right labels, clearly weren't as expensive as Simon's, yet they seemed to hang more naturally on him. Guy glanced at the queue behind him and took one slow practice swing. The real thing was identical: a perfect arc in both directions, a satisfying swoosh as club hit ball, which flew long and high and straight and landed just short of the green. There was a spontaneous ripple of applause from the line of golfers awaiting their turn. Guy looked cautiously at Simon, who had flushed slightly and fidgeted uncomfortably as the ball rolled to a halt, and decided not to acknowledge the spectators.

It was amazing, Terry thought, how much you could find out about people from just a couple of shots on a golf course. Now it would be interesting to see if Guy had really got it - how he'd handle the fact that he was clearly capable of thrashing his boss today if he chose to. Career versus competitive instinct. If he came through that one with a mention in dispatches, then one evening during the next month or so Terry would have to find out what really made him tick. What did he look like he would go for? A couple of Thai girls perhaps, for starters?

Terry wiped the sand from his face as Simon's second attempt to exit the deep bunker behind the twelfth flew past and just stopped short of the sand-trap the other side of the green, leaving him with a good thirty-foot putt. Ignoring their respective handicaps - Simon was the only person Terry had ever known to insist on playing to a lower figure than he was capable of, which said a lot about him - and adding back the couple of shots that Simon appeared to have 'forgotten' amongst the trees on successive holes, Terry was now a couple of strokes ahead of him. Guy was playing to the same handicap as Simon, and was having to resort to careless chipping and barely-aimed putting in order to keep his lead to reasonable proportions. He'd given up trying to lose after three or four holes; he'd been clever enough to work out that beating his boss by a few strokes was better than being seen blatantly to let him win. Terry was impressed by that. But with only six holes to go, it was time to move things on and get down to some real business.

"I think that's a gimme," Terry said as Simon's return putt from the far side of the green ran out of steam about four feet from the hole. For confirmation Terry looked at Guy, who nodded enthusiastically. Simon accepted, and tried not to look too grateful. Terry smiled encouragingly at him.

"So how *is* business?" Terry asked, walking directly alongside Simon as they made for the next tee.

"Good," replied Simon.

"But could be better?"

"Well, it could always be better, couldn't it?"

"Of course. Goes without saying."

Half way up the next fairway, having allowed Simon to count an air-shot on the tee as a practice swing (and given Guy a knowing wink when Simon wasn't looking) Terry thought it was time to come to the point.

"How do you find our service, Simon?" he asked seriously. "Generally. Compared with the competition?"

Simon sounded slightly surprised by the question. "Yes, good, I think."

"You think?"

"Yes, well, David Kelsey handles most of it. Seems happy enough with your performance."

"Great. Good guy, David," Terry said warmly. "Don't you think?"

"Yes," said Simon, but the momentary pause before he replied and the lack of conviction in his voice told Terry everything he needed to know.

"I've known him for years," Terry offered. "Used to think he would be a real high-flyer."

"No, David's a great guy," Simon said with more vigour but no more belief.

Terry nodded thoughtfully. "He's had a bad time over the last couple of years."

"Of course."

"Perhaps he needs something to get his teeth into. A new challenge."

"Possibly."

"Well," Terry continued as though the thought had just occurred to him, "I've got quite a few irons in the fire at the moment. Perhaps - and it's only a suggestion - if you tell David he's in charge of liaison from your end, and we put a project together that makes sense - obviously with you having the finally yea or nay, Simon - then he'll feel he's achieving something, get his confidence back and we all end up winners. If nothing comes of it, well, no-one's lost anything."

The expression on Simon's face suggested that the idea appealed, but that he had some inkling that he was being manoeuvred or manipulated, yet wasn't sure why - or how - to extricate himself. "OK," he said finally. "Have a preliminary talk with David on Monday. I'll mention we discussed it."

"Tell him he should have been here!" Terry let out a friendly laugh.

Simon laughed too. Guy joined in, though he hadn't heard the conversation.

"Now," said Simon with renewed authority in his voice. "I need your advice again, and don't tell me it's against the rules because I don't care. How many yards is that to the pin? About one twenty?"

"About that," agreed Terry, who thought it was one seventy if it was an inch.

Chapter Five

David watched impatiently as the water ran too slowly into the bath. There was a half-full can of beer next to the taps that he intended to finish off while lying in the bath – the sort of behaviour that Sonia would have been appalled by and one of the few consolations of his new life. And a reward for having successfully navigated another weekend with his daughter. It hadn't been great, but he thought it had gone OK.

The film they'd seen after leaving McDonald's had been fairly entertaining (Amy seemed to have enjoyed it more than David had himself), and then in the evening he'd rung for takeaway pizzas and they'd sat and watched a film on DVD - not VHS, which Amy now found too old-fashioned. On Sunday they'd even gone for a walk together, taking a detour through the park after leaving the newsagent, which added about fifteen minutes to the round trip. He'd seen kids on the swings and pictured Amy on similar ones, what seemed like yesterday but was probably about six or seven years ago now. He'd been tactful enough not to remind her.

They'd walked in comfortable silence back to the flat, where he'd cooked his special spaghetti bolognese for lunch. For the rest of the time he'd tried hard not to be the over-eager divorced parent, had played it as though they were in a normal family situation. Amy had spent a lot of the afternoon in her room, worn her headphones much of the time, used her phone incessantly, and, when she came out into the main room, lain motionless on the sofa staring at the TV. She hadn't seemed desperate to go back to her mother's, which, David thought, was as much as he could hope for.

The temperature of the bath water was finally right and, beer can placed carefully on the rim where he would be able to reach it, David was just about to immerse himself when the phone rang. He almost let it go to voicemail, but decided he would have a more relaxing soak if he dealt with whoever it was first. It was Sonia's number. Perhaps Amy had left something behind.

"Hello."

"I can't believe you." It was Sonia's voice.

David's heart rate went up; how many conversations had started like this prior to the separation? This time he could think of nothing that he had done until Sonia spoke again, and then he knew straight away and felt instantly nauseous as the muscles in his stomach involuntarily tightened.

"I've tried so hard to be even-handed, David," Sonia was saying, her voice breaking with anger. "I've never said anything bad about you in Amy's presence. I've always defended you if she started to have a go about something. And now I hear you're telling her our splitting up was all my fault."

"I didn't say that," David tried to reply firmly but calmly.

"Well, Amy says you did. She's lying, is she?"

"She misunderstood what I was saying."

"Which was?"

David sighed. "She asked why I left. It sounded like she thought it was my idea. I wanted her to know it wasn't – I thought she already knew that."

"And then she says you practically pulled her arm off, ripping the phone out of her hands."

"Bollocks. I took her phone away for a couple of minutes to get her attention."

"There's a big bruise."

"There is not. You know perfectly well I would never..."

"Just thank your lucky stars I managed to talk John out of coming round and having it out with you."

"Tell John he can mind his own fucking business."

David wasn't entirely sure who hung up on who. He didn't know either how much time had passed before he became aware that he was standing in the middle of his sitting-room, stark naked, with a can of beer in one hand, and that he was shaking.

Chapter Six

David was sitting in a crowded carriage on a crawling train. The examples of petty antisocial behaviour which usually bothered him were all around, but today he didn't care. He hadn't slept all night. He'd kept going over the conversations with Amy and then with Sonia in his mind. Anger had turned to anxiety and then back to anger again. Several times he'd run through in his head what he should have said to Sonia but hadn't. The most positive scenarios he had imagined involved John coming round to his flat and leaving with a broken nose.

David hadn't a clue what to do next. He didn't think that Sonia was deliberately trying to manufacture a situation where he wouldn't be able to see his daughter any more; she wasn't generally vindictive, and David was certain that she liked the idea of spending some time alone with John (God only knew why) from time to time. Which meant that she almost certainly believed everything she had said on the phone, and that in many ways made things worse. It appeared to David now that Amy was manipulating all of them.

Beyond the odd facial expression, David had never been able to see much of himself in Amy, whereas her physical resemblance to her mother appeared to become more striking each time he saw her: the thin nose, the slightly turned up lips, the eyes that, when she smiled, were always a split second or so behind the mouth. Sometimes he wondered whether Sonia had quietly murdered all his genes in her womb and simply cloned herself.

David had read somewhere that forty percent of divorced fathers lost contact with their children. He didn't want to be one of them, but it was difficult to see how he was going to be able to turn up in a couple of weeks and pick Amy up as though nothing had happened.

The train was finally pulling into the terminus. People were standing up and collecting jackets and bags from the luggage rack. Someone standing next to David had strong onion-breath, and David turned away from him. He noticed how shiny the right sleeve of his own suit jacket had become, and there was clear sign of fraying at the end, as well as on the shirt cuff that extended just beyond it. He had been meaning to buy a new suit and a couple of shirts for a while now, but they were expensive and he couldn't seem to raise the enthusiasm to go shopping during his lunch hour. When buying clothes he liked to have a woman come with him to stop him making stupid and expensive mistakes, but there was currently no obvious candidate. Sonia had been great at it before they got married; that had been the only time in his life that David had enjoyed clothes shopping. He had loved the way she looked him up and down when he tried something on; it was a buzz to buy something simply because Sonia found him attractive in it. He'd been young and naïve, but he'd undoubtedly been happy as well.

David was one of the last to leave the carriage. He walked slowly along the platform making no attempt to catch up with the rest of the throng. The station clock told him that it was just after eight thirty, so he would be in the office by a quarter to nine. He could remember a time when that would have been forty five minutes early, but now it was late by at least the same margin. Rumour had it that Simon was regularly in by half past seven. If that was the case, Guy was probably in at seven thirty-five. Good luck to them. They clearly had more willpower than David did, or maybe their alarm clocks didn't have snooze buttons. They certainly weren't divorcees with troublesome daughters, which, David guessed, made things easier for them in the cold light of morning.

David waited his turn to feed his ticket into the turnstile then took the escalator up to street level. It had started to rain. He fumbled in his bag and brought out the small telescopic umbrella that he routinely carried.

There was a *Homeless Truths* seller standing a few feet away to his right, under the awning of a station concession that sold various types of pastries. Either the rain had come on very suddenly or she had stayed out in it too long hoping to sell magazines to the flow of commuters because, although she was now sheltered from the downpour, water was still running from her almost black hair onto the dark-green jacket she wore, which was saturated in several places. She was trying with one hand to brush water off the pile of magazines she held with the other. Her face wore no particular expression. She looked up and briefly made eye contact with David, who awkwardly looked away.

David found a space large enough to enable him to put his umbrella up without injuring anyone and became part of a large wave of workers marching gravely towards their offices. Not for the first time he wondered who all these people were and what work there could possibly be for so many of them.

The rain was easing off. A narrow band of sunshine had forced its way through a gap in the clouds and was illuminating the façade of the TLO building just as it came into view. Rumours about the nature of God's sense of humour seemed to be true.

The office was bustling. There were about thirty people in the department and it really did appear that David was the last to arrive. If the others hadn't long been there then that wasn't the impression they gave. Two or three of them were leaning back with their hands behind their heads and phone receivers cradled between chin and shoulder; one was laughing so loudly that you could hear him from the other side of the office.

David bent down to switch on his computer and hung his wet umbrella over the side of his wastepaper bin. While the machine went through its elongated start-up routine, testing network connections and probing itself for viruses, David walked to the kitchen area to get himself the first cup of coffee of the day.

"Ah, good afternoon," said a guy called Adrian who was taking water from the cooler. David generally avoided him; the man thought he was funny and he wasn't. Happily he wasn't very important either. This morning David just ignored him.

Back at David's desk the computer was still warming up. There didn't appear to be any new paper on his desk that he could look at while he waited. But the round red light on his phone was illuminated, indicating that he had at least one voice-message. He couldn't think who it might be. He took a sip of coffee and pressed the sequence of keys on the phone that would play the recording.

There was only one message, and the system gave out the helpful information that it had been left at eight fifteen.

"Hi, David," said Terry's cheery voice. "Where are you? Met some bird at the weekend who's got you chained to the bed? Don't deny it, you dirty sod! Give me a call when you eventually get in. Cheers!"

The computer was finally ready. David clicked on the email icon and trawled through the ten or so messages that had appeared since Friday evening; he did have a company BlackBerry but rarely looked at emails at the weekend, unlike his colleagues who seemed to send them on Sunday afternoons. Nothing urgent today. David wondered why anyone would invite the entire company to their birthday drinks. He deleted most of the messages unread.

David looked up and saw that Jill was standing in front of him, leaning forward across the half-height screen that divided his desk from the gangway.

"Hi," she said with her air-stewardess smile. "Good weekend?"

"Not bad," he lied. "Better than coming here!" What had it come to when even that wasn't true?

"Tell me about it!" Jill nodded and grimaced sympathetically.

"How about you?" David asked. He didn't want to know the answer but hoped that the question would at least deflect Jill from her recent preoccupation with his post-divorce sex life.

"No, very good, thanks." She hesitated for a couple of seconds. "Nothing particularly special - it's just good to be able to chill out for a couple of days."

David nodded in agreement.

Jill also seemed to want to change the subject. "Er, Simon was wondering..." she began.

David was sure that it hadn't been that long ago that Simon had been capable of wondering in person. "Yes?" he asked.

"...Er, nothing urgent. Just whether you had heard from Guy at all."

"Me?"

"Well, no-one else had, and I told him your red light was on, so perhaps..."

"No, that was... someone else. Have you looked at his calendar?"

"Yeah, of course."

"He'd call if he was stuck on a train, so perhaps he's gone to the dentist or something."

"Thanks. I'll tell Simon."

"It's only a suggestion."

"OK. Thanks."

Jill started to walk away.

"Or maybe," David said quietly into the air in front of him, "tell Simon to look up his own arse and see if Guy has finally moved in."

Chris, at the desk to David's right, still leaning back and making interminable phone calls, turned towards him and smiled.

"Just kidding," David smiled back. He hadn't intended to be overheard. The way things were going, he thought, it wouldn't be that many years before he would be working for Guy, if he had a job at all.

When David arrived at the coffee house Terry was already sitting at a table, mechanically stirring a cappuccino into which he had just poured two sachets of demerara sugar. David ordered the same from the severe-looking Hispanic waitress and sat down. It was only half an hour since he had returned the call, but Terry had been insistent that they meet up as soon as possible and David had nothing pressing in his diary. He was also happy to get out of the office, where the speculation as to where Guy might be was becoming increasingly tiresome.

"Good weekend?" Terry asked ritually.

"So-so," replied David. "I had Amy."

"Oh, yes, you said on Friday."

"She's at a difficult age," David explained unprompted. "You'll find out when the boys are older. Perhaps boys are easier, I don't know. How are they anyway?"

"Oh yeah, they're fine," Terry replied vacantly, as if it were an odd question. "More Serena's department." He knocked back his coffee in one go, then gestured at the waitress to bring him another.

"I had a pretty good weekend," he volunteered as he wiped the froth from his mouth with a paper serviette. "Took twenty quid off your boss for a start."

David looked at him blankly.

"The golf?" Terry said with a hint of impatience in his voice.

"Of course, the golf," David said warmly, relieved to have something to talk about that didn't involve families. "I'd forgotten all about that. So you beat him?"

Terry nodded. "Him, but not that other little bandit."

David laughed. "I've heard he's good. I bet he tried hard not to beat Simon!"

Terry nodded knowingly. He waited for a moment as his new cup of coffee was delivered. "Anyway, Simon and I had a very good chat about how we might develop the business relationship between our companies. Has he spoken to you?"

David shook his head. "Haven't set eyes on him today."

"OK. Good. Well, I don't want to put words into his mouth, but the gist of it was, and is, that you should be the point-man for TLO, and I should run a few of the things I'm working on past you to see how you want to get involved. Simon seemed very keen."

David thought this was unlikely: his boss regarded Terry as a wide boy who should be avoided unless and until at a particular time and for a specific deal he might happen to be useful. So either Terry wasn't telling the truth, or he had somehow got to Simon on the golf course. Or maybe he'd got him drunk: Simon had a notoriously small capacity for alcohol. Safely back in his office Simon was likely to have cooled towards anything Terry might be proposing.

David shrugged. "Well, he's the boss. So when would you like to come round and discuss these deals?"

"Better still," replied Terry, with sudden enthusiasm, "why don't I buy you dinner tomorrow night? Boys' night out!"

"I don't think so…"

"Yeah, go on. Let your hair down a bit!"

Terry waved at the waitress and mimed signing a piece of paper with his hands. It was a way of trying to bring the conversation to a close.

"Come on," David said scornfully, "you've known me long enough. Call me old-fashioned, but I don't do business in restaurants. Or strip joints."

Terry's expression was half that of the offended innocent, half that of the lovable rogue who has just been found out.

"Fair enough," he said as the bill arrived and he brought his wallet out from his jacket pocket. "How could I have forgotten you and your high principles. Tell you what: how about I come round tomorrow, say ten thirty, and walk you through what I'm proposing?"

"Fine."

"And we also have a boys' night out tomorrow."

David hesitated. The idea really didn't appeal. But the alternative was another empty evening by himself in the flat, and he'd had too many of those recently. "OK," he said finally. "But don't get upset if I bail out early: I'm a bit of a lightweight these days."

Terry grinned broadly, picked up his change and stood up to go. "We'll see," he said.

"Have you heard?"

Jill was standing in a huddle in the middle of the office with Adrian and one of the secretaries from the other end of the floor, a tall girl who wore flowery dresses whatever the weather and whose name David didn't know.

"Have I heard what?" David asked flatly.

"It's terrible." The tall secretary held her hand in front of her mouth, as though she might otherwise vomit, and shook her head.

"What is?"

"It's Guy," Jill said solemnly, looking directly into David's eyes and then pausing so that the news could sink in.

"*What* is?"

"There's been an accident," Adrian added gravely.

David ignored him and turned to Jill. "Well come on," he pleaded. "Spit it out. What's happened?"

Jill looked offended. "He's been in a car crash," she said softly.

The tall secretary began to cry and Jill put a hand on her shoulder.

"What? Is he...?" For some reason David didn't feel able to say 'dead' but no suitable euphemism came to mind.

Jill shook her head. "No. He's alive. They managed to cut him out and get him to hospital. Simon's just come off the phone. That's all I..." Now she too began to cry.

Three or four more people had got up from their desks and joined the group. Jill composed herself and looked earnestly from face to face as she spoke.

"He's still unconscious...," she told them, but David spied Simon through the doorway of his office and moved away from the crowd to talk to him.

Simon was sitting quietly at his desk, looking down at the writing surface. He didn't appear to be aware of David's presence. David knocked on the open door and Simon looked up, beckoned him in and motioned to him to close the door behind him.

"You've heard?" he asked simply.

"Sort of. What exactly...?"

"A bit of a mystery. Went off the road on the way to work this morning. Just after seven. No other cars involved, according to his mother."

"You spoke to her?"

"She rang from the hospital."

"How was she?"

Simon shrugged. "Well, she wasn't in floods of tears or anything like that. I think she's quite a practical type. She was waiting for the doctor to come round again."

"What did you say?"

Simon made a wide exasperated gesture with his arms, and then let them fall back by his sides. "What *do* you say? I don't know. I guess they don't tell you about stuff like this on the TLO fast-track management course."

David smiled sympathetically. It was the first time in years he could remember Simon sharing a personal confidence.

"Still," Simon continued with an embarrassed cough, "there's nothing we can do now, so we might as well get on with our jobs."

"Yes," was all David could find to say. "If you hear…"

"I played golf with your friend Terry on Saturday."

"He's not…Yes I know."

"Expect a call."

"Already received it."

Simon looked both surprised and wary.

"Be careful."

"I will. Don't worry."

"Good."

David turned to go. "And you'll let me know if you hear…"

Simon waved him away impatiently. "Of course."

"Any news?" two or three voices asked as David re-emerged into the open office. There were now about a dozen people milling about, drinking coffee and wearing worried frowns. David wondered where genuine concern ended and enjoyment of the excitement of the moment began. He shook his head and forced a path through them.

"Guy has an old 3-Series," Adrian was authoritatively telling someone. "If he'd had a modern one he might very well have walked away. I saw this test on TV…"

"Not for the money they get," someone else was saying. "It's dreadful. Imagine the sights they have to see!"

David sat down at his desk. Chris, once more on the phone, turned to him and shrugged. David nodded, opened the 'to do' list on his computer and then began drafting an email to a client.

Chapter Seven

David hadn't slept well again. He'd hoped he would, particularly after his miserable failure the previous night, but he hadn't honestly expected to. He recognised the state of mind that would keep him awake into the small hours. There was nothing fancy about his anxieties; it was all run-of-the-mill stuff: personal confrontations, decisions he found it impossible to make, decisions he *had* taken but now regretted, responsibility he candidly didn't want, responsibility without power, estrangement from his daughter, sometimes even scenes of graphic violence on the TV news or shots of the faces of people who knew they were about to die. As he got older the list got longer.

Most nights watching mindless television programmes until late, then reading in bed, would eventually send him to sleep. Sometimes the relief was short-lived and he would wake again an hour or so later in a state of even greater mental agitation. Then sleep would desert him completely and he would turn over and over, trying to force his mind to concentrate on anything - sex, football, a song - that might drive from his mind the fixation which constantly dissolved and reconstituted itself in ways that were not rational, that would not let him rest. Finally the feeling of panic as dawn approached, and with it the realisation of how little time there was before he would have to get up and try to bluff his way through a day at work with a body that ached with fatigue and a mind that couldn't properly process the simplest thought.

David thought he should probably go to the doctor, or even the occupational health woman that TLO periodically provided. But GPs only ever gave you thirty seconds to describe what was wrong with you, then told you it was normal or nothing; and as for the alternative, how could you be absolutely certain, whatever she told you, that what you were saying wasn't getting back to your boss? And what would the diagnosis be? That he was stressed, and that he was stressed because his life was shit? Well, he knew that already.

At least this time his night hadn't been entirely sleepless. David reckoned he had had a total of about four hours which, compared with some nights in recent months, wasn't so bad. During the sleepless periods he had thought about Guy's crash a few times, but he couldn't pretend those were the thoughts that were keeping him awake. His phone conversation with Sonia on the other hand was still a major contributor to his agitation; each time he replayed it they were both getting angrier and angrier, and although in his own mind he always won the argument, the emotional confrontation drained him more and more, leaving him shaking and breathing abnormally as if he were in shock.

There were two other images that wouldn't go away: one was Terry's head, grinning, grotesque, ghoulishly lit. And then there was another face, a woman or girl. David hadn't been able to place it at first, had thought it was an invention of his feverish mind. The realisation that it was actually the face of the *Homeless Truths* seller had made him start and open his eyes.

David left the flat too late to catch the train he usually took. The following service was very overcrowded. David squeezed himself into some space grudgingly yielded by the passengers who had got on at earlier stops, and managed to find a metal pole to hold onto. As the train picked up speed he leaned against a partition screen and closed his eyes. He could hear some girls talking and the hiss of music leaking from headphones. One person shouted into a phone while several others were furiously texting. David wondered whether it was possible to fall asleep standing up and, if it was, whether you immediately fell on the floor.

The train stopped again, the door opened and somehow more people got on. David hated them; he wanted them all to go away. Miraculously the doors managed to close. David closed his eyes again.

Maybe he *had* fallen asleep, because already the train had arrived at the terminus and David was being carried out of the door and along the platform towards the concourse. He took a deep breath and tried to make sense of his surroundings. A shaft of light from the area where the escalator rose to street level suggested that it was bright outside today even if it wasn't actually sunny.

David stumbled onto the escalator and stood aside while more urgent types bulldozed their way past. He reached the top and was momentarily startled to find himself looking directly at the *Homeless Truths* girl. She was still wearing the same green jacket. She was in the act of selling a magazine to a girl who appeared about her own age, and who was engaging her in conversation. David started to walk on, then checked himself and looked back again. Someone forcefully collided with him from behind and they both apologised. David moved to one side, out of the stream of people exiting the station. The girl was alone once more and glancing around as if she wanted to be noticed. David took a two-pound coin from his pocket and started to walk towards her. He hesitated for a moment. No, it was fine: no-one he knew was in the vicinity.

Embarrassingly, the girl didn't appear to notice David as he approached from the side with his outstretched coin and sympathetic smile, and after a few seconds he had to move round into her line of vision. She looked up, saw his coin and with a placid almost business-like expression held out a magazine in his direction. He took it and dropped the two pounds into her hand without touching her fingers.

"Thank you," she said, and there was an accent that he wasn't able to place. It could be Middle Eastern or Eastern European or something much closer to home; in two short syllables he really couldn't tell, except that she wasn't originally from London. Even in today's bright conditions her hair looked black, and her facial skin was a tone or so darker than his own. Her nose was quite prominent and her large eyes were of a deep brown shade. David found himself wondering whether her skin was naturally so dark, and then became conscious of his reluctance to touch her hand and noticed that he was trying not to breathe in too close to her.

"Thanks very much," David heard himself say. "Much better than yesterday," he continued, pointing skywards, "not so much rain." And God, if he wasn't now making a pitter-patter rainfall mime with his free hand.

"Yes," the girl agreed pleasantly, turning to attend to a young man with spiky ginger hair and an earring, who was patiently waiting for a magazine, "a lot better."

"He's gonna be OK," Jill told David breathlessly as soon as he walked into the office. "I thought you'd want to know straightaway."

"How do you mean 'OK'?" David replied, hearing the terseness in his own voice but making minimal effort to change it. "'OK' as in 'absolutely fine'?"

Jill shook her head gravely. "He's conscious now. Apparently it was very touch and go, but he's out of danger. But the hospital want to keep him in for tests. On his spine. They think he's probably done some damage there."

"Permanent?"

"We don't know. Let's pray not."

"Jesus." David shook his head. "Poor sod."

Jill shrugged and nodded sadly at the same time.

David sat down at his desk and shivered. Nothing in life, except perhaps blindness, terrified him more than the prospect of a broken back. In fact if death itself were sudden and instant, then the other two held far greater terror for him. He shivered again. He couldn't bear to think about it right now. He switched on his computer and went to get the first coffee of the morning.

"David?"

"Speaking."

"It's Terry."

David's heart sank. He thought he knew what Terry was going to say.

"Hi Terry. How are you?"

"Fine, David. Listen, mate. I've got a problem. Something's come up. I'm not going to be able to make our meeting."

David reproached himself: he knew he should have anticipated this.

"What's come up?"

"Do what? I can hardly hear you. The battery's going on this thing. I'll explain later. Cheers." Terry ended the call.

David sat back. Surely he'd been around long enough not to let himself be suckered like this? He should cancel dinner. He definitely should, but he didn't relish the idea of another night in, alone. And a little alcohol, drunk slowly over a period of hours, would help him sleep. He would just need to be very careful, that was all.

Chapter Eight

David didn't like hospitals. He couldn't imagine that anyone did. Oddly he had warm memories of having his tonsils removed as a kid: of the ward, the nurses, the attention he'd received, the other kids he'd met, though the details were all pretty fuzzy now. Amy's birth had been a great moment as well, but what he remembered feeling most on visits to the maternity ward was a huge impatience to get both his daughter and her mother back to the family home as soon as possible. Otherwise hospitals were always bad news: David had been to see his grandparents and his great aunt close to their last, and memories of the indignity and of their discomfort had remained with him. And then there'd been his own short stay after the 'incident' in Cambridge. He shuddered at the recollection.

Now, as he passed through the swing doors with Simon and Jill into the disinfectant-laden atmosphere of the hospital corridor, David found himself trying not to look at the crumbling remnants of humanity - attached in various undignified ways to items of life-prolonging equipment - that he glimpsed through the doorways of the wards they passed. He saw an old lady with straggling, matted hair and an ashen, lined face, half-obscured by some sort of breathing apparatus, lying prone on a trolley. He tried to imagine her as a mother, a young woman in love, a child. He hoped she had family who came to visit her.

"Did everyone sign the card?" Simon was asking Jill.

"Pretty well, I think," Jill replied, taking the card in question out of the envelope as they walked along and trying to read the signatures scrawled at various angles across it.

"There I am." David pointed to his own name.

Jill ignored him. "Shame we haven't bought him anything," she said. "Hope he won't mind."

"Least of his worries, I would have thought," Simon said philosophically.

The name on the sign over the swing doors to their left told them that they had arrived at the ward they had been searching for. A further, smaller sign told them it was the spinal-injuries unit.

Simon took the initiative and went to talk to the young West-Indian woman at the nurses' station in the friendly but slightly patronising tone he also adopted towards employees in hotels. The nurse was listening and pointing, and then she asked them all to wait. She walked into the ward and returned a few moments later with a stocky, fair-haired woman of about thirty-five, who introduced herself with the most fleeting of smiles as the ward sister. She seemed to sense that Simon was in charge and began to address her remarks to him. David couldn't make out every word she said, but it appeared to be something to do with not overtiring Guy, not staying too long, being supportive and not being surprised that Guy might look different from when they'd last seen him. He'd had a very nasty accident, she was saying, it was bound to be a shock to the system.

"Of course," Simon was agreeing sympathetically. "Whatever we can do."

"Sister," Jill asked tentatively. "What about his back? Any news yet?"

The nurse shook her head slowly. "Not yet. The consultant is coming in later."

"I see. Well, no news is…"

"..Just no news in this case. I wouldn't get your hopes up too much."

"I see," Simon interrupted before Jill could speak. "Thanks very much."

The first sight of Guy in bed, despite the sister's warning, wiped away all David's pre-planned matey speeches and left him looking on in silence. Moments before entering the room the visitors had all adopted their hospital smiles, but Jill's had dropped immediately, and although Simon had just managed to maintain his, his reddening facial skin conveyed the extent of his shock.

The young man was lying on his back with his neck in a brace, and nothing was visible except his head. The face was recognisably Guy's, but, David thought, it was as though it had been a few years since they had last met, not four days. Guy's skin was grey-green and puffy; under the strip lighting it appeared wet. He looked as though he was wearing a clay mask that had not yet set. His hair lay disordered on the sheet beneath him. His eyes were tired and yellow and peered passively out through the layers of inflated flesh.

"Hi there," said Simon in a cheery voice that was very nearly convincing. "How's it going?"

Guy blinked a couple of times, as if he hadn't heard the question, or hadn't understood it, or was trying to compose himself to answer it. He swallowed and then blinked again. "OK," he said finally in an almost inaudible whisper, the hoarseness of which confirmed David's worst fears of the extent of damage to Guy's spine.

"Great," Simon shouted with exaggerated bonhomie, "we'll have you back at work in no time!"

Guy fixed Simon with an imploring stare as if he had so much faith in his boss and mentor that he thought he could get him out of even this predicament. Simon looked suddenly unnerved. He smiled in embarrassment and looked at his companions.

"We've got you a card," Jill interjected brightly to prevent the onset of the silence that they all feared. "Everyone's signed it."

Simon and David nodded in eager agreement.

Jill produced the card from its envelope and advanced towards the bed. Simon and David gingerly followed her.

"Here," Jill said awkwardly, holding the card out towards Guy, "can you...? Oh, no perhaps not. Best not to for the time being anyway."

It wasn't clear whether Guy found it painful to move his arm, had been advised not to, or was unable to. David found that for the moment he preferred not to know.

"I'll hold it here," Jill continued. "Is that close enough? How about if I turn on this little light?"

Guy was doing his best to focus on the scratched signatures and messages held out in front of him, but it was obvious that his thoughts were elsewhere, and after a few seconds Jill took the card away and propped it up on the cabinet by the side of the bed.

"I trust they're looking after you?" Simon asked breezily.

"Yes," croaked Guy.

"Lots of pretty nurses?!" David added. He had become aware that he wasn't saying anything, and had decided inanity was better than silence.

"Maybe you'll come out fit and have found a wife!" Simon chimed in.

"You never know," said Jill, smiling and winking at Guy. "Stranger things have happened."

Guy tried to smile weakly back.

Simon's mobile rang. "Shit," he exclaimed, removing it from his jacket pocket. He went to press the button to turn it off, but then looked at the screen and stopped himself. "Oh God, I'm sorry," he said, looking first at Guy and then at David, "I do need to take this. I'll go outside. Back in a tick." He set off down the corridor with the phone to his ear, already talking into the mouthpiece.

David noticed that there were two wooden chairs in the room by the window. He picked them both up and put one each side of the bed. He sat down and Jill did the same.

For three or four minutes David half-listened to Jill filling Guy in on two days of office gossip, and laughed, smiled and made whatever other encouraging noises he thought were expected of him at the appropriate moments. He took in the cold, white antiseptic room, with its clinical, insect-speckled lighting, exposed piping, clumsily painted walls and smells of linen, rubber, old lino and medication. He looked back at Guy and felt a wave of sadness wash over him.

"Gosh," Jill exclaimed suddenly, looking at her watch. "Do you think Simon's got lost?"

Guy looked blankly at her. David shrugged; he didn't think Simon had been gone that long.

"Well, if you'll excuse me, gentlemen," Jill continued, "I just need to find the ladies' room for a minute. Won't be long." She smiled at David and then winked at Guy again. "Give you time for some boys' talk!" She got up and left the room.

To forestall what was likely to be an awkward silence David quickly stood up, went over to the window and looked out.

"Well, you're not missing much here," he reported to Guy. "Nothing but dustbins and an overflowing car park." He could also see a large chimney, but felt that it wasn't appropriate to mention it. He turned and smiled at Guy. "I hope you didn't pay extra for a sea view or I'll have to have a word with the management on the way out."

"Can I talk to you please?" Guy asked urgently.

"Of course." David immediately stopped smiling, slowly returned to his seat, sat down and leaned forward so that he would be able to hear. He could feel himself begin to sweat.

"Look," Guy began. "I can't tell Simon this, and if I tell Jill it'll be all round the office by tonight. The truth is…"

David could see tears start to well up in his young colleague's eyes. He tried to sneak a glance towards the doorway to check whether anyone was coming.

"...I'm fucking terrified."

Tears flowed over Guy's cheeks onto the bedding. David wondered whether he should offer to get a tissue, but decided Guy wouldn't want him to draw attention to the tears.

"Well," David said finally, "that's entirely understandable." He immediately thought that he'd used the wrong word.

"Have they told you?" Guy asked suspiciously.

"No," David replied, managing to hold Guy's piercing gaze, which was searching for signs that his visitor might be lying.

"I'm not going to be OK," Guy said firmly. "I can't feel my legs."

David looked at the lump in the bedclothes made by Guy's motionless limbs. "Well," he said with assurance, "I'm pretty sure that can be temporary."

"Maybe."

"Definitely."

"I can feel my arms."

"Good. Well, that's a start."

"Perhaps."

"Definitely. Two out of four already. Fifty percent. That's a pass."

David immediately found the remark crass; but the expression on Guy's face told him the young man was desperate for any form of encouragement. "And," David continued in a matey tone, "it's the two that we need at TLO. You can't write much or use the computer or the telephone with your feet!"

"I'd be OK, then?"

David hesitated for a second. "I don't see why not."

Guy's face seemed much calmer now, but then it suddenly clouded over as if an unwelcome thought had passed across his mind, and he closed his eyes, screwed up his facial muscles and started to cry again.

"I just want to close my eyes and open them again, and it'll all be OK. Like using the PC at work: 'Click, edit, undo'."

"Yes. That would be great," David agreed.

"I keep seeing it over and over in my head."

"The...?"

"Over and over again. And I keep trying to do it differently."

"That's natural."

Guy looked searchingly at David. "Don't tell Simon this," he said, "or my mother."

David had no time to agree before Guy continued: "I was late. I remembered I'd forgotten to email Adam Davies at Carson's about our ten o'clock. I thought I'd text him. So I did. Then I hit this huge tree. And now this."

David pinched the bridge of his nose and closed his eyes for a second. "I don't know what to say," he said truthfully.

Guy's face was screwed up with grief. "I want another chance," he pleaded.

They both heard the exaggerated sound of footsteps, echoing along the cold, stone corridor. Guy seemed to sense that it was Simon and retreated behind the empty, emotionless expression that David had grown used to seeing in the office. There was nothing to suggest the conversation that had just taken place except for rapidly-drying salt deposits around slightly reddened eyes, noticeable only if you looked closely, and Simon wasn't likely to.

"Hi again," said Simon. "Sorry about that. Jason at NTU with a promising new offer." He looked at David and Guy in turn and suddenly appeared uncomfortable, as though their displays of indifference to the news genuinely surprised him. "Where's Jill?" he asked in a slightly aggressive tone.

"Right here," replied Jill, re-entering the room behind her boss. "Needed to powder my nose."

Simon and Jill hovered awkwardly around the empty chair. Simon furtively consulted his watch.

Guy sensed the atmosphere. "I'm pretty tired…," he began.

Simon seized the opportunity. "OK. Maybe we should let you get some rest. And I'm afraid the company won't run itself. Particularly with you skiving off!"

Guy attempted to smile.

Jill nodded in enthusiastic agreement with Simon. "We'll call later to find out how you are, if that's OK."

"Yes." Guy seemed to be having difficulty in swallowing. "Thanks for coming in," he added huskily.

"No problem," said Simon. "Hopefully we'll pop back later in the week."

"See ya," said David, giving Guy a friendly, conspiratorial wink on the way out and only belatedly realising that Guy had already closed his eyes.

Chapter Nine

"Charlie, this bottle is corked," Terry told the attentive, nervously smiling waiter, who had scurried over to the table on being summoned with a cursory raising of the customer's hand.

"Oh, really?"

"Yes, really. Would you change it for one that isn't?"

"Of course, Mr Ransome. Very sorry."

Terry dismissed the waiter with a curt nod of the head. As far as he could tell there was nothing wrong with the wine, but he had read somewhere, or maybe someone had told him, that on average one bottle in twenty was corked, and as a result he had taken to sending back about one in ten to be on the safe side. It kept the waiters on their toes in the restaurants he regularly went to, and he found it didn't do any harm when you were trying to impress a guest. He felt no need to impress David Kelsey, who was currently sitting opposite him; on the other hand, it did no harm to remind him that Terry Ransome was someone who commanded respect in whatever setting he happened to find himself.

"You don't seem to have much luck with wine," David commented drily, continuing to stare down at his place-setting.

"How's that?"

David pushed his cutlery slightly apart before looking up.

"You seem to send a lot back."

Terry shrugged defensively. "I have certain standards. I don't like accepting second best."

David's face wore a wry, knowing smile as though there was some joke that Terry wasn't in on. There was something wrong with the guy tonight, Terry thought: he'd been chippy from the moment he'd walked into the restaurant, a quarter of an hour previously and ten minutes after the agreed time, without offering any apology or explanation for his tardiness. Terry had been left standing on his own at the bar for five minutes, which could have been embarrassing for him if any market A-lister had seen him (thankfully they hadn't) and didn't say much for the regard in which Kelsey apparently held him.

The waiter reappeared with another bottle of wine, showed Terry the label and then unctuously poured a small amount into his glass. Terry picked it up, swirled it around and sniffed the bouquet; then tilted both his head and the glass and slowly poured the wine into his mouth. He waited a second before nodding knowledgeably.

"That's much more like it." He paused to enjoy the look of relief on the waiter's face. "Thank you, Charlie."

"Thank you Mr Ransome." The waiter filled both glasses and then fussed over a few crumbs by Terry's side plate before moving away.

"Where do you think he comes from?" David asked as soon as the waiter was out of earshot.

"Charlie?" Terry seemed surprised by the question. "I don't know. Where do these people come from? Asia, the Middle East, Eastern Europe."

David laughed. "Doesn't narrow it down much."

Terry planted both elbows on the table and held out the palms of his hands towards his guest. "Well, he's not English, I can tell you that much."

"Or called Charlie."

Terry shook his head. "Probably something un-pronounceable. 'Dshkshpsh' or something."

"More than likely."

One of the most irritating things about David Kelsey, Terry thought, was that you could never be absolutely sure when he was taking the piss. He might be now, because he seemed to be in that sort of mood. But that was OK; let him enjoy his little triumph for a few moments more. He could and would be sorted

out without too much difficulty; it would only take a few
drinks. For all his prim superiority, Kelsey did like to let
himself go once in a while, and the while had got progressively
shorter since his marriage break-up.

"Cheers," said Terry, holding his glass out across the table.

David raised his own and gingerly clinked it against Terry's.
"Cheers."

Terry knocked back two thirds of his wine in one go and
then placed the glass back on the table. David took a sip,
watched Terry for a moment, appeared to have second thoughts
and then brought the glass back to his lips and took a full
mouthful.

Terry gave David a smile of encouragement.

The waiter returned and set a large plate of beef carpaccio,
through which the blue pattern on the crockery was clearly
visible, in front of Terry. He then lowered a similar-sized plate,
in the middle of which a small leek tartlet with two lengths of
asparagus looked pitiably lost, between David's knife and fork.

"You won't get fat on that," Terry remarked amiably, leaning
across to refill David's glass, this time to the brim.

"Good. I don't want to get fat."

Terry watched David take another large mouthful of wine.
"Very sensible," he agreed. "You won't find another woman if
you turn into a lard-arse. Now if on the other hand, like me
you've already got a good woman," he pointed at himself with
the fork on which a long slice of beef was speared, "then it
doesn't matter if you do let yourself go."

David rubbed his chin. "I'm not sure I want another woman."

Terry pretended to splutter. "Of course you do! Everyone
does. It's natural. Otherwise you'll go blind. And end up
cooking your own food."

A couple of minutes later they had both finished eating and
the waiter came back to clear the plates. He refilled both glasses
and Terry ordered another bottle of the same wine. David sat

passively, gazing around the room, trying to appear uninterested in what he saw. Terry noted with approval that his companion's eyes returned a couple of times to the two blonde twenty-something girls at the next table, who laughed as they leaned across to each other to exchange whispered confidences, their faces almost touching.

Terry picked up his glass and David obediently did the same. Terry looked at him for a couple of seconds through narrowed eyes, and decided this was the right moment.

"Terrible about young Guy from your shop. What's the news?"

David took a while to respond. He looked down at his cutlery and then played with the fork before replying.

"I went to see him in hospital this afternoon," he said quietly. He looked up. "Simon and I did."

Terry was a picture of concern. "Is he going to be all right?"

David shrugged. "They don't know yet. But my money..., that's not the way to put it, is it? His back... You know..." David sounded reluctant to hear himself say the words. "I think it might be fucked." He took a long swig from his wineglass. "I hope I'm wrong."

"Christ, that's terrible," said Terry, leaning across to refill David's glass. "I played golf with him, what was it, *three* days ago? Unbelievable, isn't it? Nice kid. Natural player. Bright as well. Lot of promise. What a waste."

David slowly shook his head. "Don't write him off yet. You know, I could be wrong. And even if I'm not, there's no reason..."

"Of course," Terry interrupted. Send him my best. If there's anything I can do..."

"Appreciate it."

"Do you know what happened?" So far as market gossip went, Terry found that it was always good to be in the know.

"No. Not really. I've no idea."

Terry thought David was lying, but couldn't see why. Not that he frankly cared much in this instance. He enjoyed another eyeful of the two young blondes.

"Almost young enough to be your daughters," David whispered, now smiling and appearing relieved to be able to change the subject.

Terry reached for the wine bottle. He would see who had the last laugh.

"I thought you'd fallen down the pan!" Terry said cheerily as David returned to the table after his second visit to the toilets.

David hesitated for a moment and tried to come up with a witty rejoinder, but couldn't think of one. "Sorry about that," he said finally.

"No problem. I got you a brandy. I assume that's OK."

"Great. Thanks."

David felt a pleasant warmth inside him. He saw that not only did he have a double brandy, but his wineglass was also filled almost to the brim and a fresh bottle was standing on the table. Terry, on the other hand, had no digestif and his wineglass was two thirds empty.

"So how much longer are you going to keep me in suspense about this great new business idea of yours?" David asked. The thought had just come into his head. He was vaguely aware that he shouldn't be bringing this up, but he was suddenly curious.

"You want to talk about it now?" Terry sounded surprised.

David hesitated for a moment. "Sure," he replied. "No time like the present."

Terry looked round the restaurant as though he were concerned that someone might be listening. "OK," he said. "Your call."

"Shoot."

Terry still sounded reluctant. "I'll give you an outline now," he suggested. "I expect you'll have to discuss it with Simon anyway."

"Not necessarily," David replied, though he knew he was lying; the truth was too humiliating in his current state. "It depends."

Terry ignored the remark and started to explain his plan. As far as David could comprehend, it wasn't that radical: Terry's company would offer all its best business to TLO on a preferential basis. In return TLO would have to give up some of its rights of selectivity, and pay Terry's company a percentage of the extra profit it would make as a result. It had to be a lot more complicated than that, though, because it seemed to be taking Terry a very long time to explain it, and David was finding that each time he processed one sentence and thought he understood it he lost his grasp of the previous one. There was always a glass in his hand. Whenever he noticed it he put it down, but it kept coming back again. He began to feel sleepy.

Terry was saying something about an initial twelve-month period, extendable at the option of either party, when the kitchen door swung open and a waiter emerged silhouetted against the bright, cold, fluorescent lighting behind him. The door was open only for a fleeting instant but it was enough for David to see into the kitchen and to make out three or four figures moving towards the back wall. One of them looked like the *Homeless Truths* seller from the station. Same height, same hair colour and shape. David thought that it was very unlikely that it actually was her. What did it matter? He was surprised how often she had come into his mind during the day, because she wasn't what he would ordinarily have called attractive. It really didn't matter. No, it did: he needed to know whether or not it was her. Someone was still talking from across the table, but almost all of David's attention was now focused on watching the infuriatingly closed kitchen door out of the corner of his eye.

"Which is about the size of it," a voice was saying. "What do you think?"

David forced himself to pay attention to the man in front of him. "I'll have to think about it," he replied distractedly. "Get back to you." The girls at the next table were getting up to leave, and they were very beautiful.

"And talk to Simon?"

David could no longer be bothered to defend himself. "Probably," he mumbled. Why wouldn't that door open?

"OK," Terry continued earnestly. "Well, he seemed pretty positive about the idea at the weekend. I expect he mentioned it."

"He said you'd said something." It sounded funny; David wanted to laugh.

Terry wouldn't let it drop. "But if he said yes, then it would be all right with you?"

David barely repressed a hiccup. "Well, as you know, I work for him, so even if it wasn't."

The kitchen door finally swung open again. The waiter coming out caught it with the heel of his foot so that he could hear what someone behind him was trying to tell him. David could see the dark-haired girl more clearly. She had some sort of overall on and her hair was loosely held in a net. She was standing at a sink from which clouds of steam were rising into her face. She momentarily looked up. The line of her nose convinced David more than ever that it was the girl from the station. She was wearing a pair of large, blue rubber gloves that came up almost to her elbows as she scrubbed at something obscured from view. David looked away with a feeling of embarrassment and mild disgust.

Terry didn't appear to have noticed anything. "So if it's fine with him it's fine with you?" he asked firmly.

David's interest in the conversation had long since waned. "He's the boss," he replied wearily.

"Well, he seemed keen on Saturday."

David yawned and drained his wineglass. When he looked for a refill the bottle turned out to be empty, as was his brandy glass. "Then I'd have to go along with it," he conceded simply.

"Thanks," said Terry. "I appreciate it."

The cab ride was very strange. It seemed to consist of a small number of distinct moments, like still photos, in a particular order but not joined together, and David was aware of voices, including sometimes his own, but not really of any distinct words or sentences. The taxi lurched round side streets that all seemed alike in the dark, past the restaurants and bars and Victorian theatres of the West End. There were some girls in short skirts, walking along holding beer bottles and shouting about something. And then David and Terry weren't in the cab at all any longer, but making their way down some narrow steps to the basement level of what appeared to be a row of Georgian terraces, and David bumped into Terry twice and apologised each time, and there was this meathead of a guy with a shaved scalp and Desperate-Dan stubble, looking awkward in a penguin suit a size too small, who didn't seem to like the look of David but relaxed when he saw who he was with, and smiled when Terry put something in his hand for his trouble and clapped him on the shoulder. And there was some sort of chrome bar, and lights that moved, and girls in spangly outfits that revealed pretty well everything you wanted to see, and none of them seemed to be English, and some didn't even seem to understand English, or at least what David was trying to say to them, and there was champagne, and he definitely got hiccups at one point, but stopped them by holding his nose, which the girl he was talking to at the time seemed to find strange for some reason. And after that there wasn't anything at all.

A mid-week visit to a club like the *Inferno* was nothing out of the ordinary for Terry. It was the usual booze-and-fanny routine which was pretty foolproof in business. It worked better on the younger guys, but it worked to some extent on almost all of them, especially the bored husbands. David Kelsey had always been a bit of an exception, a curiosity: during all the time he had been married to Sonia it had been impossible to get him near a titty bar. He'd always gone home as everyone else was getting in the mood and making noises about moving on. He'd said things like the places didn't interest him, or why would you go to a restaurant where they only showed you the food, which he presumably thought was a clever remark, but a lot of the market guys just thought he must be gay, and Terry would have thought so too if he hadn't known about Sonia and the kid.

Terry hadn't been absolutely sure that David was going to surrender tonight; he had come quite prepared to just have a meal and a few beers - he was quite tired, he wouldn't mind an early night - so long as by the end of the evening Kelsey was better disposed to push his plan with Simon. But then Kelsey had started throwing back the sauce and getting emotional and his eyes had kept wandering to a couple of barely-above-average-looking giggly girls at the next table. Terry even thought he had caught him giving some menial in the kitchen the once-over, at which point Terry had become convinced that Kelsey couldn't have had any for months, maybe not since he'd split up with Sonia a couple of *years* back. Christ, think of that!

Terry had taken advantage of David's long absence in the toilet to ring ahead to the *Inferno* to find out who was working and to ask a couple of favours. Irina the Romanian kid with the piercings was on; sexy, but hard. She wasn't what David

74

required now, whereas one of her heavenly blowjobs was exactly what Terry himself needed and intended to get later in the evening. Something softer for Kelsey, one of the little Orientals with the smiling lips and sad eyes and names like the teletubbies. The guy at the *Inferno* had said he had exactly the girl.

Almost as an afterthought Terry had rung Mac from his office, someone he knew would be out on the piss in town and who was always up for a bit of gash. Mac had immediately agreed to meet Terry at the *Inferno* without asking for any explanation. Which was good because Kelsey had started to become a bit of a handful: he'd talked a load of crap in the cab, mainly about his brat of a daughter, who sounded like she just needed a backhander to sort her out once and for all. And then something about had Terry ever wondered how people came to be homeless, which he hadn't even bothered to respond to.

On entering the club, allowing Kelsey to lean against him for support, Terry found that Mac was already there, with his trademark smirk, a glass of something yellow in one hand and his free arm wrapped round an unsmiling, heavy-featured Russian-looking girl Terry hadn't seen before, who seemed to be struggling to overcome her natural distaste for the sweaty young man.

Mac smiled and nodded in Terry's direction as he and David approached. The girl looked even more uncomfortable.

Terry nodded back. "You know David Kelsey."

Mac held out his hand again, but David didn't appear to see it.

"I do indeed," Mac said. "Not quite the sort of place I expected to see you, if you don't mind me saying so."

Terry glowered at his colleague.

David smiled sheepishly from behind glassy eyes, and mumbled something about the world being his oyster, and then something else about a nightcap.

Mac laughed. "I think we can do better than that." At a nod from Terry, he turned to the bar and ordered a bottle of champagne. The barman was a small man of at least sixty with a few slicks of hair left on his otherwise bald head. He scurried around behind the counter like a performing monkey frightened of being whipped by its master and quickly, silently opened the bottle.

At Mac's instruction four glasses were filled. Three were handed out – the Russian girl dutifully took hers - and David's was placed on the bar. Terry decided it wasn't necessary to have David drink any more; in fact it would probably be better if he didn't.

The Russian girl, although her facial expression told you that she clearly didn't like the taste of champagne, managed to empty her glass in a few short gulps. Terry leant across with the champagne and gave her a refill. She visibly relaxed as he nodded at the barman to open another bottle.

Terry motioned them all over to an empty table, pulling David along with him while Mac carried his glass.

Some other tables were occupied, but the lighting in this place was perfect for privacy. You really couldn't make out the faces in the other groups of people: you could hear the hubbub of voices, the occasional laughter; you could smell some of their drinks and the girls' scent; you could make out the silhouettes of women on men's laps; but outside your own group you could be completely anonymous.

Terry leant across to the Russian girl - Olga, he'd decided to call her, whatever her real name was; there weren't many real names in this club anyway - and asked her if she'd mind pissing off for a few minutes. She scowled and then looked nervously at a tall long-haired man in a dinner-suit who had been standing near the bar since their arrival. Terry waved at him and he nodded emotionlessly at Olga, who now smiled politely and moved away.

"Don't worry," Terry whispered to Mac, whose face betrayed his disappointment. "You'll be shooting your load in that later. A bit of business first."

Terry, Mac and David sat down.

Mac punched David on the shoulder. "Enjoying yourself so far, mate?"

David nodded and smiled amiably.

"Great," Mac continued with his face close to David's. "How was your working dinner?"

David seemed momentarily not to recognise the description. "Fine," he replied eventually. "Thanks for asking."

"Did you come to any decision on Terry's proposal?" Mac asked, suddenly more serious. "Sounds like a no-brainer to me. We win, you win."

"Mac, for fuck's sake," Terry interjected, throwing his hands up in a gesture that pointed out the surroundings. "This is hardly the time or the place." He turned to David. "Sorry about that, D. You know how over enthusiastic these young guys get. Can't tell business from pleasure. How long do we go back, mate?"

David seemed to be trying to work out the answer, but it wasn't coming to him. "Long time," he said after a pause. "Long, long, long, long time." He waved his head in time to the repeated phrase and then started to laugh.

"And he's had a shitty couple of days," Terry continued. "You heard about Guy in his office?"

"Yeah," Mac nodded gravely. "I was sorry to hear it, of course."

David had produced a crumpled tissue from his pocket and was clumsily blowing his nose.

"So," Terry told Mac sternly, "business isn't everything."

David was staring intently at Mac in an attempt to focus on his face. "This guy here's a very good friend of mine," he informed the blurred features. "He's old school."

77

"Exactly," Terry agreed enthusiastically, leaning forward and patting David on the knee. "And you, my friend need cheering up."

Terry turned and made eye contact with the man in the dinner-suit, who nodded almost imperceptibly. Within a minute three girls had been sent over. Olga began feeding olives to Mac, while Romanian Irina was on Terry's lap, smiling a mindless druggy smile and letting her hands rest first on his thighs, then almost too soon on his cock, as if she had a job to do and wanted to get it over with so that she could call it a night. Terry knew the score, but even so this was a bit out of order. If it had been someone else, he might have asked the management to change her. But Irina did give the most amazing head.

She'd have to be patient for a couple of minutes, though, because Terry's attention for the moment was directed towards the third girl, little La-La. Fair play to the girl: she was doing her best to follow instructions, nestled against Kelsey's semi-comatose body in the corner seat, running one hand up and down his leg. But he was smiling at her as if she was a friend of his, and he seemed to want to have a friendly chat. The girl was nodding earnestly in reply to whatever he was saying, following his face with those big mournful eyes of hers, which was almost funny because she didn't speak much English and Kelsey was trying to tell her about his ex-wife, and his teenage daughter, and he'd even managed to dig out a photo from somewhere. Terry decided that something needed to be done before David asked for a cup of cocoa and passed out.

Irina had decided that if nothing else was working her thick, tressed, black hair might be a turn-on, and Terry had to push it out of his eyes so that he could continue to watch David. La-La looked round the room a couple of times, with a worried expression on her little face, then at Terry and finally at the man by the bar. David appeared not to be conscious. Terry pushed Irina off his lap, got up and went to have a word.

A couple of minutes later Terry watched in satisfaction as David was carried to the room out the back by a couple of gorillas while La-La followed apprehensively behind. The man in the dinner-jacket framed the scene on a small digital camera. Terry signed the bill on his corporate card and headed out with a slightly sulky Irina – did she think they were fucking married or something? - to find a hotel.

Chapter Ten

David woke and looked at the clock next to the bed. Ten past ten. He blinked and looked again. Still ten past ten. Morning or evening? He tried to sit up but spots appeared before his eyes, his stomach threatened to heave and sweat started to run down his skin.

He didn't recognise the clock. He didn't recognise the bed. Or the room. He felt a fierce thirst, and a desperate need for a piss, but every time he tried to move a searing pain in his head forced it back on the pillow. He retched.

Memories began to return. There were a couple of still shots in his head: one of someone putting him into a cab and the other of his trying to sign something at a reception desk. He remembered dinner with Terry, but what had happened after that?

He shivered at the contemplation of what he might have done or said. He had lost control when he had been so determined that he wasn't going to. He despised himself.

He figured that he must be in a hotel somewhere in West London. The room was large and ornate but the ceiling plaster was cracked and there was bare wood on the sash-window. Someone was using a vacuum cleaner in the hallway. There was a smell of laundry soap.

David breathed deeply several times then forced himself out of bed into the bathroom, where he just reached the toilet in time to throw up. His stomach continued to retch when there was no longer anything inside it, but eventually it subsided and David sat on the bathroom floor feeling curiously euphoric for a minute or so before the pain in his head reasserted itself. He drank as much of the musty water from the basin tap as his stomach would stand and then clambered into the shower, fumbling with the controls until a spray of water erupted into his face. The shower was noisy and dark, either very hot or ice-cold, but the torrent of water on the outside of his head gradually brought relief to the hangover inside it, at least while the deluge continued.

He dried himself and began to collect his thoughts. Whatever he'd done, he couldn't undo it. Today was a write-off, he told himself, but tomorrow he could at least try to limit the damage.

He called in sick. He made sure that he spoke to Jill rather than to Simon. Jill said she was sorry to hear he had stomach trouble, that there was no further news of Guy's condition, that there were no messages, except one from Terry Ransome, who had said it wasn't urgent and he would call back later. She said hopefully she would see David tomorrow, if he was feeling better by then. David said he was sure he would be.

Putting on the previous day's clothes, with their smell of wine and sweat - and there was also a powerful scent of cheap perfume, where had that come from? - made David feel nauseous again, and he opened the stiff sash-window and gulped in some fresh air. There was no sign of vomit anywhere in the bedroom, which was at least something. It was a relief as well to find that he still had his wallet and that it still contained his credit cards.

David went down to reception and asked to settle his bill. He didn't recognise the hotel at all, but the deep-red carpet on the wide, spiral staircase, the mosaic floors, the wrought-iron banisters and the smart green livery of the staff suggested it wasn't cheap. The cost would obviously have to go on his personal card, which was getting very close to its limit. He lived pretty frugally, he thought, and tried to pay off the card each month; but recently it seemed that Sonia wanted extra amounts every month for something - different each time - that Amy couldn't possibly do without and that the regular allowance he gave her apparently didn't cover. As a result he had started making just the minimum credit-card repayment each month, promising himself that he would pay off a lump sum as soon as he could, perhaps at bonus time.

"That's OK," said the serious, bespectacled, young Asian man behind the counter when David waved the credit card in his direction. "The account has been settled."

David winced. "If I put it on my company card last night I'll have to switch…"

The young man shook his head gravely and looked at his computer screen. "By a gentleman who rang this morning."

"I see." David knew exactly who the gentleman was and that he should absolutely insist on paying for himself. He went to say so. But what might Amy need this month? Whatever it was, he wasn't having John pay for it. He hesitated, then put his wallet away and asked for directions to the nearest Tube.

He got home via a circuitous route, avoiding the City. On all the trains he took people seemed to be avoiding him. He slept for the rest of the day.

He woke up at seven thirty in the evening and opened a tin of stew that needed only to be heated, then tried to watch TV, but wasn't able to concentrate on the screen. What had he done the previous evening? What had he said? And what use was Terry going to make of it?

David was relieved when his eyelids started to droop once more and he could go back to bed. He woke several times during the small hours, and each time a newly retrieved recollection prevented him from immediately returning to sleep. By the time morning arrived he could visualise a seedy club with Mac and Terry, though no sound accompanied the pictures. And he could see a pretty little Oriental girl with doleful eyes. And smell her scent and feel the warm touch of her skin.

Chapter Eleven

One face of the concourse clock said eight twenty; the other one that was visible from David's vantage point maintained that it was a couple of minutes later. Eight thirty in the office might just be achievable. Hastily but without enthusiasm David climbed the stairs two at a time and exited onto the street.

The girl was there, as, he had to admit to himself, he'd been hoping she would be: in her usual place, wearing the same coat and holding a stack of *Homeless Truths* at her hip. A serious-faced young woman brushed past David, carrying a copy of the magazine that she had just paid for. He glimpsed the cover and saw that it was not the edition he had bought two days previously. Which meant that he could now buy another one if he chose to. Should he? Or maybe wait till early next week? David took the change out of his pocket and contemplated it for a moment, then swiftly went across and held out the two coins to the girl, who smiled as she handed over the magazine. It was a business-like smile, not a greeting or a sign of recognition. David wanted to tell her he'd seen her on Tuesday night. But that was too awkward because the fact that he could afford to eat in the restaurant where she did the shitty jobs didn't amount to something they had in common.

"No rain again today," he heard himself say.

"No," the girl agreed, smiling faintly once more. "Hope not." She held up her stack of magazines. "Wet is bad news."

David nodded in agreement, thanked her quickly and walked away.

"I hope you aren't turning into some sort of bleeding-heart pinko liberal," said Adrian as David came through the door into the office.

David ignored him but quickly put the copy of *Homeless Truths* into his desk drawer.

He sat down, turned on his computer and pressed the voicemail button next to the illuminated red light. There were three messages, a disappointingly low tally after an unplanned day off. Two were from people wanting to set up routine client meetings. The third was from Terry, who didn't say much beyond enquiring as to David's health, but there was a knowingness in the otherwise friendly tone that David didn't care for. Presumably Terry would have guessed that David had failed to make it into the office.

David had conflicting instincts: on the one hand he was sure it would be sensible to avoid Terry for a few days, until the memory of Tuesday night had begun to fade and some sense of normality had returned. On the other hand he wanted to know as soon as possible what Terry was playing at with the hotel bill, and what he intended to do next.

David got himself a coffee and returned the other two calls first. As he talked he looked round the office to see if anyone was looking at him oddly, pointing or smiling in his direction. Not as far as he could tell. And to his relief no-one was telling him that Simon wanted to see him either.

He decided to take the initiative and call Terry, but when he did so around nine thirty – having a couple of times picked up the receiver and then replaced it - he was almost relieved to find that Terry wasn't at his desk. He left what he hoped was a neutral-sounding message stating flatly that he was returning Terry's call from the previous day and hoped he was well.

Terry rang back ten minutes later. He sounded friendly enough, but there was a small change to his tone, a slight hint of condescension, so that when he suggested they meet in a coffee bar that was more convenient for himself than it was for David, David felt that it was best to agree.

David deliberately arrived a couple of minutes after the appointed time and was disappointed to find that Terry wasn't already there. He sat down at the last available table and ordered a cappuccino from a pushy waitress who did not seem able to understand that he was waiting for someone and preferred that they should both order together. For the next five minutes David looked repeatedly at his watch and resisted, with increasing impatience, attempts by other customers to take the unoccupied chair from the other side of his table.

The coffee arrived and David stirred it absent-mindedly. He stared through the glass shop front, between words in large gold back-to-front lettering promoting the café's special deals.

In the gap between 'mocha' and some other phrase his brain didn't attempt to read backwards, David could see the exit of his station and the *Homeless Truths* girl, or rather her green coat. The wind that had come up in the last few minutes and was causing a few leaves to swirl and knock against the glass had also led her to change her stance; she was now huddled in on herself with the magazines held closer to her body, and there was a greater urgency to the way she thrust them out whenever someone passed. She didn't seem to be meeting with much success at this time of day. David wished someone would buy one.

Terry came through the door talking intently into his phone. David was about to greet him when Mac entered too, a couple of paces behind. David sat up. He automatically looked around for another door but couldn't find one.

Terry sat down in the chair on the opposite side of the table but looked over David's head and continued to talk into his phone. As far as David could make out it was standard self-inflated Terry stuff: we have a deadline, you need to move your position so that we can make a deal. Terry was speaking loudly enough for everyone on the surrounding tables to hear him.

David wondered if there was in fact anyone at the other end of the line.

Mac smiled pleasantly but without warmth at David, who stood up and shook his hand.

"You'll have to find a ...," David began, "I didn't realise.."

"No problem," Mac replied, dragging a chair from the next table without enquiring whether or not it was available, and sitting down between David and Terry. He looked over to the waitress, raised his arm and nodded. The woman shuffled over and languidly took the order for an americano and a latte.

Terry had now turned his body so that he was sitting at right angles to David.

Mac pointed at Terry and smiled again. "Sorry about this. You know what he's like once he gets started. Probably be off the phone by lunchtime."

David smiled back. "So how are things with you?"

"Fine. Better than fine actually: pretty good at the moment. I've been promoted."

"Oh, congratulations."

"And I got engaged!"

Vague memories from Tuesday made David hesitate for a moment.

"Congratulations again," he stammered.

Mac was suddenly serious again. "How about you?"

David scratched his chin. "Work-wise it's OK. We're going to be a little off budget, but who isn't in the market at the moment?"

Mac nodded. "Screw top line. Bottom line's the thing. You chase top line at the moment and this time next year you're toast."

David nodded slowly in agreement.

"Not that there aren't some great opportunities out there if you know where to look."

"Possibly," David replied guardedly.

Terry's conversation was becoming more animated as it became more circular: David thought he had heard Terry make the same point at least three times, and whoever it was he was talking to was apparently doing the same.

Mac was staring at David as if he expected him to say something further. David smiled unassumingly back. He didn't want to discuss Tuesday night right now, though he supposed it couldn't be avoided indefinitely.

"You haven't heard any more from your daughter?" Mac asked.

David didn't remember discussing his daughter with Mac. He shuffled uncomfortably in his seat.

"I'm sorry," Mac went on. "You don't have to… It's just that you were telling us on Tuesday night, and I thought…"

David thought for a second. "I probably told you a lot of things on Tuesday evening," he said with what was intended to sound like friendly candour. "I'd had quite a few by the time I left the restaurant."

"Nothing wrong with letting your hair down every now and then."

David nodded and held up his hands. "I hope I wasn't too embarrassing."

"Well, we've all done it."

David made a physical effort not to blush. He clasped his hands tightly together under the table. "I suppose telling people about my family is better than starting a fight," he offered, in order to break the silence.

"I suppose it is," Mac agreed, as though there wasn't much in it either way.

"What's that?" Terry had finally finished his phone call. The waitress came over and unloaded two ceramic mugs of coffee onto the table. "Cheers," said Terry, waving his mug vaguely in David's direction. "Sorry about all that."

"Problem?" David generally wasn't interested in Terry's business dealings with other people, but thought he would rather discuss those than pick over his own behaviour on Tuesday night.

"Yes," replied Terry. "Well, no, not really. Nothing I can't handle. Some little chancer at Carson's thinks he can say one thing one week and then change his mind the next. Out of his depth. Which is why," he turned to look at Mac and pointed at David with the hand that wasn't holding his mug, "I much prefer to do business with guys like this. Straight. Knows what he's talking about. Old school."

Terry's expression didn't change, but Mac looked away and appeared to be trying to stifle a smirk.

"Anyway, to cut to the chase," Terry went on, reaching down into his briefcase and producing a small, black ring-binder, "here is our detailed proposal for your perusal. I expect you'll need to get Simon's final approval, but hopefully it'll just be a question of dotting the Is and crossing the Ts."

David regretted his own stupidity more keenly than ever. It was clear he should have held the meeting in the office and taken a colleague along, but Tuesday night had made that very difficult. "I'll take a look," he replied with all the authority he could muster.

"Of course. My girl will send it electronically as well. As I say, Simon was very positive on the golf-course last weekend. Everyone's a winner."

Terry looked at his watch and got up to go. Mac took a quick mouthful of coffee and followed a couple of seconds later.

"Always a pleasure, D," Terry said in a slow, measured voice, holding out his right hand and patting David on the shoulder with his left. "Thanks for the coffee."

"I'll be in touch," was all David could find to say, and by then Terry was half way out the door, with Mac close behind.

David sat alone at the table for a couple of minutes going through the conversation in his head, trying to figure out what he should have said; what he had said but shouldn't have. He drained the cold froth from the bottom of his coffee cup, then picked up the folder Terry had left behind and tried to read it. He couldn't take it in. He felt very lonely. The café was full of people in business suits holding their important meetings, doing their deals. He hated all of them.

An idea that had previously occurred to him came back into his head and no longer seemed a strange thing to do. He stood up, went over to the counter, paid the bill and ordered two more cappuccinos to go. He fought against a loss of nerve for the seconds he was obliged to wait for the drinks, then, with the two warm cardboard cups held out in front of him and the ring-binder under his arm, went out through the door as another customer came in. Once on the pavement he put his head down into the wind and gripped the cups so tightly, in order to prevent them being blown away, that they began to burn his fingers. He saw a gap in the traffic and scampered across to the other side.

"I thought you looked cold, so I've brought you a cup of coffee," he told the startled *Homeless Truths* seller. He had rehearsed what he would say several times in his head, but it sounded lame in the open air. The girl instinctively moved back a couple of feet and looked around nervously.

David looked around too. There were quite a few people in the area as it happened; it was no longer the rush hour, but a central London train terminus was never going to be a quiet place. Maybe he ought to repeat what he had said; maybe the girl simply hadn't heard him, or had heard but not understood. Except that she was vigorously shaking her head and holding her hand up in a gesture that firmly rejected the offered cup and told him not to come nearer.

David knew the sensible thing would be to walk away immediately. But then the girl would think she had been right to be suspicious, to recoil from him, and she wasn't. He was trying for one small minute to do one small good thing.

"I didn't mean to startle you," he began, shouting across the distance that divided him from the girl, taking care not to advance into it. "You looked cold and I thought you might...It seemed like a good idea. Please don't think..."

"I'm fine." The girl was keeping her distance, and there was now an aggressive edge in her voice.

"It'll be wasted otherwise," David argued. "I can't drink two."

"No thank you," the girl said firmly.

"Don't you like coffee?" David was surprised to hear himself persist.

"Just leave me alone. *Please*."

David knew he needed to give up: otherwise he was risking arrest. "OK," he said sadly. "I suppose you have to be careful. For all you know I could be some weirdo out to poison you or give you something disgusting to drink."

The girl said nothing. She shrugged and nodded slightly.

David felt encouraged. "They gave me this voucher for a free coffee," he said, bending forward to put the coffee cups down, letting the ring-binder fall to the ground and beginning to rummage around in his inside jacket pocket. "How about if I give you that?"

"OK," the girl said quietly.

David handed the voucher to her. "Look, I'm going to stop hassling you right now," he promised. "I'm really sorry if I've upset you at all. But just so as you know: I'm going to go now and stand over there by those steps, where you can see me, and I'm going to drink both of these. And when I come past tomorrow morning I'm going to wave and you'll see that I'm not dead and the coffees were fine."

The girl made no response. David bent down to retrieve his belongings, but found that it was very difficult to stand up once he had a cup in each hand and the ring-binder under his arm. He pushed himself up very slowly, but as he did so the binder slid out and clattered to the ground and he fell backwards. To his surprise the girl laughed out loud and came forward, picked the binder up in one hand without dropping her pile of magazines and held it until he was upright. Then she forcefully pressed it against his side.

"Hold it tighter," she said firmly.

"Yes," David replied. "Thanks. I will."

David bounded up the stairs to the office three at a time, having given up all hope that a lift would ever arrive. Three large cups of coffee in less than an hour had gone straight through him. He dumped the ring-binder on his desk and headed quickly for the toilets. On his return he found Jill leaning across his desk affixing a sticky yellow note to his computer screen.

"Ah, there you are," she said. "Simon says he knows it's short notice, but can you do lunch today with Premier of Wyoming?"

"Just me?"

"And him."

"They're the nutty religious guys."

"He didn't tell me that."

"And they don't drink."

Jill half suppressed a smile. "I'm sure you'll survive."

"OK." David scratched his head. "Well, I am free and I can't think of a good excuse, so I'll have to do it. How come such short notice though?"

"I think Guy was going to…"

"I see," David interrupted quickly to put an end to the mutual embarrassment. "How is he, by the way. Sorry, not 'by the way'. How is he?"

"I rang the hospital yesterday. They said 'about the same'."

"Is that good?"

"I don't know. What do you think?"

"I hope I'm wrong, but I, you know..."

"Yep."

"I hope I'm wrong."

"Simon spoke to his mother again this morning."

"Did he? In that case I'll ask him if I get a chance at lunch. Any developments etc."

"Understood."

"Thanks."

Eva couldn't make her mind up about the guy who'd offered her a coffee. She'd been close enough to him to be fairly sure that he hadn't been drinking. Perhaps he was religious and thought she needed saving; she'd encountered a few of those types, and offering food and drink was one of their tactics. Some of them were nice and others seemed a bit unhinged.

Maybe he'd done it for a bet. Perhaps his City mates had been watching at a distance. Somehow she didn't think so; not because it wasn't the sort of thing some of these people would do, but because if the idea was to humiliate her at some point they would have let on. And when he'd fallen over and dropped his file his mates would have laughed.

He couldn't fancy her. Not the way she looked now. Unless he was one of the creepy guys who liked rough. Not that she thought she was, but, well... But those guys approached you at night in quiet places, not in broad daylight outside a major train station.

Maybe he was just a lonely middle-aged bloke who wanted someone to talk to. She wondered if he had any money. His clothes didn't look expensive, but anyone working in the City wouldn't be earning peanuts. She smiled at the thought of him trying earnestly to get her to take the drink, falling over and attempting to get up holding two cups and the file that kept slipping from his grasp; then finally downing two hot drinks in quick succession in order to prove that he wasn't a poisoner!

He probably wasn't dangerous then. And if he wasn't dangerous, maybe the guy was an opportunity. She needed to work out how she was going to play it if, as he had promised, he waved at her tomorrow. She decided that she couldn't afford to ignore him, because he might just give up. Better to look amused rather than friendly; that way she remained in control.

A serious young man in a blue windcheater was silently holding out some money. Eva resumed her practised grateful smile as she took the coins and handed over a magazine.

Chapter Twelve

Simon had chosen to book what in David's view was pretty much the dullest restaurant in London, but it was at least a place where there was no danger of rowdy behaviour that might offend the sensibilities of his American guests. The place had hardly changed in almost twenty years: it still had bare-brick walls decorated with signed photos of sports stars, a number of whom David didn't recognise; the majority of the rest, it seemed to him, must have long since retired. He was sitting next to Simon at a table for six, facing the door through which they had for the past ten minutes been expecting the imminent appearance of the Premier of Wyoming people. They were experiencing their longstanding difficulty in making small talk with each other, and for the most part Simon was speaking while David half-listened.

There were about a dozen tables with place-settings hopefully laid out, but only three were currently occupied. The head waiter had already twice enquired in a thick Mediterranean accent whether the rest of Mr Stevens' party was going to come, much to Simon's visible annoyance. It was clear the restaurant needed the business.

"Jill says Guy's about the same," David said to break the silence.

"Does she?" Simon replied with audible impatience in his voice. His eyes narrowed as he looked over David's shoulder.

"She also says you spoke to Guy's mother again this morning?"

Simon picked up his fork and stared at the prongs. Then he put it down again and silently looked at David for a couple of seconds as if he was trying to size him up before deciding whether or not he was worth the effort of an explanation.

"What do you think of Jill?" Simon asked finally.

"In what way?"

Simon unsmilingly looked David straight in the eye. "Just answer the question," he said coldly. "For once I want to know what David Kelsey really thinks. Do you know something? You are one of the most difficult people to read I think I've ever met."

David smiled nervously. "Is that a compliment?"

"It might be if I was doing business with you, but you and I are on the same team. So now I want to know what *you* think. Not what other people think, or what you think you ought to think or what you think I want to hear. Your independently arrived-at opinion. That's a major management skill, by the way; you don't progress in our business without it."

David bridled at the implied criticism but decided not to react to it. "What do I think of Jill?" he repeated the question to give himself time to think. "Well, she seems to be pretty efficient at what she does, work-wise..."

Simon's hand made a circular motion to indicate that he wanted to hear more.

" ..but as a person she does have a tendency to try to make herself the centre of attention, even with something like what's happened to Guy."

"I think I'd agree with that," Simon said decisively. "Give me another straight answer. Do you care?"

"Do I care?"

"Yes. About Guy?"

"Yes...Yes, I do." David thought again. "No, I do."

"OK." Simon picked up the fork again. "How much?"

"What? Out of ten?"

"No. Answer the question."

"OK. Well, less than I would if it was my daughter, obviously. More than I would if it was, I don't know, that waiter over there or Bob from First Denver."

Simon seemed to like the answer. "Do you like Guy?" he asked.

"I didn't…not particularly. But I think that's human nature – you care more about people that you know, even if you don't necessarily particularly like them."

Simon looked down at the table and nodded. Then he slowly raised his head. "I did speak to his mother."

"And?"

"And... Guy's back is fucked," Simon said simply.

"Oh. I'm..."

"Guy is never going to walk again."

"Shit." David put his hands between his knees and looked down at his lap. "Does he know?" he asked quietly.

Simon put the fork down again and slowly shook his head. "Not yet."

They sat in silence for a few seconds.

"I don't know what to say," David said finally.

"There isn't anything to say," Simon replied flatly. "And I don't suppose there's anything to do either, though I went through the ritual of telling Guy's mother we'd do whatever we could."

"Good."

Simon said nothing.

"Well we will, won't we?"

Simon leaned back in his chair and looked at David directly.

"Will we?" he asked significantly. "Do you really think so?"

David wasn't willing to concede the point. "I hope so."

"What can we do, David?"

David thought aloud: "Visit him for the moment. Do everything we can to make it possible for him to come back to work if he wants to. Make sure the permanent health insurance pays out if he doesn't or can't."

Simon's face suggested that he his companion's responses were only confirming the naivety he suspected him of.

"You really think he'll be able to come back?" he asked combatively.

"A few years ago probably not. But the building's been fitted out for disabled people now: the entrance, the lifts, the corridors, the toilets. It's the law, isn't it?"

Simon let out a derisive snort. "And how many physically handicapped people do you know in our market?"

David didn't have to think very long. "None."

"Precisely." Simon slapped the table with the palm of his hand. "This market is tough and unsentimental, as you well know, and we can't carry anybody, and no-one's going to make special allowances. So 'TLO is an equal opportunities employer' and we've spent a packet on ramps and braille signs in the lifts, and I'm sure our team in the London Marathon next year will be raising money for research into spinal injuries. But the bottom line is that the board are going to tell me, off the record obviously, to quietly pay Guy off and, you know what, in the real world I'm not sure I'd do anything different in their place." He smiled grimly. "Now do you want my job?"

"I've never wanted your job," David replied spontaneously before he could stop himself.

Simon looked back quizzically. "I don't think that's true," he replied. "You don't now, I accept that. But you used to, when Frank was still here."

David shrugged. "Things change. People change."

"Maybe. How's your daughter?"

David laughed nervously. "Amy is teenage and stroppy," he replied, realising as he spoke that this was becoming his stock answer.

Simon smiled. "That's normal, isn't it? Not that I'd know, I guess. Do you see her much? Sorry - am I being too personal here?"

David shook his head unconvincingly. "Not at all. Every third weekend usually. I saw her last week. That's why I didn't come to the golf."

"Of course. Your friend Terry is a strange guy."

"He's not my friend," David protested quickly.

"Well, people think he is. Impressions count. There are a lot of more legitimate operators in the business to hang around with."

"I do know that."

"Did you have dinner with him on Tuesday?"

"I did."

"Where did you go?"

"Abbington's."

"Not really the VIP treatment, then," Simon replied dismissively.

"It's OK there." David remembered in time the reason he'd given for staying at home the previous day. "Usually it is. This time they managed to poison me."

Simon's face wore a quizzical look once more. David tried not to blush; he knew he wasn't a good liar.

"OK," Simon said ambiguously. "Leaving that aside, does Mr Ransome have anything in his proposal I should be getting excited about?"

"Possibly," David replied hesitantly. "I don't know. I only received it in detail this morning. I'm going to read it this afternoon."

"Well, look," Simon sounded more emollient. "They don't pay us to turn down good business propositions, whoever they come from. So if you like it and can sell it to me, then fine. But we don't owe Terry Ransome anything. He needs us far more than TLO needs him. No favours for mates. Understood?"

"He's not.."

Simon's phone rang and he answered it.

"Hi, Jill" he said. "No, go on. Well, what are they doing there? No, I said we'd meet at the restaurant. We've been sitting here for twenty minutes. Well, can you send them down? Yes? Jill, you still there? On second thoughts, to be on the safe side, you'd better *bring* them down here."

Chapter Thirteen

David had read the same page at least a dozen times, and it still wasn't getting into his head. He had booked a meeting room for the afternoon: it was small and had no natural light, but it was a haven from the noise of the office. He forced himself to concentrate and flicked through the contents of Terry's folder. There were several sections, neatly divided by coloured cards, on each of which the applicable heading name had been written in what looked like precise, rounded female writing. David doubted that Terry had had much to do with it apart from signing the summary letter, or that he understood it. It was mainly numbers: various worked examples setting out the profit TLO would have made from the proposed arrangement if it had been in place for the last one, three, five and ten years. And then projections into the future, using various different assumptions as to how the market might move in the meantime, with suitable disclaimers. There was also a version on a memory stick, tucked into a small slot inside the back cover. All David needed to do was to plug the numbers in on the PC, check the assumptions made by Terry's company against the TLO standard model, perhaps add some of his own and stress-test the entire package. If it stacked up, then the question of how much he might be influenced in his judgment by what Terry knew about Tuesday night wouldn't have to be addressed.

An hour later David was feeling much more upbeat. The proposal did make sense: the numbers added up, there were no bogus assumptions. The projected profit margin using TLO's own model was in the top half of the deals the department had done over the last twelve months. So David could recommend it to Simon in good conscience. It was good business. There was only one small change that he would need to make to the contract to meet TLO's standards, and that wasn't controversial.

David called Terry from the meeting room to give him the news.

Terry's voice was unexpectedly cold and abrupt when he answered; he sounded as if he had been interrupted.

David had rehearsed in his head what he would say, how he would sound. Friendly but assertive. "Hi, Tel," he said brightly. "It's David. How's it going?"

"Good." Terry sounded slightly surprised. "Yeah, good, mate. What's the S.P.?"

"I've looked at your proposal."

"Terrific. Can I just put you on squawk, D? Mac's with me here."

David heard unintelligible muttering at the other end of the line, and when Terry spoke to him again his voice was accompanied by the echo of the phone's speaker.

"OK," Terry said. "So you loved it and you've sold it to Mr Stevens and now he loves it too."

David laughed. "Very nearly."

Terry's tone was frosty again. "What's 'very nearly'?"

"Well I think it does add up and I want to recommend it to Simon."

"Good. But..?."

Mac said something in the background that wasn't audible.

David continued in what he hoped was a confident voice: "There's just one small change I'd like to make."

"I don't think..."

"It's no big deal, Tel. I suspect it's just a drafting oversight at your end."

"Try me."

"The annual review clause."

"What about it?"

"It doesn't have one."

Terry hesitated. David imagined that he was turning to Mac for advice. "Is it that big a deal?" he asked uncertainly after a couple of seconds.

"No. It's standard these days."

"And everything else is OK?"

"Fine. With me, anyway. I'd just need to get Simon to sign off on it."

"And he would?"

"Well, I can't guarantee it, Terry, but I can't see why he wouldn't."

"I'll call you back."

David started to say that he wasn't at his desk, but the line went dead.

Terry thought for a second or so before coming to an executive decision. He waited five minutes before calling back. Kelsey answered immediately.

"Sorry, mate," Terry pronounced calmly. "No changes. Hello? You still there?"

When David spoke again his confidence had ebbed away. "You can't?" he said in bewildered disbelief. "Why not? I thought.. I mean, it's standard stuff now, Terry. Ask Mac. It'd be a shame to…"

"Sorry, mate," Terry said firmly. "We've put a lot into this. It stands or falls as it is."

"But…"

"You're gonna have to speak up, D: I can hardly hear you."

A long pause at the other end of the line and then a nervous-sounding voice. "Sorry, Terry. It's company policy. I couldn't change it even if I wanted to and, to be honest with you, I wouldn't even if I could. So… it'll have to be 'no'."

Terry drummed his fingers on the desk and sighed loudly into the mouthpiece. "This makes things very difficult for me," he said quietly and deliberately. "Just a sec. I'll take you off squawk. Mac, would you mind?"

There was an awkward pause and then Terry was back, talking directly into the handset. "Look, mate," he said in a half-whisper, "we go back a long way, you and me, so I'll give it to you straight."

"Go on." The voice was hesitant.

"I have a problem, let's call it a small difficulty, arising out of Tuesday night."

It was three thirty in the morning and David was still sitting in front of the television. This time he hadn't even tried going to bed. There was some sort of black-and-white film on with Jimmy Stewart playing opposite the curly-haired simpleton of a blonde who seemed to have cornered the market in wide-eyed, clingy wives in all these old movies. David realised that he had no idea what the film was about or how long it had been on. It didn't matter. The volume was turned down low so that the neighbours wouldn't be disturbed, but it was surprising how quiet it was at this time of night when the noise of the day, noise that you didn't even notice at the time, had gone away.

This sleep thing was becoming a real shit. Perhaps he should see a doctor. But it wasn't an illness, either physical or mental; his body was reacting in the way it was programmed to in the face of fear: it refused to shut down until the danger had gone away.

Against his better judgment he had drunk the best part of a bottle of wine, not because he thought the alcohol would pick him up but in the hope that it would send him to sleep. It hadn't worked.

It looked like the little blonde woman was giving Jimmy Stewart a serious telling off in front of one of his friends but Jimmy just beamed indulgently back at her. Any moment now the friend was going to admire the pluck and spirit of the little treasure.

David had recently begun to regret how careless he had been in maintaining his personal friendships during his married years. For that whole period friends had come not singly but in couples, or sometimes in whole families. Now they were Sonia's friends or hers and Amy's. Which meant that he couldn't think of anyone he could confide in, use as a sounding-board to help him figure out what Terry was up to and how to respond.

He flicked through the channels again on the remote. An even older British film, so washed out that the actors were almost two-dimensional; Argentinean football; some sort of racing with motorbikes; US cop shows he didn't recognise. News about the Middle East. Back to Jimmy Stewart. The three of them at the dinner table. "That's a mighty fine wife you got yourself, mister. You look after her, you hear?"

For the hundredth time David ran through in his brain the few, confused recollections he had of the *Inferno Club*. He could see the bar. And a man in a bow-tie. And some of the girls; one particularly. Unfortunately there was nothing that he could recall to contradict what Terry was saying.

There were pages and pages of credits rolling down the TV screen and a cheerful young female voice was telling viewers not to go away because the wrestling would be right up. David stared at the adverts that followed and wondered who in the world could be persuaded to change their brand of washing powder at four in the morning.

Chapter Fourteen

Terry realised that if he wasn't more careful he was going to cut himself. He needed to concentrate on the razor he was holding in his hand. He'd had a few drinks after work with Mac by way of a sort of celebration, and then they'd met some of the guys from Newton's and ended up down some pole-dancing joint, which had been pretty tame to be fair and not really his thing: he'd spent most of the evening at the bar, and several hundred quid on low-grade champagne. A couple of the pushier kids from Newton's had tried giving him a hard time, saying what was the matter with him, was he scared or something (him, of all people, a bloke who'd been regularly putting it into all sorts of fanny when they were still waiting to come out of one!). But the little shits had both ended up with baby oil all over what looked like expensive suits and seriously big numbers on their credit cards that they'd have trouble explaining to their boss. They'd learn.

There was something almost uniquely satisfying, Terry thought, about the way a razor ploughed through shaving foam, leaving dry, hairless skin behind. He had tried electric shavers - Serena had bought him one for Christmas a few years previously, not much in return for the Merc convertible he'd got her - but it wasn't the same experience at all; the thing just made a lot of noise and left half of the hair where it started out.

His head wasn't quite clear as yet, but he'd had worse. This time he'd been home around twoish, and yet Serena still seemed to have the hump this morning. Perhaps it was women's things.

Terry carefully focussed on his face in the mirror and then slowly drew the razor up from his throat, over his chin and towards his mouth in a series of parallel strokes. Tiny narrow white stripes were left behind, which was normal but annoying, as were the mounds of foam that collected on his ear-lobes and had to be wiped off at the end.

In normal circumstances he might have stayed in bed: it was Friday, he'd had a couple of heavy nights and there was nothing pressing at work that wouldn't wait till Monday. But today he had to go in to make sure that David Kelsey did as he was told and the deal got wrapped up. The guy had sounded so petrified on the phone that Terry didn't think there was any danger that he wouldn't, but in business you couldn't be too careful. Terry admired his own footwork. Nothing so blatant as blackmail; quite the opposite actually: tipping off a friend about the stuff that some unpleasant people at the *Inferno* had on him (after Terry had left, naturally) and how much money they might want in order to forget about it. An amount that, unfortunately for him but predictably, David didn't have. But that a good friend might be able to lend to him, without the good friend's wife wondering where the money had gone to, if said good friend had a sudden increase in his commission income. It was so good that Terry wanted to kiss the handsome face staring back at him. It surprised him that Kelsey had bought the idea that Serena knew what Terry's income was and where he put it, but the guy had been so pussy-whipped by his own ex-wife that maybe it wasn't a surprise after all.

There was one small nick on Terry's chin. Why did it take so long for blood to get to the surface? He rinsed it under the tap and then applied a tissue. A minute or so should stop it.

The funny thing was that most of this was just for his own entertainment. Kelsey would have gone for the deal anyway (which begged the question as to whether it was too generous) with a review clause, and Terry didn't actually care whether it had one or it didn't. But that wasn't the point. People said that business was about compromise, but that was complete bollocks. Business was about who blinked first; business was about achieving unconditional surrender. Kelsey was now on the ground with his sword broken, and for all future business dealings that was exactly where Terry would ensure that he stayed.

In some ways the fact that David was already so fucked up by his recent personal failings made the victory less satisfying, but that was the way of things. Work wasn't so different from school: everyone got probed for their weaknesses, and the weakest of the lot was in for repeated kickings. If that kid's parents took him away then it would only be a day or so before the crowd identified the next weakest, and so on. It was natural and normal.

Someone was hammering on the bathroom door and now Terry could hear a voice at Serena's pitch shouting something at him. Couldn't he even have a few minutes peace in his own bathroom now?

"Do what?" he replied sharply through the wood.

"I said are you going to make it home in time for Charlie's play tonight?"

Terry tried hard to keep calm. "Sorry, love," he shouted back. "No chance. I've got meetings all day." Fucking school play with a load of ten-year-olds? The woman was unreal. Now she'd go all whiny.

"You said you'd try," Serena reminded him. "He'd really like you to go."

Terry couldn't remember ever having discussed anything of the sort. "Would he?" he replied with rising indignation. "I daresay he'd like me to be able to pay his school fees as well, wouldn't he? Which means muggins here has to work while you and the kids are off enjoying yourselves."

This was usually unanswerable, but Serena was unusually persistent today. "Just this once wouldn't hurt. He'll be disappointed."

Disappointed? Terry wondered what *his* dad would have said if anyone had asked him to go to a play that Terry was in.

Smacked them in the mouth for cheek, and smacked Terry in the mouth for being nancy enough to be in a fucking play in the first place!

Terry didn't bother to reply. He knew Serena would go away if he ignored her. His blood was up, and he had very different plans for this afternoon and evening.

David woke up and found that the train had already arrived at the terminus and that the last passengers were leaving the carriage. Twenty minutes sleep. His head was groggy, there were spots before his eyes, his ears were ringing. He didn't seem to have any physical coordination, and stumbled his way up the stairs at the end of the platform. He thought he might be about to be sick.

Outside the station the *Homeless Truths* girl wasn't in her usual spot. Despite the awkwardness and embarrassment of their encounter the previous day, David had been looking forward to keeping his promise and waving at her to prove he wasn't a poisoner. He'd thought there was a reasonable chance that she would smile in return. At least there wasn't anyone else in her place. Maybe she'd just gone for a moment.

"Hi," Jill said kindly as David came through the doors into what seemed to be an impossibly busy office, bustling like a street scene in a stage musical. "How are you?"

"I'm fine," David lied. "You?"

"Not too bad," Jill replied with a small shake of the head. "In the circumstances."

David looked at her blankly for a moment.

"Of course," he said. "How is he? Any news?"

"Nothing new." Jill looked sadly into David's eyes and then back at her desk. "I guess we just need to keep praying."

David didn't answer. He felt a twinge of guilt that he had given so little thought to Guy in the last twenty-four hours. On the other hand it seemed to him that Jill wanted to make caring into a competition, and he wasn't getting into that. He fixed himself a double-strength coffee from the machine and then went and sat at his desk. The sight of the red voicemail light caused sweat to run down his sides, but it turned out that the message was internal and trivial. It could wait.

David still hadn't worked out exactly what he was going to tell Terry as he picked up the receiver and dialled the number, but he knew if he left it any longer it was going to make him physically ill; he gagged a couple of times trying to drink his coffee. He looked around but it appeared that no-one had noticed.

"Hi," said Terry in an exaggeratedly friendly voice. "What's the word on the street?"

David cleared his throat and looked around him. Chris wasn't at his desk; no-one else was within earshot if he kept his voice low. "OK," he said quietly. "It's not that big a problem. I'll recommend it."

There was a pause. "Exactly as it stands?" Terry suddenly sounded very serious.

"Yes," David sighed heavily. "I'll recommend it as it stands to Simon."

"Good man. And you'll see him today?"

"If I can get hold of him, Terry. It isn't always…"

"Where there's a will," Terry interrupted. "I'm relying on you! I just need a director, another director, to sign for us and then I'll get someone to walk the contract round to you."

"And the other thing?" David asked in a low whisper, shielding his mouth with his free hand until he realised how suspicious it made him look.

"I'm on the case," Terry replied.

"Thanks."

"My pleasure."

Terry started his celebration afternoon at *Kimono's*. It suited his mood. To his mind the place was a lot more sophisticated than any of the City pubs: it had marble counters, chrome fittings, uncomfortable wooden designer chairs set round impossibly small metal tables and the beer, such as it was, came in bottles and cost a small fortune. But if you were doing well you wanted things to be expensive: for one thing it was reassuring to know you were successful enough to be able to afford these things, and for another it kept out the hordes, the mob of average Joes.

Terry and Mac had arranged to meet a client for lunch. The man was a bit of an old woman and a bore, but his presence gave Terry a name to put on his expenses claim form (there were only so many you could get away with making up) and the guy was always suitably grateful when it came round to business. Terry guessed the bloke didn't get bought many lunches; he certainly didn't seem to know his way round a menu or a wine list.

Happily the old bore left around two forty-five, saying he really ought to get back to the office. If that was his view on a Friday afternoon, Terry thought, the guy was even more of a wanker than he had previously imagined.

On the way out, up some stairs that seemed a lot steeper now than they had two hours previously, Mac was looking at his phone. "I'll see who in the market is up for it this afternoon," he said by way of explanation. "Shouldn't be a problem: it's summer, it's Friday." He flicked through a few numbers and then dialled one. "Otherwise," he grinned as he stood with the phone to his ear awaiting a reply, "I'll go back to the office and do an inventory of my paper-clips."

"I'd like you to walk the contract round to TLO," Terry said unsmilingly.

"Me?"

"Yes, you!"

Mac scanned Terry's face to see whether he was serious, and quickly concluded that he was. "OK, boss," he replied quietly. "I'll get it round there this afternoon."

Sometimes it was necessary to remind these people what was what and who was who, Terry told himself as he watched Mac scuttle back to the office with his tail between his legs. Furthermore, the afternoon he had planned didn't involve male company.

Terry found a small alcove at the top of the restaurant stairs, away from the noise of the traffic outside, somewhere he was sure he couldn't be seen or overheard. He rang the *Inferno* and when the phone was eventually answered asked to speak to Andrew. But Andrew wasn't there, and the dour Eastern European on the other end of the line didn't seem to know either when he would be back or where he was at the moment. Terry tried without success to put a face to the voice he was hearing. He tried to keep his temper in case it turned out that he was talking to one of the owners.

"Who's in charge?" Terry asked slowly.

"Not open now. Not necessary."

"You have a little Chinese girl..."

"Lots of girls. All very nice. Open tonight."

"I wanted to ask a favour."

"Favours, yes. Not a problem. All tastes."

"I'm a very good customer. I'm sure if Andrew was there..."

"Andrew not here now. Thank you very much. We hope your custom tonight. Goodbye."

The line went dead. Terry stood for half a minute staring at his phone and then went back downstairs to the bar and ordered himself a double cognac. Two drinks and half an hour later he saw Ted McClelland weaving his way across the room towards him and quickly got up and left.

Chapter Fifteen

Eva was sitting in an underpass smoking a cigarette but, beyond that, she was literally doing nothing. She had sold all her magazines, and even taken some from Taz, who wasn't doing so well at the other side of the station. Eva had sold those without too much problem as well.

It had been a good day today, but Eva didn't think she could cope with this job (if it was a job) much longer. It was boring, it made her feet ache and although some of the people were nice, a large number were patronising and expected her to be abjectly grateful for their two pounds, or to give them her life story in return for it. And then there were the ones who didn't buy the magazine, but wanted to subject her to their opinions instead. Why didn't she get a proper job? Why didn't she go back where she came from? Her coat looked too smart for a homeless person. How come she could afford luxuries like cigarettes and mobile phones? Had she thought of welcoming Jesus into her life?

A lot of people were walking past Eva now without paying her any attention at all, which was normal. She knew it didn't necessarily mean that they hadn't noticed her: in London people instinctively avoided eye contact, and if anything was potentially unsettling they pretended it wasn't there.

Eva was a little pissed off that she hadn't seen the coffee guy this morning. Having decided how she was going to play him she was impatient to get on with it. Maybe he had deliberately used another exit today.

There was a fat middle-aged man in an expensive-looking suit who had been up and down the walkway three times now and had looked at Eva each time. She wasn't comfortable with his presence, but it was no big deal: it was the middle of the day, there were a lot of people about; she wasn't going to let this creep force her to move. The first time he had come past she had felt his eyes on her but ignored him; the second time she had met his gaze blankly for a couple of seconds and then looked away. Now he had stopped at the wall opposite, folded his arms in a self-satisfied way in front of him and started staring directly at her. Eva stubbed out her cigarette and looked up and down the walkway with what she hoped looked like an expression of calm irritation on her face. The man unfolded and then re-folded his arms and continued to stare. Eva could feel that her face was beginning to redden, which meant that he was winning. She stared back, wide-eyed and open-mouthed, in a gesture that was supposed to say 'What the fuck do you think you're gawping at?' But this was obviously a bad idea, because now the guy was coming over and suddenly Eva felt vulnerable and wanted to get away. In a couple of seconds she was on her feet, but by now the man was standing directly in front of her. She was certain that she would be able to outrun him, but for the moment he was blocking her exit.

"Do you want to earn some money?" he asked quietly.

Eva moved slightly to one side, but the man came with her.

"It's a perfectly civil question," he said with a cold smile.

"Doing what?" Eva replied.

The man laughed and Eva could smell the alcohol on his breath.

"What do you think?" he leered.

Eva pretended to laugh back in his face. Sometimes humiliating these guys worked. "Fuck you," she added when she got no response.

"You are homeless?" he asked.

"No, I live in Buckingham Palace."

The man laughed again. "Sounds more like Balmoral to me. So that'll be 'yes' to my question."

"What's it to you?"

The man shook his head sadly. "Expensive place, London, sweetheart. And I'm offering you a hundred quid for half an hour's work. Hotel across the street there, back here in half an hour. One hundred quid. How many of these fucking magazines do you need to sell to make that?"

Eva shivered; she wondered how long the man had been watching her before she had noticed him.

"Piss off. Go home to your wife."

The man grinned. "A hundred and fifty. I'm having a good day, feeling generous. Final offer. Half an hour. With a condom. Lie back and think of Scotland, darling, if you want. I'll give you one minute to change your mind, otherwise someone else gets the money. Think of all the nice drugs you can get yourself with a hundred and fifty notes. Nice drugs to blot out this nasty, horrible world."

Eva knew there had been a time when she would probably have done it. And, God help her, she might be tempted now if it really was only what he said it was. But London was full of nutjobs and the scary thing was that most of them looked quite normal.

"Fuck off now or I'll get the police," Eva screamed so loudly that it was no longer possible for the steady stream of passers-by to pretend they hadn't heard her. A few looked round, hesitated but then nervously hurried on.

The man laughed so hard that he started to cough. "You're in England now, love. What police?" He looked at Eva contemptuously one last time. "Your loss," he said casually. "Plenty more where you came from. You people are two a penny round here. See ya."

Eva remained rigidly still, watching the man's outline gradually recede towards the station concourse. She sat down and tried to light another cigarette, and it was only when she struggled to strike the match that she realised she was shaking. She finally produced a flame and applied it to the tobacco and then took a couple of very deep drags. For the next few minutes she remained propped up against the wall, chain-smoking and staring blankly at everyone who passed by. Some looked unnerved. She didn't care.

She stood up and brushed her coat. She needed to compose herself before she went to her other job. It occurred to her that, even by the girl's own very low standards, Taz was taking her time today to finish. Taz's problem was that she couldn't really ever be bothered, looked like she didn't know why she was standing in the middle of a station selling magazines, and wasn't any good at smiling gratefully. Apart from that there was a very good chance that a lot of potential buyers were simply put off by her appearance. She also got bored and tore strips off the end of her magazines, so that the few buyers she did manage to attract got something that looked like a failed origami project. It was no use trying to tell her, though. Eva smiled at the thought.

She finished her latest cigarette and began to walk slowly towards the main concourse. The place was starting to fill up with commuters going home early for the weekend. A red-faced man knocked his briefcase against Eva's stomach as he ran for a train and ritually apologised without stopping.

Eva rounded the corner and stopped suddenly outside the newsagent's shop. The low sunlight of late afternoon accompanied the busy flow of travellers coming in through the wide doorway at the far end of the concourse. There were two copies of *Homeless Truths* blowing dismally in the wind. But Taz was nowhere to be seen.

Chapter Sixteen

Sonia no longer knew what to think. Lunching with Jane had a habit of doing that to her. A lot of her friends would lend a sympathetic ear and agree with everything she said, which could be good, depending on how much she needed reassurance and how sure she was of her own case in any particular instance; but Jane never did that. If she agreed with you she said so, but if she didn't she told you that as well, and along the way she challenged pretty well all of your assumptions. Which could be invigorating or infuriating, particularly if you were convinced that you were right but still couldn't get the better of her, because then you simply felt intellectually inferior.

Today was no exception. The force of Jane's reasoning had already undermined the comfort of Sonia's previous view; and yet Sonia couldn't help wondering whether, subconsciously, that had been precisely what she had been trying to achieve by arranging to have lunch with Jane in the first place. Otherwise she could have called someone like Maureen, who cooed sympathetically, put her arm on yours, tutted and moved her head like a nodding donkey in response to every accusation you cared to come out with.

Jane wiped the carbonara sauce from her lips, dropped her napkin and once more held out a hand to stop Sonia in full flow. "OK," she said briskly. "Let's look at it from his point of view. Who left who?"

"Well, I…"

"You left him."

"Yes, but…"

"Did he beat you?"

"No."

"Was he cruel to you or Amy? Was he having an affair?"

"No, you know perfectly well he wasn't. It just got very, I don't know, stale. Boring. He got boring."

"And you were scintillatingly interesting all this time?"

"No. Of course not. I don't know. But then I met John and that gave me another option."

"So what's your problem?"

"My problem is that he's trying to re-fight old battles through Amy. He shouldn't be doing that."

Jane finished wrapping more tagliatelle round her fork and then pointed it at her companion. "So what did he say to her that wasn't true?"

"Nothing," Sonia conceded. "But he didn't have to say it at all. And he didn't have to say it the way he did."

Jane shrugged. "How do you know how he said it?" she asked through a mouthful of pasta.

"Amy told me."

"And there's no chance she was…exaggerating."

"Don't you start!" Sonia snapped back. "I've already had a row with David for calling her a liar."

"Oh, come off your high horse, Sonia," Jane protested incredulously. "All teenagers are liars."

Sonia's stare was intended to tell Jane that she had gone too far this time, but Jane simply looked down at her plate and ignored it.

"I should know," Jane continued unfazed. "I've got two of them. They lie all the time. Not because they're terrible people, but because they've got to the age where they don't think they're children any more and you don't think they're adults yet, and so you get this sort of power struggle where they tell you as little as possible. And they think it's perfectly acceptable to lie to you if you're trying to interfere as they see it, or exercising control where they don't want you to."

"That's a bit of a sweeping generalisation," Sonia protested, but she didn't try to go on; she wanted to hear what Jane was going to say next.

"Don't look so offended," Jane smiled at her. "I'm only telling you that Amy is normal. It wasn't any different when we were their age. For example, when did you have your first cigarette?"

"I didn't."

Jane's face showed her surprise. "OK, goody two-shoes. First snog, then, something like that."

Sonia laughed. "Miss Beale's class. Ian Redford."

"OK. Did you tell your mother?"

"Of course not. Oh, God, but I remember she noticed the love bite and I told her it was an allergy to my new wool scarf!" Sonia felt simultaneously shocked and pleased by her own revelation.

"There you are," Jane declared triumphantly. "Incidentally, I don't suppose there's one chance in a hundred that she believed you, but there are some things that mothers learn to let go. Tell me something else: what does Amy say when you ask her what she did at school today?"

Sonia sighed sadly. "The dreaded 'nothing'."

"I bet she hasn't always done that."

"She used to come home full of stories when she was little. It was worth listening to just for her enthusiasm, even if I couldn't always follow what she was on about." Sonia smiled at the recollection.

Jane gave up trying to chase the last strip of pasta round her plate, put her fork down, sat back and folded her arms. "Do I need to continue," she asked smugly, "or are you going to retire gracefully from the field?"

"No I'm not!" Sonia replied vehemently. "I can't see what this has to do with David trying to set Amy against me, and then trying to rip her arm off."

"Yes, you can. I'm saying perhaps she thinks if she can set you against each other then both of you will have less control over her. Perhaps it's working already: one down, one to go."

"So you're saying she made it all up."

Jane's expression suggested that she wasn't completely discounting the idea. "Well," she sighed, "something obviously happened, it's just how you interpret it. What was David's version?"

Sonia stared at a crumb on the table. "I don't know. I was so angry I suppose I wasn't really listening." She looked up and caught Jane's gaze. "You're a horrible cow, do you know that? Next time I'm talking to Maureen."

Jane arranged her mouth in a pout and put her hand on Sonia's shoulder. "You poor thing," she mimicked, "he's such a beast."

Sonia's face had broken into a broad smile. "Seriously though," she said, "you really could make a great living as some sort of therapist."

Jane winked at her companion as she raised her arm to get the bill. "Why would I want to do that," she asked, "when I can be a wife and mother with a part-time job in a local estate agency?"

Chapter Seventeen

Almost the worst part was that Taz wouldn't talk about it.

Eva had walked around the station for almost an hour looking for her friend before she'd had to go off to her job at the restaurant. She'd spent four impatient hours hoping Taz had simply wandered off somewhere – it wasn't unknown with her limited attention span – and that she would be back at the hostel when Eva returned.

And she was. Eva experienced a feeling of huge relief on coming into the room and seeing the shape of Taz's body asleep on her bed. Part of her wanted to hug the girl; the other part wanted to shake her awake and ask her what the fuck she thought she was playing at. She was too tired for either. She needed to sleep. She walked softly across the room, stopped and just looked at her friend for a moment. But what she could see, even by the dim yellow half-light of the energy-saving bulb, was not reassuring. There was a long bruise, intermittently green and brown and black, along the whole right-hand side of Taz's face. Her hair was matted and appeared to contain clotted blood. Her t-shirt was torn; so, on the floor by the side of the bed, was her jacket. Taz winced as she turned over in her sleep. Eva bent down and listened to the girl's breathing. It sounded normal. There was nothing to be gained by waking her now; what better for Taz at this moment than unconsciousness? Eva retreated to her own bed, sat on the side, hesitated for a moment and then got under the sheets. She fell quickly asleep. But every noise in the night, and every nightmare of her own invention, woke her, and each time she woke she looked and listened through the gloom to assure herself that she could still both see and hear Taz.

She woke again and this time light had penetrated the room. Taz's eyes were open. "Are you OK?" Eva called across to her. What a stupid thing to say: did the girl look OK?

"Fine." The voice sounded hollow and breathless.

Eva got up and walked barefoot across the room to Taz's bed. Daylight had rendered the colours of Taz's skin and hair much more stark and vivid. Eva wasn't able to contain herself now. "Oh, Christ," she said softly, "look at you. Who did this? What happened to you?"

"I'm fine."

"You're not!" Eva could hear the high-pitched screech in her own voice. "Go and have a look in the mirror."

"I'm fine."

"Taz, yesterday there was this fat middle-aged guy in a suit at the station..."

"I fell over."

"OK, then. Show me your hands."

Taz pushed herself further into the bedclothes; now only the top half of her head was visible.

"If you fell over you'd have tried to stop yourself," Eva persisted. "Show me your hands." She advanced towards Taz with the intention of pulling the bedclothes away, but Taz, with the sheets around her, suddenly darted towards Eva and fixed her with a look of such violence that Eva instinctively retreated to her own bed.

Eva avoided further eye contact. She decided it would be best to leave Taz to calm down. She got her things together and went and had a shower. When she returned Taz was fully dressed and was wearing a hoodie so that only the front of her face showed, and that largely in shadow. She was sitting on the side of the bed watching her feet swinging above the carpet.

"I'm here whenever you're ready to talk," Eva said quietly.

Taz didn't react.

"At least get yourself cleaned up," Eva pleaded. "Have a shower. Get something put on that cut on your head before it goes septic. You should have done that last night."

Taz gave a slight shrug. "Didn't want to be thrown out for fighting," she mumbled.

"But you fell over. You told me."

Eva felt immediately that she had made a cheap shot. Taz said nothing but got up and started to walk towards the door. She was limping, and the movement in her lower trunk suggested that her whole body was in pain.

Eva was blocking her exit and made no attempt to move out of the way. She encountered no resistance as she gently enveloped Taz in her arms. "It's OK," she whispered soothingly into the girl's ear. "We're going to kill him. We really are. We're going to kill him."

"Really?"

"Yes."

"And then?"

Eva was surprised by the question. She let Taz go and looked her squarely in the face. There were no tears. "Then? Then he's dead, Taz!"

"Yeah," Taz agreed. "But what do we do then?"

Eva understood; they had had this conversation a hundred times, but Taz didn't tire of it. "Then," Eva said, reaching for her jacket and rummaging in the pocket for a cigarette, "we are going to leave this shitty hostel and all these wankers behind, and go off somewhere really nice and get a nice house and real jobs and have money to spend, loads of it, and it'll be really great."

"Somewhere in Wales," said Taz, who appeared to be trying to imagine it.

Eva put a cigarette in her mouth, struck a match and lit the tobacco. She inhaled deeply and her eyes narrowed as if she was trying to work something out. She tried speaking with the cigarette in her mouth then changed her mind and removed it.

"What's it with you and Wales?" she asked. "You told me before you don't think you've ever been there."

"Horses," answered Taz. "I want to work with horses."

Eva felt able to laugh. "They have horses in a lot of places, not just Wales," she pointed out.

Taz shrugged.

"Wales it is," Eva conceded. "Anywhere you want," she continued almost inaudibly, "so long as it ain't Scotland." She took another long drag on the cigarette then turned to offer it to Taz, who took it.

"So now we can see about getting you sorted out?" Eva asked with more confidence and cheerfulness than she felt.

Taz nodded silently.

Chapter Eighteen

David found himself at the beginning of another weekend. His New Year's resolution had been to make sure that he did something worthwhile during the two-day break. *Carpe diem,* or whatever weekend was in Latin. From Amy's birth until his separation from Sonia his Saturdays and Sundays had been taken up with the sort of things that parents with largish houses tended to do: mowing lawns, pulling out weeds, painting window frames, gutters and soffits, wallpapering, assembling furniture; running Amy to dancing or horse-riding or violin lessons (nothing really to show for any of those) or to friends' parties; taking the whole family for days out at the coast or in the country; shopping, DIY centres; having people round for meals and barbecues or attending theirs. It had been OK most of the time and at occasional moments, particularly during the tragically short period when Amy had been small, wide-eyed, affectionate and trusting, it had allowed him a glimpse of the kind of contentment in adult life the possibility of which he wanted to believe in.

He had never during those times allowed (or had time to allow) work to intrude too much on his thoughts during the weekend. These days it was different, and the office was never far from his mind, in no small part, he realised, because he did not have much else to focus on. This Saturday morning he had woken wondering whether he was due to see Amy, and that had led to a nagging sadness that had dogged him during his solitary TV breakfast and in the shower. Thereafter work took over: images of Terry, of Mac, of Simon. The little Asian girl. As he drove to the supermarket and then walked around its aisles with his small trolley, David was still trying to work out what to do, how to play it when Monday came round. By the time he returned, removed his washing from the machine, checked that there were no voicemails on his landline and sat down again in front of the television for lunch he was no closer to a decision. Half of him dreaded the beginning of the next working week while the other was impatient for it to arrive.

It was a warm, sunny day; he shouldn't be wasting it alone and indoors. He should definitely go out. There were things you could do alone: the driving range, for example, if not golf itself. Art galleries and museums as well, though he had to be in the mood for those and they were best left for winter. As was reading during the day: he had always wanted to read more but now felt that he read too much. He was too old for most team sports and too young for bowls. He was a lousy tennis player. Watching live sport alone was just about OK, and if you were really desperate you could even go to the theatre, a concert or the cinema by yourself. Though the latter could be almost excruciatingly awkward if you found yourself, alone and middle-aged, queuing between two groups of boisterous teenagers. Otherwise there were just long walks, and though David did enjoy those, and they were free, you did not need to make many in order to exhaust all the alternative routes of any interest in the vicinity of his flat.

None of the possibilities filled him with any enthusiasm. He was tempted to sleep; he was still tired after another bad night. His mind had been filled with confused notions of work, of the *Inferno Club*, of Sonia shouting down the phone: furious, raging, not done with him yet. And a dream of a cold, dank, cemetery-like hospital in which someone who should have been Guy but wasn't was lying paralysed and David was someone with powers that could do something about it; but his limbs were heavy and when he tried to move towards the bed something was stopping him.

He fell asleep after lunch in front of the television. Then he did the lunchtime dishes, changed the bedclothes and ran the vacuum cleaner around the flat. He rewarded himself with a cup of tea. Now there was a rugby game on TV, which wasn't really his sort of thing, but it was surprisingly interesting and went on for almost a further hour after he started to watch it. Then he made another cup of tea, took the bedclothes out of the washing machine and went through the mail that had been accumulating all week. There was more than he expected, though it was all impersonal and mostly involved payments, and by the time he had finished it was time to start on dinner. When that was ready he sat down in front of the TV again. There was a quiz, which was more interesting than he remembered it from past editions, and he watched it for the full hour before getting up and once more doing the washing up, which took a while because some of the chilli he had made had welded itself to the bottom of the pan.

He watched TV for most of the evening until there was no longer anything of conceivable interest on any channel. Then, with an oddly heavy heart, he switched the set off and picked up *A Tale of Two Cities*. He had got to page fifty-four. It was good. It really was. He read four more pages. It was too quiet. He put some music on and winced at the tinny sound from the cheap stereo. He read two more pages. He read the same paragraph three times. He thought about Terry and Mac. And Simon. He thought about Sonia and Amy. And John. He thought about Guy, wondered what was going through his mind at that very moment. He felt a sense of rising panic. His stomach muscles tightened. He read ten more pages but when his eyelids began to close he didn't try to stop them.

The next day he stayed in bed until almost ten, though he wasn't sleeping. He got up, dug out his address book and rang a couple of people who weren't in, and one who was but couldn't come for a drink at such short notice. He made meals, cleaned the bathroom, went for a walk along dreary suburban side roads, watched TV, read a little. He thought about work. He thought about Amy, he thought about Guy. He thought about work.

The weekend was almost over; it had never started.

The ringing phone startled him in the silence of the flat. For a couple of seconds he watched it uncomprehendingly. He realised that he had not spoken to a single human being face-to-face since he had left work on Friday night. He ran to pick up the handset before it rang off and found himself talking to his ex-wife.

Sonia had already picked up the phone twice and put it down again. She wasn't sure what was making her hesitate. It couldn't be fear: there was nothing frightening about her ex-husband, even when he got angry. And she'd told John she was going to make the call, so there was no problem there. Amy didn't know, but, well, she was fourteen; sometimes her opinion genuinely wasn't important.

She picked up the phone again, called her former husband's number and was about to hang up when he eventually answered. He sounded a little confused and disorientated.

"Hi," Sonia began in her most emollient tone. "It's only me. How are you?"

"Yes, I'm fine," David said after a moment's pause. "You?"

"We're fine too, thanks," Sonia replied.

"Good. Good."

OK so far, but suddenly there was a new wariness in his voice. "What's up?" he asked.

"Oh, not a lot really," Sonia replied chirpily. "This and that. Mundane, mostly. Amy's been practising her big speech for next week at school, driving us nuts!"

"I didn't know she was making one."

"Didn't you? Well, no… It's no big deal. Well, it is to her, obviously, but it's just an internal presentation her class is doing."

"Oh, right. What's she talking about?"

"The Great Wall of China actually."

"Big subject."

Sonia laughed. "They aim high at that school. If you ever want to know how many miles there are, how many towers, how many bricks, how many men it took to build it, your daughter is the one to ask."

David didn't reply, and Sonia felt embarrassed by her own tactlessness. She tried to fill the silence. "We're about to book a holiday as well."

"Excellent. Anywhere nice?"

"Sicily. John's just got a surprise bonus."

"Right."

"Oh, and we went shopping today. Got some holiday clothes and I'm afraid I gave in and bought Amy that jacket she's been on about."

"I see." David still sounded distant and reserved. "Do you want some money?"

"No. Well, yes, I mean I will eventually, no hurry. That wasn't why I rang."

"Let me know how much, I'll see what I can do. And for the holiday, Amy's bit of it."

"Thanks, that's kind of you."

"Though it'll be difficult before pay day. If it can wait…"

"That's fine. As I say, that wasn't why I rang. John's pretty flush at the moment, with his bonus."

David's tone became colder. "I'm not asking John to pay for my daughter."

"He doesn't mind."

David wanted to say that he did mind. But he knew that he didn't have the money and that the only practical solution, much as it grieved him, was to let John pay and reimburse him at a later date.

"I'll give it to you when I've got it," David replied without conviction.

"Thanks. Anyway, why I called..." Sonia found that for all her pre-conversation preparation she wasn't quite ready for this. "Well, you know," she continued hesitantly, "after how we left it last week, I didn't want to, I mean, perhaps I shouldn't have - I'm not saying there weren't two sides to it - but I think we should move on."

"That's fine with me," David agreed immediately.

"Good. I mean, don't think I'm apologising."

"I wasn't asking you to. How's Amy, I mean apart from the speech thing?"

"She's fine." Sonia allowed herself a short laugh. "You know, she's Amy!"

"And the weekend after next?"

Sonia reproached herself for not having anticipated this question. Amy had been a real handful all week; Jane might well have been right. Sonia feared that it might be disastrous to get Amy and David together at the moment.

"Well," she said finally. We'll see. It's a little early for her. She'll come round, but it might need a bit of time."

"Does she still hate me?"

"No, of course she doesn't. But, well, she sort of thinks she does; you know what kids are like. It won't last."

David considered Sonia's reply. "Let's at least provisionally say the weekend after next," he suggested.

"It really would be best to play it by ear," Sonia replied firmly. She didn't want to imagine the scene if Amy refused point blank to go with her father. "Trust me on this one," she added more calmly.

A pause. An intake of breath.

"As you wish," David said with quiet resignation.

There was an awkward silence.

"I'll call you," Sonia declared with finality. "Take care."

Chapter Nineteen

David's general sleep problem was fairly recent, but he had not had a satisfactory night's rest on a Sunday evening for as long as he could remember. When the alarm sounded at six fifty on a Monday morning he was usually already awake and waiting for it. He mechanically pushed the snooze button, wrapped himself in the bedclothes and tried to wrest some life-quality from nine minutes (why was it always nine, why couldn't they programme these fucking things for ten?) of warmth and comfort. And then the mournful siren sounded again and he routinely spent a few seconds asking himself what difference it would make if he ignored the alarm and simply stayed in bed. The money would very soon run out, which would affect Amy to some degree and himself to a larger extent, particularly when it reached the point where he starved to death. Otherwise the world would go on; his absence would certainly have very little effect on TLO.

Fortunately, so far, he had always managed to get himself out of bed. He wasn't sure he would always be able to. Today unconsciousness seemed so much preferable to the office.

But he did get up, eventually. Perhaps it was just force of habit. He had a vague sense that he was dressing himself and then that he was walking to the station, and the next moment he had arrived in London and was emerging into the sombre, overcast daylight and fleetingly made eye contact with the *Homeless Truths* girl. Someone behind him on the steps stood on his heel. They both apologised and David stepped to one side to assess the damage.

Still tottering precariously on one leg, he tried surreptitiously to look over at the *Homeless Truths* girl again. He had intended to give her a friendly wave, but there was something different in her demeanour today that made him think better of the idea. Her hair had a wild, unkempt quality to it this morning that David had not seen before, and which was continued in her face: her eyes were impatient, her mouth turned down and sullen. She had moved herself directly into the path of the City workers issuing from the station, obstructing the pavement so that they had to walk round her. She was holding her magazines aggressively in front of the faces of the passing commuters and showing signs of increasing anger and disdain each time someone failed to buy one. It was as if she wanted to fail, or to be physically pushed aside. David thought that he would like to ask what the problem was, but maybe not; he took one more quick look at the girl's contemptuous face and dropped the idea.

The pain in his heel had subsided and there was no obvious damage. He rejoined the flow of people and crossed the road.

A conversation between two people he didn't recognise in the lift.

"Good weekend?"

"Yes, thanks. Too short though."

"Tell me about it! Delighted to be back here, then?"

Ironic laughter.

"Of course."

The sound of the Monday morning office: the whoosh of the air-conditioning system that you mostly only noticed when it was suddenly switched off; the voices of countless people simultaneously on telephones or talking to one another. It was difficult to believe that some of these people went home at all; that they weren't put away in cupboards on Friday nights and brought out again on Monday mornings.

Jill smiled weakly at David, made a short polite enquiry regarding his weekend, which he parried noncommittally, and then told him that Simon was already looking for him.

As he entered Simon's office David could see that his boss's face wore an irascible expression which, David concluded, meant either that he was getting grief from above or that he didn't approve of the hours that David now kept: in Simon's brave new business world eight forty-five, even on a Monday, was in the afternoon.

"Problem with the trains?" Simon asked, dispensing with any kind of greeting.

David weighed up whether or not to lie. "No worse than usual," he replied flatly.

"Right," said Simon. "Now you are here can we get this thing of Terry Ransome's out of the way? What do you think?"

David had been anticipating this conversation for three days, and yet he involuntarily hesitated before replying.

Simon became visibly impatient. "Well, what is it?" he snapped. "Yes or no?"

"Yes," David answered. He thought he sounded hoarse and stopped to clear his throat. "I think we should do it."

Simon leaned back in his chair and put his hands behind his head. "OK. Pitch it to me."

David explained the main characteristics of the proposed deal: what potential profit it offered, what the possible downside was, why the first outweighed the second.

"Have you done the cost-benefit analysis?" Simon interrupted.

"Not formally, but I've just told you…"

"Informally is no good any more. I'll need the C-B forms filled out."

"OK, I'll do that this morning."

"And the contract?"

"I've got it."

"You've read it?"

"Yes."

"And?"

"It's fine," David told Simon steadily.

"Really?" Simon looked both unconvinced and unimpressed. "I don't think anyone's ever sent me a contract I didn't make at least a couple of amendments to."

David hoped that Simon had sufficient residual respect for his experience to accept his opinion if he gave it forcefully enough.

"It's OK, really," he insisted.

"I think I'd like to take a look over it," Simon said firmly. "Could you bring it in?"

"Sure," David said quietly. "If that's what you want."

Simon looked directly at him and smiled weakly. "Two pairs of eyes are always better than one," he said in a more conciliatory tone.

David only nodded.

"Jill!" Simon shouted, though there was a phone on his desk. A couple of seconds later Jill appeared in the doorway. "Get hold of Terry Ransome at NCG, would you and ask him to get his arse round here at ten. Tell him I've got back-to-back meetings from ten thirty onwards if he starts whingeing. Thanks."

Jill disappeared. David got up, gloomily impressed despite himself by Simon's decisiveness. "Any news on Guy?" he heard himself ask mechanically.

"No," replied Simon, who appeared preoccupied with searching his desk drawer for something. "Nothing new."

An hour and a half later Terry sat opposite Simon, fidgeting like a nervous schoolboy watching a teacher mark his essay. He had the same ingratiating smile on his face that he had worn when he had walked into Simon's office five minutes previously, having patiently sat outside for almost a quarter of an hour while Simon finished an unhurried phone call. David was sitting next to him; uncomfortable at finding himself on the same side of the desk as Terry, he had already shuffled his chair across the carpet in order to put more distance between them.

Simon had his head down and was tugging at his left ear lobe at the same time that he was speed-reading the contract that was lying on the desk in front of him.

"Blah blah blah blah blah," he said as he turned the page with his free hand. "Fine, yes. No, hang on. No, no, no!"

"What's the problem?" Terry asked politely.

"The problem," Simon replied coldly, "is 15% commission. I'm not giving you 15% commission, Terry. I'll give you 10%."

"There's a lot of work involved on our side, Simon," Terry protested.

"I'm not paying you 15% commission, Terry."

Terry looked searchingly at David, who gazed hopelessly back at him. "Well, look," Terry told Simon. "I don't want this to be a deal breaker. Let's say 12.5% for the first year, and we'll discuss again in twelve months."

Simon picked up the contract and held it out across the desk. "Let's say 10%, Terry, or we walk."

Terry was silent for a couple of seconds. He coughed and ran his hand over the top of his hair. "And we can talk again in a year, assuming it's run well?" he asked.

"Maybe."

Terry looked at David again, folded his arms, looked round the room and then at Simon. "OK," he agreed.

Simon smiled to himself, picked up a pen and made the amendment to the contract.

"Good," he said. "We have a deal."

He stood up and offered his hand to Terry, who took it.

"Are you going to sign now?" Terry asked hopefully.

Simon shook his head.

"David can do that for you. There's one other thing: you've left out the annual review clause, but I'm assuming that's just an oversight."

"Have we?" Terry asked apologetically. "I'll get it put in. Sorry about that."

"No problem." Simon now had his hand on Terry's arm and was subtly moving him towards the door. "Thanks for coming in. I enjoyed the golf the other day, by the way. We'll have to do it again some time."

David stayed in his seat and avoided catching Terry's eye as he departed. He had a more immediate problem in the shape of Simon.

Simon closed the door, unhurriedly came back and sat down at his desk. David felt his heartbeat rise. Simon bent down and brought something out of the bottom drawer. David could no longer see Simon at all, but from the vigorous scuffing sound and the aroma of polish that reached his nostrils a few seconds later he deduced that his boss was cleaning his shoes.

Simon's head appeared at an angle above the desk. His face was red from the blood that had flowed into it while he had been bent over; in other circumstances David would have found it amusing. The brushing stopped.

"You were prepared to agree to fifteen?" Simon asked aggressively. He picked up the tin of polish and placed it on top of the desk. He dabbed the brush into it and disappeared from view again. "Fifteen's way too much in the current market," he added in a voice strained by the unnatural angle of his body and the exertion of the resumed brushing.

"The margin's still good," David replied in order not to appear easily browbeaten, though he knew it was probably the wrong thing to say.

"That isn't the point," Simon countered immediately. "The point is this is a competitive market, and if everyone else is giving twelve and a half, I don't want TLO giving fifteen. A few years ago, maybe, in a few years' time, who knows, but not now. We don't have to do it, David, so we don't."

"OK," David agreed contritely. "Understood. They're not going to be happy with ten though."

Simon came up for another dab of polish and grinned. "That's Terry's problem, isn't it? He should have called my bluff."

"So you would have gone with twelve and a half?"

Simon stopped and winked at David; it was the first friendly gesture of the morning. "Of course," he said more quietly as though he thought someone might be listening in. "Why not. As you say, the margin's very good."

"And if he'd held out for fifteen?"

"Well, he isn't that stupid, is he? He knows where the market is. But if he had, the precedent would have been too damaging. I would have walked."

"OK."

Simon bent down again and came up with a larger brush that he brandished in David's direction. "No more fifteens, got it?"

"Got it."

"And another thing. What was the idea of no annual review clause? That could have been an absolute disaster for us."

"I'd already discussed that with Terry," David replied, trying to maintain steady eye contact with his boss.

Simon appeared to be taking his time to decide whether or not to believe him. "Well, you didn't mention it to me," he said curtly.

"Because it was just an oversight, as you said yourself. It wasn't an issue."

The two men sat in silence for a few seconds while Simon collected his shoe-cleaning kit together and put it back in his drawer. He drew a tissue from a dispenser on his desk and wiped his hands. He threw the tissue away, swivelled his chair round ninety degrees and leaned back. His shoes shone like mirrors.

"Here's the thing," he said finally. "I'm one man down already, what with Guy, which means that I've got to have the whole of the rest of my team firing on all cylinders at all times. That includes you, David."

David nodded and then noticed that Simon wasn't looking at him. "Of course," he said quietly.

"So I want you," Simon continued, "no, I am going to *expect* you - to produce more business. And on better terms." He turned to face David once more. "No more fifteens."

"No, OK, I didn't…"

"I'm going to get Jill to book you on a negotiating skills course. I think it would be useful for you."

"OK," David replied meekly, standing up at the same time. "I'll talk to Jill about dates. And I'll sort out the amended contract with Terry."

"Good man."

David's mood became more despondent as the morning progressed, and he found himself continually looking at his watch in the hope that lunchtime would arrive. No-one called him, while everyone around him seemed to be constantly on the phone. It wasn't a good sign if Simon was now monitoring his production and expecting it to increase. And from watching his colleagues it was clear that as many of their calls were outgoing as incoming. He tried telling himself that he needed only to do the same: he had become complacent and lazy of late, hoping and expecting that business would come to him on a plate, but surely he still knew who was who in the market? It was just a matter of pressing the accelerator. The question was whether anything would happen if he did. But not only that: the biggest problem was finding the necessary enthusiasm to press it in the first place.

He decided to go to lunch early at twelve thirty. He had no plans to meet anyone, and it was only when he was on the pavement outside TLO's office, walking against a stiff breeze that had come up during the morning, that he suddenly felt a strong desire to see Guy.

As he walked down the long corridor, past scenes of human dereliction similar to those he had seen on his last visit (some of the faces had changed already though, and it wasn't possible to believe that the previous occupants of the beds had recovered) David asked himself what he was doing here, and why he was doing it alone. Jill would certainly have come with him if he had suggested it, and she would doubtless be offended when she found out that he had gone without her. But in his current mood he didn't want company.

He came up in sight of the nurses' station and slowed down, then stopped. He began to think that this whole thing was a mistake. Perhaps he would come back another time.

But the staff nurse had spotted him. "Hi," she called out in the optimistic-even-if-the-bombs-are-actually-falling tone that, David reflected, only medical professionals can truly carry off, "come back to see your friend? I'm sure he'll be pleased. We've just given him his lunch, so he must be awake. You can go in right away, same room as before."

David thanked her. He wanted to ask her something, but he wasn't sure exactly what. But he had missed his opportunity: she had turned away and started talking to one of her colleagues.

David could see the open door and hear sounds coming from the other side without being able to make out what they were. He expected the room to be dark, the air to be fetid and oppressive; but when he stopped on the threshold and gingerly put his head through the doorway he discovered that the curtains were drawn back, the window was open and the room was filled with both fresh-smelling air and sunlight. Guy was lying down but someone had rigged a television close to the ceiling so that he could see it. He was watching cricket.

"Oh, hi," he said as if David were making a social visit to his home, and one that he had been expecting. "On your own?"

"Just thought I'd pop down here during my lunch-hour," David answered rapidly. "Everyone else sends their best. Obviously."

"You ought to do more client lunches, you know," Guy observed calmly, with half of his attention still directed towards the television screen. "Give the corporate Amex a bit of a pounding."

David laughed. "Are you saying you would rather I wasn't here?"

Guy smiled weakly. "Grab a seat. England need about another twenty before they can declare."

David drew up one of the chairs he and Jill had used previously and sat down. He tried to look up at the television but found that doing so hurt his neck.

"Clever rig-up," he said admiringly. How did you manage that?"

Guy winked. "You just have to say the right things to the right people and things get done," he replied.

David didn't know whether or not to be pleased that the man in the bed once again sounded like the Guy of old. He certainly didn't look like him: he still had almost no head mobility, and his face betrayed little in the form of expressions, though it had reverted to a more natural colour. The features were less sunken too, the skin seemed less clammy; but this was not the look of a fit, healthy young man.

"Christ, that was close," Guy exclaimed. "Did you see that? Watch the replay. Looked plumb lbw to me. We're very lucky if we get away with that."

"Who are we playing?" asked David, eager to develop a conversation that didn't dwell on Guy's future health prospects.

"Who are we playing?" Guy mimicked incredulously. "The West Indies. It's the Lords' Test!"

"Sorry. I don't really follow cricket."

"I should be there," Guy informed David. "Carson's invited me. So did RN&R actually, but Carson's had a box, so I was going to go with them. Didn't you get any invites?"

David shook his head awkwardly.

"No, but as I say, I'm not much of a cricket fan."

"Not the point is it," Guy replied. "It's a good day out and excellent for networking. Here's a thought: maybe next year we should host some hospitality at the Oval or Lord's. I'll raise it with Simon when I get back."

"Why not," David agreed quietly. He paused. He thought this was the right moment, if there was ever going to be one, to put the question. "And what is the, you know, the prognosis, or whatever?" he asked gingerly.

"What a shot!" What would normally have been a cry of approval sounded today more like a loud, hoarse whisper. It was accompanied by a volley of applause from the television. "A couple more of those and the Windies will be batting again!" Guy continued enthusiastically. "Sorry. What were you asking? The 'prognosis'? Well, as far as I understand it, and I still don't think the doctors are telling me everything they could, but I believe the technical medical term is that I'm completely fucked. The damage to my spinal column is irreversible and I am never going to walk again. Hey ho."

David was going to say that he was sorry to hear that, but the words sounded so crass in his head that he stopped himself and just nodded.

"But I'm OK above the waist," Guy informed him.

"Well, I guess that's something."

"I suppose it is," Guy agreed sarcastically. "Compared to nothing, it is definitely something."

"You seem a lot better in yourself as well," David observed positively.

"In the sense that I'm not crying my eyes out or screaming at God?" Guy replied, and for the first time there was a hint of emotion in his voice. "I've always been an achiever, David: when I try to do things I invariably succeed. I am where I am and I can't change it. I have to start from here, but I *am* going to continue to be successful for the rest of my life. I guarantee you that."

"Good for you," David responded, though he could hear how trite the phrase sounded. "I think that's exactly the right attitude to have."

"Yep," replied Guy, who once more appeared to be only half listening. "Oh, no, you fucking idiot. Run out at a time like this, you useless Yorkshire tosser!"

Chapter Twenty

Eva was higher than she had intended to be. It wasn't particularly strong stuff, but she hadn't done any for a while and she thought that might explain her reaction to it. It wasn't that she didn't like it - far from it, the feeling she had right now was so much better than dreary, depressing, frightening reality - but it was fucking expensive and she wasn't going to become like all those losers who spent every last penny of the little they managed to get on drugs or alcohol and were never ever going to get off the streets, except eventually in a box. The money stayed the same, the dependency got worse, and then they ended up letting strangers fuck them for money until their bodies gave up or some creepy head-case finally killed them. Eva told herself she was too smart for that. Things had got unexpectedly worse in her life; they could get better again. She just needed an opportunity.

Eva had bought the dope today because someone had offered it to her at the hostel at a reasonable price (though it wiped out everything she had earned from her previous day's work) and it looked clean and genuine. She'd told herself she was taking it to the station just in case, to use if things went very badly and she needed to fall back on it. But it was soon clear that she was going to need it very quickly. The commuters were no worse today than usual: most of them always ignored her, and those that stopped gave off an aura of smug superiority that made her feel very small. Humiliation turned quickly to anger, but normally she managed to keep it firmly under control, at least to the extent that it was not outwardly visible. But today was different. Today she hated all of these people: the women who gazed pityingly at her, the men who smiled politely but looked embarrassed. What were they thinking about when they looked at her?

She had hardly sold anything all morning, which was bad enough in itself, but it was also clear that she was going to alienate her regular purchasers, who had been growing more and more numerous of late. This was a good pitch; it had a stream of well-off people with troubled consciences. Eva didn't want to lose it. Her sensible self told her to go away and come back when she'd calmed down.

She went to the far end of the station and stood just outside the door, a few yards away from a huddle of cigarette smokers, in an inconspicuous spot where she hoped the fresh air would quickly carry the telltale aroma away. After a while she leaned against the railing at the bottom of some steps for support. Hundreds of people continued to walk past without paying her any attention at all. The temptation now that she had had one smoke was to have another, and maybe another, until it didn't matter any more; but then there'd be none for tomorrow, and she wasn't sure she could face that. Telling herself it was for her own good, and for Taz's, she pushed herself upright, checked her balance, breathed in deeply, picked up her pile of magazines and began to walk slowly back to her post.

After leaving the hospital David really didn't feel in the mood to go back to work, but realistically he knew that he had to. He had a long-scheduled afternoon meeting with the guys from Patriots' who were making their annual visit to London. Patriots' was one of TLO's oldest accounts, and one of the few that David could genuinely lay claim to have produced. Simon had tried to muscle in on the deal a couple of years back, and it had been gratifying to see him quickly rebuffed by the client. Simon's settled opinion now, for anyone who wanted to hear it, was that Patriots' were a bunch of hicks from the dark ages, and that the account wasn't large enough for him to spend his time on.

David therefore knew he had a big incentive to pay attention at this meeting, but once it started he soon found it hard to concentrate. Larry, the boss at Patriots', was doing almost all of the talking, as was his normal practice. He had brought a couple of younger colleagues with him this year. One was a bespectacled guy with a laptop computer, who reminded David of Clark Kent, though without the developed musculature of a Christopher Reeve in his heyday. He barely spoke at all; his role was evidently to drive the PowerPoint slide-show. David guessed that he was probably an accountant. Maybe a lawyer. There was also a woman in her forties, with a great stack of unnaturally blonde hair, whose job it seemed to be to agree with everything Larry said.

Larry was clearly still the main act. David guessed the man must be in his seventies by now, despite the shock of ginger hair that was dyed at best, a wig at worst (Simon said it was definitely the latter) and he wondered why, with the money Larry must have made over the years, he couldn't find anything more interesting than business to occupy his time.

Larry was talking at length about Patriots' new headquarters building – there was a slide on the screen showing it in all its burnished, mirrored glory - and David was doing his best to concentrate on the data and offer congratulations in the right places.

He wondered what was really going through Guy's mind; whether he had really come to terms with his new situation so quickly. David asked himself how he would face up to the same challenge.

"Those are a great looking set of figures, Larry," David heard himself say in a voice in which even he could hear the beginnings of a Simon-like mid-Atlantic twang.

"We've been consistently first-quartile for the past eight years," Clark Kent interjected.

David grinned and nodded enthusiastically. "I bet you have."

The conclusion you had to come to was that Guy was genuinely strong and courageous, someone who wouldn't give up. David found that he was instinctively reluctant to believe this: something inside him essentially didn't like the man - pitied his new situation hugely, but hadn't changed its basic appraisal of Guy's character. Except perhaps that it had to admit to grudging admiration for the first time. Because the answer to the other question, David was sure, was that he himself would go to pieces in similar circumstances.

"That's terrific news," he said in response to a bar chart where the figures to the extreme right looked satisfyingly larger than all the others.

He wondered why the *Homeless Truths* girl had looked so angry this morning. He couldn't even begin to guess. Was she literally homeless? He doubted it. Maybe she lived in a hostel or something like that. He wanted to know her name. Was that odd?

There was another chart with a line for Patriots' and another, lower, line which represented the industry average. Larry was touching the screen to point out the difference.

"That's very impressive," David agreed.

What was Sonia up to? David found her more and more difficult to read. He thought other people influenced her too much. He wondered how he was going to patch up his relationship with his daughter.

"You guys are always ahead of the curve on that one!"

What was Terry's next move going to be? Simon had humiliated him this morning; he wouldn't take that lying down. But in business terms, Simon was out of Terry's league. David hadn't properly appreciated that before. What if Terry tried to get heavy again with David himself? Could he simply call his bluff?

"Which is it?" the woman with the unfeasibly blonde hair was asking.

David hadn't heard the question. "In what way?" he replied.

The woman was on her feet and giving him a strange look. "In the way that either the bathroom is through this door or it is through that one!"

Clark Kent was smirking. David didn't care about him, or about the woman; but Larry was eyeing him curiously now, and he couldn't afford to offend the old man.

"Both are equally good," David responded quickly with a mollifying smile. "Right through that one, left through the other."

"Thanks."

"You got it."

"Excuse me?"

"Either one will do."

"Oh. OK." The woman smiled and made her way to the nearest door.

"Maybe while Lori is out of the room," Larry suggested with laid-back bonhomie, "you could bring us up to speed with what's been happening at TLO over the last twelve months."

David relaxed. He had done this speech so many times now that it required next to no mental effort.

"Sure thing," he began. "I'd be happy to. Just like Patriots', TLO has had another great year..."

It was four thirty. David knew that for certain because he had consulted his watch five times in the last ten minutes. Patriots' had left, and David thought that the meeting had gone OK, though Larry had declined his offer of dinner for the following evening, saying that the London visit was regrettably short and his contacts numerous, so that to fit everyone in meant using lunch and dinner for meetings as well and not duplicating. David had said that of course he understood and that he wasn't in the least offended.

A very young girl from NCG - she didn't look much older than Amy - had come round to drop off the revised contract, about which she appeared to know nothing. Terry was maintaining radio silence; David had no desire to talk to him, but he was surprised that there was no email or voice message. David quickly read through the document. All the changes that Simon had so easily won were there. David signed where it said 'authorised signatory'; at least for the moment he was still one of those. He paused and thought for a moment while he watched the ink dry.

He looked at his watch again, closed the contract and replaced the cap on his pen. Then he stood up, put on his jacket and quickly left the office.

The coffee guy was back. The high from the spliffs was fading but Eva was having trouble remembering how she had decided she was going to play him. He had enquired after her health and was now mumbling something about not having poisoned himself the other day

"Do you want to buy a magazine?" she asked firmly.

He hesitated and then nodded.

"Good. Then you give me two pounds, and I give you this highly interesting reading material."

He rummaged around in his pocket, brought out a two-pound coin and handed it over. His fingers accidentally brushed her palm, which she quickly withdrew. She held out the pile of magazines and he politely took one, rolled it up and stood clutching it in both hands. She looked away. He didn't move. Why didn't he move? He looked like he was trying to get up the courage to say something. He should go away. Today really wasn't the day. She should tell him to piss off.

"Would you let me buy you a coffee today?" he asked nervously. "Sit down, in the coffee bar."

Eva looked around her. There were few people coming in or out of the station; the rush hour wasn't due to start just yet. Why not get a free drink and take the weight off her legs? The coffee bar was safe, and anyway this guy looked more pathetic than dangerous.

"What's in it for you?" she asked sharply.

He seemed surprised by the question. "Does there have to be anything?"

"Yes."

He shrugged. "A cup of coffee and a bit of conversation."

So he was lonely. Eva waited for a moment. "In my position nothing is for nothing," she replied. "You want to talk to me it'll cost you. Ten pounds. Plus the coffee. And I come back as soon as I like."

The man hesitated for a moment. Eva began to think that she'd misjudged the situation; maybe he wasn't so desperate that he needed to pay people to talk to him.

"I'll tell you what," she began.

"OK," he replied. "It's a deal."

They crossed the road in silence. Coffee-Guy opened the door for Eva but she gestured to him to go in first and he nodded and did so. They found a table without difficulty. There was no sign of a waiter so late in the day. Coffee-Guy asked her what she would like and when she shrugged and said he could choose he went up to the counter. In his absence Eva did her safety checks. No problem: there were about fifteen other customers and the exit was close by. She put her magazines on the unoccupied stool next to her, took off her coat and laid it on top of the pile. She caught the eye of the guy behind the bar, who was giving her and her suited companion strange looks. What was he thinking? Fuck what he thought.

Coffee-Guy returned with two large cappuccinos and set them on the table.

"Both the same again," he smiled, holding his arms out away from the drinks. "Your choice."

Eva began to take the cup that was closer to her, then changed her mind and took the other one.

Coffee-Guy drew the remaining drink towards him. "Cheers," he said. He picked the cappuccino up and began to drink it. Eva watched him carefully; she ran her fingers along the sides of her cup but made no effort to lift it.

Coffee-Guy laughed nervously. "Very sensible," he said.

Eva felt slightly embarrassed. "It's hot," she said simply.

Coffee-Guy smiled and said nothing.

"So, I'm here," Eva said abruptly. Her instincts told her that being a little rude for the present wasn't going to do her any harm; might actually increase the guy's interest. "What do you want to talk about for your ten pounds, which I haven't had yet?"

"Sorry." The man opened his wallet and took out a ten-pound note, apparently his last, and passed it across. Eva glanced briefly in the direction of the barman as she took it. "I don't really know," he went on. "You're from Scotland?"

"Well done!" Eva replied sarcastically. "I can see why you're such a high-powered businessman."

Coffee-Guy smiled almost shyly. "I'm not. I thought you might be Eastern European or something at first."

Eva shrugged. "Fair chance in London. Disappointed?"

"No, not really. Not at all, actually."

"Good."

"Whereabouts?"

"In Scotland?"

"Yes."

"Near Glasgow."

"Oh, OK."

149

"Do you know Glasgow?"

"I've never been to Scotland."

"You should. Some of it's quite civilised."

"And are you actually, well, you know…?"

"Homeless?" Eva gazed at the man steadily across the table and for a few seconds said nothing. What was it to him? Perhaps coming here had been a bad idea. She should go. She looked around. It was mainly curiosity that now kept her in her chair. That and the anticipated tedium of standing outside the station once again and then hours at the restaurant. She picked up her cup and began to drink from it. The relief that spread across the man's face as she did so almost made her laugh.

"I don't sleep on the streets, if that's what you mean. I did," she answered in a tone that was meant to suggest that it was nothing to be ashamed of, "but I don't now. I'm in a temporary hostel."

"Whereabouts?"

Eva stopped drinking and glanced round at the door. "Why do you want to know that?" she asked aggressively.

Coffee-Guy backed off immediately. "No reason. Sorry. If you don't want to say."

"How about you tell me something?" Eva suggested. "You look like the married-with-kids type; you're not wearing a ring though."

The man hesitated. Eva had imagined that he wanted to talk about himself, but now he seemed unexpectedly reluctant. She tried looking at him more sympathetically.

"Divorced," he replied finally, and the embarrassment in his voice was clearly audible. "One daughter."

"How old?"

"Fourteen."

"Bad age?"

"Oh yes." The man nodded sadly. He moved uncomfortably in his chair. "Have you... never considered going back to Scotland?" he asked.

"No."

"Why's that?"

"That's my business."

"Sorry again."

Eva shook her head and pushed her cup away. "Are we done?"

Coffee-Guy shrugged, looked round the walls of the bar and then drummed his fingers on the table.

"I suppose so, " he replied. "I thought I wanted to talk to someone, and I also thought the best person would be someone who doesn't know me. The idea seemed better in my head than it does now we're actually here."

Eva ran her hand through her hair and leaned back. It was going to be quite difficult to hate this guy.

"So why did you pick me?" she asked.

The man seemed to find Eva's gaze uncomfortable. His eyes began to wander around the room. "I don't know," he sighed. "Maybe you have a sympathetic face."

Eva said nothing and tried to maintain a neutral expression.

"Apart from this morning," Coffee-Guy ventured with a hesitant smile. "You looked like you wanted to kill everyone."

Eva remembered her mood. "I did," she confirmed.

"Well, I won't ask you why, because I'm sure you won't tell me."

"Correct."

There was now only one other occupied table. The barman had produced some sort of long-handled broom and was sweeping up, making an ostentatious noise that was presumably intended to tell his remaining customers that he wanted to close.

They were sitting in silence. Eva slowly finished her drink.

"Thanks," the man said out of nothing. "I don't really know why I…"

"No problem," Eva interrupted. "It's the easiest tenner I've made in a long time, believe me. If you ever want to do it again, er, …"

"David," the man volunteered readily. And you?"

Eva hesitated.

"Or a nickname, whatever," he suggested. "Just something to call you by. Doesn't have to be your real name."

"Eva."

"OK, thanks Eva."

Eva allowed herself a smile for a split second, then reassumed her blank expression.

They left the coffee bar and re-crossed the road as if they were not together. It was five o'clock and the first wave of commuters was heading through the station entrance. Eva took up her usual position and watched David being subsumed into a growing crowd that carried him unresisting into the station.

Chapter Twenty-One

Of all the shitty jobs she had had - and there had been a lot - this had to be one of the worst. Cleaning filthy, greasy pots and pans in a restaurant kitchen for six pounds an hour was just about the pits. It was smelly, you sweated like a pig - it was worse now that summer had come - and whatever you did someone, some nobody who got off on having just that little bit of power over another person who daren't answer back, would say it wasn't good enough. The problem was that they knew they could get away with it: there was a stack of other people, homeless or illegals, who would gladly do the job if she wouldn't. A lot of people came and went; as far as the management was concerned it didn't matter: there was no skill involved, no training lost. People got sacked, or lost it and walked out, or just didn't turn up one evening.

Eva had been here over a month and was a veteran already: she had seen about six people come and go on the other two identical jobs, if you could call them that. Tonight working alongside her were a tall, muscular African guy who didn't seem to have any English and a boy in his early twenties who sounded like he was from somewhere in Eastern Europe. Locks of his curly light-brown hair peeped around the comical hygienic caps that they were all obliged to wear, and Eva thought that outside of this environment he might perhaps be quite good-looking.

The danger was that you started to believe that you had actually become the grease and muck and shit that you had to work with. But perhaps to some extent you did; Taz told Eva she smelled strange when she came back from her shifts, like sour fat and pungent, cheap detergent. Not that smelling nice was always Taz's best feature, but Eva hadn't bothered to make that point.

One sleaze-ball of an oily-haired, puny waiter had pinched Eva's arse on her first day and told her it was an initiation ceremony that she had to put up with. She'd thought the look she'd given him would deter him from trying it again - she was sure she would be able to break him in half if she wanted to - but three days later he'd done it again, just to show that he could. She'd done nothing that time.

For some reason the worst thing was when the door swung wide open and for a couple of seconds you could see into the restaurant. Because the lighting of the kitchen was much brighter you couldn't make out faces, just silhouettes: mostly middle-aged men in suits, looking down their noses at the waiters who fluttered attentively around them, the same waiters who looked so dismissively at Eva. She hated the idea that one of these fat businessmen might catch a glimpse of her at work. What would he think? That she was scum, the lowest of the low, someone who was doing what she was doing because that was all she was capable of. She hated these people. She wanted to kill them. She wanted to poison them. It was a small consolation sometimes to watch food dropped, scooped up, rearranged and sent out into the restaurant. One plate of food that was costing someone, or more likely their company, about what Eva was getting paid for a four-hour shift.

She felt tired and angry. She felt like that most of the time lately. The African and the Eastern European were very obviously getting through more pans than she was tonight; the supervisor was bound to notice and say something soon. One large metal dish seemed to have been occupying her for about ten minutes. There was baked-in gravy on the bottom and she had scrubbed and scoured and sprayed, but although the size of the stain had reduced there was still a stubborn, brown island in the middle that wouldn't go away. Her hands were sweating

154

inside the thick rubber gloves that were now starting to slip against her skin.

Couldn't she even do this pathetically simple task properly? Eva wanted to cry and she wanted even more to sleep. By the time she left here tonight it would be fifteen hours since she had started at the station this morning. Fifteen hours work for what? A bad day for magazine sales, though that was partly her own fault; only about fifteen quid clear. Twenty-five quid here. Enough to keep going, to eat and sleep, but if that was all there was to look forward to, why bother? And if she got tempted to buy more dope for tomorrow...

There were tears now on her cheeks. She tried without success to blink them away, but her nose was starting to run and she had to struggle out of the gloves, which stretched and clung to her sweaty skin, and then rummage around under her workwear for a tissue. She collected herself quickly.

The Eastern European boy was looking at her with a puzzled expression on his face. "Just a bit of an allergy," she told him with a smile. He nodded and looked away again.

Eva wiped under her nose. She could smell rubber on her fingers; she hated that.

The supervisor was approaching. The gloves felt cold and clammy as she put them back on. She squirted the pan again and started scrubbing at it as vigorously as she could. A couple of minutes extra soaking seemed to have dissolved the stain a little; it was definitely giving way.

More positive thoughts: she'd forgotten the other, easy ten quid she'd made today, from the man in the suit, just for having coffee with him. She couldn't really figure him out. Her best guess, and her hope, was that he really was just a sad, lonely guy who wanted someone to talk to. She hoped he'd do it again. She reproached herself for not being friendlier.

"You're getting behind," the supervisor said predictably. "You aren't going till it's done and we don't pay overtime."

Eva nodded and speeded up her scrubbing; she didn't want an argument at the moment. She was saving it all up for the day she left.

She had tried to work out how wealthy Coffee-Guy was. The signs weren't good: his suit didn't look expensive and the trousers were starting to become shiny. His wristwatch looked quite smart, but dated; he didn't seem to wear any other jewellery. There hadn't been much money in his wallet. Well, that wasn't surprising: divorces and children weren't cheap. Even so, at his age in the City he must be earning a reasonable amount. It was going to be worth stringing him along for a while, to try to divert some of whatever money he did have in her direction. If that didn't work on any serious scale then she could at least make a tenner every time just for drinking coffee and listening to him whingeing about his ex-wife, his boss or his teenage daughter.

The stain finally yielded and Eva lifted the pan and deposited it on the counter. She looked up at the wall clock. An hour and a half to go. Her mood had quickly improved. She prayed that nothing she had said or done had put this David off, that he would come back for more. Her instincts told her that he would. She was impatient to get back to the hostel and, if Taz was still awake, tell her that maybe today was the day they had been waiting for.

Chapter Twenty-Two

Guy tried for the millionth time to look at the clock on the bedside cabinet. He could hear it ticking; he knew that if he could only achieve the simple feat of turning his head forty-five degrees to one side, something he had done thousands, maybe millions of times in his life - something billions of people in the world had each done scores of times that day without giving it a second thought - it would tell him what time it was, how many hours he had to endure before he would have at least the small consolation of intermittent human company, of some of the commonplace sounds of everyday life: the nurses walking along the echoing corridor, the engines of cars going in and out of the car park, even the binmen arriving to take away parcels of God-knew-what.

But he couldn't.

His brain didn't seem to get it. It wanted to know the time, it instructed the head to turn. Over and over again. It wouldn't learn.

He wished they would leave the TV on during the night, even if permanently on one channel, however bad it might be. Old black-and-white westerns would be some company, some way of passing the time. But they said it disturbed the other patients and that it was important for the healing process that he sleep. Which was easy for them to say. He had slept tonight, probably, he thought, for about two hours and had woken up maybe half an hour ago. He wanted to sleep now. A long sleep, waking only when his back was once more fully healed and, if that wasn't going to happen, well, then never.

He had two types of dream. In the first everything was as it had always been: his back and his legs worked, he played sport, he went to work. It brought an instantaneous descent into aching despair when he awoke and realised where he was, and why.

In the other type his mother, her face grotesquely distorted like the reflection in one of those novelty seaside mirrors, loomed over his hospital bed and screamed and pulled at the skin on her face until it bled.

His mother had been in to see him, every day. She was doing her best to preserve at least the façade of a positive outlook. She told him about her conversations with the doctors (though, he suspected, not everything) and about the various rehabilitative programmes they could put him on. Between visits she busied herself with things like talking to Social Services about the support staff and special equipment they would need at home once Guy was released from hospital. If there were any grants going, she was going to have them. That was how his mother was: positive and practical. 'No-nonsense' to her had no pejorative connotations. Guy supposed he was basically the same. But he wondered how his mother coped at night, when she was alone in the big house. She was so real in the dream that it didn't seem outside the realms of possibility that they were sharing it, each living it from their own perspective. How then did he look to her? When each morning came and she returned to see him she looked visibly older than the previous day. Her hair had been grey for a while, but now it was brittle and arid, like straw. Her eyes were red and the skin below them was a pellucid grey-green. Had she been crying? Guy could only remember seeing her cry once, when his father had died, and even then she had quickly immersed herself in the practicalities of the arrangements to be made. He wondered whether she knew that he himself had several times in recent days given way to tears. He supposed she might have guessed, but he hoped not. He wasn't routinely going to pieces, he was too strong for that; but there were moments such as the present one, in the depths of the night, when there really seemed to be no hope at all; then he closed his eyes and could feel the wetness, and sometimes he just let it flow.

Days were better. Daylight and sunshine and the nurses and other patients bustling about. Phones ringing. In the middle of the day Guy could almost recover his normal positive outlook on life. When David from work - nice enough man, but not much get-up-and-go - had come to see him a few hours previously he'd been able to tell him how he, Guy, was an achiever and no accident was going to change that, and he'd believed everything he'd said.

But the night somehow was different. He was haunted by The Thought: the scenario that had played itself out in his head a thousand times since he'd woken up in hospital. It was so simple. He was driving to the station and the idea came to him to text Adam Davies but he decided it wasn't urgent and didn't do it. Then he arrived at the car park, just like every other day, and got on the train and went to work. And his back and legs worked quite normally. Why wouldn't they?

Part Two

Chapter Twenty-Three

David was meeting Eva almost every day. Their cups of coffee together had become the part of his working week that he most looked forward to. The remainder comprised mostly meetings with interchangeable American clients; encounters with increasingly slick (and young) business introducers who made Terry look like a lovable old rogue, the sort who could shake your hand and stab you in the back in one movement; and occasional visitations from senior management. The latter had become ever more remote as TLO had grown over the years, to the point that they now occupied their own floor and rarely left it; Simon was now the main conduit for what the 'fourth floor' did and didn't want, though some of the other guys on David's floor imagined they were in the know. Chris said that what the fourth floor really wanted was to sell the company to a cash-rich, probably American, bidder.

Adrian talked about the board directors as if he knew them personally: "What Stevie Allen wants to do", he once said in David's hearing, "is to cash in his fifteen mill and get the hell out before it all starts to go pear-shaped."

Chris, his phone clamped to his ear like the style statement it possibly was, would nod sagely, push out his lips and agree: "The guy's been there, done it; he's headed for the golf course."

David remembered when 'Stevie' had lived in a bedsit in Plumstead and driven a Vauxhall Chevette; the two of them had even propped up the odd bar together. Steve was now pleasant but distant if they met in the lift; his expensive suits were immaculately pressed, his hair suggested he went to the salon every morning, one of several chunky expensive watches clung to his wrist and even his aftershave gave off an odour of wealth. Given the chance, David now avoided him.

Eva's company was much more pleasurable. Whenever possible, David had started to arrange his business meetings so that there was a half-hour gap beginning at ten thirty, when he could sneak out of the office and meet her. The venue was now a coffee shop in the heart of the station. The change had been David's idea and thankfully Eva hadn't asked for a reason. David still felt that there was something semi-clandestine about their meetings, and that gave him a buzz, as did the notion that he was doing something which was outside the expected norms of City behaviour. He knew all of that was childish, but he felt it nonetheless.

Eva texted almost every day, either to confirm ten thirty or sometimes to cancel, usually without giving a reason. David himself rarely cancelled, though he had no option if Simon suddenly called a meeting at short notice. He had stood Eva up once when Simon had summoned him into his office at nine forty-five with a few of the other guys and talked for over an hour. Eva hadn't been very put out: she'd said it was only a cup of coffee, which David had found both a relief and a disappointment.

On most days David and Eva drank coffee and ate Danish pastries. After six weeks or so of this David thought that he had told Eva almost everything about himself, but for all his own candour he had still learnt next to nothing about her. That wasn't entirely true. He thought he knew a lot about her personality: what made her laugh, what annoyed her. And her physical mannerisms: the finger curling the hair in front of her ear, the way she licked her coffee-stirrer and then waved it in front of her when she wanted to make a point. But he still knew next to nothing about her current life or her history. He thought he knew her name, and her accent gave away her nationality. She lived in a hostel, which presumably wasn't far away, though she wouldn't say exactly where. She had a friend called Taz, who she would sometimes refer to without giving many details.

Reading between the lines it seemed that this Taz was quite young and a bit mad and Eva felt responsible for her. If Eva had a boyfriend she never mentioned him, and David found that he preferred not to know. After a couple of weeks Eva had been prepared to tell him that she had the casual job in the restaurant kitchen, and even where it was, and David had pretended to be surprised at the information. He had said he had heard of it and thought he might have eaten there once, though he wasn't absolutely sure because he went to quite a lot of restaurants, which immediately struck him as a crass thing to have said.

Eva had found a good way of changing the subject when it looked like she might have to talk about herself, which was to ask about Guy's progress. David would tell her what he knew, some of it second-hand: about the surgery, with its limited success; Guy getting into a wheelchair for the first time; the physiotherapy; going back to live with his mother; his mother's plans to adapt the house for use by a disabled person. Eva listened and sometimes contributed practical suggestions, which generally seemed useful and sensible. On the other hand any sentimentality seemed to bore or even irritate her and David quickly learnt to avoid it.

David enjoyed the conversations. He really did. He even began to find that he missed them at the weekends. He knew that this was partly due to the sporadic nature of his human contacts outside the working week, with Amy still refusing to spend time with him, though she would now briefly come to the phone if Sonia felt inclined to ask her to. But that wasn't the whole story, and David had to admit to himself that given a guilt-free choice of companion for Saturday lunch he would take Eva over his daughter most of the time.

He knew that he had to do more for Eva or she would get bored and drift away. He couldn't see what possible interest she could have in listening to him droning on every day, beyond the free coffee and pastries, which at about three quid a time were hardly valuable. He did sometimes give her money and she didn't refuse it, but she didn't ask any more. Sometimes he thought that maybe she really liked him, but he quickly dismissed the idea as a middle-aged delusion. His big fear was that one day she would simply no longer be there. David would come out of the station and find someone else selling *Homeless Truths,* someone who would claim to have no knowledge of Eva or of her whereabouts.

Eva lay back on the bench and took another drag. There were people who claimed to smoke spliffs in the hostel, and occasionally you could smell one, but it wasn't worth the hassle. Here in the park no-one gave you any grief: you got filthy looks from a few old dears for being sprawled out with your feet up, but OAPs were easily outstared; and there were enough benches to go round anyway, so they could fuck off. Towards nightfall, if you were stupid enough to hang around that long - and the area got very creepy, so why would you? - you might get trouble with tramps, the pisshead psycho types, who didn't appreciate you lounging about on their bed; but otherwise, assuming it didn't rain, it was cool. The police never came within a mile of the place; the pile of discarded needles in the flower-beds showed that everyone knew that. Sometimes, if you wanted to, you could watch someone shooting up under one of the trees, though it wasn't a good idea to stare too long.

Without attempting to sit up, Eva held out the spliff to Taz, who leaned awkwardly across to take it. She was crouched in a small area at the far end of the bench, the only part that Eva wasn't occupying, looking like a restless bird on a perch and constantly shuffling her feet to prevent herself from toppling over. She put the cigarette in her mouth and inhaled deeply, narrowed her eyes and gazed in the direction of the grey, lifeless pond fifty metres in front of her.

"What's he like?" she asked.

"Who?" Eva shaded her eyes in the bright sunshine and looked uncomprehendingly at her friend.

"Coffee-Guy."

Eva sat up, waited for the younger girl to take another long drag and then gently took the cigarette out of her hand.

"I've told you. He's just a guy, a bloke in a suit, OK? I get a coffee and a doughnut, he gets to go on about how crappy his life is and I pretend to listen. End of story."

"Why's his life crappy?"

"I've just told you, I don't listen." Eva paused. "I don't know, something about his wife's left him, his daughter won't speak to him, his job's boring." Eva decided that the spliff was finished, threw it down and ground it into the gravel with her heel. "I'd like his problems."

"Can I come along one day?" Taz asked.

Eva stared at her friend, who gazed back blankly.

"Why do you keep doing that?" Eva asked, laughing.

"What?"

"Coming out with the same questions over and over again."

"I don't."

Eva rolled her eyes and sighed loudly.

"What do you mean, you don't? What's the point of saying that? You do! You know you do! You've asked me forty thousand times what 'Coffee-Guy' is like, and about thirty-nine thousand times if you can come along one day."

Taz pushed out her lower lip and shrugged. "Wouldn't cost anything," she said quietly, without conviction. "I don't like coffee."

"For the thirty-nine thousand and one-th time," Eva replied, "how do you think he'll react to you? Look at you! You'll freak him out. He'll run away just as I'm getting somewhere."

Taz nodded and looked out towards the pond again. Eva moved along the bench until she was sitting next to her. She went to put a hand on Taz's shoulder, but then decided it would not be welcome and withdrew it.

"Look," she said sympathetically, "it's not you. I don't mean *you'll* freak him out; I mean anyone would. You know, what's he going to think? 'Now there's two of them, how many more? What are they after?' Next day he doesn't show up. No Coffee-Guy, girl, no horses in Wales."

Taz smiled. "You're shitting me."

Eva laughed and finally put her arm around Taz's shoulder.

"OK, you win. I'm shitting you a little. Trust me. I've told you: we're getting out of that arsehole of a hostel very soon, you and me. Don't look at me like that! Watch my lips: together, you and me, OK?"

"Where are we going?" Taz asked suspiciously.

Eva thought for a moment. "Somewhere much better."

"Wales?"

"Maybe next year."

"And the creepy guy."

Eva smiled patiently: she understood now that Taz knew the answers to the questions she asked; she just needed to hear them in someone else's voice. She drew Taz closer towards her.

"That's easy," she said. "We're going to kill him."

Chapter Twenty-Four

'Dissing', Terry thought, seemed to be the modern word for it. Young people all seemed to use it, even one of his own kids, though he couldn't remember now which one. He'd meant to tell Serena that he didn't want the boys sounding like blacks, but something more important, something to do with work, must have sidetracked him because he'd never got round to it. All kids these days tried to sound black: England had lost its self-respect and English kids just reflected that.

But 'dissing': against his better judgment Terry liked the word. It was supposed to be short for disrespecting, but it was stronger than that, and suggested retribution. Some of the young guys in the market occasionally tried to diss Terry, but their time would come. Mac had tried it and been put in his place. Simon Stevens had severely dissed Terry over the contract - fortunately in front of no-one except Kelsey - but it had been noted and would be rectified in the future. At a time and place of Terry Ransome's choosing.

But for the moment Kelsey himself was the main problem. Weeks had passed and he hadn't so much as rung to apologise for the changes Stevens had made to the contract. Maybe he was lying low, but that didn't get away from the fact that he must either think that Terry would simply take it on the chin and sort out the business at the *Inferno* for him anyway; or, worse, have concluded that Terry had made it all up, and so decided to call his bluff.

So was David Kelsey 'dissing' Terry Ransome? It seriously pissed Terry off just thinking that he might be. The man was playing dangerously out of his league. The question was how to bring that home to him.

The contract with TLO was in place, business was flowing through it and Terry was receiving his commission - more from that source in fact than from anything else he had on the go at the moment, despite the cut from fifteen percent to ten. Serena would be pleased because she kept complaining that her SLK was the old shape, and they could now change it; come to that they could chop in the X5 for a Discovery as well, seeing that every other house these days seemed to have the Beemer. But it wasn't about the money - this was another thing that Serena, and women in general, didn't get - and it never had been. What business was primarily about was business itself.

Much as it hurt him to do it, Terry realised that he would have to make the first move. He made sure that there was no-one else in the office when he picked up the receiver and dialled David Kelsey's office number. The phone rang several times and Terry was just about to give up (he had no intention of leaving a message) when it was finally answered.

"TLO," came David's breathless voice.

"Hi, TLO," Terry replied sarcastically. "This is Mr Ransome from NCG. Long time no hear. How are tricks?"

"Oh, hi, Terry."

The voice was quiet and distant and Terry couldn't quite get a handle on the tone. There was a pause; it appeared David wasn't going to say anything else.

"Thought you'd disappeared off the face of the Earth!" Terry continued with forced joviality.

"No," David replied. "I've been around."

"Great," replied Terry, who was uncomfortably aware of the difficulty he was having in trying to sound calm and friendly. "You been running or something?"

"Not really. I heard the phone as I came back in the office from a coffee meeting and ran over to pick it up."

"Anyone I know?"

A slight laugh. "Very much doubt it."

"Try me. I know most of the people in this market."

"Not this one, you don't."

Terry exhaled loudly. "Have it your way. Listen, I thought we should touch base now that the contract has had a few weeks to bed in. From our side it's looking pretty good so far, apart from the obvious disappointment over the commission. I'm giving you a heads-up now, David, we could struggle with 10 at renewal. TLO is a good client, but there are other games in town, if you understand what I'm saying."

"You'll need to talk to the organ-grinder about that, Terry. You heard the man."

Kelsey sounded completely unembarrassed by his own lack of authority. How pathetic was that? Or was the guy taking the piss? If he was, how was he? Terry struggled not to lose his rag.

"Well, let's cross that bridge when we come to it," Terry said emolliently. "How are you fixed for lunch?"

There was an intake of breath at the other end of the line, then a pause as though David was consulting his diary or giving the matter some thought. "Tricky for the next few days," he replied eventually. "Not sure about next week. We're having server problems and I can't access my calendar at the moment. Can I get back to you?"

Terry didn't believe that TLO really had a computer failure, but he knew that lunch one-upmanship was one of the standard status games in the market, and he thought he played it as well as anybody.

"Sure," he replied. "Though I'm going to struggle to do anything in the next two or three weeks unless you can come back to me really quickly."

"OK."

"Good talking to you, D. Speak to you soon."

"Cheers."

Terry sat in silence for a couple of minutes after he had replaced the receiver. He looked around to ensure that no-one could have overheard. He really was overdue his own office. He played back the conversation in his head. He was certain now that Kelsey was dissing him, but what made the little fucker think he could get away with it? Or didn't he care? If not, why not? Unfortunately for him, Terry Ransome was one of the sharpest operators in the market; it might take him a short while but he'd dig a bit here, probe a bit there, make a couple of calls to the right people somewhere else. It wouldn't be long before Terry had the full s.p., and then Kelsey wouldn't know what had hit him.

Chapter Twenty-Five

Guy knew he owed everything to his mother for looking after him over the last few weeks, but he wished she'd just fuck off and leave him alone. Less than two months ago he had been a twenty-seven-year-old man with an excellent career in front of him, and now it was as though he was two again, at home all day being fussed over by his mother. He did still have a job, in theory and certainly legally, but although Simon sporadically - and decreasingly - called to ask how he was, he didn't seem in any hurry to have him back at work. The TLO building had been fitted out in the last few years to comply with some Act or Directive on disabled access - Guy had to admit that he'd thought it was a waste of money at the time and said so - and now had ramps at the front entrance, wide exit and lift doors and so on, so there was no reason why he couldn't work there. There were two major problems, though. One was getting to the office: for all that modern buses had low-level access, you were bound to encounter at least one impossible step before you even got to the bus stop. He could use trains (overground at least), but it meant involving station staff and holding everyone else up each time you travelled, and that would be just too frustrating, as well as humiliating. In time he could relearn to drive - thank God there was nothing wrong with his arms - but it would take a while, mean buying an adapted car, and even then he'd have to find a way to get from the car park to the office. And then, how would he get around to meetings? Guy had always thought the reason there seemed to be too many disabled parking spaces at supermarkets was the retailers' over-eagerness to be seen to be being nice to disadvantaged people; now he took the view that the number of spaces probably did accurately reflect the proportion of disabled people in the population: it was just that a lot of them were defeated long before they ever got to the car park.

So problem one was a practical one. It could probably be overcome if he really set his mind to it. But problem two was potentially far more difficult. Problem two was that the market was completely unsentimental. Business was business. The large majority of the people - certainly the successful ones - were white, male and healthy and had the vital self-assurance that came from being either privately-educated types like himself or cockney wheeler-dealers. Beyond the odd corporate donation or sponsorship they didn't care about cripples any more than they cared about increasing the job prospects of women and ethnic minorities. Their rude health, the gym workouts, the competitive sports they played and the level they played them at were badges they wore with pride, part of their identity. When you were negotiating business with people like that you had to believe that you were at least their physical equal. If you weren't quite there you knew it and they knew it; they looked down on you and you had lost before you started.

Guy found himself reflecting along these lines a lot now because he had far too much spare time. Sometimes his eyes welled up and he quickly tried to think of something else. Other times a black despondency settled in his head and wrenched at his stomach, and for a while he couldn't find the will to do anything, least of all the painful, repetitive, tedious exercises that were supposed to restore some of the strength in his body and legs, or at least prevent them from wasting away.

The simple truth was, for all his own brave words and those of others, however well-meaning, Guy no longer wanted to wake up in the morning. Everything was an effort, and he couldn't think of anything to look forward to. His mother appeared cheerful – in her reserved sort of way - and bustled about being practical; but she was having to do again for her son things which she couldn't possibly have expected to be

174

doing at his age. At least his greatest fear hadn't been realised: his bowels worked OK and he could get himself into the bathroom, which now had so much equipment that it felt as though it was in a hospital (his mother's careful, understated, slightly rustic decoration had been ruined in the process). But he couldn't get out of bed or dress himself without his mother's help, and that was a status you associated with babies.

Guy wondered how other people coped in the same situation. It wasn't difficult to believe that most of them had more friends. In the six years since leaving Uni Guy had consciously devoted the large majority of his time to developing his career, which meant drinking with market acquaintances and going to dinner with clients as often as possible. Other contacts, beyond the occasional reunion, had somehow melted away. Guy didn't reproach himself for that: it was the accident he regretted, that he wanted to change, not anything that he had done in the pursuit of his career.

He was relieved that he hadn't had a girlfriend at the time of the accident. That would be just too awful, too awkward for both of them. But sex, or more accurately semen, was becoming a problem for him. Guy thought that all unattached men, with the exception of the Pope, wanked on a fairly frequent basis, even though most of them wouldn't admit it. Now he wasn't able to, and his dreams at night were full of encounters with more and more ridiculously overendowed, faceless women. Each morning he felt the sheets, as he had as a fourteen year old, to find out whether or not he had embarrassed himself. So far he hadn't, but it was becoming more difficult each day. He had hoped that after a time his body would give up and the urge would go away, but to date there was no sign of that.

There was no-one he could talk to about any of this, least of all his mother. His specialist seemed too old, too cold and unworldly. Guy now had regular fantasies in which the nurse who made regular visits to monitor his progress - she was probably over forty, but she was still slim and she had friendly blue eyes, smiled a lot and gave off a warm, perfumed smell – undid his flies and helped him out.

Beyond the physical there were the mental aspects of his disability. For a couple of weeks after his return from hospital they had sent a woman round every few days who was supposed to talk to him about the emotional side of his new circumstances. She was in her mid-fifties, plump, motherly and entirely unattractive with her sensible, greying pudding-basin haircut. Guy had never been entirely clear whether she worked for the NHS or some charity or other, but either way, and whether or not she was being paid for her time, she had seemed well-meaning enough. He hadn't been surprised though when she'd suggested after only four sessions that she wouldn't come any more unless he asked her to, because he had barely been able to find a word to say to her, and those he had found had almost all been sarcastic. The fact was that unless she could undo his accident, she wasn't of any use to him. Trying to find words to describe his new situation, in Guy's opinion, wasn't helpful. It changed nothing. Worse than that: it was embarrassing and intrusive. Guy had snapped at the woman a couple of times in answer to what he had thought were pointless questions, and now she had gone and he wouldn't miss her.

He had been surprised by the degree of indignation he had felt at the suggestion that he might want to attend the meetings of a group of similarly disabled people in his area. Although it would at least get him out of the house, he had turned the idea down flat. Clearly the people suggesting this weren't looking at him the way he wanted to be looked at. He wouldn't have anything in common with the others in the group: unlike them he wasn't a disabled person; he was a normal, able-bodied person who happened to have had a car accident.

This morning the boredom had suddenly overwhelmed him. Everything looked and felt and tasted and smelt exactly the same as it had the previous day, the previous week, the week before that. Daytime TV was shit. The sickly odour of lemon surface-cleaner pervaded the house. No-one had called him for three days. Guy impulsively picked up the phone - even that required complex, tiresome manoeuvring with the wheelchair to get close enough - dialled David Kelsey's work number and told him pretty much straight off that he wanted to come into the office.

David sounded slightly unsure for a moment at the other end of the line but quickly, as Guy had expected, adopted the tone of a man who was going to do the Right Thing. He even volunteered to come and collect Guy if for any reason his mother was unable to take him. Guy was able to affect to be surprised and touched by the suggestion before quickly agreeing to it.

Guy replaced the receiver and smiled to himself for the first time in days. In the short-term at least the future no longer had the character of an entirely empty space.

Eva licked her coffee-stirrer, as she habitually did, but this time she left her tongue in the hole at the far end of it as she considered what David had just told her. She put the stirrer down on the table, arranged both hands around her mug and leaned forward.

"So, what's the problem?" she asked. "The man wants to come to your office. Why shouldn't he?"

David put his own mug down, picked up a serviette and wiped his mouth. Somehow he didn't feel he could enter into this conversation with a moustache of froth.

"I agree with you," he said. "Of course he should."

"Well, there you go, then. Problem solved."

David scratched his head. "Yeah, but it isn't that simple, is it?"

"Isn't it?" Eva replied shortly. "It sounds simple to me. But I'm a simple person."

"Well, no," David hesitated. "I don't know how to explain it."

Eva tore a hunk of pastry off the end of her croissant and stuffed it in her mouth. "Try me."

"I don't know." David sighed heavily. "It's difficult out of context, if you don't know our company, or the way the market works."

Eva looked directly at David and continued to chew her croissant. She didn't have her mouth fully closed as she did so, which David found mildly disgusting, but he didn't want to risk offending her by saying so. She appeared to be waiting for him to expand on his comments.

"My boss won't want him to," David explained, "because he'll say it'll disrupt the office and give him false hopes of coming back permanently, when we all know that what is really going to happen is that the company's permanent health insurance scheme will pay out, Guy'll be looked after, at least financially, and we'll then be in a position to hire someone else who'll be able to do the job without all the issues of mobility."

"Nice guy, your boss," Eva remarked sarcastically. "This is Simon, right?"

David nodded. He was pleased at this evidence that Eva did sometimes listen to what he said. "I don't think he thinks of it in those terms," he replied. "He thinks he's operating in a competitive market and he has to have the best people to survive. It's not personal, it's business."

"Are you one of the 'best people', David?" Eva asked.

David did not detect any irony in her face. He smiled. "Probably not. I think Simon would happily replace me if he got the chance. He certainly wouldn't hire me now. But I'm not bad enough to sack. Yet."

"Sounds like a pretty shitty company to me," Eva declared roundly as she dunked a piece of pastry into her mug.

David could see the crumbs randomly arranged like wood chippings on top of the coffee. He laughed. "You're probably right."

"You're doing the right thing," Eva said with conviction. "Screw your boss. Poor Guy's in a wheelchair, for fuck's sake. I feel really sorry for him."

"Do you?" David replied in surprise before he could check himself.

Eva looked offended. "Yes I do," she said with passion. "You think it's strange that I should feel sorry for someone else?"

"No."

They sat in silence for almost a minute.

"Are you embarrassed about being seen with me?" Eva asked finally.

"No, I'm not," David answered clearly with what he intended as a hint of indignation in his voice.

"Sure?"

David indicated all the people sitting around them. "Does it look like it?" he asked. "This is not a hideaway, is it?"

Eva nodded slightly as if she grudgingly conceded the point. David fidgeted uncomfortably in his seat.

"OK," Eva said more brightly, "so why don't you invite me round?"

"Where?"

"To your place."

"Well, I would."

Eva looked down and began to drum on the table with the fingers of one hand. "Except..?"

"Well," David replied, "except nothing really. I thought you might think it was a bit funny if I started inviting you round to my flat. You know, a bloke on his own. I couldn't invite you to a party or something because, well, since my divorce I don't have them. My wife got custody of most of our friends."

Eva laughed. "Poor thing. See, now I feel sorry for you as well. How does it feel?"

David smiled. "Fine." He felt his body begin to relax.

"Great," Eva continued. "How about this weekend?"

"This weekend?"

"Sure. Why not?" Eva looked questioningly into David's eyes.

"Well," David thought aloud, conscious that he should not say anything that sounded like backtracking, "it's not an Amy weekend, as she still refuses to come round." He stopped for a second. Now that that he considered it, the prospect of Eva's company was hugely more appealing than the empty, solitary weekends he had experienced of late. "OK, then," he replied, trying not to show too much enthusiasm. "Fine. Let's do it!"

"Great!" Eva grinned back at him. "We'll come down Saturday morning."

"We?"

"Me and Taz. Didn't I say? Can't leave her behind. You'll like her." Eva narrowed her eyes. "Well, probably. When you get to know her."

"Great," David replied. "Looking forward to it."

It wasn't an easy journey from David's flat to Guy's mother's house by public transport. When he had offered to collect Guy David had had the notion in his head that he would take the car. He had had no idea where he would park in the City, but he guessed they'd find somewhere. But then he'd realised that the SEAT had a small luggage area and there wouldn't be enough space for a wheelchair. So here he was at five thirty in the morning boarding a train at his local station.

He felt in surprisingly good spirits. There was a freshness about this time of day, particularly in late summer, that he wasn't used to. The air looked clearer and smelt cleaner. It was quieter too; he had actually heard birdsong on the roads along the route. It really was as though the world started afresh each day. The other people in the carriage, the usual early-bird mixture of traders and builders - asleep, texting, looking blankly ahead from under headphones or partly hidden by newspapers - didn't look as though they had the same appreciation, but then this wasn't a novelty for them.

David almost took a cab between the two London terminuses, but eventually decided he couldn't afford it. Twelve stops on the Tube took an eternity, but finally David found himself on the concourse of the station that would take him to Guy's. The last stage of the journey was slow; the train stopped at almost every station, though often it appeared that no-one was getting on or off. David used the time to study Guy's e-mailed directions.

Guy had done a good job. As he made his way on foot through the ample streets of solid pre-war suburbia with their generous gardens and tall hedges - this area really was something from a Betjeman poem - David had to consult the directions no more than a couple of times, and he arrived at the address he was looking for without any inadvertent detours.

The house was a large nineteen-thirties semi with a long but narrow path that looked as though it would struggle with the width of modern cars; a round-arched porch with an incongruous and obviously newly-fitted ramp; and ivy growing across the brickwork but not yet fully covering it. It wasn't a place, David thought, that you would associate with Guy – you could imagine him in a self-confident apartment development in Docklands - but then it wasn't his place.

David looked at his watch as he pushed the doorbell: seven twenty-five, five minutes early. A dog started to bark; the sound suggested it was a large animal. David could hear voices shouting, then footsteps coming down the stairs.

The door opened and David saw a grey-haired lady in late middle-age together with an overexcited black labrador that was trying to push past her. The lady looked harassed and irritable: a lock of hair had fallen over her brow and she was holding the dog back with one hand as she shouted something to someone behind her in the house.

The dog's attention was suddenly attracted by something it found more interesting and, to David's relief, it ran away. The lady was now able to open the door fully and give some attention to the visitor.

"Mr Kelsey?" she asked.

"Yes," David replied. "David." He held out his hand, which seemed to surprise her. She took it briefly and limply, as if doing so was an inconvenience, and then let it go.

"Please come in," she said in a tone that to David's ear sounded courteous but not friendly. "I'm Guy's mother. He won't be a minute."

David walked into the hallway. The dog had clearly already become bored by whatever had distracted it and now came bounding back. David felt its snout collide with his leg. He looked down and saw a small wet patch on his suit trousers.

"Sorry," said Guy's mother. "Is he going to worry you?"

"Well, a bit," David admitted without taking his eyes off the animal. "I'm not the greatest with dogs."

Guy's mother smiled wanly, as though David were giving her one more problem that she didn't really need. "OK," she said, grabbing the labrador unceremoniously by the collar, "I'll shut him in the kitchen."

As she walked off with the protesting dog a door opened to David's right and a figure in a wheelchair emerged. David's immediate impression was that Guy looked thinner and his hair, although it bore signs of very recent grooming, no longer gave off the old sense of slick self-assurance. He was wearing a pair of chinos, black shoes and a blue blazer that refused to sit symmetrically on the trunk of his body; instead it rode up on one shoulder, despite Guy's repeated attempts to pull it back. In one hand he was holding a tie.

David smiled weakly. "Ready for the off?" he asked.

"Sort of," Guy replied in a voice that, David thought, was trying a little too hard not to sound disconsolate. Guy looked up from the wheelchair and returned a cold smile. "As ready as I'm ever going to be."

"You'll do," David said perkily.

"Right," said Guy's mother, returning from the kitchen and rubbing her hands together as though brushing imaginary dust off them. "The dog is dealt with. I hope you're feeling strong Mr Kelsey: that chair is very heavy, I can tell you, and it's uphill to the station. I did offer to take him by car, but apparently my son has no need of my help."

David wondered why he had been expected to come all this way if he could simply have met Guy at the front of the TLO building, but Guy's impatient face suggested this was a conversation he didn't want to revisit. David decided to let it go for the moment.

"I've been working out in preparation for this," he replied jauntily, flexing his biceps and smiling at Guy's mother in an unsuccessful attempt to ingratiate himself with her.

"Good luck, then," she replied coldly, before turning to Guy. "Shall I expect you when I see you?"

"Yes," Guy replied in a barely audible voice. In his eagerness to go he had already begun wheeling himself towards the door. His mother overtook him and opened it.

David only now realised he had no previous experience of wheelchairs. He placed himself awkwardly behind the thing, clumsily manoeuvred it through the opening and almost fell over trying to prevent it accelerating down the ramp onto the path.

Guy quickly suppressed a look of alarm in the hope that his mother wouldn't see it, but she appeared nonetheless to take some small, grim satisfaction from the discomfiture of her son and his new helper.

"Bye," she said. "You've got your phone, Guy?"

"Yes" he replied shortly. "Don't fuss."

"Have a good day."

It was indeed uphill to the station - far more so than it had appeared to be downhill in the other direction when David had had no weight to push - and he was forced to stop three times in order to get his breath back and so that his rarely used arm muscles could stop shaking and recover their strength. Guy said almost nothing along the way, and David tried to conserve his own energy by speaking only when absolutely necessary.

They managed to find the one entrance to the station that had a ramp, and the lift to the platform was operational. To David's relief, when the train arrived, a burly, thickset porter was available to help lift Guy and his chair into the carriage. It was a crowded rush-hour service and David thought that the glances of a number of the other standing passengers suggested that they thought Guy should be travelling at another time of day. Guy seemed to sense it too and stared back at each of them until they looked away.

"I appreciate your coming down," he said to David, who immediately felt embarrassed. "I really do."

"No problem at all," David replied breezily. "Happy to help."

"Mother means well," Guy continued, as if this followed logically from his previous remark. "I do appreciate what she's done for me…"

"It can't have been easy for her either," David tried to agree.

Guy slowly shook his head. "Are you an only child?" he asked.

"I am," David replied awkwardly.

"Is your mother the same - I suppose you're a bit older, so it's different."

"I haven't spoken to my mother in years," David said in an embarrassed, quiet voice.

"Really?" Guy sounded for the first time as though he thought something about David might be interesting. "Why's that?"

"It's a long story," replied David, though in fact it was a very short one.

"Fair enough," said Guy, whose interest in David's life had apparently waned as rapidly as it had arisen. "Anything different I'll notice in the office?" he asked after a pause, but it sounded like no more than a polite inquiry.

"Pretty well all as you left it," David replied. "Dull as ever."

"Dull?" Guy looked up in amazement. "Working at TLO has never been dull!"

It was only two stops on the Tube between the mainline terminus and TLO's office, but this was no longer an option. There were a number of bus stops in the vicinity, but neither Guy nor David could work out which services went in the right direction. They were both equally ignorant as to whether a standard black cab was or was not set up for disabled access. It was spotting with rain and neither of them had thought to bring an umbrella. David tried to press on as quickly as he could but, with a stream of commuters coming in the opposite direction, weaving in and out was difficult. They made slow progress, with some enforced rests along the way, and took over half an hour to reach the TLO building. David could feel and smell the sweat on his body. His arms were moist with rainwater, which had also blunted the crease on his trousers; the material also bore a couple of marks that suggested inadvertent contact with the wheels of the chair. Guy, who had presented a larger target for the rain, was looking bedraggled; in his hair there were droplets of rain, some of which would periodically drip onto his jacket. His upper legs were simply wet. He didn't complain.

Access to the building presented no problem; because of the recent alterations, there was a ramp and the door was wide. A look of pleasure spread across Guy's face when he found that his pass still worked the security turnstile.

A couple of minutes later Guy was in the middle of the office with a paper cup filled with coffee in his hand and a large crowd of people gathered around him. David had quickly realised he wasn't needed and gone to the washroom to dry himself off, sort out his hair and straighten his tie. He returned with some paper towels in case Guy needed them, and found that Jill had got there first: Guy's face was no longer wet, the colour had returned to it and he was smiling.

It was noticeable that most of the people immediately around Guy were female. Many of them David barely recognised, and he wasn't sure that Guy knew them well either. A number of men from the immediate office area were there too, but they were mostly hanging about at the back of the crowd and offering no more than the odd witty comment. One or two were conspicuously still at their desks, continuing with their business phone calls, much as they did if a woman on maternity leave came in with her new baby.

"God, give the rest of us the opportunity never to have to come to this place again and you wouldn't see us for dust!" one of the girls was saying.

"New company vehicle, then?" It was Adrian, walking past with a file under his arm. A couple of people closed their eyes in embarrassment and others glared at him.

Someone thought it would be a good idea to wheel Guy round to his desk, but when they got there he discovered that Rob, who sat next to him, had been using it to store some of his papers. Rob apologised and muttered something about lack of cupboard space before hurriedly collecting his files in a tall pile under his chin and depositing them on his own desk. Guy watched him in silence.

Guy sat at his desk for a couple of minutes, rubbing his hands across the wood, picked up the phone and put it down again, then asked everyone to excuse him because he wanted to use the bathroom. There was a lot of clucking and offers of help, but Guy waved them all away. He manoeuvred himself into the gangway and the crowd parted to let him pass.

David was pleased that he had made the effort today - though his arms still ached - and only slightly peeved that no-one had commended him, or even asked him about it. He looked over his shoulder and saw Simon standing in the doorway of his office. Simon saw him too and beckoned to him before retreating into the room. David left the crowd and went to see what his boss wanted to say to him.

"What's this all about?" Simon asked in a half-whisper.

"Guy's come in to say hi," David replied cheerfully.

"And how did he get here?"

"By train."

"What, on his own?"

"No." David hesitated. "He asked me, and I went and got him."

Two people walked past. Simon said nothing until they had gone, then retreated a few more steps into his office.

"And you didn't think to clear this with me?"

David didn't answer for a moment. "Well, no, Simon," he said finally. "He works here. He's on the payroll."

The redness of Simon's face clearly showed how angry he was, but he remained wary of being overheard. "We've had this conversation," he continued in a shouted whisper. "You know he isn't coming back. So what's the point of this? And don't look at me as if I'm some sort of unfeeling bastard. You're getting his hopes up when I've already told you there's no prospect. That's far worse."

David searched in his head for a reply that wouldn't sound weak. "He just wanted to see people, that's all," he said quietly. "And I still don't really see why he can't come back."

"Are you trying to undermine me?"

"Of course not."

"Uh huh. Uh huh. So it's something else. You're Guy's best friend now, is that it?"

"No." It was David's turn to suppress the growing anger in his voice. "I'm just trying to help, the same as anyone..."

"Bullshit. You've never liked him. I know that, you know that, he knows that, everyone else knows that. You saw him as an arrogant little upstart who was intent on overtaking you on the career ladder."

"You're right," David conceded, his eyes narrowed.

"OK," Simon nodded. "So why would you suddenly want to help him now?"

"Because," David replied, and he knew that his voice was too loud and that he wasn't going to have the time to consider the wisdom of what he said next before it was out in the world, "he's got exactly the same right to come into this building as any able-bodied person I can't stand!"

Both David and Simon had been looking out for potential eavesdroppers at head height, and now realised their mistake.

"Thanks" said Guy who had quietly wheeled himself along the carpeted corridor with the intention of saying hello to Simon. "I really appreciate that."

Chapter Twenty-Six

David felt nervous. Now that Saturday morning had arrived he wished that Eva wasn't coming. It was all too complicated.

He had hoped to sleep well so that he would be relaxed and mentally sharp for the visit, but his rest had been fitful and peppered with dreams in which Eva didn't turn up; or she arrived but looked completely different; or she brought twenty aggressive, mainly male, friends with her. There were others too, but their memory hadn't survived his regaining consciousness.

Much of the morning passed. There was no phone call, no knock on the door. David tidied the flat a little and repeatedly looked out the window to see if anyone was approaching. He was beginning to think that it was all an elaborate wind-up, that Eva would laugh in his face on Monday, when she called from the train to say that she and Taz would soon be arriving. David hoped he had managed to sound pleased; he told her he would pick them up from the station. On his way out he had second thoughts and went back to hide his Longines watch - something that Sonia had bought him years previously - in the wardrobe inside a shoe that he rarely wore. He put his chequebook under his underwear in the drawer - he wasn't convinced that this was really secure, but couldn't come up with a better location - and did up the button of the pocket in his jeans that held his wallet. He felt guilty, but convinced himself these were all sensible precautions: after all, he knew next to nothing about Taz.

He drove to the station feeling slightly sick, and did not switch on the radio that he usually listened to when travelling alone. Parking wasn't difficult on a Saturday - during the week it was all but impossible - and David arrived well before the train. He had been standing by the ticket barrier for a few minutes, idly staring at the advertising posters on the walls, when Eva and her companion suddenly appeared in front of him.

David smiled at Eva; she returned the expression but with the detachment of their early acquaintance. David had imagined that she would either kiss him on the cheek or at least shake hands with him, but she made no move to do either and he decided it would be better for the moment not to try to instigate any physical contact.

David had had no fixed idea in his head of what Taz would look like, but he was still surprised by her appearance. Her wild shock of spiky hair - that you could believe naturally grew like that were it not for the fact that it was partly dark, partly blonde, with a few other colours besides - together with the studs in her nose, her eyebrows and her bottom lip, gave off an air of aggression that made you instinctively want to take two steps back. And yet that impression was completely undermined by the unassuming gaze of her large eyes, the softness of her skin (though it appeared unhealthily white as though starved of sunlight) and the petite physique of a child still in transition to young adulthood. She was looking at David with no more than mild curiosity; there was no other emotion discernible in her expression, except the sense that the encounter had made her think of some sort of joke, one that she would only be able to share with her peers. Amy wore that expression all the time.

The short journey back to the flat was made almost in silence. David and Eva discussed the rain, which was coming down steadily but was far from torrential, and whether it was likely to ease later. Taz fidgeted in the back and flicked the cigar-lighter cover up and down. Eva seemed to be disappointed by the SEAT, as if she had been expecting something grander, which surprised David: he had told her what car he had more than once over coffee. Maybe she just didn't know much about cars.

Eva came out of the bathroom as quietly as she could with the intention of giving herself the opportunity to look round the flat alone. She had left David and Taz together, which she imagined would probably be excruciating for the former (who would try, without the least prospect of success, to make conversation) but not for the latter who, if she got bored by the silence, would as likely as not help herself to the TV remote control and see what was on.

It was immediately obvious that Coffee-Guy (she had warned Taz on the train, on pain of death, not to call him that to his face) either wasn't well off, or didn't spend his cash. Everything looked quite new but cheap, as if it had all been bought at the same time on a tight budget: the furniture was all low-priced self-assembly stuff with visible screw-heads, a lot of which weren't flush to the wood - either the guy was no good at all at DIY or the cabinets were really badly manufactured. Most of them wobbled if you touched them. It was preferable to the furniture at the hostel, which looked like it came from house clearances and prisoner-of-war camps, but not by much. The bed in the main bedroom, a flimsy pine effort, looked like the sort of thing people had in their least-used guest rooms. The white wardrobe, one of the doors of which didn't hang properly on its hinges, didn't match the teak-effect table on which stood a small, framed picture of a teenage girl whose sullen expression suggested that she didn't want to have her photograph taken.

The kitchen was cluttered and the cabinets oppressively dark wooden things from the nineteen eighties, with tarnished, brass-effect handles, or none at all. There was ground-in grime around the gas rings on the hob, though the rest of it looked as if someone had made an effort to make it presentable. Maybe Coffee-Guy was more house-proud than the previous occupiers, or maybe he employed a cleaner. Eva wasn't sure that he could afford to. There was a vestigial smell of lemon cream-cleaner in the air; Eva liked the idea that David had tidied up especially for her visit. He hadn't quite succeeded: the floor was still slightly sticky, occasionally crumbs crunched underfoot, but for a guy it wasn't a bad effort.

But no man should be allowed to be in charge of a bathroom. There was a powerful smell of pine as you entered it - actually it wafted out into the hallway - but it didn't properly mask the hormonal stink of male piss. There was mould on the window and on the sealant around the bath. Flowery nineteen-seventies wallpaper was peeling off the wall. The paper on the toilet roll had been torn off at an odd angle instead of at the perforation, there were only a few sheets left and no sign of a replacement. And the single towel in the room, a large bath sheet, was damp and had soap on it.

The decoration of every room, Eva thought as she walked back along the hallway, was tired and old-fashioned. By most people's standards it was a truly crap place. Eva breathed in deeply. And now, despite all that, she was going to do her best to move in. Because compared to the hostel with its head-cases and body smells and atmosphere of barely suppressed aggression (when there wasn't actual violence) this flat was fucking paradise. She would have privacy and space. She wouldn't have to keep everything she owned of any value on her body all the time. Eva had almost forgotten what that would be like.

David seemed lonely and vulnerable and just a bit sad. Which meant that moving in shouldn't be too difficult. Just be friendly, sympathetic. And hope that Taz would behave herself.

"What's this?" asked Taz, sounding bored.

"It's a bottle of vintage port," David answered, nervously watching the girl hold the glass-fronted wooden case casually in front of her as though it wasn't fragile. "It was given to me at work because I'd been with the company fifteen years."

"Not a lot, is it?" said Taz.

David smiled.

"No, it's not," he agreed. "It's about five centilitres a year."

Taz looked at him seriously before sliding the box back into its position on the shelf. "Why haven't you drunk it?" she asked artlessly.

David winced and then shrugged uncomfortably. It was a painful question, the honest answer to which was that the case contained two glasses besides the bottle and he had hoped to be able to share it with a new woman in his life. He really hadn't expected when he split up with Sonia that he would be alone for so long. He continued to expect, or hope, that he would meet someone any day.

"I'm waiting for the right moment," he replied quietly.

"Coffee-Guy won't let me smoke," Taz complained as Eva came back into the living room.

Eva threw David a quick apologetic glance then decided the most important task was to stop Taz saying anything further.

"Well, it's his flat," Eva told her young companion. "It's up to him, isn't it? Why don't you go outside and have a smoke? It's not raining now."

Taz stood up wordlessly, took her jacket and walked out of the room. David and Eva heard her scurry along the corridor and then bang the door behind her.

"Sorry about that," said Eva.

"No problem. Is she going to be OK?"

"She's fine. She's perfectly happy now."

"I think it might still be raining a little."

"I know." Eva smiled. "I lied. She'll be fine under the porch."

David laughed. "Please have a seat."

Eva sat down on the sofa, taking care to cover up the marks of Taz's shoes.

"Journey no problem?" David asked after a couple of seconds of awkward silence, though Eva had already indicated in the car that it had been fine.

"No problem at all," Eva confirmed. She hesitated for a second. "Look, about this 'Coffee-Guy' thing…"

"It's not an issue," David replied. "I am the guy you meet for coffee."

"Well, I know that. But I don't want you to think that I call you that. It wouldn't be very nice. There's another bloke we know called David, so when I'm talking to Taz I sometimes say 'David, the coffee guy'. Does that still sound bad?"

"Not at all. Should I live up to my name? Would you like one? No cappuccinos here, only instant though."

"Instant's fine."

David got up. "What about Taz?"

"She doesn't like coffee. Hyper enough without caffeine."

David went out into the kitchen and left Eva alone. She reflected that Taz seemed to be taking a long time to smoke one cigarette and hoped she didn't come back stoned.

David returned a couple of minutes later with two full mugs of black coffee, a bag of sugar, two spoons and a plastic bottle of milk. He put them on the coffee-table and invited Eva to help herself.

"Do you tell Taz much about our conversations?" David asked.

Eva leaned forward and started scooping sugar into her mug. "She asks a lot," she replied, relieved to be saying something that was true. "I think you've been built up into quite an exotic character in her mind. She thinks you're very important and very rich."

"Thought," David replied, by way of a correction. "This place must have changed her mind." He chuckled to himself. "And my car."

Eva smiled. "Nothing wrong with this," she insisted. "It's very nice."

"It's OK," David conceded. "The natural habitat of divorced man."

The front door slammed. Taz reappeared with water dripping freely from her hair, onto her clothes and the carpet. Rain didn't bother her, she said. Eva looked at Taz, saw David's bemused expression and spontaneously roared with laughter. David tried to smile sympathetically at Taz then went to fetch a towel.

David took them to the cinema. The idea seemed to appeal particularly to Taz; Eva, somewhat less enthusiastically, said it was a while since she had been, though that didn't necessarily mean, David thought, that she wanted to go now. He had to admit to himself that his own motive was largely to avoid having to find things to talk about for an hour or two, as well as the knowledge that the film itself, whatever it was, would be something to discuss afterwards.

He let his guests choose the film - or thought he had, though they didn't appear all that interested in his opinion in any case - paid for the tickets and bought the food they asked for. He held back while they decided which of the remaining seats in the almost full auditorium were the best. They sat down with Eva in the middle, which seemed the natural arrangement.

David didn't take in much of the film, which was some sort of American blockbuster with a lot of special effects and smashed-up cars and wry one-liners. Taz had started acting up early on: she kept talking; she threw her food wrappers on the floor; her feet were pressed into the back of the seat in front of her. She took no notice when people shooshed her, and when the woman in the seat in front turned round and looked pointedly down at her feet Taz stared back so aggressively that, even in the limited light coming from the screen, the threat of violence was unambiguous. The woman then looked at Eva, who glared unsympathetically back. David avoided eye contact until the woman turned away. But the next time Taz shouted out in response to something on the screen Eva turned and said something into her ear which kept her quiet until the credits appeared at the end of the film.

Eva wondered how long it would be before David's politeness gave out and he asked them when they were intending to go home. She had been keeping an eye on the time on various clocks throughout the evening while ensuring that David never saw her do so. When she would eventually claim to have no idea how late it was there was a very good chance that he was going to believe her.

Everything was going as well as could be expected. Taz had been a bit of an embarrassment in the pizza place they'd gone to after the cinema, piling her plate so full of salad that the waitresses and other customers stared at her, and then eating all of it, but maybe giving Coffee-Guy the impression that they didn't know where their next meal was coming from was no bad thing. Right now Taz seemed quite happy sprawled on the sofa with a beer bottle in one hand. They'd all had two beers already and Eva was trying to force the pace a little, without giving the impression that she had some sort of drink problem. Her idea was that David was going to be far more receptive to the idea of them crashing over if he had a few inside him when he had to make the decision. At this time of night she hoped the alcohol would send Taz off to sleep rather than make her aggressive. And from Eva's own angle, she might want to be drunk because, having turned it over repeatedly in her mind, she had taken the decision that if staying here rather than returning to the hostel meant fucking the guy, then that was what she was going to have to do. He seemed to be a gentleman to the point where he appeared plain naïve, and he was so easy to manipulate that it almost didn't seem right to do it. But you could never be entirely sure, not where men and sex were concerned.

Eva and David engaged in all sorts of immediately forgettable small talk, which became less structured with each bottle of beer, without any of the embarrassing silences there had been when they'd been sober. Taz chipped in when she felt like it and didn't seem put out if no-one responded.

"When's your last train?" David finally asked. "Not that I'm trying to get rid of you!"

"Ten o'clock," Eva replied, using every effort not to allow her facial muscles or her voice to betray the fact that she knew it was already well past that.

"Ten?" David replied. "Oh, bugger. It's eleven fifteen!"

Eva sat forward quickly and pretended to be looking for a clock. "Shit," she said, fixing on the one she had checked every five minutes for the last hour and a half. "Shit, shit, shit."

"I don't know what to suggest," David said with the exaggerated thoughtfulness of someone who was beginning to slur his words. "I would drive you to another line, but I think I'm probably already over the limit."

"I don't want you losing your licence for us," Eva replied. "That wouldn't be fair."

"I could phone for a cab," David said brightly. "They're pretty good round here, and obviously I'll pay."

Eva found herself having to think quickly. "That's very kind," she said, looking at the clock once more for effect. "Problem is, even if we get a train, I don't think we'd get back into the hostel at that time of night. Particularly smelling of beer." She got up and picked up her jacket. "Still, it's a warm night and it's our own fault." She looked over at Taz, who appeared to be drifting in and out of consciousness, until David directed his gaze in the same direction. "Come on, you," she said sternly. "Stay awake: we're off in a few minutes."

"Well, look," David said hesitantly. "I don't like the idea of you being on the streets all night."

Eva smiled and shrugged. "Believe you me, we've slept rough loads of times before."

"Perhaps," said David, and Eva was pleased to hear that her words, together with the alcohol, had produced the hoped-for sentiment in his voice. "Perhaps. But then I wasn't in a position to do something about it."

"So what are you saying?" Eva asked with feigned innocence.

"Well, look," David said earnestly. "No pressure or anything, but if you both want to stay here I have a spare room that you can have if you don't mind sharing, with each other. Up to you. As I say, no pressure."

"That's really kind" Eva replied. "What do you think?" They both turned to look at Taz who was now sound asleep, with that look of untroubled youthful innocence on her face that she never had when she was awake. Eva noted to herself that it was often the parts that you didn't plan that worked best.

"Well, looks like it'll have to be a 'yes'!" she told David with a bashful smile. She threw her jacket back onto the chair and sat down. "I guess I'll get to finish this beer, and you can finish telling me about Amy's sports day."

Chapter Twenty-Seven

David woke up with a headache, the sort that was probably going to be in for the day. He looked at the clock. It was ten fifteen. Sunlight was streaming through the thin curtains at his bedroom window. How could it possibly not have woken him earlier? Normally - if anything during the last two years could count as normal - anything could wake him up or keep him from sleeping in the first place, but last night he had slept he didn't know how many hours. He had definitely still been talking to Eva at two, and he remembered helping her to put blankets over Taz, who had looked so tranquil on the couch that it seemed pointless to move her. So the chance was he had had at least seven hours sleep, and possibly somewhere near eight. Despite his headache he felt almost euphoric.

He listened out for signs of activity in the flat but couldn't hear any. The drone of a far-off lawnmower meant that quieter sounds wouldn't be audible, so perhaps, he thought, the women were trying not to disturb him, or maybe they were still asleep.

He wondered how long it had been since either of them had been woken up by someone offering them a cup of tea. He decided it would be a really nice thing to do. He got out of bed quickly - so quickly that he had to pause for a couple of seconds while the spots cleared from his vision and the percussion in his head subsided a little - put on his dressing gown and shuffled out into the living room.

Taz wasn't there. David thought that perhaps she had got up in the middle of the night and gone to join Eva. The blankets were still on the sofa, arranged as though someone had made a half-hearted attempt to fold them. The door to Amy's room was slightly ajar. David approached it gingerly; there didn't appear to be much light coming through the gap, which suggested that the curtains were still drawn. It wasn't possible to tell conclusively without opening the door a little wider, and there was no way David was going to risk doing that and appearing to be some sort of Peeping Tom.

He went into the bathroom to take a piss while he decided what to do next. There was a dampness to the air, and water droplets in the bath. A large towel was hanging from a hook on the door. David reluctantly touched it with the tip of his fingers, as if he was doing something wrong. It was wet, so wet that it must have been used in the last hour or so.

David came back out into the hallway. No-one that he knew of got up, had a bath and then went back to bed. So where were they?

He walked slowly into the kitchen, looking around him as though he expected someone to jump out and attack him at any moment. He saw two upturned mugs on the draining board that he didn't think had been there the previous evening, and then his heart sank as he noticed the folded scrap of paper on the worktop. He picked it up, but then found that he didn't want to read it. With the paper held tightly in his hand he went round the flat again. He found himself looking to see whether anything of value was missing; he reproached himself for the thought but continued anyway. Finally he sat down in a chair and opened up the note. The handwriting was long and spidery and heavily slanted. David assumed it was Eva's, though as far as he could remember he'd never seen her write anything.

"Thanks for yesterday," the note began. "Got to go (ought get back). Taz says thanks too." Then at the bottom corners, at different angles, two apparent afterthoughts: "See you in week?" and "didn't want to disturb"; finally a scribbled signature that could be read as 'Eva' if that was what you were looking for.

David walked over to the bin, put his foot on the pedal, screwed the paper up into a ball and was about to throw it away when he changed his mind, opened it out again, reread it then folded it and put it into the pocket of his dressing gown.

He pushed cautiously at the door to the spare bedroom as though he wasn't sure what he might discover behind it, but all he found was a slightly dishevelled duvet and a chair out of its normal place. The air was slightly stuffy, and he instinctively went and opened the window, pulling back the curtains at the same time. In fact, he thought, once mixed with the freshness from outside, the scent wasn't bad at all: it was a soft feminine odour, not unlike the smell of Sonia when he had first met her, except that this was less complicated, unperfumed. It was quite unlike Amy's scent when she stayed in the same room, which was still ingenuously childlike, at least to her father.

David straightened the bedspread and then went and made himself a mug of tea and toasted two slices of bread. He had breakfast sitting in front of the TV, watching rolling news that he soon realised he was not taking in. He couldn't remember the last time he had felt so lonely.

He took a long shower, letting the water soak into his scalp until the hangover started to subside. He dried himself slowly and went to hang his towel over the other one on the door, but thought better of it and instead put it over the radiator in the living room.

There was no message on his phone. David hoped Eva might call to say that they had got back safely, but realised it was just an instinctive thought: she wasn't going to.

He folded up the blankets on the sofa and put them back in the cupboard. He thought of Taz's sleeping face. He wondered what her real name was; he supposed Taz could be a diminutive of something, but more likely it was some sort of nickname.

David got dressed and then, finding that the previous night's alcohol was still sapping his energy, sat down again. The TV was off and he had no interest in turning it on. His entire CD collection looked tired and overplayed. He tried to remember what he usually did on a Sunday, but although memories of past family Sabbaths came back to him, both from his time with Sonia and Amy and, more curiously, from his own childhood which he rarely thought about these days, nothing more recent suggested itself.

He didn't have the stamina for cleaning the flat or ironing his work shirts. He just managed to raise the energy to get himself out of the chair, collect his keys and wallet and walk out of the flat and along the street the few hundred yards to the nearest newsagent, where he bought the largest newspaper he could find, one with enough sections to last for the rest of the day.

As he came back through his front door he was surprised by, and his mood was momentarily lifted by, the unaccustomed smell, the scent of other humans. But as David sat in the chair once more, trying to make sense of the news section, the scent soon faded, either because it was naturally dispersing, or because his own breath was replacing it, or because he had simply grown used to it. He went into each room in turn and breathed in the air. His yearning for human company had become almost physical. Mostly the apartment represented a sanctuary, but today it felt like a prison.

The phone rang. David almost ran to pick it up. Please let it be Eva.

It wasn't. It was Guy.

David almost let it go to voicemail, but changed his mind at the last moment. He picked up and heard himself exchanging the standard bland pleasantries. At both ends of the line they were saying that they were fine, but Guy sounded anything but: his voice was hoarse and hollow, as if he were very dejected and near to tears. Either that or he had just suffered some sort of shock. There were a couple of uncomfortable pauses and a number of strained jokes about work.

"That's right," Guy eventually said in a distracted tone in answer to some inane remark of David's regarding the management set-up at TLO. "Look, what I rang up about was..." There was another pause, and then Guy continued in a whisper: "Look, I know she means well, and it's difficult for her as well, but my mother is absolutely fucking driving me crazy. It's just her all the time, her and me, never anyone else."

"Oh, God," David replied sympathetically, "that doesn't sound too good. How about your mate Hugo at RN&R? And whats-his-name, the guy at Carson's?"

There was silence at the other end of the line for a moment. "Good question," Guy replied quietly. "I've left the odd message, they're busy guys obviously... I haven't seen either of them since, you know..."

"Well," David interrupted cheerily, "you and I should definitely get together again one day soon. I mean, if you'd like to."

"Yes," Guy agreed readily, and the hoarseness had returned. "Look," he continued after a small nervous cough, "this is embarrassing, but I'm sort of desperate. I really don't want to wait. I was wondering if, well, if I could come round to yours this afternoon?"

To his own surprise David found that he didn't hate the idea. He really didn't want to be alone today. And he genuinely felt sorry for Guy, tried to imagine being in his place and involuntarily shivered.

"Sure," he replied. "Why not?"

The voice at the other end of the line sounded very surprised and almost childlike in its excitement and gratitude.

"That's great. Oh, that's so great. Thanks a lot."

A practical problem immediately occurred to David. He had to think quickly in order to couch it in terms that wouldn't give the impression he was having second thoughts.

"How are you going to get here?" he asked brightly. "I mean, I could come and get you, if you need me to. It wouldn't be a problem; the traffic isn't usually too bad on a Sunday."

"No need. I'll tell mother I'm getting a taxi," Guy said decisively. "And if she doesn't offer to bring me then I really will get a taxi."

David smiled to himself; something of the old Guy had clearly survived the accident.

"Whatever you want," David replied; he didn't want to emulate Guy's mother's big mistake, the constant violation of her son's sense of independence.

Guy sounded almost pathetically happy now and listened intently as David gave him the address and basic directions. He rang back a quarter of an hour later to say that his mother was bringing him and that, although she drove unbelievably slowly, he still expected to get to David's place by around two thirty.

David made some half-hearted attempts to tidy up in the flat, but the previous night's alcohol was still sapping his strength and he decided the place didn't look too bad as it was; it would do for a male guest. He sat down again and briefly considered how he might entertain Guy when he arrived; then he picked up the newspaper again. From time to time he looked across at his silent phone.

Eva and Taz hadn't got very far. After leaving David's flat they had gone about a mile to the local park where they sat on a bench watching some ducks until Taz got bored and Eva began to worry that her friend might start throwing sharp, heavy objects at the birds, not out of any particular malice, but just to see what would happen. It wasn't that Eva had any sentimental attachment to ducks, but today she didn't want anything to occur that would draw the attention of strangers.

She bought Taz off with all the food and drink the girl demanded, shared a spliff with her and kept her in coins when they came across an amusement arcade. For once money wasn't too much of a problem today: Eva still had all of the cash David had given her for train fares, plus the note he had left as a tip in the restaurant the previous evening. No-one who did her kitchen job had any time for waiters and waitresses.

As Taz stood in front of yet another arcade machine, her face a picture of rapt concentration, her eyes darting around the screen as her hands deftly pushed various combinations of buttons, Eva tried to work out how much longer they needed to wait before they went back to David's flat. From the time they had left it would be twice the journey time plus twice the walking period at each end, adding on a realistic amount for waiting on platforms. Not forgetting a few minutes for arguing at the hostel.

Just as Eva was deciding that enough time had been killed and that the moment might finally have come to start walking slowly back to David's place, the arcade manager, an untidy middle-aged man with thinning hair and an unkempt grey moustache, shuffled up to Taz and told her she was underage and would have to leave. Taz's response, almost as though it were a reflex action, was to kick him hard between the shin and the kneecap, watch him fall to the ground clutching his leg and shouting out in pain and then, with an expression of mild surprise and growing pride on her face, slowly walk away. Eva saw that there were at least three potential witnesses within a few feet of the incident. She grabbed Taz's arm and pulled it as urgently as she could.

They ran through the onlookers, round the lake and out of the park, then weaved through traffic on a main road before Eva was able to satisfy herself that they weren't being followed. She shouted out breathlessly to Taz, who by now was several yards in front, to stop. They sat down behind a small embankment where, in Eva's judgment, they couldn't be seen from either the park or the road.

"I ought to slap your stupid fucking little face, you know that?" Eva screamed.

They looked at each other and both laughed.

"OK," Eva smiled, "that *was* funny. But that's your lot for today. Do exactly what we talked about when we get back to Coffee-Guy's flat, OK? You understand how important this is?"

Taz nodded gravely and appeared to be going through some sort of plan in her head. Eva wanted to hug her.

"I have to think about something very sad."

"Yes, when I say." Eva agreed.

"The creepy guy."

"Maybe not that sad, Taz," Eva replied, surprised by the sudden reminder; Taz hadn't mentioned the man-they-were-going-to-kill recently and Eva had deliberately not brought him up. "Just something that will make you *look* very sad."

Taz affected a sad face, her lips pushed out and wide eyes gazing up from a lowered head. After a couple of seconds she burst out laughing. Despite herself Eva joined in.

"OK," she said. "Maybe you just let me do the talking."

David had no idea how long he had been asleep when the doorbell rang. Part of one section of the newspaper was still stretched across his lap, but the inner pages had cascaded onto the floor, where they had joined the myriad other sections that he was never going to have time to read, even if he stayed in his chair until next Sunday.

He got up, quickly collected the paper into a concentric pile, placed it on the sofa and walked towards the door. He stopped momentarily and looked round to ensure that nothing embarrassing was on display; then he hurried out of the flat and along the corridor, smoothing his hair down as he did so in case it had become unkempt while he had slept. He tried to think of what he was going to say to Guy's mother, but hadn't come up with anything by the time he opened the door and saw Eva and Taz standing on the doorstep.

"Hi," said Eva in a friendly but downbeat tone, "remember us?"

"Of course," David replied, trying not to sound as disorientated as he felt, "but weren't you...?"

Eva nodded. "It's a long story. Can we come in?"

David glanced at Taz who appeared to be about to burst into tears. But at a look from Eva she instead adopted an expression of confusion before turning her gaze towards the ground.

"Well, er, yes of course," David replied. He stood aside to let them pass and at the same time looked out into the road in the expectation of seeing Guy's car arrive at any second. There was no sign of it; maybe Guy's mother really did drive as slowly as he claimed.

David hurried back along the corridor. Instinctively he wanted to get rid of Eva and Taz as soon as he could: a few hours earlier he would have been elated to see them return; now it would just be too awkward and complicated if they encountered Guy, and vice versa. He didn't know what he wanted. Maybe that Guy wouldn't come after all.

Inside the flat the Eva and Taz had resumed their positions of the previous evening, as though they had never left. But instead of sitting down himself, David perched on the arm of the free chair.

"Shoot," he said, instantaneously realising that, although he heard the word a lot at work, it wasn't one that he himself could carry off. "What's the problem?"

"The problem is," Eva began. "Oh, shit, this is really embarrassing. I don't know you that well, really."

"Well, it's up to you," David said. He looked automatically at his watch and realised that Guy was now overdue.

Eva looked as if she had been expecting greater encouragement.

"Well, it's really difficult," she continued. "Basically, the hostel won't let us back in. We missed a night, so we lost our places."

"Shit," said David. "Sounds a bit harsh. What, forever?"

Eva appeared to be thinking as she spoke. "Yes," she said, and then, as though she had read something on David's face that had changed her mind, "well, no, but you have to join the queue again. Could be a few days."

Taz had a look of exaggerated, wide-eyed pathos on her face that David found the more endearing for being so obviously contrived. Amy had perfected that expression years ago but long since abandoned it.

"It's very cold," Taz said suddenly.

"So, you know," Eva continued, "if we slept rough it wouldn't be the first time - as I said last night, for Christ's sake, we've done it enough times - but not in this sort of weather if we can help it. As Taz says, it's been cold recent nights with no cloud cover."

David was distracted by a strange wailing sound that turned out to be Taz in tears, her face red and contorted and her cheeks wet. Eva went across and put her arm round her to comfort her. The sobbing gradually subsided.

David found that half of him wanted to be sympathetic and the other half wanted to laugh. He wasn't sure what that said about him as a person.

The doorbell rang again.

David stood up. There was no way he was going to be able to prevent Eva and Taz meeting Guy now; he would have to make the best of it. But then, it suddenly seemed to him, why not?

"Friend of mine," he said by way of explanation. "Well, more work colleague, really." He turned to face Eva. "Do you remember I told you about Guy?"

Eva looked up. "The bloke who had the crash?"

"That's him."

Eva looked uncomfortable and ran her free hand through her hair. "Do you want us to leave?" she asked quietly.

"No," David answered firmly and by now sincerely. "Not at all. Why should you?"

He hurried out of the flat and along the corridor again - if he didn't run sometimes people rang twice before he got there, and for a reason he couldn't explain he found that very annoying - and opened the door to find Guy alone, in his wheelchair. His mother was watching from behind the wheel of her car, parked in the road. David instinctively waved at her, but she did not return the gesture.

"Shouldn't we invite her in?" David asked Guy, nodding towards the car as he did so.

"Please don't," Guy implored him.

"Seems a bit rough when she's driven all this way."

"I know, I know," Guy agreed. "But sometimes it helps me to feel more normal if she can just be, well, as invisible as possible. I think she does understand. Just give her a thumbs-up or something to say it's OK."

David did as suggested and Guy's mother, without acknowledging David's signal, slowly drove off.

Guy and David grinned nervously at each other for a few seconds.

"Nice area," Guy said finally.

"It's OK," David replied. "I mean, there isn't much in the way of drugs or gang warfare round here, which is about all you can hope for these days." He gave Guy a friendly smile.

Guy nodded vigorously, but seemed preoccupied with the doorstep which stood between himself and David.

"Yes," said David, looking down. "Sorry. They didn't do ramps when they built this place. Still, a run-up and a bit of a shove should do it."

"We could go out somewhere," Guy suggested hopefully.

David didn't know whether or not to be offended. In any event it wasn't a bad idea.

"Where's good on a Sunday?" David asked himself aloud. He was also wondering how he was going to make the introductions.

"You've got company?"

"Well, yes. How did you...?"

"Hi," Eva called out from the doorway of the flat. Guy smiled, raised a hand and waved at her. David heard footsteps behind him, turned and saw Eva just as she reached the front door. Taz was about four steps behind her, now dry-eyed and scowling warily.

"It's great to meet you," Eva was telling Guy enthusiastically as David returned from the bar with four bottles of beer. They were in the *Pear Tree* which, to David's mind had little to recommend it other than the fact that it was the only pub within walking distance of his flat. The main reason that he usually didn't go there, its popularity with young people, a number of whom looked suspiciously underage, was now a positive feature, since it reduced the possibility of someone refusing to sell alcohol for Taz or asking her to leave.

"One, two, three, four," David said as he placed the bottles on the table. He realised that Guy wouldn't be able to reach and handed his beer across to him. "And I've brought some nuts as well as the bar menu if anyone wants anything more substantial. Sorry it's a bit sticky: I think someone's got some brown sauce on it or something."

It was a strange, incongruous sight to see Guy and Eva talking to each other: they seemed to David to belong to two entirely different parts of his life. No, more than that: to two different lives. And, oddly, the fact that they now appeared to be almost ignoring him in favour of conducting their own conversation seemed a positive thing. Taz had her lips round the neck of her beer bottle, but didn't appear to be tipping the contents into her mouth. She was still eyeing Guy suspiciously.

David tried to think of something to say to her, but failed to think of anything. "Cheers!" he said, holding up his own bottle.

Eva and Guy fleetingly looked at him as if they were wondering who he was, and then joined in. Eva moved her chair back slightly as if she was symbolically letting David into the conversation, though physically it wasn't necessary. David found himself doing the same for Taz.

Guy turned his wheelchair towards David. "Your friend here seems to know everything about me, but I don't know anything about her," he said in a tone of friendly accusation.

Eva looked round at David as though she thought the answer might be interesting. Taz seemed to be studying the frame of the wheelchair.

"I know almost nothing about her myself," David said simply. He shrugged and took a swig of beer as if he had nothing further to say.

Eva laughed. "That's a good answer," she said. "It's true, he doesn't."

Guy looked as if he thought he might be the object of some sort of joke.

"So what is it?" he asked. "You're not related or something?"

Taz blew a musical note on the mouth of her bottle.

"Yeah, I'm C-G's grandmother," she said.

"Who's C-G?" Guy asked in a kindly tone, as if he was relieved to have an opportunity to include the unnerving young girl in the conversation.

Taz blew another note, then waved the bottle in David's direction.

"He is," she replied.

Guy smiled at her.

"Why do you call him that?"

Taz stared back at him, put her tongue into the bottle and tried to say something that the glass rendered inaudible.

"It's complicated," Eva said with embarrassment. "And not very interesting."

"But his initials are 'DK'," Guy pointed out. "'DRK' actually I think." He turned to David. "I've just thought, that's a bit unfortunate. No-one ever called you 'Dork' did they, like at school?"

"No," David replied quickly. "And I don't want them to start now, thanks."

Taz smiled with her teeth clamped together. "Dor-k!" she said slowly.

"So come on," Guy continued patiently. "Talk to me. What's with 'C-G'? Share the joke if it is one."

Taz didn't respond.

"I think it stands for 'Coffee-Guy'," David explained to Guy with a sigh. He looked to Taz for confirmation.

She held her bottle aloft.

"Two points to the man in the hat," she replied.

"I think that means 'yes'," David told Guy.

Eva glared at Taz then looked uneasily at David.

"Eva and I meet up for coffee most mornings," David explained. And sometimes she tells Taz about it. But I hadn't met Taz until yesterday, so she thinks of me as the guy Eva has coffee with. No more to it than that."

Guy smiled at Taz. "My name actually is Guy," he told her amiably.

Taz took in the information. "Crippled Guy," she suggested flatly.

Guy's expression didn't change. "Yeah, but that would be 'CG' as well, so you'll have to think of something else for me," he said softly.

Eva was holding her hands between her knees and looking down at the floor. David was watching Guy and finding that his pity for the young man was giving way to something more positive.

"That chilli was awful," Guy complained as David directed him towards the toilet that, to his relief and surprise, had genuinely been adapted to allow disabled access.

"I know," David agreed. "But it's the least awful thing they do here."

"The best thing," Guy laughed, "was the vegetarian option."

"I suppose it has soya or something."

"Yes, but the name."

"Not many Spanish speakers round these parts, Guy."

"Yes, but even so, 'vegetarian con carne'!"

They both laughed heartily at the shared joke, even though it wasn't that funny.

Guy was clearly reluctant to make the phone call. David didn't want to remind him, though it was approaching ten o'clock and it would take Guy's mother at least an hour to get to the flat, even if she drove more quickly than she seemed to be naturally inclined to. From a selfish perspective, David didn't want to be tired and hung over on a Monday morning: it made the day so long, and sometimes had a knock-on effect on the rest of the working week. Whether it prevented him from doing his job to the best of his ability was no longer the consideration it once might have been.

The conversation around the table was still easy - though it was difficult to remember what had been discussed only a couple of minutes earlier - and there was a lot of laughter. Eva was still insisting that she was David's long-lost Scottish cousin, and Guy was playing along with the idea; he had invented a Great Aunt Morag that he voiced with what seemed to David a more-than-passable Highland accent.

It was the best Sunday evening David could remember in a long time. The pub was full of young people having their own noisy conversations, and no-one was paying any unwanted attention to the unlikely combination of a middle-aged man, a bloke in a wheelchair, a twenty-something woman and a spiky, liberally pierced young girl all sitting together at the table by the bar. Anxiety about returning to work wasn't tightening the muscles in David's stomach the way it usually did at this time of the week. He was on his third beer - he had bought two and Guy one - and was hoping he wouldn't succumb to a fourth. Guy had bought a second drink for Taz, but she was still nursing her first, and both Guy and David were looking at the full bottle on the table and wondering whether they dared take it.

They moved very slowly through the door of the pub and out into the street. It seemed to surprise them all that it was now dark and cold. Guy, it turned out, had called his mother from the toilet; the thought of doing so in a public place had apparently embarrassed him. But the pub was now shutting, and it was necessary to dawdle in order not to arrive back at David's flat well before Guy's mother was likely to arrive. Guy, now silent and subdued, pushed himself along, aided by either David or Eva whenever any obstacle presented itself. Taz seemed to be kicking something along, but David couldn't tell whether it was real or imaginary.

David thought there was something sad and lifeless about the moonlit brickwork of his flat as they approached it, but he told himself the alcohol was making him sentimental. He realised that he hadn't actually told Eva that she and Taz could stay the night again. He rather hoped they'd just assume it; it could be awkward otherwise.

There was no sign of Guy's mother's car. Both David and Guy checked their watches several times. Guy started to rub his hands together and he and David concurred that it was cold. Eva said that it wasn't especially, and David was about to disagree with her when he thought better of it. He stretched his palm out;

he thought he had felt a spot of rain, but he couldn't be sure. The wind was getting up, so he guessed it might just have been the sensation of a sudden gust.

Guy's phone rang. It was his mother again. The conversation did not last long, and Guy impatiently rolled his eyes as he spoke to her.

"Car's broken down," he told the others. "She's waiting for the RAC."

"Any idea how long?" David ventured.

Guy momentarily tried to shrug. "No idea," he said sullenly.

They stood in silence for a few seconds. Taz started to rub the soles of her shoes together.

"Oh, for God's sake, go in, will you," Guy snapped. "I'll be fine."

David looked at Guy and then at Eva.

"I'll stay with you," he suggested. "If you two want to go in…"

Eva nodded. David rummaged in his pocket for his keys and threw them to her. She opened the door and disappeared inside. Taz stared at the back of Guy's head for a couple of moments then blinked, yawned and wordlessly turned and walked into the flat.

David saw lights go on, and after a couple of minutes the sound of a shrieking TV audience was audible through the window. He imagined Taz was back on the sofa with the zapper in her hand.

It seemed to be getting colder. As far as David could tell, Guy, hunched forward in a grey despondency, wasn't actually shivering. David wondered whether he should borrow the blankets Taz had slept under or maybe bring down a thick coat or even his own duvet.

"This is when it really gets me," Guy said quietly.

"Won't be long," David replied cheerfully.

Guy ignored him.

"I mean how stupid, how fucking stupid not to be able to do something so utterly fucking simple as to walk through a doorway."

"Probably something minor with the car," David answered, guiltily aware that embarrassment was causing him to try to change the subject.

Guy still wasn't listening. "You know," he went on in an impassioned voice, "that's what gives me the flashbacks: the road, the tree… just do something slightly different…don't send the text, or just concentrate a bit more on steering. That's all, then everything's OK, I get to work, everything's normal."

David looked away. Guy's features were half in shadow, and the rest of his face poorly lit, but if Guy was going to cry David preferred not to know about it.

Eva came along the hallway with two mugs of tea and a packet of sugar with a spoon sticking out of it.

"Any news?" she asked warily.

David took a mug. "Thanks. Not so far." He glanced at Guy. "Shouldn't be long."

"We're just sort of…same as last night, if that's OK," Eva told David.

"Perfect," replied David. "No, that's fine."

Guy's phone rang once more. He listened in silence for about a minute. "So what am I supposed to do?" he asked finally. There was another pause. "Taxi?" he said in a tone of deep exasperation. "Half way round London at this time of night? With disabled access? Get real! No, calm down, I'm not saying it's your fault, but what do you expect me…I'm sitting outside David's flat like a cabbage, mother, and… Why's that selfish? You'll be fine, the RAC will…Because just once I want to get out of the house, that's selfish is it? Hello?" He wheeled himself round to face David and Eva. "Christ," he said, "now my own mother has hung up on me."

Eva handed the remaining mug to Guy who nodded a peremptory gloomy thanks.

"Taxis a non-starter?" Eva asked.

"Pretty well," David replied. "That distance, this time of night. You could probably do it if you had booked in advance."

"We could try getting him into the flat," Eva told David.

"I *am* here," Guy reminded them.

Eva turned to him. "We could try getting you into the flat. Unless it would damage your back."

"It's as damaged as it's going to get. But I'm thirteen stone."

"What's that between three people?" Eva asked.

"Four and a bit," said David."

"Piece of piss."

Guy hesitated. "Oh, shit, why not?"

"OK," David agreed. "We'll need to be quiet for the neigh…"

Eva already had her head through the doorway.

"Taz," she shouted, "get your arse out here now."

David was beginning to think that there was something freakish about Taz. It simply wasn't possible that a girl that small could have so much strength. He had seriously imagined that he and Eva would be hauling Guy over the threshold while Taz opened doors if she did anything at all; but the girl had single-handedly tipped the wheelchair back while the others were still considering how best to tackle the problem, and then propelled it in a single movement into the hallway. The step now bore the scars of the exercise and had come loose at one end; and Guy would have fallen face first into the hallway if Eva had not been there to stop him; but David nevertheless could only admire the achievement.

"How come she's so strong?" he asked Eva in astonishment once Taz was out of earshot on the sofa in front of the blaring television and Guy was installed in an armchair.

Eva smiled and shrugged at the same time.

"Because it's never occurred to her that she isn't, I guess," she replied.

Taz was channel-hopping at intervals of approximately ten seconds. Guy was looking at her with a mixture of admiration and bemusement, but she appeared uninterested now in anything that wasn't on the TV screen.

"That was amazing," Guy told her.

Taz continued to flick. A black-and-white film became a colour one. Then Melvyn Bragg appeared fleetingly, seated opposite a man with a beard.

"Whatever," Taz replied.

"You're so strong," Guy continued.

Taz seemed to sense an opportunity. She looked round.

"I'll arm-wrestle you, fiver for the winner."

Guy laughed and shook his head.

"Not me," he said. "I'm a cripple, remember. But I'm sure David would be up for it."

David was walking into the room with the last few cans of beer he could find in the flat. They were a bit warm, but he figured they would do. "Me?" he said. "No thanks."

Taz looked him directly in the eye. "Why?" she asked. "You scared?" She looked very serious; there wasn't a hint of the childlike expression she had when asleep.

"Of course I'm scared," David replied. "Why wouldn't I be? I'm supposed to be going to work tomorrow. I don't want a broken arm."

David thought this was a good answer, but it didn't go down well in the room. Eva looked unimpressed and Guy disappointed. Taz continued to stare.

"All right," David relented. "Just once, though. No double or quits or anything."

"Fine," Taz said simply. She stood up, licked her fingers and wiped her hands on her trousers.

David and Taz knelt down at opposite sides of the coffee-table. David rolled up his sleeve and was surprised that Taz kept hers in place, covering the whole of her arm and wrist. They both deposited their elbows on the surface.

Eva decided she should act as referee. "OK," she said, "lock hands when I say so, but don't start pushing until I count to three. If you cheat you automatically lose. Understood?"

David nodded in Eva's direction. Taz continued to stare at him.

"OK, lock."

Taz's hand was small, but David could sense the strength as soon as he made contact with it. He could also feel the muscles strain lower down her arm. He could also smell her breath, stale and redolent of the cigarettes she had been disappearing to smoke all evening. There was a look of absolute concentration in her eyes. Her nose was screwed up, her lips drawn forward.

"One, two…"

David had resolved that he had to lose, even in the unlikely event that he was able to win. For a start he didn't suppose Taz had five pounds. And the tiny girl was supposed to win; that was the whole ironic point of the show. But he had at least to appear to make an effort, otherwise it was all worthless.

"Three!"

They both pushed. For a split second David thought he might have the advantage. He eased off slightly and instantaneously his arm started to move backwards. And now the momentum was such that he couldn't save it even if he wanted to. Within less than ten seconds his arm was pinned to the table. But Taz wasn't done: she continued to hold David's hand in a tight grip until she judged that his face adequately registered his defeat. Then she let go and beamed triumphantly at Eva. Guy began to applaud and Taz smiled at him too and raised her arms aloft.

David examined his hand; it was throbbing a little, but otherwise seemed to be undamaged.

Taz turned back to face him.

"Five quid, C-G" she reminded him.

"Fine," replied David, "just give me a minute to get my breath back." But getting his pride back was going to take longer: he thought he'd seen poorly concealed scorn on the face of Eva as his arm had gone down, and he now wished he hadn't agreed to the challenge in the first place.

Guy's phone rang. He listened for a few seconds.

"No problem," he said finally. "They got me into David's. What? Well, they just did. OK. Don't worry. Talk to you tomorrow." He hung up. "They've taken mother home," he told David simply. "Be a good bloke and pass me a beer."

David was aware that it was two o'clock in the morning and that he needed to go to bed in order to have any chance of being fit for work in the morning. But his flat was full of people, and although Taz had curled up on the sofa and gone to sleep Eva and Guy showed no sign of wanting to stop talking.

"Come on," Guy was saying, stop teasing me. "You can't be related to David."

"Why not?" Eva wasn't ready to give in just yet.

"Well, for a start, he isn't Scottish. And secondly," Guy pointed slowly at Taz, who turned over in her sleep as he did so, "neither is Popeye over there, so you aren't even related to each other."

Eva looked at David. "Do I tell him?" she asked.

David yawned and rubbed his eyes. "Why not," he said. "As long as I can go to bed straight after."

Eva nodded.

"OK. This is the truth. No shit. I'm not going to repeat it, so listen."

"I'm listening," Guy assured her.

"We're a couple of pikeys of no fixed abode. Bit of rough."

Guy smiled weakly and looked at David in the expectation that he would share this latest joke, but he quickly saw that David wasn't laughing.

"Aren't we?" Eva persevered. "Tell him C-G."

"I wouldn't put it like that," David said.

"I would," Eva insisted. "I have."

"And you two…?" Guy waved at them each in turn.

David wanted Eva to reply to this. He wanted her to laugh, but not too loudly.

"Us?" Eva grabbed David's hand, "we're like this, aren't we darling?"

David couldn't be bothered to join in; he could hardly keep his eyes open. He vaguely registered that Eva's hand was much larger than Taz's and that the skin was quite hard. Also that his own hand still hurt.

Eva quickly relaxed her grip. "No," she told Guy firmly, "nothing like that. We're just acquaintances." She looked directly at David. "Maybe sort of friends?"

David nodded, mumbled "I hope so" and shut his eyes again.

"So how did you..?"

"I sell *Homeless Truths* at his station."

"Seriously?"

Eva stared back and said nothing.

Guy tried to read her face. "This isn't some sort of wind-up?"

Eva appeared to be enjoying Guy's incredulity. David shook his head slowly without opening his eyes.

"Fuck me," said Guy when he'd finally convinced himself that this wasn't a strange joke. "That's all I've got to say."

Chapter Twenty-Eight

Everyone in the office today looked as though they thought nothing in the world had changed since the previous week. Jill smiled knowingly at David as he came through the door - but what she knew or thought she did he couldn't fathom - and mouthed a 'morning' to which he responded with a small wave. The voicemail light on his phone was already illuminated, which was unwelcome so early. Chris, as usual, was on the phone. And Adrian was hovering, with the expression of relish on his face that usually suggested he had some boring scrap of office politics to impart.

Jill came over as David was taking his jacket off.

"I've told all the others, but as you're last in: Simon has called a departmental meeting at ten."

"OK," David replied. "Thanks." He could see that Jill wanted him to ask what it was about; it gave him a small mischievous pleasure on a Monday morning to disappoint her.

But Adrian didn't need a cue. "Junior's sending us out shovelling shit," he said excitedly.

David sat down at his desk and picked up the telephone receiver.

"Excellent," he replied cheerfully. "I'll look forward to that."

Terry had had the crap weekend to end all crap weekends. The football on Saturday had been boring, and on top of that a couple of the invitees had cancelled at the last minute, leaving empty seats in the box, which always looked bad. Then almost ditto on Sunday when a couple of twelve-year-olds from Newton's - it had been borderline as to whether it was beneath him to invite them - had blown him out for golf. Which meant he had had to spend several hours with Serena and the kids.

Endless distractions while he was trying to watch Sky Sports and Movies plus Serena bleating on about why didn't he go out in the garden and play football with the kids like other fathers did. And that sulky look on her face when he explained, yet again, that he worked very hard to keep her and her kids in this sort of style and he was therefore entitled to be tired at the weekends and relax and do whatever he pleased. His own father would have given her a backhander and probably taken his belt to the kids as well for good measure. Serena was really pushing her luck these days. And she wasn't even making the effort to be attractive any more.

And there were fucking great mortgages and two car loans and pressure at work, because, despite the new TLO deal, production overall wasn't quite what the top nobs at NCG in their infinite wisdom deemed that it should be. Well, Terry had a few irons in a number of fires - he always did - but nothing that was going to translate into a lot of commission in a hurry. Short-term, then, take the lowest-hanging fruit: time to yank Kelsey's chain again and see what more could be squeezed out of him.

Simon looked as if he was in two minds as to whether to get up onto a chair or a table. In the event he didn't, figuring, David speculated, that he might look ridiculous if he did, or that he had enough authority that it didn't much matter whether or not people could actually see him.

"I'll be brief," he began.

"That'll be the day," Adrian whispered. David tried to move away from him, but there were thirty people, the whole department, obstructing the corridor and standing untidily between rows of desks, and there simply wasn't room.

"We're all busy people," Simon continued," so I'll come straight to the point. As you know Mr Tweddle has been making a number of changes in the company since he took over the reins as CEO, from his father. And these changes are not merely cosmetic: he feels that there are some cultural changes that we need to make too. In particular he believes that we are too isolated from the communities amongst whom we live and work. We are privileged to work here at TLO: this is a great company. We work hard of course, but we are rewarded well for what we do. We have comfortable home lives as a result."

He paused for a moment and shuffled some small white cards on which there appeared to be handwritten notes.

"Yet you don't have to go very far from this building - just outside the limits of the City in fact, walking distance - to find pockets of great poverty and deprivation. The fiftieth anniversary of TLO is, as I am sure we all know, in a couple of months' time, but instead of congratulating ourselves, Mr Tweddle believes that we should instead say thank you, give something back to the community. As a result, for one day, it has been decided that instead of coming here we will be going out into the community and working on a number of community-based projects."

"Shovelling shit," said Adrian with a smirk.

"We have a couple of ideas already," announced Simon, who looked increasingly uncomfortable, "but fairly obviously we can't have thirty of us turning up in the same place at once, so further ideas are welcome. I want and expect this department to make a good showing on the day; I'm fully behind this idea, as are the whole fourth floor. Any questions, quickly, before we get back to work?"

"What are the ideas so far?" someone asked.

"I believe one is some sort of City farm?" Simon looked across at Jill who nodded in confirmation. "And the other is painting something or other..."

"A community hall," Jill told the meeting.

"Yes," said Simon. "Anything else?"

"Is Mr Tweddle going to take part?" Adrian shouted out, as if he were at school and someone had dared him to do it.

Simon shielded his eyes with his hand as he searched for the source of the question. He identified Adrian and then fixed him with a cold stare. "I'm sure he is. As am I. As are you, Adrian."

There was a small ripple of laughter, but it quickly subsided.

"Thanks everyone," said Simon, turning to walk back into his office. "Ideas to Jill please."

David half expected Eva to call and arrange to meet up for coffee. He had left the flat in a hurry without finding out exactly when Guy's mother was expected and what Eva's plans were. The reason was partly that he had been genuinely late, but he also knew he had wanted to avoid any sort of encounter with the others. He had had enough of the solitary life: he craved company, their company; but how to say so without appearing pathetic or weird? He hoped it wasn't too late; he dreaded the idea of going back to an empty flat tonight. Why couldn't Eva and Taz move in? Eva could get a proper job once she had an address. As for Taz, it wasn't clear whether she should be at work or at school. Whatever: they could support her between them. It would be good if Guy stayed for a while as well, if he wanted to.

David stopped daydreaming: he knew he was getting much too far ahead of himself.

He tried to concentrate on some files on his desk. They didn't seem very important or, if they were, he was having great difficulty taking in the contents. It was a relief when the phone rang, until he answered it and heard Terry's jaunty tones.

"The thing is," Eva told Guy in the firm, slightly testy voice of someone who thinks the person they are talking to is assuming too great an intimacy too early in a relationship, "I want to help, but I have other things to do for the rest of the day."

Guy nodded. "Sorry, I was being very selfish. Old habit." He looked up and smiled sheepishly. "Ask my mother. Ask anyone for that matter."

"You see I've got a job to go to," Eva continued, "two actually. I need the money. And we've got to find somewhere to stay as well..."

"I'll look after him," said Taz, who had appeared to be flicking between the shopping channels on the TV without paying any attention to Guy and Eva's conversation.

"Sorry?" Eva asked, though she thought she had heard correctly.

"What's to do?" asked Taz, who appeared mystified as to why these two people were looking at her so strangely. "Food out of the cupboard, drinks out of the fridge."

"Well, there'd also be..." Eva began to warn her.

"Yeah, I know." Taz sounded as though the conversation was beginning to bore her. "I did that last night."

Guy's face reddened with embarrassment. "It's true," he told Eva quietly. "She did. She was the only one who was awake when I..."

Eva shrugged. "It's up to you. It suits me fine." For a second she watched Taz, who was now concentrating fully on a chunky gents' wristwatch on the screen and its rapidly reducing price. Eva turned back to Guy. "You should be alright," she told him in a low voice. "Taz either likes people or she doesn't, and it looks like with you she does." She smiled grimly. "Of course if I'm wrong she may have set fire to you by the time I get back, but it's a very small probability."

"It'll be twenty quid," Taz said without looking up.

Eva saw Guy's expression of surprise, shrugged again and then nodded seriously. "Sorry," she said. "Nothing's for nothing. Not if you're in our position."

"Cool," said Guy. "No, I understand. That's fine."

David very rarely had lunch with Chris and Adrian, and he wasn't sure why he was doing so now. He could only think that the lack of his usual coffee meeting with Eva had impelled him to seek some sort of company at lunchtime, without which a day largely devoted to paperwork would be almost devoid of human contact. Unless you counted a possible meeting with Terry later, and these days he definitely didn't. As Chris had made his way up the company, he spent more time having lunch with clients, and David still did the same to some extent, so that it was now rare for them both to be free on the same day. Adrian was a different matter: TLO, wisely in David's opinion, generally didn't allow him contact with clients. David couldn't really understand why Chris tolerated Adrian to the extent that he did; but then again unlikely friendships were one of the things that made people human.

There was something depressing and at the same time reassuringly familiar about the canteen at the foot of the TLO building, with its individual chicken and ham pies and vegetarian curries congealing under strong lights; the daily pauper's option of sausage and chips that David himself often selected; the worn carpet tiles thick underfoot with today's dropped food and the sticky evidence of last week's; the long queues to checkouts manned by scowling middle-aged women with no-nonsense iron-grey hair; the certain knowledge that at the other side there would be either no knives or no forks, and that when the missing implements did arrive they would not be properly clean.

The strange thing was that Chris and Adrian always seemed to negotiate the system better than David did. Today was no exception: by the time he located them at their table they were already half way through their meal and in the middle of a conversation. David deposited his tray quietly and sat down.

"The thing is," Adrian was saying at the same time that he was forking a piece of pie into his mouth, "what right does Junior have to order me to go out shovelling shit? Does he think we couldn't get a job anywhere else, so we'll do whatever he fucking well tells us to? Read my contract: it says I work for TLO so many hours a week, and what I do. We're a financial services company: if I want to go out shovelling shit I'll get a job in a fucking farm!"

"You'll do it anyway," Chris said simply.

Adrian put down his cutlery.

"I will not," he said firmly, "and I can't believe anyone else is going to unless they're right up Junior's arse and have no self-respect at all. Seriously, Chris, Are you going to do it?"

Chris had a mocking smile on his face. "Sure," he said, "why not?"

"I've just told you why not," Adrian snapped.

"Chill out," Chris replied. "It's one day, and it's out of the office, which will make a change. Might be fun."

"Shovelling shit?"

"Not necessarily. Must be possible to find some sort of cushy indoor number, I don't know, maybe painting something or teaching someone something or other."

Adrian's face was getting redder. "And that's going to change the world is it, in one day?" he asked sourly.

"Of course it isn't."

"So what's the point?"

"None that I can see. Massages Junior's ego, I suppose."

"So you agree with me: it's a waste of time."

"I agree with you that it's a waste of time. I don't agree with you that that's a reason not to do it."

Adrian turned to David as if noticing his presence for the first time.

"I give up with him," he said with a loud sigh, rolling his eyes as he did so.

"No, seriously," said Chris, who for the first time appeared to want to do more than just wind Adrian up. "It isn't. We will achieve absolutely nothing, I agree. But we probably don't do any lasting harm, we get a day doing something different, and I get to suck up to people who can help or block my career at this company. QED."

Adrian now looked so angry that it wasn't clear he was going to be able to finish his lunch. "Are you going to do it?" he asked David.

David had a particularly gristly piece of sausage in his mouth; he chewed on it for a couple of seconds and then removed it. "I suppose I will. No, of course I will. No choice. Never know, might brighten up someone's day. Maybe some people will want to go back and do some more in their own time." He hesitated for a moment while he gauged his audience. "Though if TLO really wanted to help the less fortunate I guess they could have started by trying to find a way for Guy to come back, instead of which it looks like they're intending to pay him off as if he was some sort of embarrassment."

"Ah, yes," interjected Adrian. "Your old mate Guy. Because you really liked him!"

David shrugged. "Isn't the point. A lot of people who work here I don't like. You for a start."

"Love you too," Adrian grimaced.

Chris finished his risotto, laid down his fork and wiped his mouth. "Have you had a personality transplant over the weekend, or something, David?" he asked, "because I would have had money that you were going to agree with Adrian on this."

David tried to think of ways to deflect the question, which was going to lead into areas he wasn't comfortable discussing with Chris and Adrian, certainly not yet, and possibly ever. He succeeded only in stammering and going red.

Adrian looked triumphantly at David and then addressed himself to Chris. "Must be a woman involved!"

"God," said Chris, joining in the joke. "David's found some new totty at last. Hallelujah!"

"Who is she?" Adrian asked brightly. "Someone we know?"

"Eat your cold pie," was the best retort that David could come up with. But then his phone rang and he saw Guy's number on the display. He might otherwise have taken the call away from the table, but now it seemed better to give his companions something that would divert their attention. "Hi, Guy," he said loudly into the handset, "I'm here with Chris and Adrian. We were just talking about you."

Terry was looking forward to this. The fact was that all the trump cards were held by TR. To put it another way, despite Simon Stevens' unwelcome intervention over the deal – a temporary setback - Terence Ransome had Kelsey by the short and curlies in a way he'd never had anyone before. If the man didn't realise that now he soon would.

David was now walking into the coffee bar finishing a phone conversation and looking very pleased with himself. Terry didn't mind that: there was less pleasure in beating up someone who was already half battered before you started.

"Hi Terry, how's it hanging?" David held out his hand but his handshake was perfunctory.

"Great," Terry replied with the same exaggerated bonhomie. "Never better. What can I get you?"

David sat with his hands on his lap; his torso swivelled towards the menu on the wall, his eyes squinting to read it.

"Mocha, I think," he said finally.

"Mocha and a strong americano," Terry told the waiter, who had been hovering for some time and was beginning to look as impatient as Terry felt. The man nodded and turned away.

"So," David began brightly before Terry had a chance to speak, "what's cooking?"

Terry ignored the remark; he intended to control the conversation himself. "No," he said, "I thought it was time that we had another chat."

A look of concern passed fleetingly across David's face, but he recovered his composure with a speed that Terry found frankly disappointing. "Shoot," he said.

Terry almost laughed; where had he heard that one?

"OK," he began. "What it amounts to is this. I want some more business before end of the financial year…"

"Don't we all?" David interrupted him. "You're behind budget?"

Terry imagined his fist smashing into Kelsey's face. "I am *not* behind budget," he said firmly. "You know me: I have never been behind budget in my life, and never will be. But maybe this year I'm not as far ahead of budget as I want to be, let's put it that way."

"OK," David agreed. "And?"

Terry imagined the crack of the bone and the splash of the blood as the knuckles impacted the nose. "So," he said, "cards on the table: you owe me a favour and you could do more to direct some new business in my direction."

David smiled weakly at the waiter, who had brought the drinks and was setting them down on the table. For a few seconds after the waiter had gone he said nothing, but busied himself with stirring his coffee and trying to break into the small cellophane bag that held two thin biscuits.

Terry decided to remain quiet too, tactically though, not because he felt any sense of weakness.

"Why do I owe you one?" David asked quietly.

Terry began to laugh before he saw that David appeared to be serious. "Well all I can say is you've got a fucking short memory," he replied in a shouted whisper, looking round as if to point out that other people might be listening. "All the money I spent, my own money mind, digging you out of the shit you got yourself into at the *Inferno Club*, just because you're a mate."

David nodded. "And you got your deal, Terry."

"Sure. And your boss cut the commission."

"To normal market level. It's still a good deal, Terry."

"For you it is."

"And for you."

"I don't believe this," Terry spat, and some of his spittle ended up close to David's coffee. David spotted it too, and pushed the mug to one side.

Terry was confused; none of the potential scenarios he had played out in his mind had been like this. He decided very quickly that aggression was his only option. "Now you listen to me," he said, pointing his finger directly towards Kelsey's face. "Let's have a little reality check. There's not a single version of events that night - and by the way that doesn't mean I'm changing mine - that does you any credit at all. If any of it, I mean *any* of it, got out in the market Simon would sack you."

"Possibly."

"Definitely."

David shrugged as though he couldn't be bothered to argue."Do you know who Samson was?"

"Who did he work for?"

David laughed. "Some sort of Jewish outfit, I think. What I'm saying is – and I'm sorry it's come to this - if anything did get out in the market you'd seriously damage yourself as well. And you have far more to lose than I have. I have a small rented flat and a second-hand SEAT. A large part of what I earn goes to Sonia for Amy. But if I'm not working and I haven't got it, she can't have it, can she? Doesn't make much difference to me. Think about it."

Terry knew that he had somehow lost control, but didn't understand how; he wanted to rewind the whole conversation and re-examine it. The person he was talking to looked like David Kelsey, but didn't sound like him at all. If he really didn't give a fuck about his career any more, then the existing business with TLO might go for a walk as well. If that happened Terry Ransome would be well and truly screwed. Tactical withdrawal, he told himself, then regroup.

"Look," he said quietly. "This is getting out of hand. We're both going to say things that we regret, which would be a shame after all these years. Let's leave it for now, re-convene in a couple of days when we've both calmed down."

But David was on his feet and having none of it. "'After all these years' you've come here and tried to blackmail me, Terry. That's going to take some getting over."

And with that he slapped a five-pound note on the table, turned and walked out of the coffee bar. Terry sat and watched him go, then spent the next couple of minutes staring gloomily at the table, trying to work out what had gone wrong: either TR was genuinely starting to lose his touch, which didn't seem likely, or some freak element was at work here. He hadn't seen Kelsey so confident since he couldn't remember when. Yes he could: around the time when the bloke was not long married and his kid had just come along. Confidence went with happiness and, although he found it difficult to credit it himself, he knew there was usually a woman behind such transformations. In case David started mouthing off - and that still seemed unlikely despite his newly acquired bravado - it might be worth finding out who she was. Even better, if there was someone else she was currently married to.

David couldn't believe what he had done. He walked back to the office very quickly in some sort of euphoric adrenaline rush, but once back at his desk he found that he started to sweat and

233

then his left leg began to shake uncontrollably. He got up when he thought no-one was looking and went into the toilets, where he entered an empty cubicle and locked the door behind him.

What *had* he done? He had had no plan on entering the coffee bar except to try not to appear intimidated and to give away as little as possible. Where had his words come from? Had he perfectly called Terry's bluff or had he done something very stupid? For all that they clearly hadn't liked each other for some time, he and Terry had at least kept up the appearance of still being friends. That was well and truly over now. What would Terry do next? It was pretty certain that he wouldn't take this lying down; too much 'face' was at stake. He might not buy the idea that circulating the *Inferno* story in the market would cause him as much damage as it would David. Fortunately Terry wasn't very subtle. But if Terry did decide to bring down the ceiling, then there was the real prospect that David would literally find himself with no income and his assets wouldn't last long. He could end up homeless.

Well, then, maybe he'd be with Eva and Taz! Guy had called him at lunch to ask whether it was OK for Eva and Taz to stick around, because he was sure they wanted to stay but Eva didn't want to say so. David hadn't wanted to talk in front of Adrian and Chris but called back as soon as he left the office. He had said, sure, no problem and Guy had sounded really elated and said he would give them the good news.

Now for the first time in years David was looking forward to going home, not just because it meant not being at work, but positively, for its own sake. The last memory he had of home as a positive attraction was when a small Amy used to run squealing to the front door to greet him when she heard his keys in the door. The feeling he had now wasn't as powerful as that, but it was something, a start.

Guy was having trouble hiding his fascination with Taz. He tried telling himself that it was just an idle, bored curiosity since there was nothing else in David's flat that was of any interest, and Taz was the only company that he had had for several hours or would have for the next few. Unless you counted the television, which Taz still wouldn't leave on the same channel for more than a minute at a time, so that at any time Guy had a partial, disjointed view of about six programmes, ranging from news to cookery to old movies.

He thought about asking, politely and with the friendliest possible smile, whether they could watch the whole of a programme, even something that only lasted half an hour, but thought better of it. Part of the fascination with Taz was that, for all her diminutive size, she was a little bit scary. Despite what Eva had said, Guy didn't think that Taz was likely to set fire to him if he upset her, but he didn't think it was impossible that she could get physical, wheelchair or not. And as he needed her assistance each time he wanted to go to the toilet (assistance she gave in the most matter-of-fact way as though it were the most natural thing in the world, so that he was already almost ceasing to be embarrassed by it) he thought it better by far to remain on the right side of her.

He was conscious that they had not exchanged many words all day, and he wondered whether it was his fault, and whether he ought to try harder. But he had started all the conversations they had had, and Taz had generally responded in a few words: to answer a question if it interested her or avoid it if it didn't, but without ever trying to give Guy anything to build on. He didn't think she was being deliberately rude: she just spoke when she had something to say or if someone asked her something; beyond that she didn't bother, and sitting in silence with a near stranger clearly wasn't something that made her uncomfortable.

In fact Taz seemed entirely content lying on what was already becoming her habitual spot on David's sofa. For the present she was fed and housed and warm and Guy guessed that was enough for her. Although there seemed to be a lively intelligence in her eyes as they darted from the screen to the remote control and back, Guy had no sense that she was thinking about anything beyond what she saw in front of her. Guy contrasted her with his own pre-accident self: everything he had done since school, from choosing his university and course, to selecting a career, to networking and developing business at TLO, had been with one eye to the next stage and the greater plan, which had always been to be as rich and successful as he possibly could. Probably if he had seen Taz on a TV documentary about the homeless he would have despised her. He would have said that anyone young and able-bodied could make something of themselves if they were prepared to study, get a good job and work hard; he was proof of that.

He certainly didn't despise Taz now, but he didn't exactly feel sorry for her either. He was sure in any case that she wouldn't want his sympathy, any more than he wanted hers, or anyone else's. He was conscious though that he was spending more and more time watching her rather than the TV. Luckily she didn't seem to notice, or if she did it obviously didn't worry her.

Guy supposed that part of Taz's appeal for him was that she was unlike anyone he would ever previously have come into contact with. There was nothing either exotic or glamorous about living on the streets, but for someone with Guy's solid middle-class upbringing it was undoubtedly a novelty. And then there was the age thing: she could be anywhere between fourteen and nineteen, which was mysterious in itself. Guy wasn't going to ask Taz, at least not yet. There was a strong possibility, he thought, that she wouldn't want to answer, or that she might decide to lie; and it wasn't inconceivable that she didn't know.

There were so many paradoxes about Taz: she was small but very strong; sometimes childlike and yet, by necessity, probably far more resourceful and self-reliant than 'normal' kids of her age; tough, which made you wary of her, but also vulnerable so that at the same time you found you instinctively wanted to protect her.

And then there were the thoughtful, expressive eyes in the small face, the smooth-skinned innocence at odds with the proliferation of rings and studs and the explosion of multi-coloured hair that she shook every couple of minutes.

"You OK?" Taz suddenly sat up and looked round. "You want to go to the toilet or something?"

Guy gave her what he hoped was an ingratiating smile, but one which he suspected didn't fully hide his embarrassment. "No," he replied, "I'm fine for the moment, thanks."

Taz let her eyes rest on Guy's face just long enough to discomfit him; perhaps, he thought, he had unintentionally been staring at her, and maybe it did bother her after all.

"Cool," she said, settling back down on the sofa and changing channels for the four-hundredth time.

Eva had agreed to do a lunchtime and afternoon shift at the restaurant. It was shit as usual; it was always going to be shit. Nobody here, from the manager downwards, was really at all successful in their lives, and they were all taking out their resentment on whoever they could. The shittiness of the place, the bullying, the aggression was really nothing more than the highest of the low taking out their frustrations on the lowest of the low. Until the previous week Eva had recognised herself as the latter, but now she could foresee a future in which she would feel sorry for these people, and the realisation of that possibility offered a huge emotional release. So for the four hours that she spent loading and unloading dishwashers and scrubbing at pans in the oversized sink she was efficient, cooperative and friendly to superiors and co-workers alike, even to waiters - almost annoyingly so, and that was the key. The steamy detergent smell that would cling to her clothes when she left the restaurant was no longer a problem; nor were the incomprehensible comments of today's batch of young unshaven East Europeans, or the way they looked at her arse every time she bent over.

Eva was sure that her life had suddenly changed. She knew it could change back again quickly, but she didn't think it was going to. She had long ago abandoned the illusion that there was any such thing as a totally nice guy, but David seemed to be the nearest thing to it she had encountered for a very long time. Men never did anything without some sort of selfish motive, but she hadn't yet fully fathomed what David's was. Maybe it was no more than that he was a sad, lonely guy who wanted company or maybe he thought he was going to get himself some sex. Maybe he was right, but not just yet; it would almost certainly pay to keep him hoping a while longer.

In any event what David was doing for Guy seemed pretty selfless. She wasn't so sure about him though. Last evening, with the benefit of alcohol, Eva had found Guy charming and good company, but this morning the facade had cracked a little and it had seemed to her that the personality he presented to the world was slightly artificial and manufactured. She didn't think she would have liked him before his accident. What was strange was that, in her own way, Taz seemed to have quickly taken to him. Presumably he'd be going back to his mother's tomorrow anyway, though when Eva had called during her break to ensure that Taz hadn't killed him, either accidentally or deliberately, he had seemed very keen to tell her that David was happy for her and Taz to stay on, as if it made a difference to his own life as well.

It certainly made a difference to Eva's. She finished stacking all the crockery away, looked at the clock and saw that her shift had just finished. Everyone else was filing out. Eva joined the back of the line, smiled at the greasy, sweaty guy who gave out the money, thanked him and wished him a nice day. The bewildered expression on his pinched little face stayed in her mind as she walked out into the autumn sunshine.

Terry was in a foul mood, something that two beers and a bottle of wine had failed to mellow; had in fact aggravated.

He walked through the station looking around on the off chance. There was obviously some sort of heightened security status, which meant that the place was swarming with police, some of them openly carrying serious-looking guns. Terry found himself tottering into some of the alleyways around the terminus, but he knew from experience that you had to be careful exactly how far you went into that territory because then you lost control of the situation, and probably your wallet and watch as well. He saw a girl probably still in her teens, with pallid, grey-green skin, lying on her back with her empty eyes flickering and an almost empty syringe next to her arm. Terry stood and stared at her for at least a couple of minutes before he finally stepped over her and walked back towards the lights and sounds of civilisation.

He went into the nearest pub and bought another bottle of beer. The Indian bird behind the bar was slow and surly; the good thing was, though, what with the way their families worked, she'd probably get it from her husband when she got home, and fair play to him. In some ways, Terry thought, you had to hand it to these people; there were some things they did better than English people did. The problem was that England had gone soft. Could you imagine any Asian bloke putting up with Serena and her constant whining and what she wanted and what she didn't want, and why didn't he buy this that and the other, and do this with the kids and come home straight after work? What was he, a fucking schoolboy? Asian women were obedient and subservient, at least with their own, and if they weren't they got a good slapping and all the family joined in, uncles and cousins and all that, killed them sometimes if they were seriously out of order. It was in the paper all the time.

Maybe he'd ask one of them to take Serena in hand. She was turning into her mother, which was just about the worst thing you could say about anyone. Her flesh was looking old and it didn't smell sexy any more, however much she covered it in expensive perfumes. He, Terry, was now working his bollocks off so that this unattractive, middle-aged woman could doll herself up and go shopping and have a cushy time at his expense, and he got absolutely nothing in return, except for a little bit of grudging sex every now and then, and familiarity had long since bred contempt in that department. The woman was a complete parasite, to put it bluntly. And if she was only giving him his conjugal rights in return for material possessions, what did that make her? There was a word for women like that. There were several words.

"They're going to do what?" Guy spluttered through a thick slice of pizza. He looked hurriedly at Taz, thinking that he might inadvertently have spat stringy cheese and bread dough in her direction. If he had, he noted to his relief, it didn't appear that she'd noticed.

"A 'Charity Day'," David told him in the weary tone of someone who was sure that he had been heard correctly the first time and was only being asked to repeat himself for effect. "To 'celebrate' fifty years of TLO. Apparently Junior thinks that instead of having a staff piss-up we should give back something to the community by all doing good works for the day."

"That'll change the world," said Eva, who previously hadn't appeared to be paying attention to a conversation about David and Guy's work.

David smiled at her. "That's exactly what Adrian said."

Eva's face fell. "Isn't he the office tosser?"

Guy laughed. "That's him. God, Eva, have you had to sit through hours of David banging on and on about the office?"

"Hours and hours," Eva replied. And then in case it wasn't obvious that she was joining in a joke: "I'll put up with anything for a free cappuccino."

"Sorry," David said ruefully. "I didn't ..."

"Do you think people will do it?" Eva interrupted.

"Of course they will," Guy answered, "if Junior's behind it. Junior could announce a 'shove your head up a horse's arse' day and most of our management would volunteer for it."

David looked searchingly at the speaker: in his previous life, in David's view, Guy would have been right at the front of the queue.

"Why would anyone want to do that?" Taz asked incredulously.

No-one laughed.

"No-one would," Eva told her straightforwardly. "Guy's just exaggerating to make his point."

David looked down to conceal the smile on his face in case Taz looked in his direction. Once Taz was hidden behind a large cup of takeaway cola he thought he could exchange a knowing glance with Guy, but he received only a blank stare in return and quickly looked away in embarrassment.

"I don't know about no-one," Guy laughed, biting into a fresh slice of pizza at the same time. "You haven't met our boss, Simon."

David smiled at the comment and at the image that came into his head.

Taz had finished her pizza and was looking around to see if there was anything else she could eat. Guy saw her and motioned at the last, untouched slice in his open box. Taz quickly got up, went across to Guy, picked up the slice in one deft move and looked Guy directly in the eyes with an artless, winning smile that David had not previously suspected she was capable of. Then she fell back onto the sofa, still clasping the pizza firmly in her hand.

"So what are you going to do for this day, then?" Eva asked.

"I'm not sure yet, " David replied, wondering whether it was selfish of him to have finished his own meal without offering any of it to anyone else, even on an exchange basis, ignoring for the moment the fact that he was actually paying for all of it. "There seems to be some talk of city farms, whatever they are, which sounds a bit smelly."

"Chance to get your head up that horse's arse, though" Eva interjected.

Everyone laughed.

"I'll probably give that a miss, if that's OK," David replied, wishing he could think of something wittier.

"Don't be so boring," said Guy.

"Or," David continued, wanting to move the conversation on, "someone was talking about having a contact with a primary school in a deprived area and going in and doing the place up and maybe helping with their reading as well."

"Why don't you go for that one?" Eva suggested.

"I'd have done that," said Guy. "Sounds worthwhile."

"Maybe," David replied without enthusiasm. "Thing is, I'm not much good with kids."

"You've got a daughter, haven't you?" Guy asked.

"Yes," David nodded sadly, "but I'm particularly bad with her."

"I'm sure you're just fine," Eva told him without looking in his direction.

"Anyway, we'll see," David said noncommittally. "I'll probably just end up following what everyone else decides to do."

Eva shrugged. Guy looked impatiently at David but said nothing.

Taz had finished Guy's pizza and was licking her fingers. "You could paint the hostel," she suggested.

Eva looked uncomfortable and said nothing.

"What's it like?" Guy asked, looking at Taz and Eva in turn.

"Shit," said Taz.

Guy let out a hearty laugh. "Well, there you are, David," he declared. "There's your project!"

David smiled and nodded slowly. It wasn't a bad idea in itself, and suggesting it would appear to show initiative on his part. On the other hand, what would he say if someone asked how the idea had come to him? But if he dismissed the idea straightaway he worried that Eva and Taz would be offended, for different reasons.

"OK," he said, as if a wave of resolution had suddenly broken across him, "yeah, why not? I'll put it forward. Great idea, Taz," he added as an afterthought.

Taz looked round in response to her name, but David still saw no warmth in her gaze.

Chapter Twenty-Nine

"You've got to come over. She's in a terrible state."

"What, now? It's eleven o'clock on a Monday night, Sonia. I've got to go to work in the morning."

"This is not about you, David. Just this once I'm asking you to..."

"OK, OK," David interrupted soothingly. "What's the matter?"

There was silence on the line for a couple of seconds before Sonia continued. "I've got Serena on my sofa in floods of tears. I've got two small boys who don't know what's going on." Her voice became softer, as though she didn't want to be overheard. "John isn't at all happy about this. Amy's fled to her bedroom. I don't know what to say or do or suggest. David, you know Serena has always had a soft spot for you. I don't think she would have come here at all if she'd known your address."

David rubbed his eyes and thought for a moment. "Perhaps if you put her on I can calm her down from here."

Guy made some almost inaudible crack in the background and Taz laughed.

"Is there someone there?" Sonia sounded startled. "Do you have company?"

"A couple of people," David replied quietly. "One of them's Guy from the office."

"Hi, Mrs C-G," Taz called out, looking mischievously at Guy, who was regretting having told her who the caller probably was, and who was now looking down at his lap. Eva glared at Taz and put her finger to her lips. Taz tried once more to find approval on Guy's face, failed, and turned and pushed her head into the sofa cushion.

"Doesn't sound like Guy to me, David," Sonia snapped.

"Well, I don't know what difference it makes, but there are three other people here, two female - you don't know either of them - and one male, Guy. And we've just had takeaway pizzas, a couple of beers and watched a bit of TV."

"Fine." Sonia suddenly sounded much more conciliatory. "Look, the thing is," and her voice was almost a whisper now, "it's a bit difficult with John. All he knows about this woman who has suddenly turned up on his doorstep is that the husband she's running away from is a friend of yours."

In his head David pointed out to Sonia that she had chosen to live with John, that his moods were her look out, that he'd always known the bloke was a bit of a jerk etc, etc. He said nothing into the handset: he knew that for all the sharp words between them of late, if Sonia really was desperate and needed his help she was always going to get it. What was more, he had a sense of foreboding that told him it was more than a coincidence that something had happened to Serena today of all days. He hoped that he was wrong.

There was unfortunately going to be only one way to find out. "OK, I'm coming over," he whispered. "Give me half an hour."

"Thanks. I appreciate this. I'm sorry," Sonia hesitated, "you know, about the…"

"No problem. See you in a few."

As David once more squeezed past John's Audi, resenting the lustre of the paintwork that was clear even at this time of night in the reflection of the streetlamps, he told himself that, although he wouldn't condone anyone running a key down the side of it, should a passing bird, or better still a flock, care to do its worst then that was certainly OK by him. The SEAT, he thought, parked out in the road, looked kindly and unassuming, but also somehow down-at-heel by comparison both with the Audi and with the hulking, aggressive, bejewelled, silver BMW

X5, presumably belonging to Serena, which dwarfed the Spanish hatchback.

He rang the bell and was surprised that it was John who came to the door. John's expression was the polite but distant we-both-know-what-the-score-is look that he always wore when they met. He pointed towards the sitting room, as though David didn't know where it was, and then followed him through the door. Sonia was seated on the sofa with her arm around a weeping Serena, whose mascara had run so badly that she instantly reminded David of some sort of Gothic rocker. He was immediately ashamed of the thought. Serena was saying something, but it was inaudible between sobs and further obscured by the clucking and shooshing sounds Sonia was making, as if Serena were a small child who had fallen off a swing and cut her knee.

Serena caught sight of David and patted the free space on the sofa next to her. David dutifully sat down and in a single movement Serena disentangled herself from Sonia and wrapped herself round him instead. Her body felt warm, and there was the overpowering smell of an expensive scent that had nevertheless been applied liberally.

Sonia stood up and glanced knowingly at John, who was still standing awkwardly by the door. They left the room together, Sonia apologetically mumbling something about making a drink for everyone.

Serena seemed to be waiting for a few seconds to elapse so that Sonia and John would be truly out of earshot before she could truly unburden herself. She hung limply round David's neck sobbing quietly, and then slowly moved back and stared tearfully into his face.

"What's happened to him?" she asked between gulps of air. "It's not him. He wouldn't… I mean, I'm not saying he's a …, but not this, he wouldn't… What have I done? He was like…You wouldn't believe it."

"It's OK," David told Serena reassuringly, releasing the painful grip she had taken on his arms, "he's not here now. If you want to tell me exactly what happened."

Serena looked affectionately at David as if he were the kindest man in the world, smiled slightly, nodded, and produced a small handkerchief with which she wiped her eyes and blew her nose. "Well, he arrived home unexpectedly just after six o'clock, rang the doorbell continuously though he had a key and then, when I opened the door, he starts shouting about do I think it's OK to keep him waiting all fucking day? And then when I try to reason with him he calls me… I won't tell you what he called me … and tries to push past. I wasn't putting up with that, so I tell him enough's enough and he should piss off and come back when he's sober. He looks round, gives me a look the like of which I hope I never to see again, David, then calmly raises his hand before bringing the back of it down hard on the side of my face. I didn't try to defend myself because I didn't believe he would actually do it, and I was trying to show that I wasn't afraid of him."

Serena paused, sniffed and looked blankly round the room. "I fell backwards onto the stairs and even then I thought Terry would feel sorry about what he had done and come and help me out. But instead he bends down and grabs my head and pulls it forward as if he's going to smash it against one of the edges of the stair-treads. Then he seems to change his mind, pulls my whole body onto the floor, face-downwards, sits on my back and starts fiddling with his trousers. He stands up to free his belt and I don't know what he's going to do next so I reach up, yank at his balls and squeeze them as tightly as I can. Terry immediately crumples into a pathetic whining heap. I got up, quickly threw a few things into a bag while he's still rolling around with a purple face, scooped up the boys, who thankfully hadn't seen anything - though I suppose they might have heard it - and drove off. I didn't know where I was going to go, until I thought of you and Sonia."

David patted her gently on the shoulder and smiled weakly. He wanted to say something positive or reassuring. He was finding it hard to believe that he and Sonia had been top of the list: neither of them had seen the woman in years; surely there were closer friends? He also felt terribly weary; it was well past midnight now and he really wanted to go to bed.

"Are you going to go to the police?" he asked.

Serena shook her head. "I don't know. Should I?"

"It's up to you. Yes, I would think."

Serena's expression suggested that David wasn't telling her what she wanted to hear. "It's your decision," he reiterated.

"Sonia said I should sleep on it."

"Did she?" David was surprised: he thought Sonia would have been adamant on the subject; he wondered where she had gone and why the promised drinks had not materialised.

"Maybe she's right," David agreed after a pause. "You gonna be OK here?"

Serena nodded, and David noted that at last she was dry-eyed.

"Sonia said we could stay tonight," she told him.

David smiled again.

"That's good of her," he said brightly. He saw his opportunity to leave and slowly stood up. "I'll call tomorrow," he promised. "Let me know if there's anything I can do."

Serena got up as well, enveloped David in a broad hug and kissed him on the side of the head.

"You're so lovely," she told him, "I really do appreciate this."

He couldn't think of a sensible response and simply smiled weakly.

David was still in a bad mood with himself as he drove away. He knew he wasn't doing enough and, worse, he also knew that he wasn't really inclined to get more deeply involved. He had known Serena for many years, he told himself; she was now in serious trouble and needed someone she could rely on. And he did like her: for all her brash, surface materialism she was basically kind-hearted. And there was no doubt that she had a genuine affection for him, a sentiment he wasn't sure he fully deserved. Furthermore, he found it hard to believe that he was not at least partly responsible for the mood in which Terry had arrived home. In which case wouldn't his getting involved just make matters much worse? Or was that thought just a convenient cop-out?

It was gone one o'clock when he parked and let himself into the flat. He was still surprised when he entered the living room to encounter the scent of other people. He avoided turning on the main light in case it woke someone and made do with the limited illumination provided by the moon and streetlamps, which shone unevenly through the thin curtains. Guy was nowhere to be seen. Taz was asleep on the sofa, her face screwed up as though the dream she was having required a lot of concentration. Eva was on the floor beside her, her eyes closed but flickering; David suspected she might be awake and trying to avoid conversation at this time of night.

He made his way as quietly as he could to the kitchen, closed the door behind him and then switched the light on. He automatically poured himself a glass of water and wondered whether he could invent a good excuse to be late for work tomorrow. He noticed that someone had removed the old bin bag, bulging with takeaway wrappers, and neatly tied it up, leaving it to one side. They had also gone to the trouble of replacing it, which would have entailed finding the roll of bags under the sink. For reasons that his weary brain couldn't comprehend, he was pleased by this thought. He briefly thought of making another attempt to persuade Eva to take the bed, but discovered that he was by now too tired and too selfish. Gratefully he switched off the light and began to make his way towards his bedroom.

Chapter Thirty

It was odd David thought, remarking for the umpteenth time in one morning that he was failing to concentrate on his work because he kept thinking about other things, how quickly circumstances became normal, a routine; and there was a comfort in routine, or at least there was for him. Which explained, he supposed, why he was never going to set the world alight.

It was now Thursday and for the fourth day in a row he had got up and made himself ready for work to the accompaniment of the sounds made by other people still sleeping within a darkened flat. Eva had been stirring just as he was about to leave, and he had brought her a mug of tea which she'd seemed pleased to receive. She would have got up soon after and gone off to her job or jobs, whatever it was today. He didn't like to ask, because the work she had to do seemed to embarrass her, and the contrast with his own relatively comfortable employment embarrassed him.

After Eva had left the flat, Guy and Taz would get up whenever they did and spend the day doing he wasn't quite sure what. Whatever it was, they both seemed to like it. For the moment at least they were always in the best of spirits when David arrived home, and for the rest of the evening they exchanged knowing smiles from time to time; or little asides that David and Eva couldn't hear; or in-jokes that David and Eva could hear but couldn't understand, and weren't intended to. David had initially found this endearing, but it was now beginning to irritate him. Eva had lost patience with Taz and Guy from the moment a question had been met with a cryptic remark and a pair of matching grins, and she was now routinely ignoring them.

Guy was showing no sign of being about to depart. David hadn't asked him directly when he was going home because he thought it would sound like a hint and because, if he was honest, Guy's presence had been useful to him. He asked Eva if she knew when Guy might be off, but she shook her head.

"Do you think Taz would be OK if he went?" he asked. "You know they seem very..."

"She'd be like a five-year-old with a dead puppy."

"Really? That bad?"

"That isn't bad. I mean a lot of tears for about five minutes until something else distracts her."

David laughed. "OK. I'll play it by ear and see if Guy says anything."

So far he hadn't. At the moment David intended to broach the subject when the weekend came around again in a couple of days.

Once that was sorted, there was still the question of Serena, who remained at David's ex-wife's house. Sonia rang nightly to bring him up to date on the situation. To begin with she had been relieved to find that the kids weren't going to break everything in the house, but relief had turned to concern at how unnaturally subdued they were: she couldn't tell whether they were temporarily traumatised, she said, or whether they were always like that. Even Amy had tried and failed to coax any life out of them.

Terry had been leaving a lot of messages on Serena's mobile, but so far, at least as far as Sonia was aware, she hadn't returned any of them, though it did appear that after a couple of days she was now listening to them. David wasn't sure how this was going to play out. The longer she waited the less it seemed likely that Serena would go to the police. David was aware that he had his own reasons for hoping that she did. He wasn't cynical - or maybe brave - enough to circulate the story in the market himself though. He hadn't encountered Terry in the City and had no intention of contacting him.

Meanwhile, according to Sonia, John remained 'unamused' by the whole thing. The guy was never amused by anything, as far as David could tell. He wondered what women saw in humourless men.

David slowly became aware that Simon was standing by the side of his desk and that words were issuing from his mouth. He had no idea how long this state of affairs had existed or what the man might be talking about. He looked up, nodded a couple of times and tried to divine what, if anything, his boss had just been instructing him to do.

Chapter Thirty-One

"She's done what?"

"She's gone back to him."

"When? How? Why?"

Sonia laughed mirthlessly: "I know what you mean. I couldn't believe it either."

"So what happened?"

"Well, he rang again today, and this time she decided she would take the call and, as she put it, 'hear what he had to say for himself', and I didn't think it was my place to try to talk her out of it. I said I'd leave the room while she spoke to him, but she waved me back in, as though she could do with the support. And at first her manner was really cold towards him, though he was doing most of the talking, and she rolled her eyes and looked around impatiently. But gradually, after a couple of minutes, her face started to brighten and then a sort of smile appeared and she wiped a couple of tears from her eyes. And when she said something you couldn't believe the transformation: her voice had gone all soft, like some sort of love-struck teenager. It was all 'of course' and 'love you too' apart from a note of indignation when she kept repeating: 'we should sue them, definitely'."

"So what was that all about?" David asked incredulously.

"Well," Sonia continued. "Just a minute, John's yelling something. Hang on darling, I won't be a minute. Well, as soon as she came off the phone she said it was all sorted out. Apparently, according to Terry, he'd been taking some medication but the doctor had failed to tell him that you weren't supposed to drink with this stuff. And that had been entirely to blame for Terry's behaviour the other night."

"And she's buying that?"

"Apparently. Hook, line and sinker."

"And what did you...?"

"Well, I sort of tried, you know, was she absolutely sure etc."

"And?"

"She got quite shirty with me. Looked at me as if I had some sort of personal interest in breaking up her marriage, so I backed off. And to be honest it's her decision, and it had been getting more and more difficult with John, so I decided to let it go."

"So, she's gone now."

"Yeah, didn't hang about at all. Packed in about ten minutes flat, got the two zombies together and that was that."

"I hope she's OK."

"Well," Sonia paused. "I think she got what she wanted: I asked her whether she was going straight home - just something to say really. Brought out a huge grin on her face, drawing her cheeks into dimples, and then she winked at me. 'Not exactly,' she said, as if she was telling me a big secret that she'd sworn not to reveal. 'Terry's buying me that Land Rover Discovery I wanted, in the gold, as a 'say sorry' present. I'm meeting him at the dealer'."

David sighed. "Oh God."

"Yep." Sonia paused. "Best stay out of it though."

"I know, but even so."

"Oh God."

"Yeah."

"Listen." Sonia's tone was immediately more forceful. "It's been a pretty traumatic week for John and me, what with all this."

"Poor old John."

"Don't start that, please."

"OK, sorry."

"Anyway, we've booked up at the last minute to go away for the weekend. The two of us. So I'm assuming as you haven't had Amy for a while now you'll do your fatherly bit and take her for a couple of days?"

David found himself wrong-footed. "Of course, I'd be happy to," he began, and then as though by way of an explanation of the doubts he could hear in his own voice, and that Sonia would certainly have heard as well: "I thought she wasn't talking to me."

"I asked her," Sonia replied, "and she seems OK now. She's obviously forgiven you."

David suppressed his instinctive reaction, that there was nothing to forgive. But he was not going to rise to his ex-wife's bait, and was in any case disarmed by the unexpected strength of the desire he felt to see his daughter again. He glanced through the doorway to the living room where Eva and Taz were staring at a music channel on the TV while Guy flicked through a copy of *Golf Monthly* that David had bought for him on the way home. There were foil containers, for the most part empty, from the local Chinese takeaway scattered on the coffee-table and on the carpet. Sooner or later, David thought, someone was going to have to cook something.

"OK," David said into the phone, "that's fine. I've still got Guy and the others staying so it'll be a full house, but we'll manage."

Sonia didn't sound very interested by the news. "Great," she said, "if you can pick her up Saturday morning?"

Chapter Thirty-Two

Guy was alone in the flat. Taz had decided that she wanted to walk down to the station with Eva, who had appeared no less surprised by the idea than Guy was: usually Taz didn't seem to care whether she went out or not, a fact which Guy thought at least partly explained why the girl looked so pale most of the time; if there were other reasons he preferred not to know them, at least for the moment. He had told her jokingly that he would reduce the amount he was paying her to spend the day with him if she was away too long, not because he had any intention of doing so but because the thought of being alone for an extended period now frightened him. His fear was not merely practical, though concern about his immediate physical wellbeing did form no small part of it. What if he needed to go to the bathroom? He had suffered a loss of sensation since the crash which meant not only that he no longer had much prior warning before he had to go, but also that his ability to prevent his bladder emptying when it wanted to was greatly reduced. So far Taz had always got him onto the toilet in time, but he dreaded the moment when he would piss himself in front of her, or while she wasn't there; he had done it in his mother's presence a couple of times, in the early days. It wasn't that he thought that Taz would be shocked by it; he imagined that she had seen some squalid sights in her time, though he had never discussed the issue with her. The thing was he wanted her to like him. It pleased him when he said something that made her laugh because, although for most of the time her expression was impassive and unreadable, when she did laugh her face really lit up with pleasure. It was something that David and Eva never saw because she didn't do it when they were around. Sometimes Guy wished she would, provided that it was in response to something that he himself said or did, because he liked the idea of being able to demonstrate that there was something to this girl that only he could unlock. But on balance he preferred to keep that face entirely to himself.

He was willing to admit, if only to himself, that he had become quite attached to this strange little scrap of humanity in a short space of time. He was sure it would be temporary. It was undoubtedly the result of a number of factors: close physical proximity, the fact that she was female, and his own huge sexual frustration since the crash. He had hoped that this would gradually die down, that nature would make his body adjust to its new situation, but so far there didn't seem to be much sign of it. He knew that Taz would look completely different if he could just once find a way of doing something about his overloaded testicles. He knew already how she would look then: young, rough, boyish, spiky; someone who in his previous life he wouldn't have given a second thought to. Once he had found a way to relieve the build-up of sperm in his body Taz would no longer smell so good when she leaned over him to help him onto the toilet. She had an unperfumed but unmistakably female scent, a million miles away from the sterile, antiseptic smell of his mother. On the other hand being in the direct path of Taz's breath could still be worth avoiding at times. Guy wasn't sure how naturally cleanliness came to her - it appeared that she never planned to go into the bathroom before going to sleep at night and Eva usually had to remind her, sometimes quite forcefully. But, Guy reasoned to himself now, hundreds of generations of humans had been attracted to one another before the invention of soap and showers and toothpaste; the natural scent of each sex was designed to attract the other, so there was no shame in it if it did exactly that. Well, maybe not.

Taz had been gone for exactly twenty minutes now and Guy had nothing to occupy him except TV cartoons intended for seven-year-olds. He wished the girl would come back. His greatest need right now wasn't for practical assistance but for some sort of distracting physical presence. He did not want to be alone with his thoughts: he avoided them at all costs, because the thoughts he ended up alone with were no less suicidal today than they had been when he had first woken up in hospital and realised that his legs wouldn't move. He kept going back to The Day. He ran over it again and again, and always changed some detail - not getting out of bed, not taking the car, not using the mobile - so that It didn't happen. Then, when he came out of his reverie and looked down at his legs and at the wheelchair, his entire existence seemed to be so boundlessly bleak that he simply didn't want it.

Once he got to sleep at night he was OK; the crash didn't seem to feature and he could walk in his dreams, but the initial moment of renewed consciousness was the real killer. If he awoke during the night he often cried - he hoped the others hadn't heard him - and he was going to have to try very hard not to now.

He supposed he was going to have to go back to his mother's. She still rang every day. Her early exasperation and anger had subsided after a couple of days and she now seemed to be humouring him and waiting for the moment when he would admit defeat and give in of his own accord. It reminded Guy of his childhood, of the summer evening when he had refused to abandon the tent in the back garden and return to the house for his supper. Then his mother had simply let him stay outside until he became hungry and cold and crept back indoors, where his food, now cold and indigestible, was still waiting for him. That his mother thought she could successfully use the same tactic on him twenty years later told him that she still regarded him as a child, and was the most compelling reason of all for not going back.

But she would win. Her house had been adapted for a disabled person; it was there that the nurses went, in that locality that he was signed up for the hospital rehab services. Here he had nothing like that: only a small flat that he couldn't

259

afford to re-fit even if David (to say nothing of the landlord) was willing to let him, and no support except three untrained people in the evenings and, during the day, one small girl who, despite her freakish strength, was going sooner or later to injure herself. That was if she was intending ever to come back again.

"A penny for them," Eva said amiably.

"What does that mean?" Taz's face wore the serious expression she always adopted when she didn't understand something.

"A penny for your thoughts," Eva explained patiently. "It's an expression. It means I can see that you are thinking about something and I'd like to know what it is." She laughed. "I'm not going to give you a penny, by the way."

"Five quid?"

"Fuck off."

They were making their way through the park; they had been walking for almost ten minutes and were half way to the station. Until a moment ago Taz, despite her odd request to accompany Eva, had said nothing at all. For the most part she had looked down at her shoes or at the pavement, though her attention had occasionally been engaged by sudden noises such as a car driving past too close to the pavement, the quacking of the ducks on the pond or the distant sound of a train sounding its horn. In one sense Eva was grateful for Taz's silence: it made the two of them less conspicuous and less likely to draw the attention of the man Taz had kicked the previous Sunday.

"Do you like him?" Taz asked suddenly.

"Do I like who?" Eva replied slowly, though she knew the answer.

"Coffee-Guy."

"You ought to stop calling him that, you know. He doesn't like it."

Taz grinned momentarily. "Do you like him, though?"

Eva nodded. "Sure, he's OK. He's not exactly the most exciting guy I've ever met, but I don't want exciting at the minute. The important thing is we've somewhere to stay where we can get some sleep without having to worry about druggies and drunks and nutters. So we just need to be nice to C-G, OK? He's a man, which counts against him, but I guess he can't help that."

Taz nodded and looked satisfied by the answer, but her face suggested she wanted to say something further.

"So do *you* like him?" Eva asked after half a minute had passed, in order to break the silence.

Taz pushed out her lower lip and shrugged. "He's OK, I suppose," she said.

"He seems to like you," Eva offered brightly, though she wasn't quite convinced that this was the case.

Taz nodded again. She scuffed her feet together as she walked. She looked directly into Eva's eyes for the first time since they had left the flat then averted her gaze as if she was embarrassed. She thrust her hands into her pockets. "I like Guy," she said quietly.

"Do you?" Eva asked hesitantly. "Well, that's good, isn't it?"

Taz started scuffing her feet again. Eva found it annoying, but didn't think this was the moment to ask her to stop.

"I suppose," Taz mumbled.

"Well, of course it is," Eva said positively. She wondered whether she ought to put her arm round Taz. Sometimes she would let you; other times she would punch you. Eva decided she didn't want to risk having to wash a lot of dishes with a bruised arm; verbal consolation would have to do. "And I'm pretty sure he likes you too," she ventured.

Taz nodded slowly, but didn't appear pleased by the reassurance. She suddenly stopped walking. "Is he going to have to go back to his mother?" she asked.

Eva turned back to look at Taz and found her gaze so penetrating that she immediately abandoned any idea of lying to her, even for her own good. They had reached the end of the park. There was an empty bench in front of a flowerbed by the gate. Eva sat down on it and Taz came and perched beside her.

"The honest answer, Taz," Eva began (hearing the name sounded odd and she realised that she rarely used it), "is probably yes. We can't look after him, can we - I know you try very hard and you do a great job - but, you know, he's permanently disabled, he isn't going to get better, and he needs professional nurses and that to look after him."

Taz's face had clouded over. Eva wondered nervously what would happen if Taz found out she had talked to David about sending Guy home.

"You're a real funny one, do you know that?" Eva said more spiritedly, in an attempt to rescue the situation. "You've known him for less than a week. And he's much older than you. It was the same with that bloke Peter in the hostel. Do you even remember him now?"

Taz kicked the ground forcefully with the toes of her right foot. Eva expected her to cry out but she seemed not even to notice the pain.

"It's not the same," she said loudly.

Eva decided that it was better not to argue the point. "OK," she said, "but listen. If Guy does leave the flat at least he has another house to go to." She wanted to add that maybe Guy would invite them round, but didn't want to raise Taz's hopes when they would almost certainly be disappointed. "Me and you don't have another house," Eva went on more animatedly, "and it's fucking cold these nights and we've got to look out for ourselves first. Do you get that?"

Taz shrugged and didn't look at Eva.

"So tomorrow, for example," Eva continued, "prepare yourself for a lot of duck-feeding because C-G's daughter is coming over and we're not going to hang around if he doesn't want us to. And if you do speak to her, be very very nice. Understood?"

"C-G likes you," Taz said suddenly.

Eva was momentarily thrown off balance by the comment; she forgot to be annoyed that Taz wasn't listening to what she was telling her. "Well, I'm a likeable person," was all she could find to say.

"No, but he *likes* you," Taz insisted.

"He likes you too," Eva replied, though she was perfectly aware that she was deliberately missing the point of Taz's remark. "Look," she went on, "he's even given you the spare key to his flat so you can come and go during the day if you need to. That's nice, isn't it?"

Taz dug the key on its cheap plastic, orange fob out of her pocket and stared at it, as she had countless times on the evening that David had given it to her.

"Yeah," she said, carefully putting the key back into her pocket and checking one second later that it was still there, "it's cool."

"I need to get my train," Eva said, standing up at the same moment.

Taz remained seated. "You and C-G would be cool too," she said almost shyly. "You and C-G, me and Guy. We could get a big house together..."

"Don't tell me: in Wales?" Eva was now only partially paying attention. Her eyes were skimming the horizon for sign of her train. If it appeared now she estimated that she would just have time to run to the hole in the fence and clamber through it onto the platform before the carriages pulled up.

"Yeah," Taz said earnestly. "Or Cornwall."

Chapter Thirty-Three

Having taken the principled decision that it was right for Amy to meet Eva and Taz, David was beginning to get cold feet. He was standing in the hallway of what he had now to think of as Sonia's house, waiting for Amy to finish whatever it was she was doing and come downstairs. If Amy kept him waiting much longer - simply, he suspected, because she knew she could - then there was the possibility that he might change his mind completely.

Sonia now came down the stairs; she had been in the bathroom when David had arrived and he had been admitted by the ever dour and conversationless John. She smiled and planted a kiss on his cheek. Her perfume was different, more expensive, sexier.

"You look great," David said sincerely. She did: her hair was up, which he had always liked; her bare arms, offset against a white top with a criss-cross pattern that hinted at cleavage without actually showing any, looked tanned and healthy; a pair of tight jeans showed that she had still not begun to put on weight at the hips.

"Thanks," she said, looking down at her clothes. "Just some comfortable stuff for the journey."

"Any news of Serena?" David asked.

Sonia shook her head: "I was going to ask you."

"She hasn't contacted me and I thought it best not to..."

"Terry?"

"Our paths don't cross much these days."

"I'd keep it that way if I were you."

"I intend to."

Sonia looked slightly embarrassed, as if there were something she wished to say, but she wasn't sure that this was the moment. Her hand lightly brushed David's arm before she seemed to change her mind and withdrew it.

"You know," she said softly, "however bad things got between us I was never worried that, you know…"

"Good." David could feel the blood begin to run into his face. "Of course I wouldn't have," he said vehemently. "Ever."

"I know."

Amy appeared round the corner at the top of the stairs and bounded down them two at a time, causing her mother to step aside to avoid a collision. Her face wore a suspicious frown.

"Are you talking about me?" she asked.

"No, darling," Sonia replied. "Hard as it may be to grasp at your age, not everything revolves round you."

Amy looked at Sonia and David in turn and, realising that her disappointment might show on her face, rearranged her features into a more assertive expression.

"Whatever," she said. "Give me a hand with my bags, Dad."

Once in the car Amy hardly reacted at all when David told her that there were people staying with him. She mumbled something about her mother having told her there might be, and she was cool about it, and then reverted to her main theme of the day, which was that the SEAT must be like the only car in the whole Universe that didn't have an I-Pod socket. David replied that it did have a jolly good wireless and cassette player though, judging from the absence of the anticipated frostiness that Amy was in a good mood and that it was OK to wind her up. She responded with an exaggerated rolling of the eyes and shaking of the head and told him that was such a Dad thing to say, which he decided to take as a compliment.

Almost as soon as David turned the key in the lock Eva came forward with a broad, big-eyed smile on her face as if she was very eager to please; David worried that she might be overdoing it a little.

"Hi," she said, holding out her hand.

Amy took it and smiled back. One of the remnants of his and Sonia's attempt to bring her up well, David thought, was that she was at least polite to strangers; she reserved her surliness for people she knew well.

Eva retreated and simultaneously Guy wheeled himself forward. Amy smiled and bent down to take his hand; David half expected him to offer her a posy of flowers.

Taz was nowhere to be seen. It didn't matter, David thought: this wasn't supposed to be a welcoming committee.

"I'll take your things through," David told Amy pleasantly. He wondered how she could possibly need so much stuff for two days. He was carrying a large holdall and a rucksack while Amy had a smaller, fake designer bag over her shoulder. "You've got my room this time," he called over his shoulder. "I hope that's OK."

Amy didn't reply. She was distracted by the staccato sound of footsteps running along the hallway and then the fussy clinking of a key being inserted in the lock.

As David re-entered the room the front door opened and Taz appeared. She saw Amy and halted; then with uncharacteristic timidity she mumbled something in Eva's direction about going for a smoke. Eva shrugged then gestured towards Amy with her arm, as if to suggest that Taz should at least introduce herself before she went.

Amy was now looking Taz up and down in quiet astonishment: she studied the unkempt hair, the eyebrow, nose and lip studs, the dirty jacket, ripped jeans and trashed trainers. David was surprised how quickly he had got used to Taz's appearance; he hoped that Amy's expression wouldn't convey disdain or, worse, derision.

But not a bit of it: her father had never seen Amy appear so awestruck in the presence of another human being. She came shyly forward and didn't seem to know whether or not it might be too presumptuous to offer any physical contact. Taz looked confused for a moment, and then seemed instinctively to understand that she was in a dominant position. She helped herself to Amy's hand, squeezed it tightly as if she were giving the other girl some sort of test which, despite wincing, she apparently passed, and then pulled Amy's hand up in the air with her own, clasped as if in a joint fist.

Taz said something that David couldn't understand. Amy said something equally unintelligible, then began to smile before realising that Taz was giving her a detached visual once-over; then she attempted to look serious and cool while awaiting the verdict.

David looked at Eva who grinned and shrugged at the same time. Guy appeared baffled and confused. David didn't know whether to be relieved or worried. He wondered how Sonia was getting on.

David found himself alone with Eva again. This time they were in the kitchen, both holding mugs of tea which neither of them particularly wanted, but which seemed an essential prop of the conversation they were having. David was supporting his weight against the oven door, though slightly awkwardly, as if he was trying too hard to appear relaxed; Eva was leaning against the worktop and had the palm of her free hand flat against the surface. She had quite long hands, David noted; maybe a little too bony.

The fact that David and Eva now found themselves holding such solitary conversations had nothing to do with any increased intimacy between them, and everything to do with trying not to intrude on the privacy of the teenagers. David thought he wouldn't really mind if his daughter and her new friend wanted to go to her room, if it meant he no longer felt like an interloper in his own flat, but there was no indication that they intended to do so; and because he only had Amy for the weekend he could hardly suggest it himself. In any case her room - his room as it usually was - lacked any of the electronic necessities of teenage. The hi-fi system in the main room, David had no idea how, had quickly been adapted to take the signal from Amy's I-Pod and was even now pumping out dubious rap lyrics at a volume that made him hope the people upstairs weren't in.

"I know I'm very close to pipe- and slipperdom," David told Eva jokingly before he realised that increasingly he didn't want to draw attention to the age gap between them, "but have *you* got any idea what this music is supposed to be about? It all sounds exactly the same to me."

Eva laughed. "Don't worry, grandad," she said. "It doesn't do much for me either."

"What sort of thing do you like?" David asked tentatively.

Eva's expression became suddenly more serious; she squirmed slightly against the edge of the worktop.

"Come on," David continued in a mock-offended, half-teasing tone, "I'm not asking for your life story, just what sort of music you like."

Eva appeared to accept that; she visibly relaxed.

"OK," she said. "Fair enough. Well, I haven't had much time to listen to music since…over the last…I'm not going to tell you how long. I may be a bit out of date myself but anyway, people you've heard of? Coldplay, I used to listen to them, the Killers, we used to…I used to like them as well. Green Day…" She paused to think for a few seconds, drumming her fingers on the work surface. "My mind's gone blank. Oh, some of Oasis is OK as well. There were also a lot of great Scottish bands, but none of you English tossers have ever heard of anyone except the Proclaimers."

David nodded in agreement. "And Franz Ferdinand," he added.

"Well, I don't think I like them."

"Me neither. So that's something we have in common."

Eva was looking uneasy again.

David sighed, he hoped inaudibly. "Tell me," he continued so that the conversation wouldn't falter, "can you understand what those two are talking about?" He pointed in the direction of the living room.

Eva shook her head and smiled. "I'm not really trying to," she said, "but no. It's all so quick, and it's not all words: there's the hand gestures and all the facial expressions that are part of it." She shrugged and her eyes lit up: "They're young."

David nodded. "And there's all the American intonation, and the *so's* and *like's* and all the 'dissin' and 'fessin' and all that. Don't you find that annoying?"

"Not particularly. Anyway, your Amy does that stuff more than Taz does."

"I know," David agreed. "That's what you get after ten years of satellite TV at forty pounds a month: your daughter sounds like Buffy the Vampire Slayer."

Eva laughed. "How would you know? Were you a big fan?"

David laughed as well. "Guilty pleasure!" he admitted. He knew that Eva was mocking him, but he didn't mind at all. Quite the opposite.

"She seems like a nice kid, your Amy," Eva offered.

David wanted to agree with her wholeheartedly, but he had told Eva so much about his relationship with Amy over their coffee meetings that, unless she hadn't been listening at all, she must be well aware that it was a complex subject for him. "Thank you," was all he managed to say, before realising that it was probably inappropriate.

"I'm not sure whether I should envy Guy or go in and try to rescue him," he said to change the subject.

Eva barely reacted at all. "He's cool, I think," she replied flatly.

"I suppose so. It's just that with Amy, you know, I'm surprised, well, you know, he's almost twice her age. I'm surprised he isn't cramping her a bit."

Eva pushed herself upright and put her empty mug in the sink.

"I'm not entirely sure I know what you're on about," she said. "But it sounds like something to do with how come they're happy with Guy in the room, when they wouldn't be with us?"

"Well, sort of, something like that," David mumbled.

"Well, I wouldn't stress over it, David," Eva sighed sympathetically. "I mean, it's fairly normal." She held out her fingers as a precursor to counting on them. "a) You're Amy's father, which is going to make things more awkward; b) Guy's a lot older than her but a lot younger than you; and c), and most importantly at least for the minute, Amy seems happy to go along with whatever Taz wants, and Taz wants her new pal Guy there, so that's where he's stopping."

David nodded thoughtfully. "Guy's only a few years younger than you though," he remarked, thinking aloud without being sure what his own point might be.

"You haven't spoken to him yet, then?" Eva asked quietly.

David shook his head. "Not yet. It's difficult, you know. Not just with him, but Taz is obviously attached to him now, and with Amy here it seems a pity to rock the boat. Monday would be much better."

Eva gazed back impassively and said nothing.

"And," David continued, surprised that Eva wasn't arguing with him, "to be honest I have enjoyed it with the four of us."

Eva smiled. "Me too. I'm not trying to tell you what to do in your own flat, David, it's just that…"

"Understood."

Eva began to make her way to the doorway. "Now," she announced, "I am going outside for a cigarette. Oh, and just so as you know, Guy is only *two* years younger than me."

She walked out of the kitchen and into the living room. David took the opportunity to position himself so that he could see through the doorway. Taz saw Eva and made a cigarette gesture at her; David noted that it was in the form of a thumb and forefinger. Eva gave a slight nod, as though to acknowledge the question without issuing an invitation, but Taz nevertheless got up and followed her. Amy looked up at Taz then guiltily round at her father. David stared sternly back at her: she wouldn't be the only fourteen-year-old who had ever had a cigarette, and if she did from time to time he really didn't want to know about it; but he wasn't going to have her doing it just outside his flat.

Amy seemed to get the message and turned back towards the television. David decided that this was the moment to take back his space, if he didn't want to spend the whole of the rest of the evening trapped in the kitchen. He walked into the living room, asked Guy if there was anything interesting in the football results and sat down in the armchair. Amy turned to look at him, then at Guy, then once more at the screen; her face was confused, a troubled mixture of guilt and hostility that David had seen on many previous occasions. Guy was continuing to summarise the day's main sporting headlines, but David was only half listening; at the same time he was asking himself why Eva, who had previously always refused to answer questions about herself, had suddenly volunteered the information that she was twenty-nine years old.

David was surprised at the request and initially failed to say anything at all.

"It's no big deal," Amy was protesting, "I just want to go out for a while with a friend. I do it all the time at home. Mum's cool with it. I mean, it's not as if I'm like ten years old or something."

David turned to look at Eva to gauge her opinion then checked himself because he didn't want to give his daughter the impression that he couldn't make up his own mind. But he did have time to notice that Eva was staring reproachfully at Taz. Maybe though, he reluctantly convinced himself, Amy had a point: it really wasn't fair that she should have less freedom of movement just because her parents no longer lived together. She had sat patiently in the flat ever since she had got up - though like most teenagers, her Sunday mornings were very truncated - as David had struggled to cook a large chilli con carne that they could all have. He didn't know why it mattered to him, but something told him that takeaways, ignoring the expense, were inherently unhealthy, though he had no evidence for the assertion. And he had another unshiftable notion in his head, which was that it couldn't be considered a proper household unless you were cooking in your own kitchen. The result was edible, but only just. David had lost most of his culinary skills and become accustomed to lazy cooking for one over the last couple of years; cooking for five entailed more than simply multiplying the ingredients by the same number. There was too much liquid and not enough chilli powder in the saucepan, and when he turned up the heat to boil away the water the kidney beans burst and the mixture stuck to the bottom. His preoccupation with the sauce led him to neglect the rice, which cloyed into lumps that no amount of later stirring and prodding was ever going fully to disguise. It was by David's own admission one of the most tasteless chillis he had ever eaten; but everyone did eat it, including Amy, who at first looked as if she had no intention of doing so, but then took her cue from Taz, who was attacking the burnt, lumpy offering in the same uncritical way that she did any food that was offered to her.

So David felt that he had some reason to be grateful to Taz, and any misgivings he might feel about her going out unsupervised with his daughter he put down to unreasonable prejudice. She'd been a pain in the cinema the previous week, but since then, when you considered everything she had done for Guy, she'd been a really good thing. He thought he could feel her gaze on his face as he vacillated over whether or not to agree to Amy's request; he didn't make eye contact until he had said yes, when to his surprise - and disappointment - he found an almost blank expression. Amy, on the other hand, for a fleeting moment looked as though she was going to hug or kiss him, which itself would almost have been worth agreeing to her request for; but too quickly she remembered how old she was and who she was with and she stopped herself. In the end she just stood there, looking in any direction except at her father, intermittently offering an embarrassed grin in Taz's direction or rolling her eyes as David told her to be careful and ensure that her phone was kept switched on in case he wanted to contact her.

Amy and Taz unhurriedly left the flat and David took up a position at an angle to the window, where he was sure they wouldn't be able to see him if they did look up, and watched them walk side by side along the pavement. He thought he saw his spare key-ring wrapped round Taz's finger and made a mental note to have a further set cut for Amy.

It now seemed very quiet in the flat. Guy, who David had entirely failed to take into account in his deliberations, was trying hard to hide his disappointment at being left behind. If they had wanted to, the girls could have taken Guy out for a walk; he hadn't been more than a few yards outside in the last week. But, David told himself, young people needed their own space. And there was no good reason why he and Eva couldn't take Guy out themselves later, assuming he wanted to go.

There was only one thing which really bothered David as he started to do the dishes, if you didn't count what Sonia was probably going to say. He decided it was best to come straight out with it.

"Don't take this the wrong way, but does Taz do drugs?" he asked Eva bluntly as she dried a plate and he, with both hands immersed in water, continued to try with the aid of an abrasive sponge, all else having miserably failed, to persuade a black patch of dried-on chilli to release its grip on the Teflon coating of his largest saucepan.

"I'm not her mother, as I keep saying," Eva replied uncomfortably.

David stopped scrubbing. "I know that," he said, "but you'd know if she..."

"Not necessarily," Eva interrupted hurriedly as though she didn't want to hear the end of the sentence. "She doesn't tell me everything. I don't ask. It's not my business. You have to understand..."

"You said something to her before they went out."

Eva was opening cupboard doors, trying to find the right place for large plates. She found it and slid the one she had just dried on top of the existing stack.

"I did," she conceded after a brief pause. "I told her to behave herself."

David looked round. He could only see the back of Eva's head.

"Thanks," he said. "I appreciate that."

"OK," Eva replied coolly as she swung the cupboard door shut, "but as I say, I'm not her mother."

Taz was bored, which was something that didn't happen to her often. Usually if she'd eaten and had something comfortable to lie on and a TV to watch she was happy. Some days that was more difficult than others. There were periods, though, like the past week where it was no problem at all. Hostels were usually OK on that score, as were squats, particularly the posh ones, but even they weren't like C-G's flat, where you could sit all day if you wanted to and no-one ever came along and threatened you or took your stuff. You couldn't smoke was the only thing, but you could outside, and you could make good money just looking after the crippled guy for a few hours. He was nice, so that wasn't boring. Taz could quite happily watch TV all day, or the same DVD three times in a row, which seemed to piss Guy off a bit but not too much.

But now with C-G's daughter Taz was bored. There was a TV in the room and she wanted to turn it on, but she wasn't sure whether it was OK. Eva had told her she had to behave and looked at her very seriously before she came out, so for now she was going to leave it alone. She wanted, needed, a smoke too, but something told her she wasn't going to be able to do that here either.

It had been OK at first. After they left the flat they just walked around for a bit and went in a café for a while, and most of the time Amy complained about her school and her mum and dad and someone called John, and said how fat or ugly or uncool most of her friends were, which seemed strange. But Taz didn't particularly mind listening, or at least appearing to, though some of the time she was imagining she was riding her horse in Wales.

But then C-G called Amy to make sure she was OK, and she said what was she, a nine-year-old or something, and she wasn't coming back just yet because they were going round to her friend Becky's. After which she called Becky and invited herself round and started to tell her about Taz and how cool she was, and looked at Taz at the same time, which Taz really didn't like.

There were a difficult couple of minutes when Amy flagged down a taxi. The driver gave them a funny look, and Taz backed away a bit until she was sure that she hadn't seen him before. Now C-G's daughter was looking at her oddly too, so she did eventually get in the car, though she left the door open. She watched as the other girl leaned in the side window and showed the driver, a balding Asian guy in his fifties, that she did have enough money. Looking straight ahead all the while, so that Taz could see his tired, cloudy eyes in the rear-view mirror, he said that OK he would take them. Taz watched him for the whole journey and he stared at her a few times too, but she was used to that.

"If Dad asks, OK, Becky's Dad came and picked us up," C-G's daughter said as they got out of the cab in front of a large yellow- and red-bricked house in a street full of other buildings that looked just as new. In the driveway they squeezed past two tall, wide cars with massive tyres and Amy, instead of pushing the bell, used her phone again to let her friend know that she had arrived.

Becky looked nothing like Amy: she was taller and bigger-boned, and not as pretty; she had curly ginger hair that clung to the side of her face and made her look like a child. She knew it; she had applied a lot of dark mascara around her eyes but it hadn't worked: she had only managed to look like she'd discovered her older sister's make-up bag. Taz wanted to laugh but managed not to.

Becky stood in the doorway and smiled at C-G's daughter without opening her mouth. She nodded and gave a small wave to Taz, who had already decided that she wasn't going to like her.

A dog barked as Taz walked across the threshold, which made her jump. She looked at the alarm box, which was obviously a fake.

The whole house had an overwhelming smell of newness: new wooden floors downstairs, new carpet elsewhere. They all had to take off their shoes and then follow Becky up the stairs and past an open door with a small, white, rectangular plate at eye-level with squiggly writing that C-G's daughter read out as 'Rebecca's Room' .

"Amy and her friend are here," Becky was telling someone, who turned out to be a small blonde girl, seated on a beanbag by the window with her feet curled up in front of her.

Amy seemed surprised to see her, and not in a good way. "Hi, Charlotte," she said with phoney warmth. "How are you?"

"I'm good," replied Charlotte, looking round Amy, "and this is…?"

"Er, this is Taz," said Amy looking round at her companion, comparing her with her new surroundings and for the first time sensing the potential awkwardness of the situation. She turned back to face into the room. "I'm having to stay with Dad this weekend because Mum and John have gone away for some sort of shagfest, and Taz is staying…well, it's a long story, but she's totally cool."

Becky smiled her watery smile again and told them to have a seat. Taz sat down on the bed and saw Charlotte and Becky exchange a very quick, knowing smirk. She didn't care: she'd seen it so many times before. Amy appeared to have seen it too, and sat down awkwardly next to Taz but then moved away. Then she moved back again, swung her legs and fidgeted. She looked worried.

A middle-aged woman appeared in the doorway and asked if any of them wanted drinks. She had large sympathetic eyes and hair that curved away from her head, the two sides meeting at the bottom so that you wanted to tie both halves together. Taz thought this must be Becky's mother. She seemed surprised at Taz's appearance – Taz knew the piercings seemed to freak a lot of people at first so it was no big deal - but her smile when she had composed herself seemed genuine enough and Taz returned it. Becky said they could help themselves, thanks. The woman disappeared and Becky and Charlotte rolled their eyes at each other.

The girls started talking but Taz soon felt left out of the conversation. It was very fast and flowing and had a lot of names of people in it that they all seemed to know. They didn't seem to like many of them, though, except for one or two boys who they all agreed were totally gorgeous: they looked upwards and squirmed in their seats and made imitation panting sounds when they talked about them. And there were a few Mr This's and Mrs That's, and hushed exchanges of what the girls said were details of the sex lives of these people. Taz guessed they were probably teachers, but she didn't really care.

The bedroom was huge, not much smaller than C-G's entire flat. Some hostel dormitories weren't as big. There were three large, white, fitted wardrobes, all with mirrors on the doors. There was a doorway through to what appeared to be the room's own bathroom. And beyond the double bed there was space for three wickerwork chairs plus the beanbag, a smoked-glass table and a large flatscreen television with a games console attached to it. There was also an expensive-looking I-Pod dock and speakers, which had been churning out hip-hop ever since they had arrived, though very quietly, perhaps so that the parents couldn't hear the words. It was Jay-Z. Taz liked him.

Taz thought she might like Becky's life as well: the house, the room, the nice, smiling mother. Not the dog though.

"I *so* do not fancy Paul Watkins!" Amy was saying to shrieks of laughter from the others. There still seemed to be something in the room, beside the conversation itself, that the three girls found constantly funny. Taz thought she knew what it was, but she didn't care about that either. She needed a piss though.

The bathroom that was attached to the bedroom reminded Taz of the celebrity places she and Guy had watched programmes about on TV, though this one was much smaller. It was all gleaming white suite and grey-white marble with a huge frameless mirror lit by LED bulbs so bright you could see every mark on your skin, every hair up your nostril. Taz examined her face: it looked almost as white as the basin. It would be different in Wales: she intended to spend most of her time outdoors - good outdoors like fields in sunshine, not bad outdoors like railway stations on cold nights; she'd had enough of that.

The toilet looked like it had never been used, but whatever. Taz started to undo her jeans. There was an urgent knock on the door.

"Excuse me," it was Becky's voice. "But we don't usually use that one."

"OK," Taz replied. "I hadn't started."

There was giggling from outside, three voices Taz thought, but it had subsided by the time she opened the door. Becky was still standing there, with her arms folded and an embarrassed grin on her face.

"Sorry to be a pain," she said, "but we've got so many bathrooms and no cleaning woman at the moment, so we're only using the main one up here, through the door, second on the left," she illustrated the direction with a sweep of her left arm, "or the cloakroom downstairs, because it saves running up the stairs every time."

Taz went quietly to the main bathroom. It was almost the same as the other one but with more room between things. The bath was huge and oval and had lots of holes in the bottom. Taz saw three toothbrushes and thought about doing the joke where you stick one up your arse and then put it back, but decided not to in case she picked the nice lady's brush by accident.

On her way back she paused to look through the door of another bedroom. There were adult clothes suspended from the wardrobe doors on hangers, so she figured this must be the parents' room, but it wasn't as big as Becky's. There was a large expensive-looking dressing table at the far end of the room, and on top of it you could see two or three rings and a tangle of chains next to a square, black jewellery box. Taz quickly looked around. She was a certain as she could be that were no cameras, no sensors. Remembering the crappy fake alarm box convinced her. Before he died, Ash had said that it wasn't really stealing from people like that, if they were that rich and that stupid: they were asking for it. She looked again. Soon she'd have nothing to smoke, and what Guy was paying her to babysit him wasn't going to buy much. The woman probably wouldn't even miss one or two bits. But in her head Taz could see the woman's nice smile. What clinched it was the memory of Eva's threatening scowl. Taz turned away. This behaving herself thing was really shitty.

She paused outside Becky's bedroom. She could hear the girls' synchronised high-pitched laughter and could see them through the slit between the hinged side of the door and the frame without being seen by them.

"I mean, not being funny, but where *did* you find her?" Charlotte was asking. "It is a 'her', right?"

Becky looked anxiously towards the doorway before adding: "Really Ay-m, is this like a bet or something? Perhaps it's 'Pet a Pikey' week!" she half whispered before collapsing into laughter at her own joke.

"Come on guys," said Amy, but her tone sounded half-apologetic.

"I mean, I've seen less rings on a sort of..." Charlotte hesitated while she tried to think of something funny, "...really old tree."

"Yes," Becky agreed, "and who's sponsoring her socks - the Swiss-cheese marketing board?"

Charlotte scowled at Becky as though she didn't appreciate people making jokes that were better than hers. She in turn glanced nervously towards the door now. "I wouldn't mind the holes," she whispered seriously, "but I think they're sponsoring the smell as well."

Becky nodded vigorously and looked earnestly at Amy. "Yeah, I assume that's her feet. Well, I hope it is."

Charlotte screeched with laughter, then abruptly stopped when she realised that the others were not going to join in.

"Chill out, guys" said Amy. "Look, I'm round at Dad's and that's like *so* boring and Taz was there and she was cool to talk to. OK, maybe I was a little desperate, but it was OK. Why don't you guys try talking to her?"

"If she comes back," said Becky.

"Perhaps she hasn't used a toilet before," suggested Charlotte.

"Guys!" Amy protested. "*Please.*"

"OK," Becky held out the palms of her hands. "No problem."

Taz counted to three before re-entering the room. The look Charlotte and Becky exchanged said they hoped she hadn't heard them, but wouldn't it be funny, later, if she had. Amy had the face of someone who wanted to be somewhere else.

Taz still felt bored, and even more in need of a smoke, but otherwise pretty chilled. She didn't expect people to like her; she was used to them calling her names. One of the foster women, a long time ago, had said no-one would want to have anything to do with her because she was bad. And something about hell that she hadn't really understood. So this wasn't a problem. She could still be cool with C-G's daughter if Eva wanted her to be.

"So," asked Becky, with the overenthusiastic smile of someone who is trying to make conversation, "what is Taz short for?"

Taz shrugged. She never understood why people kept asking her that. There were three faces looking at her, expecting an answer.

"I don't know," she said finally.

"You don't know your own name?" shrieked Charlotte in mock bewilderment, looking at Taz and then at Becky and Amy in turn. All three appeared to be trying not to laugh.

"It's just Taz," Taz said quietly but firmly.

"T-A-Z?" asked Becky.

Taz didn't know. "It's just Taz," she said once more. She looked at Amy to see whether or not she was making sense. Amy gave her a weak sympathetic smile.

"Could be short for Tasmin?" Charlotte suggested. "Do you think she looks like a Tasmin?"

Taz returned her gaze blankly. She wondered if Eva would think she wasn't behaving if she went outside to have a smoke.

"Hey, Tasmin," shouted Charlotte, looking at Taz but playing to her audience. She pointed at the frayed fibres in one area of her designer jeans. "I'm thinking maybe you can let me have those socks to go with these. I mean, you're one step ahead of the rest of us!"

Becky laughed and Amy, after a brief hesitation, joined in nervously. Taz was getting more and more bored. She would go outside for a smoke, whatever Eva thought. She started to rummage in her coat pocket for matches.

But now Charlotte was walking across the room towards her, and now she had her small, smooth, limp hands on Taz's right foot and was trying to wrench the sock off. And that was going to be a problem. Taz didn't have another pair, which would make things very difficult if she and Eva had to leave C-G's flat, because the sole was coming off one of her trainers as well. But that wasn't really it. The real thing was that you couldn't let other people take your property, whatever it was, however small it was, if you were going to retain respect; and you had to retain respect or you were done. But no sweat: this girl obviously didn't know what a fight was – you could see just by looking at her. And there was no power in her arm muscles.

Taz pushed Charlotte away with her feet as gently as she knew how, but the girl flew backwards and landed on the rug in front of the table. She looked round and saw how nearly her head had hit the glass. She got up looking startled, glanced at Becky then, with her face flushed red with anger, started coming back for more. Then the other girl, with a smile on her face as if she thought this was some sort of a game, started walking towards Taz as well and now they were trying to grab a leg each. C-G's daughter was looking away in embarrassment with her hands held in front of her face. Taz quickly decided it was best to make the other two back off right now before things went any further, she really hurt someone and Eva went mental.

In the pocket where she had just successfully located a box of matches Taz's fingers closed around the handle of her knife. She brought it out, just to show them, to make them stop.

They stopped.

Then they just stood there. Like statues or something. And then one of them screamed and the other one started crying, and C-G's daughter had her head in her hands, and there were people calling out from downstairs. Taz didn't want to be here any more: it was doing her head in. She put the knife away, picked up her shoes, ran out of the room and down the stairs; she collided with the nice lady who, wearing a startled look on her face between the two curtains of hair, was coming up at the same time. Taz tried to smile at her before opening the front door and running out into the street.

Amy sounded more bewildered than distraught on the phone, but David insisted on picking her up straight away, so that he could see for himself that she was OK. For once she didn't protest.

Eva asked him what the matter was and David relayed to her coldly what Amy had told him. Eva sat down as if she had suddenly lost all the strength in her body and looked at David earnestly and said in a husky voice that she was really sorry. David nodded as he searched for his car keys. He found that he was beginning to shake, whether from anger or shock he couldn't tell. Then Eva asked him quietly if anyone knew where Taz had gone, and he replied without looking at her that he had absolutely no idea. Guy opened his mouth as if to say something, but then appeared to think better of it. David left the flat without another word.

He felt a wave of relief when he arrived at Becky's parents' house and could see his daughter for himself. Amy didn't seem too badly affected by her ordeal: there was no sign of tears and she didn't fling her arms round him; instead she stood quietly while David spoke to Becky's mother, who thankfully seemed a fairly level-headed sort. Another girl's mother was also there, a tall blonde woman with a pair of sunglasses on the top of her head though it wasn't sunny, who kept repeating that they should contact the police straight away. Amy's friends themselves were nowhere to be seen. David said that he thought the police should be kept out of it, since no-one had been hurt, to prevent it being even more traumatic for the girls; he hoped that the two women didn't know enough to appreciate how self-interested his opinion was. Amy kept quiet and gave nothing away.

As far as David could tell Amy didn't seem to have made the leap to blaming him for what had happened. She sat quietly in the SEAT, for once without the accompaniment of music from either speakers or headphones, and looked steadily in front of her. David was dreading breaking the news to Sonia; he didn't think it was realistic, or fair, to ask Amy not to tell her mother. David was surprised that Amy had not phoned her already. She had called him first, which was the only positive from the whole thing. When Sonia did find out there would be hell to pay.

It was much colder than you would normally expect in early evening in the middle of autumn. David had had to remove frost manually from the windscreen before he had set off because the fan wouldn't clear it, and the heated rear window had also taken some time to do its work, so that he had had no idea who or what might be behind him for several miles after he had left the flat. The sky was entirely cloudless and a light kept illuminating pointlessly on the dashboard to tell him that the wheels were losing grip, as if he couldn't feel that himself through the wheel. There were very few people out, even for a Sunday night; those that were tended to be wrapped up warmly in thick coats as they hurriedly scuttled the few yards between buildings and cars, emitting short vapour trails that caught in the illuminated shop signs and street lighting. Why did it have to be this night of all nights?

"Do you think she'll be OK?" Amy asked suddenly, putting into words the thought that had been circulating in David's head for the last couple of minutes.

"I'm much more concerned about you."

"I'm fine, really."

David turned to smile at her. "Good."

"It's cold tonight, Dad "

"I can see that."

"Dad!"

"Well, she should have thought of that before she started threatening people with knives, shouldn't she?"

Amy said nothing.

They stopped at David's flat to pick up Amy's stuff. Amy remained in the car, and David went in and out as quickly as possible, making no attempt to talk to either Eva or Guy. They didn't come out to talk to him either; maybe they thought it best to avoid him for the moment.

Sonia reacted predictably when she heard the news. She enveloped Amy in her arms, bending down as though she didn't realise how tall her daughter was these days, and pulling the girl's head towards her.

"It's fine, Mum," Amy kept saying.

Sonia looked up at David, as though she had only just noticed him. "I'll call you tomorrow," she said frostily.

Now John was standing in the kitchen doorway with that smug, more-in-sorrow-than-in-anger expression of his, plastered across a face you could never tire of punching. David decided to leave before he said completely the wrong thing.

He drove home slowly. Now that his anger had subsided he began to reproach himself for his earlier behaviour, particularly his coldness towards Eva. He wished she'd call. On a sudden whim he found himself driving back to the streets near Becky's house and looking for Taz, without much expectation of seeing her and unsure what he would do if he did.

It was completely dark by the time David got back to the flat. He had rehearsed in his head what he was going to say to Eva and then changed it several times. What, it only now occurred to him as he parked the car, if Taz was there? What would he do then? But as soon as he opened the door to the flat, and before he saw the note in Guy's lean handwriting on the kitchen table, David knew that his guests had gone.

Part Three

Chapter Thirty-Four

David couldn't believe how badly you could miss something that you had only had for a short time.

It wasn't that his life was actually bad; objectively it was OK, better than most in the world, certainly deserving of no-one's sympathy. It was just that he knew that it didn't amount to very much and that, frankly, he didn't enjoy it. It had reverted to the state prior to the day that Eva and Taz had turned up on his doorstep: he worked, he ate, he slept, he drank - if he could find someone to drink with (and he sometimes felt like a whore and a hypocrite for drinking with people from work he didn't particularly like). He had even gone to the theatre on his own twice, which struck him as sad, but not as sad as staying in alone night after night. He'd planned to invent a friend if anyone at work asked him who he'd gone with, but in the event they didn't.

Amy was still coming round every third weekend. Her visits could be either the highlight of her father's month or an absolute pain, depending on what mood she was in, and her mood could change very quickly. To David's surprise Sonia had made no attempt to prevent Amy's visits, and in fact hadn't made as much of the 'incident' as she insisted on calling it as David had been expecting, beyond a gratuitous, well-rehearsed sarcastic comment every time he called to pick Amy up. He guessed she still valued the time she could spend alone with John, though God knew why.

Sometimes Amy asked her father if he had any news of Taz. She cocked her head to one side when she did so, as if to say it would be their secret if he told her, but although he now thought there were discernible signs of her growing up, even between one visit and the next, he wasn't sure that she had as yet reached the stage of maturity required in this situation: one where the resolve to keep a promise wouldn't be overruled by the desire to possess a fascinating piece of information for the attention that it would bring. David always shook his head and then changed the subject.

David did know where Taz was, and Eva for that matter. In what seemed an even more improbable household than the one in which they had lived for a week - it really was difficult to believe that it had been that short - they were now lodging with Guy and his mother. Guy had sent David a short text message the day after they had left to give him the news.

For the first few days after that David hadn't known what to do. He couldn't see that as a responsible father he should just forget that Taz had brandished a knife in his daughter's face. He had hoped that Eva would call him. The longer he left it the more difficult it became, and the more he felt a growing resentment that no-one was asking him how Amy was, or apologising, or even just thanking him for the week they'd spent with him.

At least now Guy had the specialist equipment he needed to make his unwelcome new life tolerable; it had never been a serious possibility that he could have stayed much longer in the flat. That he seemed to get on so well with Taz was more than odd, but if it worked, why not? David smiled to himself when he tried to imagine Guy's mother's reaction the first time she would have caught sight of Taz. He wondered how the dog would take to Taz, or she to it.

David couldn't believe that Eva would be happy with this arrangement, except to the extent that it brought her food and a roof over her head. Perhaps that was all she wanted for the moment. He was surprised that she hadn't called though. And disappointed. In his most optimistic scenario she was embarrassed at the trouble she had brought to him, indirectly, and to his family. More realistically, in view of the expression on her face the last time he had seen her, just before he had left the flat to collect Amy, she felt let down by him. Was that fair? How should he react to it?

Eva wasn't selling *Homeless Truths* any more (at least not at David's station - there was a burly middle-aged guy with an untidy, greying beard there most days now) and somehow David didn't like to accost her at the restaurant, assuming that she still worked there, which was also by no means certain. Which left the indirect, admittedly slightly cowardly, option of calling Guy and asking to speak to her. It had been four weeks now, and if he didn't do it soon he would never do it at all. And he had a pretext: the TLO Charity Day was imminent, and David and a team of co-workers, at his suggestion (or, perhaps more accurately, Taz's), were going to spend it doing some decorating, and maybe some simple repairs, in the hostel.

David had now picked up his home phone three times, looked at it for a couple of minutes on each occasion and then replaced it on its cradle. He walked over to the window and peered through the net curtains. It was a wet, featureless Saturday afternoon. The sky and the buildings opposite were grey. It seemed to have been raining all day, to a lesser or greater extent. You couldn't actually make out the droplets in the air now, but you could see their impacts in the two or three large puddles that had formed on the pavement outside and the overlapping, competing ripples that they created. Yet another weekend was ebbing away.

David walked back towards his chair. The TV was still playing soundlessly to itself: a rolling-news channel going over the same story he had already watched four times. The untidily discarded copy of the *Radio Times* on the floor bore witness to his futile attempt to find anything interesting to watch. Yet he didn't want to switch the set off.

He looked at the phone again. There was nothing really that needed to be done in the flat; there was a lot he would like to improve, but the flat wasn't his to alter. Of the weekly chores only two remained: ironing his work shirts, which were still too damp, and cleaning the bathroom, the worst chore of the lot, and one which for the moment he simply couldn't face.

He sat down. With the windows closed against the rain the air in the small apartment rapidly became stale. It now smelt of washing powder, of slightly singed toast and of himself.

He picked up the phone and dialled Guy's number. He heard the ringing tone four or five times and began to hope that no-one would answer. Perhaps he should hang up, in case they did.

"Hello?" said Guy in a puzzled tone.

"Hi," replied David in what was intended to be a warm, expansive voice. "It's me, David."

"Oh, hello," Guy said distantly, but with no discernible hostility, "how's tricks? It's David," he told someone in the room with him, "yeah, David Kelsey."

"Yo, C-G!"

"Hi, Taz," David called back.

"He says 'hi'," Guy told her. There was no audible response.

"How's things with you?" David asked.

"Fine," Guy replied. "Well, could be better: you know, I could be able to walk and go out whenever I want to and go to work like everyone else. But otherwise OK. Quite good at the moment, really. Did you know they paid me off, on the permanent health? Did Simon mention it?"

"No, he didn't." David felt a mixture of embarrassment and indignation.

"Oh, well, anyway, they did. The insurance company sent someone round to assess me - apparently they hate to pay out, but I'm such a hopeless case they gave in straight away. Then some woman from HR rang me and came round and talked to me as if my dog had just died. Then Mr Stevens himself favoured me with a call and explained to me in a man-to-man way why it wasn't practical for me to return to TLO."

"I had no idea."

Guy grunted dismissively.

"No, seriously," David protested. "I mean, what's the point of going to all the effort and expense of installing ramps and wide doorways if, when it comes to it, they don't, you know…"

Guy laughed cynically. "So that they don't get fined under the Disability Discrimination Act, that's why. It doesn't mean they actually want to see cripples representing the company."

David couldn't argue: he remembered his own conversation with Simon, weeks ago in the restaurant. "And you've accepted it?" he asked tentatively.

A hesitation. "Yes. It's quite generous and, you know, if they don't want you they don't want you. And the market is unsentimental. Anyway I've got some plans. For a business."

"Really," David enquired enthusiastically. "Excellent. What's that?"

"Something on the web," Guy told him confidently. And then more guardedly: "the details haven't been worked out yet."

"Good," said David, hoping there was no note of discouragement in his voice. "Good for you." He wondered if it was appropriate now for him to divulge the real reason for his call. He decided that it probably wasn't, but that it had to be now or the moment might never come again. "Listen," he began diffidently, "I was wondering whether I could have a word with Eva if she's around."

The pause before Guy replied was, David thought, exactly of the length needed for Guy to cup his hand over the mouthpiece, ask Eva whether she wanted to speak to David and receive a negative answer.

"She's…not here at the moment, unfortunately," Guy stumbled unconvincingly. "I'll let her know you called."

"Could you tell her," David said urgently, fearful that Guy was about to hang up, "that it's about the TLO Charity Day and the hostel. I just need a few pointers, that's all."

"I'll tell her," Guy promised. "When she gets back."

"Thanks. It's next Wednesday, so I haven't got much time. Perhaps she can call me?"

"I'll tell her."

"Thanks. Good to talk to you."

Eva sent a very brief text two hours later suggesting coffee at eleven o'clock on Monday in the old place. Actually there was no question mark, so it wasn't really a suggestion. David was slightly annoyed by that. It seemed dismissive. If anyone had the right to feel aggrieved, surely it was him? He sat looking at the message on the screen while minutes passed. Perhaps, he decided, he was reading too much into half a dozen words. "Fine," he texted back. "See you then."

Chapter Thirty-Five

Terry had been watching a wildlife documentary on Christ knew what channel because the other two hundred channels were all shit and he couldn't be bothered to turn the TV off and go and do anything else. Not that there was anything else to do in this house: the cleaner did the cleaning, the gardener did the gardening, Serena did a bit of cooking, on the odd occasion that he wanted food at home; he assumed that she did the same for the kids. Which only left the telly or, sometimes, the internet.

He found that he needed the internet less of late. Since her return Serena seemed to have become, how could he put it, 'more cooperative' in bed, either because she was still pathetically grateful for the Land Rover Discovery or because, and here was the real turn on, she had seen what he could do and felt the need to be more submissive from now on. "Careful!" she implored him repeatedly, as if he wasn't already taking every care with what he was doing.

A documentary. About big monkeys, or apes rather. The Alpha Male. Now there was a concept Terry could relate to. The one in charge, head honcho, the one who had first choice of all the females and ruled over all the other males. The perfect hierarchy, especially if you happened to be the Alpha Male. And what were humans but apes, albeit slightly more sophisticated? To Terry's mind that distinction was doubtful in some parts of the world - or some parts of London, for that matter. And human societies had complicated things by introducing concepts like book-learning and passing exams and class and shit like that, things that could cloud but never really overcome the natural, instinctive order by which your position in society was determined at birth, not because of who you were related to but by who you yourself were.

Terry Ransome, he knew, was innately an Alpha Male. There were people at NCG who were technically above him because they had been to this fucking school or that fucking university, but the fact was almost all of them must have spent the first few years of their lives having the crap kicked out of them in the playground. But, as the apes knew if these tossers didn't, there was a natural hierarchy in the world. These people who thought they were so superior would eventually come a cropper in business, one by one, because they had no bottle; and they had no bottle because nature never intended them to be in charge.

The interesting thing in the documentary was that sometimes one of the other males would attempt to challenge the Alpha, even though it had no hope at all of coming out on top. There literally was no possibility, genetically, that it would win, ever, yet still it would try. Why would it do that? Why wouldn't it just accept the inevitable?

Kelsey: now there was your…what came after alpha? Beta? That flattered him. Somewhere lower down the order. What else was there? Delta. Terry thought that was one; the whole Greek alphabet seemed to consist of old Italian cars. The Delta Male. Trying it on, causing a small nuisance, but inevitably about to get his comeuppance.

Of course with adult humans the Alpha couldn't win just by showing its arse, or even in most cases just by brute violence, tempting though that was. It was necessary to be more subtle. In this particular instance the Alpha Male himself had, through the odd contact, been doing some research, and he had discovered that there was a pikey sort that Kelsey seemed to have a soft spot for. The kids in the office had told Terry that Kelsey had been seen several times buying coffee for some tart that sold *Homeless Truths*; they made jokes about it, but beyond that it was nothing to them. But somebody else knew that this pair of tits worked in the kitchens at Abbington's. Which was fortunate because Terry went to the place a lot - he'd even had dinner there with Kelsey himself before he'd taken him to the *Inferno*. All Terry had then needed to do was to slip Charlie the waiter a score to find out the bag lady's name - it amused Terry that the waiters considered themselves socially superior to the kitchen staff and didn't normally know what they were called - and another score to forget that he'd ever been asked for the information. After that, presumably in search of further tips, Charlie had been falling over himself to be of assistance, and all Terry's subsequent visits to the restaurant had been greeted with a further snippet.

So Kelsey's pikey was called Eva McKechnie, or at least that was the name she used – apparently with casual labour half of them were called Minnie Mouse or something. Someone in the kitchen (Charlie had been using his initiative and sub-contracting a lot of the work) had asked her whether she was married and, so the story went, very quickly got the message that she wouldn't talk about it. But a fellow Jock had managed to get out of her the fact that she wasn't actually from Glasgow - she told English people that, she said, because it was easier - but from a small town a few miles away. Terry learnt as well that she had been living in a homeless hostel, but rumour had it at the restaurant that she had somehow managed to sweet-talk some businessman she had met into letting her move in with him. Not everyone in the kitchen believed that, apparently, because they couldn't see why with a Sugar Daddy she still needed this shitty work. Kelsey, a Sugar Daddy! What planet were these people on? The Planet Loser, obviously. Terry laughed aloud at the thought.

One day Charlie had sidled across with a particularly ingratiating, oily smile on his face and said in a conspiratorial whisper that perhaps Mr Ransome would like to see the young lady in question. So Terry had ended up paying another tenner for a distant view through a doorway of a woman whose body contours were disguised by an overall and her hair hidden by a net. She was facing in the wrong direction, so Charlie said something to her that made her turn round. She was probably in her early thirties, Terry thought. She was certainly no stunner: her face wore a tired, worried frown, her eyes were dull and unexceptional, her nose too large, her lips too thin. Terry thought he had seen her somewhere before. Well, maybe he had; he'd certainly seen a lot like her.

What was Kelsey up to? He'd gone even further down in Terry's estimation, if that was now possible. Nothing wrong, in Terry's mind, with some rough trade every now and then, but why would any sane bloke even want to talk to, let alone live with, something like that?

Terry's digging had originally been with the simple intention of putting the story round the market, because he knew how the market loved salacious gossip and that it would be possible to embroider the facts just enough to comprehensively humiliate Kelsey. David could get away with the coffee meetings at a pinch as a charitable act, but actually moving in with a bag lady was something else! If Terry judged Simon Stevens correctly, and he was rarely if ever wrong on such matters, then news like that would be enough to completely screw Kelsey's career at TLO.

But the more he brooded on it, the more somehow Kelsey's own lack of self-respect in taking up with this frumpy, jockstrap tart affronted Terry personally, called for more than the humiliation he had originally sought as revenge. The Alpha Male needed to take it one step further, to total victory.

Here was the beauty of the natural social order. Charlie still wanted to impress Terry. Some low-life in the kitchen still wanted to impress Charlie. So the low-life talked to the pikey as if he was her friend and went through her jacket pockets when she wasn't around. You could discover a lot that way. Names, addresses. A letter from a man. What would Terry have given to slap that down in front of Kelsey and then watch his reaction as he read it? Too easy though, too quick. Insufficiently entertaining. A bit of matchmaking, or re-matchmaking was called for. Terry wasn't usually the romantic type, but in this case he was prepared to make an exception.

On the screen the Alpha Male had pissed on one of his defeated rivals. Now, according to the voiceover, he was threatening to eat one of his own young. Fair play to him, Terry thought as he settled back to enjoy.

Chapter Thirty-Six

There was no getting away from the fact that he was nervous. Eva was late, and David was sitting looking at two cups of coffee. He had stirred his own several times so that the froth had become incorporated into an unappetising brown soapy mush, and it was now beginning to get cold. He hadn't drunk any because he didn't want to appear impatient if and when Eva eventually turned up.

It hadn't previously occurred to him that she wouldn't show. Maybe something over the last two days had changed her mind. Maybe Guy had talked her out of it. But why would he?

David hardly wanted to admit to himself how much he had been looking forward to the meeting even if, as was possible, Eva wasn't going to be that friendly to begin with. Sunday had been nothing more than an annoyance, an irritation, something to dispatch as quickly as possible. He had got up late, watched a lot of TV, slept in the afternoon, gone to bed early. Once there it had taken him a while to get to sleep, but he had expected that.

He ostentatiously looked at his watch several times so that anyone seeing him would know he was waiting for someone and wasn't someone who routinely drank coffee on his own. He was sick of the sight of that dial: he had looked at it about every three minutes since he had arrived at work this morning. Chris had noticed, and suggested that if David was worried about missing a meeting he should put a reminder in his *Outlook* calendar. David had smiled gratefully and apologetically muttered something about a meeting regarding the TLO Charity Day.

David was looking at his watch again when Eva came through the door. He guiltily put his arm down, waved, smiled and got half way out of his chair to kiss her before the expression on her face made him change his mind. They both sat down.

"I got you a coffee," David mumbled. "It might be…"

"Cold?" No sign of a smile. Eva was looking down, trying to arrange herself around the table leg. "Not to worry. Train got held up."

A few weeks earlier David might have asked whether Eva had forgotten his mobile number; now he didn't feel that he could.

"How have you been?" he enquired.

Eva looked at David but her head was leaning over at an angle, almost resting on the table, as she continued to try to get comfortable; it wasn't possible to read her eyes.

"I've been OK," she said.

"Good. You look well."

She did. Her face had filled out, her skin was less sallow. She was still wearing her usual green coat, but the white, ribbed top she had on underneath looked bright and new, though not expensive. David instinctively felt resentment - towards Guy - and then guilt; he tried to dismiss both emotions.

"Thanks." Eva picked up her mug and drank a mouthful of coffee. "You said you wanted to talk about the hostel," she reminded David in a business-like tone.

David had envisaged that they would have a long conversation, about events a month ago and everything that had happened since, before they got onto talking about the plan to redecorate the hostel. In truth the latter had not been much more than a pretext to bring Eva here: although she might have a few useful tips arising from her recent knowledge of the place, most of the arrangements had already been made. But now the stern expression on her face, the face of a stranger, made David rapidly conclude that talking initially about the Charity Day would be necessary to break the ice; hopefully the rest would follow.

"Yes," he began. "We're going there this Wednesday. There's about a dozen of us."

Eva was nodding from behind her cup; there was no sign that she was going to ask a question.

"We're going to do some painting," David told her limply. "And a few simple repairs, where we can."

"Good."

Silence for a couple of seconds. Eva turned to watch someone walk out through the door.

"I just wondered," David pressed on, "as you know the place, whether you have any tips for us?"

Eva shrugged. "Painting's painting, isn't it? You wash things down, fill holes, rub down then paint. A couple of coats if you have time."

"I was thinking more..." David hesitated while he tested in his head what he wanted to say. It wasn't very diplomatic and she might take it the wrong way; but it was better than allowing the conversation to lapse, at which point Eva might very well leave. "I was thinking more about," he made eye contact with Eva and adopted a pained expression which asked her to appreciate his candour, "you know, handling the people there."

Eva shook her head slowly. "What, do you think they have two heads or something?"

David laughed nervously. "No..."

"Or they smell?" Eva's indignation was rising.

"I didn't mean..."

"What, then? Are they going to rob you and stab you?"

"Look..."

Eva's eyes were wide open, her cheeks beginning to redden. "Well, yes they are. Let's hope so, anyway, I could do with cheering up."

"I see."

They both looked down at their drinks. Eva began to fidget and checked out the path to the exit, just as she had done when

David had first known her. He realised that if she left the likelihood was that he would never see her again. And he really didn't want that. "Can we talk about this?" he asked finally.

Eva glanced around at all the people on the adjoining tables before looking back at David. She leaned forward slightly. "There are a lot of people here," she told him. Some of them might be your business buddies."

"I'll take the chance."

Eva sat back. "OK. Say your piece then."

David didn't know where to begin. "That evening," he said quietly. "It was an awful situation. All I knew was that Taz had pulled a knife on Amy and her friends, then run off. The girls were distraught and one of the mothers was threatening to call the police."

"That's what you think?"

David was taken aback: he hadn't expected that Eva would dispute the bare facts.

"Well, basically it's true, isn't it?"

"It was all Taz's fault?"

"I didn't say that. I didn't - don't - care whose fault it was. The point is if someone threatens your child you just want to protect her. You don't care about anything else, or anybody."

"Yes, but you didn't have to be so cold, David. There was me sitting in your flat abjectly apologising, for what I don't know, and you just took no notice at all. You didn't care that I was worried sick about Taz."

"I wasn't listening. Until I'd seen Amy with my own eyes and made sure that she was safe I had no interest in anything else. Until you've had a child…"

"I've no idea, have I?"

"… which I'm sure you will one day, you can't understand it. You just can't."

"Well, thank you for those patronising words."

David was now sure that Eva was going to object to anything he might say; and yet he noted with surprise that she was making no move to leave. "OK. If you had been me," he asked more boldly, "what would you have done?"

"It was a freezing cold night, David. Have you any idea what it's like to be out on the street on a night like that? It's bad enough at the best of times, but when you've a constant battle to keep warm and you can't sleep - and you daren't because your body temperature drops when you sleep and you've heard of real people who have died of exposure, right here in London. And you can see the lights on in buildings and imagine the warmth inside and you're just sitting there shivering trying to keep out of the wind. Do you have any idea, I mean *any* fucking idea?"

"No, but…"

"Do you?"

"No, I've said no." David felt his own indignation rising. "But who said anything about being out on the street? I came back, you'd gone."

"You're trying to tell me you weren't going to throw us out?"

"Not onto the street, I wasn't."

"The way you looked at me…"

"I was distracted. I didn't hate you. I didn't even hate Taz. For Christ's sake, I went looking for her on the way back to the flat."

The last assertion seemed to surprise Eva. She stared silently at David as though his face would give away the lie, if it was one. "So you were going to let us stay?" she asked finally.

"Honestly, I was that preoccupied I didn't think about it, and when I got back to the flat you'd made the decision for me. I was sort of relieved, I admit: I thought the police were going to be involved. But I would never have let you end up on the street."

"Well, we couldn't take the chance. Guy said he would take us, and that was that."

"I understand that. It was good of him," David replied without conviction.

"How is Amy?" Eva asked quietly after a brief pause.

"Oh, she's fine, thanks."

"Good."

"How's Taz."

"Same as ever."

"You're still working at…"

"Crappington's?" She looked up at the clock on the wall. "I'm supposed to be there in a few minutes. Four more hours of sheer fun."

"You haven't thought about doing something else?"

Eva laughed sardonically. "All the time. But people want to pry into your life if they're going to offer you a proper job and I don't need that, not at the minute." She hesitated, as if there were something she might be about to tell David. She looked up at the clock once more. "You know what?" She leaned forward again and clasped her hands together. "I don't mind the job so much now. At least it gets me out of that weird house."

"Weird how?" David asked. Something inside him was pleased that Eva might not be happy at Guy's; he tried to repress the sentiment before it made its way to his face.

Eva gave him a how-long-have-you-got look. "I'm not sure what the fuck I'm doing there. Guy's mother puts up with both of us because she thinks we're some sort of temporary whim - is that the right word - of her precious son's. And Guy only puts up with me because he doesn't think Taz could or would live there without me; or he hopes he can rely on me to keep her in check if she has one of her funny days; or maybe he thinks somehow his relationship with Taz looks less odd if I'm there too."

David nodded. "It is strange: if you'd known Guy before the accident… but they're good for each other in a funny sort of way, aren't they?"

Eva nodded slowly. "Maybe," she admitted with reluctance. "He's trying to teach her to read and write now, did you know that?"

"Is he? I didn't realise that she…I suppose I could have guessed. Well, good for him."

Eva was looking at David as though there was something he wasn't getting. Then it occurred to him to wonder what Taz might be doing for Guy in return.

The pained expression on Eva's face suggested he was asking himself the right question. She looked at the clock again, then stood up and put her jacket on.

"So, are we cool now," David asked, surprised at the nervousness in his own voice.

Eva looked as though she would have preferred not to be asked the question. "The thing is," she said deliberately, "you asked what I would have done and, if I'm honest, you did exactly what I would have expected anyone else to do."

"Thanks. So then can we…"

"And I'd just started to think that you weren't like everyone else. And that was the most disappointing thing."

David watched Eva adjust her jacket and flick her hair above the collar and decided it was better to say nothing. He followed her silently out of the door of the coffee bar and waved tamely as she crossed the road on her way to the restaurant. He could not remember ever previously having felt two contrasting emotions so intensely at the same moment.

"How did it go?" Guy asked without taking his eyes off the TV screen that he and Taz were watching yet again. It seemed to no more than a polite enquiry, if polite was the right word for the way that Guy, and Taz too for that matter, increasingly behaved towards Eva.

"It was fine," Eva replied neutrally. "We drank coffee. We talked."

"Yeah?" Guy turned his head as far as he could. There was a note of disappointment in his voice, which he himself appeared to have heard as well. "Well, that's great," he continued with contrived enthusiasm. And then with fake nonchalance: "Everything, you know, sorted out?"

Eva stepped over the splayed legs of Taz, who made no attempt to move them, and fell into the empty armchair. It was late and she was tired; she had worked both lunch and dinner shifts in the restaurant to make extra money, because it had become more and more evident to her over the last few days that she really needed to do something to start supporting herself. Not that eight hours at the minimum wage were going to be enough to rent a flat, but it was a start.

Guy appeared to be still awaiting an answer.

"Yeah," Eva told him. "I didn't kill him." And then, as if to deflect any follow-up question: "What the hell's this?"

There was a young woman on the screen with dyed blonde hair, a crop-top which showed both cleavage and her navel and a pair of tight blue jeans. She was wielding a microphone which looked as though it was too large for her, and she kept thrusting it in the face of a random member of the group of people she was with, all of whom looked like they could be in a boy- or girl-band.

"It's a programme," Taz replied helpfully. Guy sniggered.

"No, seriously," Eva persisted patiently but firmly; she was getting fed up with answers like this.

"It's the celebrity karaoke thing we've been watching," Guy volunteered at last.

"I thought that was finished."

"It is. This is a repeat."

"No sign of any singing."

"This isn't the programme itself; it's the behind-the-scenes gossip thing they put out after it on their other channel."

"We voted for Laverne but she came third," Taz added.

"Who won?" Eva asked before it registered on her that she didn't remotely care.

"Lee," Guy told her, as if it was an important fact or something that she should have remembered. He turned and looked at Taz. "And what do we think of Lee?" he asked her in a jokey voice.

"He's a fucking dipshit," Taz replied with conviction.

Guy nodded vigorously. "That's right," he agreed, "he's a fucking dipshit. Fucking talentless dipshit too." Taz and Guy grinned at each other.

To Eva's relief no-one spoke for the next few minutes. She found that she was more than happy for that to continue; she doubted that there was anything that Guy and Taz had been doing that would be of interest to her, and there was nothing about her restaurant job that could ever remotely be of interest to anyone else. Which left only her meeting with David as a conversation point, and she wasn't going to discuss that in any detail until she had worked out what she herself thought about it. For the moment, though, she didn't want to be alone - she couldn't quite work out why, but the feeling was strong - and the silent company together with the inane droning of the television suited her perfectly.

So had today had any plus points? Well, she didn't hate David any more. And it was only now that she fully realised how much she had hated him before, as an outlet for all her stored up anger and frustration, and that she hadn't cared whether or not her hatred was reasonable. One night she had had a dream in which she had been in a warm, comfortable house and David had been outside in the cold and the rain, dirty and dishevelled, begging to come in. She had opened the door as if to let him in, then laughed in his face and kicked him repeatedly until he scurried away. The dream had come back to her several times during the interminable hours she spent up to her elbows in soapsuds and had cheered her up, like some sort of wish fulfilment.

Now that she was sufficiently calm and detached to think about it logically, there were a lot of men who had done far worse things to her than David had ever done. In fact, there were few, if any, who had been as kind to her, certainly not since her arrival in London. Cut the crap: there weren't any.

Did she actually believe that he wouldn't have thrown her and Taz out? He didn't have it in him to be a very good liar. It wouldn't have been sensible to stay at his place if the police were looking for Taz, but maybe he would have paid for them to go somewhere else, at least for a while? This idea hadn't previously occurred to Eva. No-one else had suggested it either. Why not? In hindsight, the week they had had round at David's flat had been the best Eva had had since, well... since whenever.

It wasn't any fun for either of them now - for Eva herself it was positively uncomfortable, and she imagined that David must be quite lonely. Guy and Taz still seemed happy, but Eva couldn't help thinking that one cold morning reality would suddenly intrude and the hopelessness and absurdity of their relationship would finally dawn on one of them. Guy's mother was obviously having a wretched time of it as well, feeling unwelcome in her own home, and that couldn't go on forever. What happened next?

David's sexual reticence puzzled Eva. How come he had never come onto her? That was what men did, they couldn't help themselves. She was glad in one way that he hadn't - she had had enough of men on that front - but even so she had a couple of times studied herself in the bathroom mirror at David's flat to try to work out what was stopping him. The daughter suggested he wasn't gay, though it didn't absolutely prove it. He seemed just... physically starved.

"Penny for them." Guy was looking round at Eva with a benign smile. Taz's face expressed a quiet pride that she now understood the phrase.

"A penny?" Eva told Guy in mock horror. "You'd have to do a lot better than that!"

Chapter Thirty-Seven

David found himself in the unaccustomed, and initially uncomfortable, position in which people he worked with on a daily basis, many of them senior to him, were listening to what he had to say and apparently willing to carry out any task he might want to allot to them. He had begun by making polite suggestions as to who might like to do what, but it had soon become clear that the others were relying on him and his confidence had grown accordingly; now he was unashamedly issuing instructions. He was beginning to reflect that being in management wouldn't perhaps be such a bad thing after all.

To his regret, the one thing he couldn't safely instruct his co-workers to do was to ditch the t-shirts they had all been given by the Director of Marketing as they had walked into the office this morning. On a bright yellow background these featured the TLO logo and then the legend 'TLO Charity Day: 50 Years in the Community'. David had been the last to put his on, reasoning eventually that it was better to get paint on the company's t-shirt than on his own clothes, but he hadn't fully convinced himself. The fleet of smart taxis laid on to transport the work party to the hostel had similarly troubled him with its incongruity - he wondered what the inhabitants of the hostel would make of the sight, and worried that it would look to them as though a bunch of rich people had come round to patronise them - but he had had to concede that the group needed some sort of transport in order to move its materials.

In many ways it had been an interesting experience already. David had expected the hostel to make him uneasy because of his general middle-class sense of guilt on the one hand and the place's specific association with Eva and Taz on the other, but essentially it was just a building, if a slightly run-down and sparsely furnished one. There were the smells of human habitation – cold stone, cooked food and cleaning chemicals – but no smells of humans themselves.

The TLO group had already encountered the hostel warden, Mr Lee. Eva had described him as "a bit of a shit most of the time", and Taz seemed to hate the man, but David had not taken much account of their views: he had reasoned that anyone who volunteered to work in a hostel for the homeless, carrying a lot of responsibility without, presumably, a large financial reward, had to be basically a very good person.

If Mr Lee was a very good person, though, he was trying quite hard to hide it. He had reacted coolly to David's initial contact by telephone and behaved in their subsequent conversations as though he had something that David wanted, which in truth, he probably did: the clearing of corporate consciences wasn't going to come cheap. Mr Lee had managed to dictate the hours the TLO people could come to the hostel, their numbers, what they could do, how they should do it, the quality of the materials they should use, the insurance they would need, the disclaimers they would sign. David had acceded in every case. And if he himself now didn't like Mr Lee, he did at least grudgingly respect him; the man was shrewd and he was unsentimental, and he was therefore probably ideal for his job.

David wondered whether Simon would have fared better in dealing with Mr Lee, but for once he genuinely doubted it. In fact Simon today was looking more lost than almost anyone. He was holding a paintbrush in the slightly awkward way that occasional visitors to Chinese restaurants hold chopsticks prior to the arrival of the food, trying to get some last-minute practice. It wasn't impossible, David reflected, that Simon had never personally painted anything in his life. He had certainly always mocked David for using part of his annual leave to decorate his house. Maybe, David thought with grim satisfaction, today was going to be payback time.

Disappointingly Adrian had come along too. Predictably his insistence in the canteen that he wasn't going to have anything to do with the Charity Day had turned out to be so much hot air. He had done no more than make a couple of barbed comments in departmental meetings in a voice that might or might not have carried as far as Simon; if it had, Simon had decided to ignore it. Adrian was now slouched against a wall with the cynical, world-weary scowl of a teenager on his face. His expression reminded David of Amy, but the Amy of a couple of years ago. David had hoped that Adrian, if he was going to do anything at all, would do it with another team. This project was only one of several that TLO's staff were undertaking today. David hadn't paid much attention to the others, but he had an idea that there was a city farm, something having to do with pushing people round in wheelchairs and another offering the chance to spend a day teaching computer skills to ex-alcoholics and drug addicts in rehab. David had been exhilarated to see how oversubscribed his project was, until it occurred to him that it probably appeared to be the cushiest: it was indoors, didn't involve mud or digging or necessitate, with any luck, talking to anyone whose behaviour might be unpredictable or whose appearance might embarrass polite middle-class sensibilities. And most people were confident they could use a paintbrush.

They were a team of twelve, which David was now beginning to think might be too many, unless he could spread them out into more than one room; though that would present difficulties because there wouldn't be enough stepladders. A lot of people were now holding brushes of various sizes and one or two were beginning to lever open tins of paint. David was having to explain to them, as he had feared, that it wasn't that simple, that you had to be patient and that generally, if you wanted to do a proper job - here he seemed to be losing a few people - then you were likely to spend more time on preparation than on the actual painting. He told them about the importance of washing down paintwork, of rubbing down wood, of filling cracks and priming metal. A couple of people called out that he was a sad git and he good-naturedly thanked them and kept going. As a joke he pointed out that the emulsion was for the walls and the gloss for the wood and metal, until he realised that a couple of people were nodding with interest and a third was taking notes. Simon was nervously rubbing his brush along the seam of a pair of jeans which, though probably his oldest, still looked far too expensive for the occasion.

Chris was standing to David's right, moving from side to side as though limbering up in a gym and gazing with mild curiosity around the room. His face wore its usual effortless, go-with-the-flow expression, and David registered for the first time the unassuming geniality in his colleague's face, which manifested itself in a permanent semi-smile around the mouth. David wondered idly whether that explained Chris's popularity with women, most of them younger than himself, and whether it was something it would be possible to emulate.

David was glad that Chris was here: he looked as though he would be one of the more practical types; he'd make an effort; and hopefully his presence would render it less likely that Adrian would behave like a complete arse. David didn't care whether or not Adrian actually did anything, given that the team was probably overmanned, but he didn't want to hear him.

"Anything you're not sure about, please let me know," David said encouragingly at the end of the safety briefing that TLO's HR department had obliged him to read out. Any questions?"

Adrian with his hand up. A furtive look towards the doorway, a grin on his face and a voice in a very loud whisper: "Yes. Why are we going to all this trouble for a bunch of winos, druggies and down-and-outs. Where are they? Why can't they paint their own hostel?" Adrian looked around for support, but found only embarrassed faces.

"OK, that's enough of that," Simon said sternly without bothering to make eye contact with Adrian. "Just get on with it."

"Right," David said, "that's about it. Might as well make a start. Everyone knows where the loos are, I hope, and I think Karen has brought along some fairly basic tea-making facilities - thanks, Karen - which are over there by the window."

David picked up a plastic dustsheet and started to move towards a large, iron radiator which he had set himself the task of washing down and priming. No-one else moved; they all appeared to be staring at him. Except that they weren't staring directly at him, but over his shoulder.

"Ladies and gentlemen," began Mr Lee, who, while David had been speaking, had quietly come through the doorway behind him, "if I could have your attention for a couple of moments." His voice was slow, serious and laconic, like that of a schoolteacher of many years' experience and no remaining illusions addressing a class of fourteen-year-olds. Physically he was imposing: thickset, stocky, with an obvious paunch above the belt of his trousers, hair that was slightly unkempt and a tangle of black beard, greying at the sides. David thought that he might easily be a bouncer; perhaps he had been. He had the drawn, lined, seen-it-all face of a fifty-year-old, but something about his stance suggested to David that he was probably younger, maybe forty-five. He certainly had presence: everyone was looking at him, with greater or lesser degrees of trepidation.

"I am Mr Lee," he continued. "I have the pleasure to run this five-star establishment. I appreciate your coming in today, I genuinely do."

A few polite nods and awkward self-effacing grins in response. David was sure there would be a 'however'.

"However," Mr Lee continued, "I don't know how many of you volunteered or 'were volunteered' or how many are just trying to suck up to the boss," - a few nervous laughs - "but please remember to work safely and sensibly. I know it's a day out of the office but please don't piss about. We are grateful for your time, but I would say to anyone who doesn't want to be here and doesn't intend to do a good job: please go now. It'll take us longer to undo it and redo it than it would to have done it ourselves in the first place, if you follow me. That's all. Thanks again, and if you need me I'll be downstairs." He smiled without warmth and raised his arm as a farewell salute, then started to back away towards the door. At the last moment he seemed to spot Adrian, whose pulled-in body language now suggested that he would like to be invisible. "Oh," Mr Lee began again in a quiet voice, "just so as you know, sir. We don't have any winos here. Or druggies or down-and-outs. Or tramps or hobos, or whatever. What we have is people. People who for one reason or another don't have a home today. Possibly last week they did, hopefully next week they will, but it so happens that today they don't. Maybe one day it'll be you or one of your friends here. Let's hope not, eh?" He looked disdainfully away from Adrian and his gaze then slowly swept the room. "Ladies and gentlemen," he told his attentive audience, "if you take nothing else away from today, please take this simple thought: the homeless are not a separate species."

Eva wasn't sure why she was doing this. She had just spent another four shitty hours in a steamy, smelly overheated kitchen having to endure listening to a group of three Eastern Europeans make remarks and jokes that had them in stitches but that she couldn't understand, except to the extent that they clearly had something to do with her body in general and her arse and tits in particular. So today she hated the whole of humanity even more than she usually did. She wanted to get back to the house and ignore Taz and Guy and whatever they might be up to - it was getting more and more annoying - and just go up to her bedroom and pass out for as long as possible.

But here she was, going in exactly the wrong direction, her tired feet walking the not inconsiderable distance through roads that became increasingly bleak and dilapidated the further she went, past graffiti-strewn boarded-up shop fronts and open doorways through which Asian women and their children eyed her, the mothers with suspicion, the children with curiosity.

She began to shiver, though it wasn't so cold today. Her heartbeat had increased. She stopped. It was still possible to turn round. What was she doing here? She lit a cigarette while she thought about it. Well, the answer was easy: she was here because it made a change, didn't cost anything and it would be fun to embarrass David and at the same time take the piss out of his gang of City silver-spoon hoorays trying to interact with the real world for possibly the first time in their privileged lives. She began walking again, but when she saw the grim, grey façade of the hostel across the street she came to a halt once more and stood by the kerb taking slow, careful drags on her cigarette. The thing was that something down in her stomach wanted her to cry, but she didn't do crying. Not any more. She had nearly cried when she thought David was going to throw her out. *Nearly*.

Standing here now, what was strange was that this place had once seemed like a godsend. After the streets, the days, the weeks, whatever it was; she honestly couldn't remember any more. And yet now she felt that if she ever had to spend one more night in a place like this, then....

She threw the butt of her cigarette onto the pavement and ground it into the concrete with her heel. She crossed the street and purposefully rang the bell.

There was a delay before an impatient woman's voice on the intercom told Eva that the hostel didn't open till six.

"I know that," Eva began to explain, making a conscious effort not to lose her temper, before she realised that she wasn't talking to anyone. She pushed the buzzer again, more urgently. Another long pause.

"Yes?"

"I'm with the people doing the decorating."

"Are you? Well, they're…OK, just a sec, I'll come down."

Eva realised with a heavy heart that she knew what was going to happen next.

The rain-warped door juddered open on its hinges and plain no-nonsense Maria appeared behind it. She recognised Eva in an instant.

"Nice try," she said sarcastically, staring arms-folded at this woman who clearly took her for an idiot. "How stupid do you think I am? Six it is, for everyone, you included, Eva."

She went to close the door, but Eva had put her foot in the gap and sprang through the opening and into the hallway. She tried to say something to mollify Maria, mentioned David's name, but the woman simply backed off and called out for help in a loud, high-pitched voice that was bound to get attention. There was no reasoning with the woman at all, and now Mr Lee was striding down the hallway towards Eva with a menacing expression on his face, and any moment now her arms were going to be pinned painfully behind her and she was going to be frogmarched from the premises. She had seen it many times before, and on those occasions it had usually been comforting to see a potentially violent and disruptive person ejected. But now it was her turn. Mr Lee was directly in front of her and was just about to grab her arm, and she had a split second to stop him.

"David Kelsey," she shouted into Mr Lee's face.

He stopped, but continued to bar the way.

"What about him?"

"I was trying to explain," Eva said breathlessly, relieved that Mr Lee seemed to recognise the name. "I know him. I'm why... I've just come round to give a hand."

"Stay here," Mr Lee instructed both Eva and Maria. Without further explanation he walked away and then began to climb the stairs. Maria continued to glare at Eva; neither woman spoke. Eva wanted to say: "I hope you realise that everyone, I mean *everyone*, here knows that you're shagging Mr Lee, so don't give me that I'm-so-superior shit." But it would be infantile, and now was not the moment. Maybe another time, though.

David was sipping from what he felt was a well-deserved mug of tea and surveying the team's handiwork. According to his watch, he had been working for four and a half hours without a break, which was surprising to him in the sense that it didn't seem like half that, and that usually he would be unable to concentrate for even a fraction of that time. It must, he told himself, be something to do with devoting your whole mind to very narrow physical tasks. The team was doing well: between them they had accomplished, well, maybe not twelve times what he would have managed alone but, charitably, say seven or eight times. It had been hard initially not to laugh at Simon's gauche attempts to wash down the ceiling and then paint it, but, fair play to him, he had clearly attained his position in business by being someone who, once he had resolved to do something, always gave it his best shot. The ceiling was clean and it was white and it was evenly painted; on the occasions David had looked over at Simon as he worked, the expression on his boss's face had reminded David of Amy as a four-year-old determinedly filling in her colouring book.

David felt content. Time to get back to work, though: he'd taken over five minutes out while the others continued with their labours - though most of them had taken breaks already - and it wouldn't look good if he remained idle much longer. He was bending down to pick up his two brushes and pot of gloss paint in order to transport them to the giant radiator under the main window, taking care not to spill his tea on the floor at the same time, when he heard Mr Lee come into the room behind him and clear his throat.

"Looks good," he conceded, surveying the scene dispassionately. "You are going to be done by five?"

David turned round and nodded. "Yes. We got off to a bit of a slow start, but everyone's up to speed now."

"Great," replied Mr Lee, though it didn't sound as if he had really paid attention to the answer. "Listen, there's a woman downstairs who stays here sometimes, never been any trouble or anything, but she's pitched up now, saying that she knows you and has come to help. We don't let anyone in before six, but some of them try a few ruses to get in earlier, so I thought I'd check. Scottish girl. Do you know her?"

David felt his body seize up in panic. He dropped one of the brushes, which bounced off his shoe onto the groundsheet. He bent down to retrieve it, taking his time in order to give himself a couple of seconds to work out how to respond. Simon and Chris and Jill and Adrian and seven other people who shared his work life were in the room. And now Eva, from a completely different part of his existence, was threatening to invade the same space and he found, to his shame, that he really wasn't comfortable with the idea.

"Sorry," he said, annoying himself with his own timidity. "No, I do know her."

"You don't sound sure. Either you do or you don't."

David nodded. "Positive. Her name's Eva."

Mr Lee's expression said that he was sure that something strange and possibly sordid was going on, but that he couldn't be bothered to work out what it might be. "OK," he said half wearily, half irritably. "So, I'm letting her in, right?"

"Of course, yes."

Mr Lee shrugged, nodded encouragingly at the people who, David now realised, had been listening to the conversation, then turned and walked out of the door, shouting something down the stairs as he went.

David looked to see if anyone was staring at him. He made eye contact with Jill, who returned a weak but friendly smile, and with one of the guys from accounts. He tried to compose himself as he heard footsteps coming up the stairs. His heart was racing as he attempted to work out how he was going to play this. He was sure that if Eva detected he was embarrassed by her presence then he would not be seeing her again.

But here she was already. She came through the doorway looking slightly bemused, her face flushed. She smiled ironically at David when she caught sight of him, then came over and quietly said hello. David became aware of how straggly her hair looked, how tired and worn that same green jacket, her only coat, appeared. From a foot or two away you could smell the restaurant kitchen on her too. David smiled at her while out of the corner of his eye he was trying to see who was looking, and especially whether Simon was.

"Christ," Eva half whispered, "I hate that Lee guy. What took so long?"

"I was trying to pretend I'd never heard of you," David replied with a furtive grin.

Eva said nothing and looked critically around the room.

"What do you think?" David asked her.

Eva stood with her chin in her hand and gradually turned around, surveying each wall in turn. "It's good," she said finally. "No, it's very good, really. It's cheered the place up."

"Thanks."

"Hi," said Simon, who had somehow crept up unnoticed. "I'm Simon Stevens, divisional head at TLO." He held out a hand that was almost entirely covered in dried white paint, a fact that he seemed belatedly to notice. "Sorry," he began with an embarrassed smile, but before he had time to withdraw his hand Eva had taken it.

"Great to meet you," she said warmly, "I've heard a lot about you."

"Have you?" Simon replied in confusion, looking at David as Eva continued to pump his hand. When she finally released it he pointed at each of them in turn with his index finger: "Do you two…"

David couldn't think of anything to say.

Eva glanced momentarily at him before replying. "Yes," she began brightly. "We know each other. In a roundabout way I'm the reason that you're all here today. I was homeless myself at one time. In fact I stayed here for a while."

"I see," replied Simon with what sounded like genuine interest. "That's amazing. It's really a different world: to be honest, I can't imagine it." He looked at David, who nodded in agreement and hoped his boss wouldn't pursue the matter of how he and Eva came to know each other; he was sure Eva would tell him if asked. "Well," Simon addressed Eva, "hopefully our efforts will do some good for the people here."

Eva nodded pleasantly. "I think they will."

"Fantastic," said Simon. "Great to meet you, er…?"

"Eva"

"Great to meet you, Eva. Had better go. Need to get to the loo before I burst, and then I have a skirting board waiting for me!"

Eva smiled. "See you later."

Simon walked out of the room and Eva looked searchingly up at David. "You look terrified," she said.

"Do I?" David tried to sound surprised. "I don't know why."

"Are you scared about what I might say? Would you rather I wasn't here?"

David turned away and began to pick up his paint pot and brushes. "Of course not," he said in a slightly aggrieved tone.

Eva watched him in silence for several seconds. She looked around the room again; everyone now seemed to be giving their attention to the individual tasks in hand. "Do you want some help there?" she asked finally.

David looked up at her warily. "You could help me paint this radiator," he replied.

"Cool," said Eva. "Start at opposite ends. Last one to the middle's a div."

David clashed brushes with Eva for the tenth time and realised that it was all over. Not only was the point at which their efforts joined at best one third of the way from the end at which he had started, but also in his hurry he had clearly left bare patches in two or three places, and he couldn't now cover them without drawing attention to his own incompetence. Even if he did so, the repair was going to look obvious, and that was going to bug him for the rest of the day every time he walked past it. Eva's two thirds by contrast – now that he looked again it was closer to three quarters – gave the impression of having been evenly painted with a single skilled, effortless, flowing stroke from top to bottom. Eva's face had assumed an expression of determination and concentration from the moment she had set to work, with her eyes darting around the painting surface and her tongue pressed against her bottom lip. She hadn't looked round or appeared to be aware of any distractions until she knew that she had passed the halfway mark, and then a small, gratified smile had begun to play around her mouth, where it remained until her hand and David's finally collided.

They were now looking at the finished product, and still Eva hadn't said anything; clearly it was going to be up to David to concede defeat as gracefully as he could.

"Well done," he said, deliberately trying to sound patronising for the first time since they had met. "You win. You've done this before, haven't you?"

Eva grinned smugly. "Possibly," she said enigmatically.

"As in 'possibly you used to do this for a living'?"

Eva tottered slightly on her knees and then drew herself up onto her haunches. "Possibly," she repeated, closing her eyes for a moment and continuing to smile. "Nice try."

David sat down on the floor. "Yes, well, one of these days you'll forget. Anyway, you're obviously losing it."

"Why?" Eva was immediately curious.

David smiled. "You knew you would win and you forgot to have money on it."

Eva sat down as well, carefully placed her brush on the lid of the paint can and propped herself up on her hands. David scanned the room quickly to ensure that no-one had noticed that he and Eva were not currently working.

Eva shook her head slowly. "Unfair fight," she said simply. "Taking candy from a baby."

David laughed out loud. "Since when would that have bothered you?" he scoffed.

Eva smiled back with feigned innocence.

"So," David went on, "you did do this for a living?" He looked directly into Eva's eyes in the hope that they would give him an answer if her mouth wouldn't.

Eva blinked awkwardly then sat up and retrieved her paintbrush. "You've missed a bit," she told David.

He groaned. "I've missed several. You're too quick."

Eva was crawling across towards him. "Do you mind if I...?"

"Be my guest."

David withdrew slightly to give Eva room and then watched as she expertly repainted his botched handiwork, finding fault with areas beyond those he had identified himself, so that within two or three minutes she had all but re-covered David's third of the radiator, which now looked as good as the rest; there was no longer any sign of joins in the paint, and the brush strokes, to the extent that you could see them at all, were regimentally straight.

"How do you do that?" David asked, aware too late that he was thinking aloud and that he sounded irritable and ungrateful.

Eva looked surprised. "How do I do what?" she asked cautiously.

"That." David knelt down again and pointed at one vertical area of paintwork. "That straight, no joins."

Eva shrugged. "I don't know. How else would you do it?"

"The way I do it, obviously."

"Show me."

David gingerly picked up his brush and looked at Eva. She nodded confidently as if to affirm that she didn't mind if he messed up her work; she'd easily fix it.

David dipped the brush into the paint more times than was really necessary and then timidly applied it to an upright section at the end of the radiator. The stroke petered out about a third of the way down and the impact of the individual bristles was clearly visible. There were also vertical gaps where he had simply pressed too hard.

Eva wasn't impressed. "Get some more paint," she commanded impatiently, and once David had meekly done so and was about to apply it she suddenly put her hand on top of his and wrapped her thumb firmly around his wrist.

"Just relax and follow," she instructed. David did his best to comply as she pulled the brush in a single satisfying stroke all the way from the top to the bottom of the radiator. "You see?" she asked helpfully.

"Thanks."

They made eye contact and Eva released David's hand and looked away. He noticed the pressure mark on his wrist made by Eva's thumb and at the same time registered the unexpected warmth of her skin. It was harder than he had expected, and the fingers were a little dry. He glanced at Eva, who was now looking in the other direction and getting to her feet, then let his eyes roam around the room, where his colleagues were continuing to work steadily and, apparently, enthusiastically. Someone was bound to have seen, and would take the piss later or tomorrow. Such was office life. Let them. David levered himself to his feet. The radiator looked good, all of it. He turned around. Eva was standing with her back to him, methodically and, he thought, quite violently brushing dust and dirt from her jeans. She seemed oblivious to the fact that both Chris and Adrian had had their attention drawn by the slapping sounds and were now eyeing her strangely. Chris caught David's gaze and gave him what appeared to be a sympathetic smile.

But within a second no-one was interested in Eva any longer. There was the sound of brisk footsteps in the doorway and then a number of flashbulbs went off in succession. A young woman and a middle-aged man walked backwards into the room, he taking photos while she nodded and wrote in a notebook. Behind them, striding purposefully forward, came two further men, one thin and wiry, the other short and stocky. The short man was one step ahead, and it was his words that the woman was recording while the thin one was agreeing enthusiastically. Both men wore sharp-looking suits, but the short man's had that extra degree of crispness and depth that denoted genuinely serious expense. The effect was further accentuated by a long light-brown overcoat with a felt collar, a garment which, David reflected, you only ever saw in the City of London or on the occasional bookmaker.

Eva watched the new arrivals for a few seconds before retreating to stand next to David by the wall. "Who the hell's that?" she asked.

"That," David replied in a whisper, hoping that Eva would take the hint and moderate her own voice similarly, "is Mr Tweddle."

"Oh," said Eva in a whisper so loud it was still likely to be audible to other people, "that's Junior is it? Is it?" she asked again, when it appeared that David was going to do nothing except look embarrassed.

"Yes," he agreed very quietly. "Only people don't call him that. I mean, not to his face."

"Right," Eva replied earnestly. "Got it. So what's he doing here?"

"Your guess is as good as mine."

"You didn't invite him, then?"

David checked to see whether Eva was joking; it appeared that she wasn't. "Of course I didn't invite him!" he whispered with exasperation. "I'm not in a position where I can invite him to anything, and, even if I was, I certainly wouldn't."

"I see," said Eva, who sounded as if she didn't. "I don't really get company hierarchies, not my thing. Who is the other bloke?"

"TLO's marketing director; I can't remember his name."

The nameless man clapped his hands together to get the attention of everyone in the room, though in fact Junior already had it. "Hi fellow TLOers," the man called out, "I wonder if you could just break off from your efforts for a few moments and gather round. Mr Tweddle has some remarks he would like to make."

People began quickly to put down brushes and climb down ladders. Junior surveyed their urgency with apparent satisfaction. David noticed that Simon hadn't waited for the instruction: he was already hovering a couple of feet away from Junior, and had succeeded in exchanging a couple of remarks with him as they waited for the others to approach. There was soon a tight, silent huddle of bodies in the middle of the room.

"Colleagues," Junior began with outstretched hands that seemed figuratively to embrace everyone who qualified for that description, "well, you know, I er…"

He paused in a manner that suggested he was used to being listened to and had no fear of being interrupted or of losing the attention of his audience. Then he looked around and a wry grin spread across his face. No-one spoke, moved or looked away.

"Well, you know," Junior continued. "I like to think that at TLO we are more than a company. Companies employ someone eight hours a day, five days a week for however many years. Big deal. TLO isn't like that. TLO is fifty years old this year, operating in a business arena that is so fluid, so dynamic that most of the competition think themselves lucky if they last ten years. TLO is different, and that is because we are not just a company but a team, a family if you will, and I am not embarrassed to use that term. That is what differentiates us, that is our USP: we are great because our people are great. All of them, all of you."

David stole a glance at the faces of his co-workers, and found that they were all, Adrian included, focusing exclusively on the short man in the long coat. If they felt any cynicism towards the message they were receiving, they clearly intended to save it for later.

"Now," Junior went on after another pause timed to allow the effect of his previous words to sink in, "because TLO is fifty years old doesn't mean that we are backward-looking. Quite the opposite. Happily some of our competitors make that mistake in bidding against us: they think TLO's big, TLO's traditional, TLO's slow. Well, let me tell you: TLO is big, TLO has a great tradition, but TLO sure as hell ain't slow."

He chuckled briefly to himself and there was an appreciative murmur from the audience.

"Look at this." Junior pointed vaguely around the room. Some of the listeners attempted to follow his gesture with their eyes and to work out what it was that he was indicating. "TLO teamwork," Junior went on. "All working together, using the skills we've learned at TLO, putting together a project in short order, seeing it through. That's our people. That's what the others don't have. They envy us, believe you me."

A frisson of satisfaction in the room.

"Look, you know. Hey." Junior was now at his most candid, most congenial. "We could have celebrated our anniversary in the usual way, with a dinner or a cocktail party or whatever, but instead you chose to be special: to give something back to the community in which we work and live, and I'm proud of you for that."

The marketing director leaned across and whispered something into his boss's ear.

Junior nodded. "OK," he said as though taking the audience into his confidence. "Apparently I'm keeping a helicopter waiting. You wouldn't believe how much these things cost an hour!" He winked. "Maybe you would!"

The marketing director leaned across again.

"OK, sure," Junior said affably. "Just a couple of photos for our friend here. Where do you want me?"

Junior and the marketing director were now in inaudible conference with the photographer. The audience appeared unsure whether the speech was over, and looked at one another for guidance. They exchanged wide-eyed shrugs before one or two took the initiative and withdrew towards the back of the room.

Junior had handed his coat, suit jacket and tie to the woman taking notes, who appeared surprised by her new role as ad hoc valet, while the marketing director struggled to remove a TLO t-shirt from its protective cellophane wrapping. Once it was free Junior impatiently snatched it and pulled it over his head. The marketing director thoughtfully scanned the room for a few seconds then scampered across to the radiator that Eva and David had just painted and picked up their paintbrushes. He returned and handed one to Junior and the other to Simon, who had not moved far away. After a brief further discussion between the photographer and the marketing director a ladder was commandeered and placed against a wall, next to a large vertical pipe that had been half painted by Chris and one of the accounts guys before the interruption. Simon climbed a couple of rungs of the ladder, held his brush against the pipe and smiled towards the camera. Junior did the same from ground level, but it was almost immediately clear that he did not like the fact that Simon towered above him. Without needing to be told, Simon came down and they swapped positions.

"Shouldn't we have some sort of representative of this, er, place?" the photographer asked hesitantly.

Seeing that Junior seemed to like the idea, Simon said something quietly to him and pointed at Eva. Junior nodded and beckoned her across with his index finger. Eva flushed slightly and shook her head.

"Come on," said Junior in a tone of mock jocularity in which, however, an air of impatience was unmistakable. "Just a quick picture. I'm a busy guy."

Eva shook her head again and looked towards the door.

Junior nodded silently; a joyless grin remained fixed on his face. "OK," he said quietly in a voice that was almost hoarse, "if you don't want to, my friend. Too bad. Maybe I was about to offer you a job!"

David noticed that the marketing director's forehead was now gleaming with sweat as he looked first at Junior and then at Eva and contemplated how to rescue the situation. Simon was glaring at David, who for his own part could feel his heart pound as he attempted to look like an accidental bystander. He wasn't about to try to force Eva to do something she didn't want to; it wouldn't work in any case. He was only relieved that Taz wasn't here: he was sure she would have kicked Junior by now.

Eva shook her head again. "Thanks," she said firmly, "I'm not the person you want. You want Maria."

The expression on Junior's face told the marketing director to find out instantly who Maria was and fetch her immediately. Having made eye contact with David, who pointed him towards the stairs, the harassed man nodded ingratiatingly and ran off to accomplish his task.

Junior turned to David. "You work for me, right?"

David was so taken aback by the fact that Junior was addressing him, for only the second time in the fifteen years he had been working at TLO, that for a second he didn't react at all, and then he only nodded.

"Great," said Junior irascibly, "pick up a paintbrush would you."

David complied as quickly as he could; as he did so he became aware that Eva was watching him through narrowed eyes.

Junior had noticed too. "You know her?" he asked suddenly as they lined up for the photographer.

David knew he couldn't delay another reply or Junior was going to think he was an imbecile. "Yes, I do," he heard himself answer. "Sort of."

Junior nodded and his face expressed no more than mild curiosity before it broke into a smile for the camera.

The pained expression on Simon's face, on the other hand, momentarily unnerved David. "I mean," he tried to add hastily by way of clarification between shots, "she sort of helped me arrange this…"

But Junior had completely lost interest in David and Eva. The marketing director had reappeared with a bemused and reluctant looking Maria; she barely had time to glower at Eva, who grinned insolently back at her, before David's paintbrush was snatched from him and thrust into her hand.

David went and stood a couple of feet away from Eva as the remaining photos were taken. She looked down at the floor; something seemed to amuse her.

331

"Thanks everyone," the now smiling marketing director called out as Junior headed for the door. Junior gave a last wave as he left the room, using the same hand to smooth down his hair, which had been ruffled by the TLO t-shirt passing over it twice. The woman with the notepad followed on with the photographer. The marketing director exited last, watching the rear like the final member of a military patrol in a war zone.

Mr Lee was standing silently, expressionlessly to one side as the visitors passed. He then entered the room and walked over to David, gesturing lazily with one hand towards the small groups of TLO employees, none of whom had as yet resumed work.

"If you don't mind me asking," he said bluntly in a tone that suggested he didn't care whether David minded or he didn't, "are you here to do a job of work or for a corporate photo opportunity?" He showed his watch to David and shrugged.

"Chill out," Eva said irritably. "It'll get done. It's going fine."

Mr Lee continued to look at David and then shrugged again as if he was still expecting an answer.

"You heard the lady," David replied with a calming smile. "Just a minor interruption."

"And now *you're* interrupting," Eva added assertively. "Everyone's watching you instead of working."

Mr Lee looked round and found that almost everyone was indeed watching him. He nodded slowly. "OK," he said softly, "that's fine."

"See you," replied Eva. She had already picked up her can of paint and was heading off across the room with it, in search of something in need of rapid redecoration.

Chapter Thirty-Eight

Somehow David had inadvertently become detached from Eva soon after they had entered the pub. Which meant that for the last hour or so he had been able to watch her talking to his work colleagues, but unable to make out what she was saying to them or they to her. She had had conversations with a number of people, but with the exception of Chris, and briefly Jill, no-one that David knew particularly well. Others had come up to talk to David, and he had done his best to give them his full attention. Most seemed to want to congratulate him on his choice of project and on his organisational skills, sentiments which at any other time he would have been only too happy to hear. He did try to make the effort to thank them all individually for their contribution to the success of the day, but the impact of what he was saying was clearly blunted by the fact that he had one eye and ear elsewhere.

Now no-one was talking to him at all. Eva was nodding in agreement with something a girl from Accounts - David thought she might be called Claire - was saying to her, and her conversation also seemed to include a young guy with long sideburns who David had seen in the TLO building before today but couldn't put a name to.

David sat back and drank from his third pint. It really was a grim pub this, he thought, and the TLO contingent, with one or two still in their company t-shirts, looked particularly incongruous in it. Really they should have gone back to the City, but everyone had clearly felt that it was in the spirit of the day to patronise a place in the vicinity of the hostel. The red velour on the seats was punctuated with old cigarette burns and beer stains, and the smell of cleaning fluids hung in the air. There was an aftertaste to the beer and the glasses all bore a whitish bloom that suggested careless washing. The tables were as sticky as the floor. Apart from the TLO group and the two people behind the bar, there were very few people in the place. An overly made-up dyed-ginger hard-faced woman in her forties and a tall man in his fifties or sixties, with nothing left of his hair apart from a couple of neatly combed patches above each ear, sat alone at small round tables a few feet from each other. Three skinheads were playing pool in the distance; a black couple in their mid-twenties smiled and leaned across to each other at a table by the door; and two men sat perched on high stools at the bar. One of them, apparently in his seventies and sporting a chequered cloth cap, attempted to make conversation with the less-than-interested barmaid; the other, a straggly-haired middle-aged man with eyes as red as his face, had been unashamedly watching the TLO crowd, particularly the women, from the moment they had come in.

Within the office group people seemed suddenly to be shuffling round a lot, and now a space was being cleared next to David and Eva was sitting down in it.

"Seem like a nice crowd," she remarked, trying at the same time to arrange her legs under the table. "Your colleagues," she added unnecessarily.

"Yes, they're fine," David agreed without conviction. "Most of them, anyway."

"Except the bosses," Eva smiled. "But that's the same everywhere." She spoke directly into his ear: "I'm glad that Simon didn't come along. He's a slimy shit, isn't he?"

David shrugged and laughed. "Well, yes and no," he replied noncommittally. "Still, you really hit it off with Junior."

Eva punched him on the shoulder and let out an exaggerated laugh; David realised that she had probably had rather more to drink than he had.

"What a bastard!" Eva exclaimed loudly. "I mean, how can you work for him?"

David moved uncomfortably in his seat. "Same way you work for whoever you work for," he replied flatly. "They pay me."

"I know." Eva touched him on the shoulder again. "But I was looking at him and I thought: you're standing here taking the credit for other people's work, mister, and trying to pretend you're a guy who gives a toss about other people, and at the same time you're running a company that gets rid of someone because they get paralysed in a road crash. You know what I'm saying?"

"Yes. So is that why...?"

"I wouldn't do the photo thing? Partly. I just don't like being photographed, in case..." Eva blinked and looked away in embarrassment.

David decided it was better not to press the point. "Thanks anyway," he added.

"For what?" Eva sounded genuinely surprised.

"For holding your tongue."

Eva waved away the remark. "No point getting you fired was there? Even when you tried to insert yourself up Junior's arse."

"I did not," David replied indignantly. "I work for the man. I can't refuse to be photographed with him, can I?"

The guarded smile on Eva's face suggested that she was reluctant to concede the point. "Maybe you could have walked instead of running?"

"Maybe," David admitted weakly. "I thought I'd better placate him after you'd done your best to upset him."

The expression on Eva's face was more mischievous now. "Mr Brown Nose," she taunted.

"Whatever." David tried to conceal the irritation in his voice because he knew it would merely encourage her. "So," he went on, trying to pretend that the answer was only of passing interest to him, "what have you been talking to everyone about?"

Eva was still smiling. "A lot of things," she replied quickly. "They were amazed that I'm living with Guy, wanted to know all about that and how he is."

"You told them that?"

"Shouldn't I have?"

David wondered what questions he was going to face at work now. He wanted to know what details Eva had given of the events leading up to her going to live with Guy, but realised he couldn't probe too deeply without giving the impression that he was somehow ashamed of knowing her.

"I get the impression," Eva added quietly as if in confidence, "that a lot of people didn't really like him."

David nodded slowly. "He's probably a lot more popular now," he agreed, "than he ever was before. Not that that's likely to be much consolation."

Eva looked at David curiously for a moment. "Anyway," she said brightly, almost impishly, "we mainly talked about you."

"Really?" David felt a rising sense of unease. "That must have bored them to death. I think they know most of it already anyway."

"Well, they know a lot more now. And don't be so hard on yourself."

"It's true," David protested. "I'm Mr Dull. I'm the only person that when my identity was stolen the thieves brought it back."

Eva laughed so loudly that others turned to ask what the joke was, but she either didn't hear or decided to ignore them. "You see," she told David, "you can be a funny guy as well when you want. And a dark horse: the man who keeps leaving the office to have secret meetings with a mystery girl in a coffee bar."

"You told them that?" David could hear the anxiety in his voice.

Eva shook her head emphatically. "No, they told me."

"Who?"

"I don't know. Everyone. Apparently it's something that's going round 'the market'. Everyone keeps going on about 'the market', don't they?"

David didn't answer the question. "And what did you say?" he wanted to know.

"I said that would have been me."

"I see."

Eva's smile was gone. "Is there a problem with that?" she asked waspishly.

"No," David replied unconvincingly. "Why would there be?"

"I'm asking you."

"No. No, of course there isn't."

Eva sat up straight. "Are you embarrassed by me?"

"No."

"Sure?"

"Absolutely positive."

"Good," Eva said calmly. "I won't have to batter you then. Oh," she added as if as an afterthought, "I also told them we weren't sleeping together."

"You did what?"

"The woman, the one with the hair, what's her name...?"

"Jill probably."

"That's her. Seemed very keen to know. Disappointed by the answer too. Some of them think you might be gay, you know."

"I've got a daughter!"

Eva nodded. "That's what I said."

"Thank you." David thought about it for a moment. "Just a minute – are you saying you have no other reason to think I'm not gay?"

"Have I?" Eva teasingly looked him up and down. It was an expression that David recognised, but had not seen on Eva's face before. "You've certainly always been a perfect gentleman, or maybe you are just gay!"

David quickly looked around to see whether anyone else was paying attention to his conversation. "OK. If you're saying what I think you're saying," he leaned forward and scratched his head, then became aware that he was doing it and that it looked awkward and slowly lowered his arm again, "maybe this weekend we could…"

"Or tonight."

"Tonight?"

"What's wrong with that?"

What was wrong with that, David thought, was that Eva was showing all the signs of being drunk, and he wasn't going there again, not even after twenty years. But that wasn't necessarily his only problem: he was horribly out of practice, and dog-tired, and had also been drinking. So there was a chance that he wouldn't be able…or, alternatively, he'd be so grateful after such a long lay-off that he'd…Either would be disastrous. And although he couldn't pretend that the thought of sleeping with Eva had never occurred to him, now that it appeared possible he needed a couple of days to get used to the idea.

"Well, it's been a long day," he replied feebly. "We're both tired."

"I have a lot of energy, me."

"And we've both been drinking."

"So?" Eva sniggered. "Think you couldn't…?"

"No, well I…I'm more worried about you waking up in the morning and changing your mind."

Eva's face suddenly clouded over. "I wouldn't," she snapped, "but if I did, that would be my lookout, wouldn't it? I'm a big girl, you know!"

"I know," he said, "it's just that something happened once… it's not that simple."

In his half-drunken state David found that what he wanted above everything else was for Eva and himself to sit somewhere private and tell each other their secrets. No-one, but no-one in his current life, including Sonia, knew anything about Cambridge, or Isabella, or about David's wretchedly incompetent attempt to kill himself, and all that had followed on from that. If he shared those intimate details of his past, maybe Eva would at last trust him with her story. If sex came naturally at the end of that, then...

Eva got up. "I'll call you," she said coldly.

"Don't go like this," David pleaded.

Eva was putting her jacket on. "Like what?" she asked in a loud whisper. "Like a woman who is offering it on a plate – which is not something I make a habit of doing by the way – and is being turned down by someone who is not exactly... That's pretty humiliating, wouldn't you say?"

David stood up too. "At least let me walk you to the station," he volunteered.

Eva flicked her hair back. "I know this area," she replied dismissively. "I'll be fine."

"I had a really good day, Eva."

"Yeah," Eva nodded. "Right. I'll call you."

David knew there was nothing to be gained by arguing further, and that there was still something to lose. He sat down and watched as Eva smiled, shook hands and exchanged kisses with some of his work colleagues, politely refused offers to stay for another drink, and then disappeared through the door at the far end of the bar.

Taz knelt on Eva's bed, tottering from side to side on top of the uneven, rumpled bedclothes. At any moment, Eva thought, the girl was going to fall over, either onto the floor or on top of Eva herself. She could feel Taz's bony knee push against her own right leg each time she swayed against her.

"Come on," Taz was teasing her for the umpteenth time. "What happened?"

"Nothing," Eva told her directly. I worked for four hours in Crappington's, then I went round to the hostel…"

"With C-G." Taz was kneeling over her now.

"With C-G and about a dozen of his workmates," Eva corrected her. "Who were already there. To paint the place. Your idea, remember? You could have done the same if you'd wanted."

"Nah, boring. Then what?"

Eva tried to sit up. "God, you're a nosey little mare tonight, do you know that?"

Taz giggled and grabbed Eva's arms. Eva managed to shake her off.

"Then what?" Taz wanted to know.

"Then we went for a drink."

"You and C-G?"

"Yes. Me and C-G. And at least six other people. What? What are you looking at me like that for?"

Taz was rocking triumphantly from side to side. She grabbed Eva's right arm again; this time Eva couldn't be bothered to resist.

"I know, I know!" Taz taunted her.

"You know what?" Eva said crossly, trying to pull Taz off balance and then regretting it as Taz's superior strength told and she almost pulled Eva's arm out of its socket.

Eva raised her other arm towards Taz's face so that Taz had to lean back to avoid it. "You know, do you? What do you know?"

"You and C-G!" Taz rocked excitedly up and down on her knees.

"Me and C-G what? And stop doing that before we both get seasick."

Taz slowed down momentarily. "You fancy him!"

"I do not!" Eva protested. She didn't either, she was sure of that. At least not physically, as a static portrait.

"We think you do!"

Eva's mood changed immediately; it was one thing to share confidences with Taz, quite another to say something that was going to get back to Guy. That would have been her attitude even before tonight, but something in the way his former colleagues had spoken about him, despite all their outward - and genuine – sympathy, had put her further on her guard.

"Oh, do 'we'. I really can't be bothered to argue, Taz."

After the day she had had - maybe the week, the month, the year, Christ, the life – as she looked up at Taz now, despite the triumphant, smug look on the girl's stupid little face, all Eva wanted to do was hug her. She slowly leaned forward with her arms outstretched. For a moment Taz seemed to be wondering whether this was some sort of trick that would turn into revenge for the damaged arm once she had let down her defences, but as soon as Eva had her arms around Taz's torso the girl unhesitatingly reciprocated, and then tightened her grip, not to the extent that it actually caused pain but so that Eva knew that it wasn't going to be possible to escape until Taz decided to let go. Eva cried: hot, silent tears that ran down her face, some into her mouth and others into Taz's hair and onto the shoulder of her t-shirt. Taz didn't seem to care.

Eva was experiencing high elation and an almost bottomless sadness at the same moment. This, she told herself, was what you got if you allowed yourself to open up, something she had consciously been denying herself for so long. You got emotions in their rawest state, as likely bitter as sweet; and then you lost control. And if you lost control, you were screwed.

This could be a turning point in her life, though. It was time to start thinking about how to move on. David had disappointed her once again. Now that she had sobered up she was relieved that he hadn't taken up her offer. So, in fairness, he had been

341

right about that, but the rejection itself still rankled. Eva had the feeling that David was someone who didn't grasp what life offered, not simply in the sexual sense, but in broad, general terms. That wasn't what Eva was looking for in the future. Beggars couldn't be choosers, everyone said; well, in that case it was time to stop begging.

Guy had been calling out something that Eva couldn't make out, and didn't want to, for the last couple of minutes now. Taz slowly disentangled herself from Eva, raised herself up, wiped her eyes and nose with her hand and her hand on her t-shirt. Then she wordlessly got off the bed and left the room.

David knew that he was pissed, and wished that he wasn't. He would have to go to work tomorrow, and however many pints of water he drank before he went to bed, in an attempt to stave off dehydration, he was going to feel rough in the morning and the day was going to seem very long. It wasn't even as though the alcohol had made him happy: if his motive in drinking so much, in accepting every glass offered to him by his colleagues after Eva had left the pub, had been to cheer himself up, it definitely hadn't worked. He had drunk so much that he didn't have much of an appetite and, although he had dozed off on the train – or perhaps because he had – he doubted that he would be able to sleep for a while once he got home. The prospect was an hour and a half spent watching TV programmes he wouldn't be able to take in while running through the day countless times in his mind. Then finally, if he was lucky, his eyelids would begin to droop.

According to the clock on the platform of his home station, as he and about six other people got off, it was still before ten o'clock, which meant that he had been in the pub less than three hours, half of that after Eva's departure, but enough time to put back seven or eight glasses and to start to say the wrong things to the wrong people.

To be fair to himself, a lot of people had wanted to buy him drinks as organiser of what they all said, at least to his face, had been a successful day. He'd felt the need to reciprocate in order to thank them all for their contribution. He remembered saying, to some applause, that the TLO Charity Day should become an annual event, something he didn't actually believe.

It was all Eva's fault. There seemed to be no pleasing her, and it was becoming very wearing even trying to. Logically it ought to stand in his favour that he had refused to take advantage of Eva's drunkenness, but somehow he doubted that logic was going to come into it. She had said she was going to call him, but that was often a euphemism for 'goodbye'. If she didn't call, David wouldn't initiate contact this time. He didn't want to be alone for the rest of his life, but there had to be a less complicated relationship out there for him, with someone who wasn't as... was 'damaged' fair? Someone at any rate who didn't have their defences raised all the time.

David noted the large number of people leaning patiently against the counter inside the brightly lit takeaway, with its giant pictures of pizzas and kebabs and burgers on the walls behind the serving staff in their primary red uniforms and baseball caps, but although he had been there on several previous occasions – the food was actually much better than the shop looked – this time he wasn't tempted to go in.

Normally late at night David skirted around the park – there were too many dark corners and the police seemed as nervous of the place as he was – but this time his physical and mental weariness made the prospect of the additional ten-minute walk that would be necessary to avoid it very unattractive. It was a cool, cloudless night and David wasn't dressed for it; and he was going to require a slash sooner rather than later.

He quickened his pace as he walked through the gates and his eyes searched for evidence of the presence of other people. He knew that kids did drugs here in the evenings, but he thought the area to avoid was where the benches were, by the pond. The path he needed to take was straight, and from where he was now, not far inside the park, you could see the lights at the far end, the streetlamps of his own road. You just needed to keep your head down and walk briskly.

David didn't think he had said anything career-endingly stupid in the pub, but all the same, from what he could now remember, he hadn't done himself any favours. He knew he had made some very cynical remarks about Junior's unscheduled appearance, which some people clearly - if surprisingly - hadn't agreed with; as soon as he had heard Adrian enthusiastically supporting his view David had known that he ought to shut up.

He encountered no-one in the park. The shop and amusement arcade looked eerie in the moonlight, with minimal bare strip lighting accompanied by the rhythmic flashing of armed intruder alarms, and David half expected to see people lurking in the shadows. But if they were there, he didn't spot them and they left him alone.

He was surprised how relieved he felt to emerge into his own road with its bright streetlamps and the reassuring proximity of houses and blocks of flats, most with light bulbs burning warmly behind drawn curtains, indicating the presence of other people. There was the welcome sight of his car, too, the SEAT parked patiently outside his flat, like a faithful dog awaiting its next instruction.

There was someone sitting in a car parked next to David's. It was an odd place to park, David idly reflected, because it blocked the path to the flats. Unnecessarily as there was plenty of free space, unusually, further along. David walked between the two cars and, as he fumbled for his keys, he tried to get a look at the driver of the unknown vehicle. It was a man who seemed to be in his early thirties with close-cropped light brown hair. He had the collar of his jacket up and was looking down, maybe reading something in his lap, so that it was not possible to make out his facial features.

As he opened the door to the hallway and turned on the lights David quickly spun round to see if the man was watching. He was; he gazed expressionlessly at David then unhurriedly looked away. He had a long, thin, pinched face and a prominent nose. David was about to wave at him when he decided it was a pissed thing to do. Instead he went inside and closed the door behind him, entered his own flat and made his way as quickly as he could to the bathroom. When he came out he thought he could hear an engine start up, and when he looked out through the window he saw the car slowly driving away.

Chapter Thirty-Nine

It was an uncomfortable weekend with Amy. It wasn't so much that she was uncooperative or difficult as that she seemed preoccupied and distant, and not at all interested in anything her father suggested they might do together. In fact, the idea of their spending weekends together had recently become increasingly nominal, as David didn't want to stand in the way of any plans she might have made to meet up with her friends; his aim was that the divorce would make as little difference as possible to the life that Amy would otherwise be leading. He wasn't naïve enough to suppose that this could easily be achieved in practice, but he tried to make it happen so far as he could. As a result there were times now that the only impact of a 'Dad weekend' on Amy's existence was that it was her father's flat rather than her mother's house that she – eventually - came back to, or that it was he rather than John who ended up late at night sitting in a car outside yet another god-forsaken church hall, having to endure the ear-injuring bass which emanated from the building and vibrated uncomfortably through the bodywork of the SEAT. That and the aggressive scowls of the boys and girls of Amy's age passing by the window.

It was always a relief when Amy did finally appear. David suspected that she kept him waiting longer than she did John, but it wasn't a subject he wanted to broach, and he was fully aware that for him actually to go into the hall to find her would be social death for his daughter. He liked to think that he was at least trying to be a good parent, certainly better than his own parents, though that wasn't difficult. Certain memories still annoyed him, gnawed at him, even now when it was all ancient history.

Enough of that. The immediate problem was what was eating Amy. This weekend she had had no parties, no sleepovers (though admittedly at her age they were becoming increasingly uncool) and had not required ferrying to any friends' houses. When she wasn't asleep she had for the most part stretched herself out on the sofa in a pose her father suspected she had learnt from Taz (though Amy at least took her shoes off) and spent hours doing whatever it was that kids did on their mobiles. She made a few calls, but whatever it was she was finding to talk about, it seemed she didn't want her father to hear: she shuffled uncomfortably, turned away or began speaking more quietly whenever he came close to her. Sometimes she looked at him reproachfully as if he was trying to eavesdrop. At other moments there was a slight haughtiness in her eyes and the beginnings of a grin about her lips which, together with the fact that she cupped her free hand over her mouth, made David uncomfortably aware that he was probably being talked about. The truth was, he reflected ironically, that Amy had so perfected the teenager's habits of mumbling and using a vocabulary that was entirely their own, that her father wasn't going to be able to pick up more than a few words of it anyway.

Amy went out a couple of times: once on Saturday, once on Sunday. Both times 'for a walk', which seemed like a very un-teenage thing to do; when David volunteered to go with her she said she just wanted her own space for a while. On both occasions when she returned there was something sheepish and furtive about her, David thought, and she made her way immediately to her room and then spent several minutes in the bathroom. But she was fine after that, even chatty for a few minutes, except on the subject of where her walk had taken her, on which she remained monosyllabic. David concluded that he was an overanxious father and that he shouldn't pry further; there wasn't really anything to worry about. When he returned Amy to her mother on Sunday evening, and was unable to point to anything interesting they had done over the weekend, Sonia gave him the familiar reproachful look that suggested that he was providing no mental stimulation to their daughter. He was used to it now; it no longer upset him.

Eva hadn't rung. He hadn't really expected her to, but he wouldn't have minded if she had. He wasn't going to call her though.

Eva was sitting on her bed asking herself how this could possibly have happened. The letter was lying open on the duvet and she was reading it for the hundredth time. Her heart was racing and she felt nauseous. She didn't want to touch the paper.

It had arrived at work – and nearly not reached her as the management of Abbington's didn't know who she was. She had immediately recognised the spindly handwriting but had had to wait almost two hours for her next break in order to open it. Then she hadn't known whether she wanted to. Other kitchen workers had noted her discomfort as she tried to concentrate on dirty pots and pans, and had started eyeing her strangely. No-one had asked if she was OK though.

How had he found out where she worked? When she had been so careful for so long. She wasn't registered for anything, or if she had to be, not under her real name. At least if he was contacting her at work it almost certainly meant that he didn't know where she lived. But if he'd got this far, he'd only need to pay someone a few quid to follow her. The sort of people who worked at the restaurant didn't have principles: a few notes in the hand and they'd do anything, no questions asked. And even if that didn't happen, the letter made it clear that he was going to come down to the restaurant itself unless she called him. She wasn't going to do that.

The only certainty was that she would have to find somewhere else, very quickly, a long way away. Where, she didn't know. And, worst of all, she'd have to go on her own.

She stood up and started to take her clothes out of the wardrobe and lay them out on the bed. She wiped some tears away from her eyes, pushed her head back and breathed deeply; crying was becoming a habit and it would have to stop.

She looked round for a case to put her clothes in: there was a square, battered trunk on top of the wardrobe; that would do. She would borrow it or buy it, whatever. She stood on a chair to remove the case, but through her tears she pulled at something that wasn't there, overbalanced and landed heavily on the floor.

She quickly picked herself up. She was winded, but nothing appeared to be broken. She pulled the chair upright and stood on it once more. She would pack as quickly as she could, and get out as soon as possible. No goodbyes: she'd leave a note. Where she was going to go she would work out later.

There was a knock on the door. Eva looked hurriedly around. There wasn't time to try to conceal anything.

"You dead in there?" Taz's voice.

Eva almost smiled. "I'm fine. Knocked something over, but it's OK now. I'll be out in a moment. Don't come..."

But Taz had already entered the room, with a grin on her face that evaporated as she took in the scene and slowly worked out what it meant.

"You're leaving me," she said quietly. She turned and ran out of the room and down the landing. Eva jumped off the chair and went in pursuit of her, frightened of the damage Taz might randomly inflict on parts of Guy's mother's house. Eva caught up with her outside the bathroom and instinctively grabbed the girl's arms to try to stop her lashing out. Taz turned her head and for a second Eva feared that her friend was going to spit at her, but Taz wasn't being aggressive; she wasn't even resisting. She looked up with big eyes like a bewildered child and seemed to be waiting for Eva to say something. Eva's resolve almost failed on the spot.

She steered Taz back to the bedroom and motioned to her to sit down on the bed.

Taz casually picked up a couple of Eva's recently purchased tops from on top of the duvet and tossed them contemptuously onto the floor. Eva did not react. Taz fell onto the bed and made only fleeting eye contact before looking away again.

Eva carefully cleared a space beside her and sat down. "I need to go away for a while, Taz," she said simply.

Eva expected Taz to ask why, but the girl only looked into space.

"The thing is," Eva went on, "the bloke I told you about? Him?" She exhaled sharply. "Well he's found me. I don't know how, but he has. So I need to leave. Just for a wee while. It's not you, Taz. I don't want to leave you."

"I could come."

"I couldn't ask you to. You've got a nice place to stay here, now. You've got a roof over your head, regular food, some money. You've got Guy!" Eva hoped Taz hadn't noticed the lack of enthusiasm in her last comment.

"We could kill him," Taz suggested.

"Who?"

Taz looked puzzled. "The bloke," she replied. "Him."

Eva tried to smile. "But we can't, can we?"

Taz was indignant. "Why not? We're going to kill the Creep."

Eva hesitated for a moment. "So we are," she agreed. "But that's your call. This is my call, and I don't want to kill him."

"Why not?"

"Because I don't."

"Is he here now?" Taz asked practically.

Eva shook her head. "No. He sent me a letter at work." She pointed at the sheets of paper that were now trapped under Taz's right leg. Taz leaned forward and extracted them, then held them up in front of her face. Eva guessed that, however

350

successful Guy was being in teaching Taz to read and write, and she had her doubts, it wouldn't yet extend to scrappy handwriting like this. Eva had seen Taz pretend to read before; it was endearing, but it was sad too.

Taz tired of staring at the paper, put the edge of it into her mouth and then spat it across the room. It landed on the floor by the dressing table.

"Stay here with me and Guy. Don't go to work. It'll be great." Taz gave Eva a toothy smile.

Eva sighed. "It wouldn't work, Taz. Money for a start. And then I don't think Guy would be up for it, and I couldn't blame him. And anyway he, this bloke, would be only a few miles away. That's too close."

Taz bit her lip and nodded slowly. "Why can't we kill him?" she asked again.

"Because I don't want to," Eva replied steadily.

Taz said nothing, but continued to study the ceiling.

"I'll call. Every day," Eva offered. "It's only temporary."

"That's what Ash said."

"Ash died, Taz. I've no intention of dying."

Taz sat up, produced some banknotes from her pocket and, without attempting to count them, offered them to Eva.

Now despite herself Eva was crying again and tightly embracing Taz, enjoying her warmth and her scent, forming comforting sense memories that she could draw on for strength in the days and weeks to come, until they met again. And they would; she was sure of that.

Terry sat in front of his home computer, staring into space. The images on the screen were the usual collection of degraded scrubbers and, although he wouldn't previously have thought it possible, he was beginning to tire of them. Not to mention the cost: it seemed to be mounting monthly, and he knew exactly what it was because he had had to take out a new credit card in order to subscribe to these sites without the possibility of Serena finding out about it. The statement went to his office and he paid it at his bank, in cash, posting the anonymous little envelope into the paying-in box. Just a precaution because he didn't let Serena anywhere near his bank and credit-card statements anyway – they were none of her business – but things could get left lying around and you couldn't be too careful.

There was some bird on the screen now, a bit fat around the thighs, too much loose skin on the torso. Tattoos on her right upper arm and shoulder. Not a nice look. Couldn't see the boat due to it being thrust firmly towards the carpet by the flabby middle-aged geezer rogering her from behind. Terry imagined himself and Serena in the same pose. Never say never: she kept going on about this diamond necklace she wanted; it wasn't unreasonable to expect her to do something to earn it.

Of course when he fantasised like this it wasn't Serena he imagined but something much much younger and altogether more exotic. Trying not to lose the thought from his head, Terry shut down the computer, unlocked the door to the study and made his way to the bathroom. On the way back he paused outside the living-room door. The TV was on much too loud and there was a lot of irritating shrieking and whooping that suggested some sort of inane game show programme. It was no wonder, Terry reflected, that the boys were turning into such sullen, uncommunicative little pricks when their mother not only let them watch this sort of shit but watched it with them.

Back in the study Terry decided not to turn the computer back on. The mood had passed. It was time to start thinking business again. Terry liked the saying that had caught on in the City in the last few years – it sounded as if it came from America but, whatever, that couldn't be helped – that if you started your working week on Monday morning you were already a day behind. Well, it was now Sunday evening, and apart from flicking through the financial section of the paper he hadn't done much today except eat, sleep and watch sport on TV. Admittedly he had spent the whole of Saturday with some overseas clients - first playing golf then at some god-awful West-End musical that they'd left half way through, then out on the piss till about two - but Saturday wasn't Sunday, and if you wanted to stay successful you had to know that modern business was 24/7.

Try as he might though, Terry couldn't recall anything he particularly needed to think about for tomorrow. He guessed that was a tribute to the efficient way he ran his business in the first place, unlike a lot of people in the market he could name. His mind started to wander, not away from work entirely – it rarely did that – but to things that weren't exactly central to it. He thought about Kelsey again. No story in the market yet, as far as Terry knew – and he made sure he was always among the first to hear anything – of Kelsey being confronted by a violent, mad, jealous Scotsman in a public place. Give it time. In the jungle Alpha males disposed of their rivals in a few minutes; business was a little more complicated, but the principle, and the result, were the same. There was a story doing the rounds that Kelsey had brazenly turned up with the pikey bird at some sort of company charity day. Someone said she was now living with Guy the raspberry ripple, which seemed unlikely, except that Terry had now heard it from two different sources. It shouldn't be difficult to get that address and pass it on. Just to be helpful, of course. Then sit back and enjoy.

Terry closed his eyes and imagined a really young one, bent over forwards awaiting his pleasure. Sex. Power. Alpha.

Chapter Forty

David was finding Monday mornings increasingly surreal. After a weekend it just didn't seem possible that he was supposed to get up, put a suit on, travel on a commuter train to the City of London again and spend anywhere between eight and ten hours trapped in a fake corporate persona. It wasn't that he resented working: almost everyone in the world had to do so in one form or another, mostly something they didn't enjoy, and there was no reason why David Kelsey deserved to be any different, or even wanted to be. It was more that his work involved no product except numbers on a profit-and-loss account at the end of the year, a lot of which could frankly be attributed to luck, either good or bad, and almost none of which could with any accuracy be assigned to his own endeavours. The older he got, the less he could understand why so many of his colleagues were so clearly excited by the business.

David handed over money to the new *Homeless Truths* vendor at the station - a stocky, swarthy young man in his twenties who looked like he came from somewhere in the Middle East - and tucked the magazine under his arm. He sighed to himself. It was a cold, overcast Monday morning and the whole working week was ahead of him. Would he retire if he could? Not with his current life – it was too boring. What would he do all day? What else could he do with his life? He didn't know. He started to think of Eva and stopped himself; that was just a dead end.

He walked through the doors into the TLO office, went directly to his desk without greeting anyone, sat down and turned on the computer.

It was the noise that finally alerted him to what should have been clear as soon as he came into the office: that, with the exception of himself, everyone was standing up and gathered together in informal groups from which a hubbub of voices was rising. The atmosphere was qualitatively different from the relaxed state of the previous Thursday, the day after the TLO Charity Day: where then the office buzz had oozed goodwill, if in a somewhat self-satisfied way, now there seemed to be a much greater sense of urgency and alarm.

David got up and walked across to join the crowd.

"What's up?" he asked as nonchalantly as he could of a seven-strong group which included Jill and Adrian, as well as Chris, who generally stayed above the fray of office gossip. David concluded that whatever it was that had prised Chris away from his phone must be serious.

"Redundancies," Adrian said loudly. "That's what's up."

"You don't know that," Jill told him crossly. She looked at David more sympathetically. "They've called a meeting of all the staff at nine thirty. There's some sort of announcement," she informed him.

"What else could it be?" Adrian asked irritably. "Of course it's redundancies."

"We don't know that," Jill repeated, more loudly.

"You're Simon's secretary, Jill," Adrian objected, "not his bloody spokesman. You don't have to give us the party line every time."

"I'm his *personal assistant*," Jill retorted angrily.

David walked away and got himself a coffee from the vending machine. Although he was still close enough to hear the developing argument, he tried to close his ears to it. He would know the truth soon enough. He was surprised to realise how relaxed he felt, how indifferent to his own fate. Which was ridiculous, because with a daughter and ex-wife to maintain, plus his own rent and bills to pay, and no savings either, there was probably no-one in the company who more desperately needed continuous employment than he did. Yet somehow he felt that things needed to come to a head; that they couldn't continue much longer in the present vein; and, further, that he didn't really want them to. Did that mean that he was inclined to push the self-destruct button, assuming that he hadn't already done so? He sat down at his desk, warmed his hands on the coffee cup and contemplated the idea, without coming to a definitive answer.

The fact that TLO had gone to the trouble of hiring a hall in order to make their announcement was only adding to the sense of occasion. The place had a high, ornate ceiling busy with multi-coloured cherubs and men in chariots; long windows with elaborate drapes; and dark walls of carved wood. Two panels announced that the hall belonged to the Worshipful Company of some long-abandoned medieval trade, and provided a list of Presidents who, David noted passively as he waited for the TLO management to appear, curiously extended to the present day.

It was almost ten to ten by the time that Junior, grinning broadly, took to the raised dais at the far end of the hall. The hubbub in the hall heightened for a moment, before tailing away into an expectant silence. Junior's suit was immaculately pressed, his shirt crisp and clean, his tie perfectly knotted. He was accompanied by a man David didn't recognise: taller, bulkier, in his mid-fifties, with neatly parted, receding grey hair and an expression of repressed impatience on his face, as though he wondered whether the presence of so many onlookers was really necessary.

"Colleagues," Junior began. "Colleagues, I appreciate your coming here today at such short notice, I really do. You know, what we are about to announce today is a tremendously positive development. TLO is a great company, we have a proud history, fifty years unbroken, and most of all we have great people: you people here today. Nothing has made that clearer to me than the way you reacted to my call, my challenge to you to give something back to the society we live in, through the TLO Day of Charity last week. You rose magnificently to the occasion, and I am equally confident that you will be eager to exploit the exciting new opportunities that will be occurring in the coming weeks and months."

A few nervous coughs rang round the hall while Junior quickly consulted some notes before continuing. "You know, TLO is a great company, but in world-market terms it is not a large one. The world in which we live and work, paradoxically, is both increasingly small and increasingly large - made smaller by the increasing sophistication of communications technologies and larger in the sense that a global reach is increasingly necessary. For the first years of our existence we were a player in the UK market, then a successful niche player in the global market. But in business standing still is never an option: now we need to go further, to take the next step. I am therefore delighted to announce that today the board of TLO has formally accepted an offer to become part of the Globe Two Group of Companies."

A lot of murmuring in the hall, a few intakes of breath. David looked round to gauge reaction but found that most of the audience was still staring intently in the direction of Junior and his anonymous companion.

"It gives me great pleasure," Junior continued, "to introduce Tad Crocker, President, Chairman and Chief Executive Officer of Globe Two Companies, who has kindly taken time out of an unbelievably busy schedule to fly to London and be with us today. On a personal note, I should say that my wife and I have got to know Tad and Patty pretty well over the last few months as we conducted our negotiations, and I've found Tad to be a man of the greatest integrity and decisiveness, and a straight-shooter. When he says he's going to do something he does it, and we greatly appreciate that. Tad, please."

Junior smiled at the thickset, middle-aged businessman and began to walk to one side, pointing as he did so at the place on the stage that he had just vacated. Tad slapped him on the shoulder as their paths crossed.

"Thanks, Charles, I appreciate that," Tad began in a slow southern-state American drawl. "Hey, maybe it should be 'Chuck' now that you're a Globe Two guy!"

Junior threw his head back and laughed. A few members of the audience half-heartedly joined in.

"Well, what can I say," Tad continued amiably, "except that you're all fired." More nervous laughter. "No, but seriously you know – say, does someone have a chair?" A couple of men each picked up a chair from the stacks that had been pushed against the walls and raced to deliver it to the stage. One arrived just in front of the other, who retreated in disappointment. A frisson of amusement in the hall.

"Thanks," Tad said summarily to the winner, without looking at him. "You know, I'm gonna take off my jacket if you don't mind." He did so and threw it casually across the chair. "And I'm gonna take off my tie and roll up my sleeves." The tie soon joined the jacket; the sleeves were folded back to just above the elbows. "You know," he told his audience, "I'm a kinda no-jacket, tie-off, rolled-up-sleeves guy. And Globe Two is a no-jacket, tie-off, rolled-up-sleeves kinda company. And I kinda like it that way. So, how about you guys here give it a go? Ladies, you'll be let off this time round."

He ceased talking. David looked around him and found that most of the men were looking at one another for guidance. Some appeared to be attempting to pick out their own boss within the crowd. Gradually all eyes focussed on Junior, who looked fleetingly at Tad and received a smile of encouragement in return. Junior slowly took off his jacket. The marketing director David had seen at the hostel, but hadn't previously noticed today, rushed across from a position a couple of yards to the left of the stage, took the jacket and neatly folded it over his arm. He received the tie and seemed about to help with the sleeve-folding until he was irascibly waved away.

All around David people began to follow Junior's example. David looked to the back of the hall to see whether it would be possible to retreat there unnoticed, but concluded from the flurry of activity and the acres of visible shirtfronts that it wouldn't. Thinking what Eva might say if she could see him now, David reluctantly joined in the disrobing ceremony. He dropped his tie once and then struggled to roll up his sleeves and hold onto his jacket at the same time. He didn't want to be the last person to finish. He spotted Simon for the first time that day; his boss had taken up a position just in front of the dais, with his legs set slightly apart in a purposeful posture and his jacket hanging casually over his shoulder. David tried to emulate the stance but didn't feel comfortable with it. He ended up with his feet together and his jacket held out in a bundle in front of him.

"How about that?" Tad was saying, smiling and nodding at the audience with approval. "How about that? Two minutes ago you were a bunch of buttoned-up Brits. Now you look to me like a team, a Globe Two team, ready for action!"

David looked at Junior. No-one else appeared to be doing so. Junior's face was flushed and he was blinking rapidly. He was trying to force a smile, but the disquiet in his eyes and the tension around his mouth wouldn't allow it, so that he ended up looking faintly ghoulish. And he gave the impression that he felt half-dressed, as though a dream in which he had appeared in the office in his underwear had suddenly come true.

Tad was no longer paying any attention to him. "So what do you say?" he was asking. "Shall we get back to work?"

Loud assent from Simon and a few others. Otherwise sheepish murmurings. Tad cupped his hand to his ear. "Come on guys, we can do better than that. I said, 'Shall we get back to work'?"

A loud if, David thought, less than wholehearted cry of 'yes'. Tad grinned with satisfaction. "OK," he said. "Any questions for me before we do?"

Adrian's voice from near the front, almost inaudible. A lot of faces turned towards his, with expressions that said 'don't do this'.

"Excuse me?" Tad scanned the audience, uncertain where the sound was coming from.

Adrian's voice again, louder now. "I was just asking whether there are going to be any redundancies, particularly as you already own TBE in the UK."

"Pardon me?" Crocker was looking directly at Adrian now, and didn't appear to like what he saw. Adrian had removed his jacket, but his cuffs were still buttoned and his tie around his neck, though at half mast.

"To translate into American," Adrian tried again and the audience's collective wince was palpable, "are you intending to fire people where there's an overlap with TBE?"

"Well," Crocker replied, still looking intently at Adrian, "thanks for translating for this simple colonial guy. I appreciate it."

A few sniggers. Adrian looked uncomfortable but appeared to be expecting an answer.

"I don't know if you all got that at the back," the Globe Two CEO said to the audience. "Our friend here wants to know if there'll be any terminations as a result of this acquisition. That's a fair question. The answer is this: the board of Globe Two intends this acquisition to be accretive. However, where there are synergies, naturally we intend to recognise them." He looked at Adrian in a mock-kindly manner. "Hopefully that answers your question."

Adrian slowly nodded but said nothing.

"Great," Crocker continued. "One more time. What do you say we all get back to work?"

"What's the matter?" Guy asked for the third time. It was often like this now. It was a question of ensuring Taz got fed up with the repeated question before he got tired of asking it.

"Zip," Taz replied almost inaudibly and without turning her head. She was sprawled once again in front of the television, which was spewing out some sort of cookery show that she wasn't really watching. She was propped up on one elbow, wearing baggy grey tracksuit bottoms and a shapeless black vest; she looked like a pile of abandoned clothes.

"Well, something must be," Guy sighed. "You haven't said anything for over two hours. Even by your standards that's going some."

Taz moved so that she was now lying horizontally. She continued to watch the TV screen from a sideways angle. "Bored," she replied through an unstifled yawn.

"Well," Guy said with carefully restrained exasperation, "you will be if you just lie there all day. There are a lot of things we could be doing. I mean, I know there are things I can't do because of my, you know, but that still leaves some. Mother was suggesting…"

"Your mother hates me."

"No she doesn't," Guy protested.

"She does. She wants me to fuck off. I wish she'd fuck off."

Whether or not his mother actually hated Taz, Guy knew it was less easy to deny that she would prefer not to have the girl in the house. By contrast she seemed sometimes to enjoy talking to Eva (it was far from clear whether the feeling was mutual) though Guy realised that this was not the moment to point that out, if ever there would be. Instead he laughed. "Well, it is her house, you know, so you can't really expect her to fuck off."

"Whatever."

"Come on, Taz, don't 'whatever' me. Why don't we have another go at the reading thing? You were doing really well."

"Arsed."

"'Zip', 'Bored', 'Whatever', 'Arsed'. This is a great conversation, Taz! You sound like some sort of stereotype of a sketch-show teenager. Come on, tell me what the matter is."

A couple of seconds of silence. Then Taz rolled across the sofa and hung her head down the side so that Guy was looking at her face upside down.

"I don't want Eva to leave," she said quietly.

"Neither do I," Guy answered forcefully. "So what's the problem? Your face is going red, Taz – you're going to pass out if you hang like that too long!"

Guy expected Taz to smile or pull a face, but she did neither. It was difficult to read an upturned expression.

"People leave me," Taz said simply.

Guy wanted to change the subject quickly. He had soon learnt that it was never a good idea to go into Taz's past. She got very moody very quickly, and what she did tell you was such a confused litany of homes, foster-carers and life on the street that Guy doubted that he would ever understand still less be able to relate to any of it. There were various 'Aunts' and 'Uncles' and someone called Ash who featured a lot, both for what he said and what he did. He was male and apparently a lot older than Taz; beyond that she gave few details and Guy found that he really didn't want to know too much more.

"Come on," Guy tried to cajole Taz, "let's do some reading. Do it as a favour for me, if you like."

Taz rolled off the sofa onto the floor. She propped herself up on both elbows and gazed up at Guy with a serious expression on her face. Guy subconsciously put his hands onto the wheels of his chair in order to be ready to retreat.

"Why d'you wanna do it?" Taz asked aggressively. "I thought you could read already."

Guy ignored the sarcasm. "I like teaching you," he replied in a friendly tone.

"Why?"

"Honestly? Because it makes me feel useful. It keeps my brain going – you know, I used to get... from work. It's difficult now... and I like to see you succeed. It's something you have to have to get on in life: you can't get anywhere if you can't read. I mean, when you're older..."

"You can read things for me, like you do now."

Guy sensed some sort of trap and hesitated before replying. But the girl was staring at him, expecting a response. Guy cleared his throat. "Yeah, and I like doing that as well, but wouldn't it be great if you could do it yourself? And you were doing so well before, Taz, I was really impressed. Honestly. And you never know what's going to happen in the future - what if things change and for some reason I'm not there?"

Guy immediately realised that he had said the wrong thing. Taz's face reddened and her eyes narrowed. She started to crawl towards him.

"Why wouldn't you be there?" she shouted.

"Well," Guy tried to think quickly. "I mean you could be out at the shops while I'm here doing something else."

Taz stopped for a moment, but the fear in Guy's eyes told her that he didn't expect her to believe him. So he must be lying. Eva was leaving her, and now so was Guy.

She stood up and began to walk across the room. Guy tried to retreat but only collided with the wall behind him.

Taz was upon him now, and it was not until he looked directly into her eyes that he realised the extent of the trouble he was in. His mother had gone out, Eva was at work. Whatever Taz wanted to do to him, no-one was going to stop her. If she still carried a knife and wanted to carve him up, that was what was going to happen. The rage on her distorted features wasn't going to respond to reason, and she was past the point where she might respect his attempting to face her down.

She drew back her fist and Guy cowered and tried to cover his face with his arms. But instead of the expected impact of Taz's knuckles Guy felt the side of the wheelchair being lifted up. He was suspended in mid-air for a couple of seconds and tried to brace himself for the fall; but instead of simply pushing it until it overbalanced, Taz retained control of the chair and slowly lowered it onto its side. She bent down and looked at her victim with an expression of triumphant satisfaction. And yet there were tears on her cheeks. Guy could smell her breath. He closed his eyes; whatever was going to happen next he wanted to get it over.

"Fuck you," Taz screamed as she stomped out of the room. "Fucking cripple."

If there was one consolation for Eva in her present circumstances, it was that she wouldn't have to work at Crappington's in future. She had told them today that she wouldn't be coming in any more and the man had just nodded and said that in that case they didn't need her today either. She hadn't been expecting a gold watch or a speech by the Head Chef, but bearing in mind that she had been there longer than any of the other casual kitchen staff, 'thanks for all your work' or 'give us a shout if you ever want to work here again' might have been in order. But nothing. Well, she'd wanted anonymity and she'd got it. Oddly one of the waiters she didn't remember having previously had any dealings with had overheard the conversation and suddenly shown an interest in her future plans. She hadn't told him anything, of course.

Eva had booked a one-way ticket to Birmingham for the following morning. Not that there was anything particularly special about Birmingham except that, after London, it seemed the best place to go if you wanted to melt into the crowd. Using Guy's computer late at night she had found some hostel addresses, the names of some agencies who dealt in casual catering staff and, if all else failed, she also had the address of the local *Homeless Truths* office. With a bit of luck she wouldn't starve or die of exposure. She had some money, including the not insubstantial amount that Taz had given her – the girl had refused to take it back and, in the circumstances, despite feeling guilty about it, Eva hadn't tried very hard to persuade her.

Eva slowed down as she walked back from the station to Guy's place for the last time; it was as though she didn't want to get there because arriving would hasten her leaving. She was going to miss Taz terribly; she was finding it increasingly difficult to come up with a plausible, real-world scenario in which they would ever get back together again. Maybe, from Taz's perspective, it was for the best. Eva found now that she was also going to miss the warmth and certainty of Guy's house and even his mother and that stupid dog.

Maybe the future would be bright. Maybe Birmingham would give her the opportunity to set up her own little decorating business. You just needed to be able to put away a few quid for materials and advertising and a little van – that might be easier in Birmingham if things were cheaper than London. But what if Alastair found her again? What then? Run once more or face him down? The latter would be a lot easier if there was a new man in her life. Eva smiled ruefully at the thought of David and the disappointment he had turned out to be.

She had decided that there would be no goodbyes. Taz knew she was going early tomorrow and could tell Guy and his mother. Eva doubted that the news would be greeted by great outpourings of grief. If David ever made contact again, one of them could fill him in.

Eva was lost in her own thoughts as she turned into the road and Guy's house came into view, and it took her a couple of seconds to register that there was an ambulance standing outside with its back doors open.

Her heartbeat increased; she tried to stay calm; to think rationally. Maybe it was for a different house – the people next door were quite old. She didn't wish them any harm, but if it was them or…but someone in a uniform was standing on the path to Guy's house.

Eva didn't know whether to run towards the house or run away. Maybe something minor had happened to Guy's mother – she wasn't so young any more - and she was being taken in as a precaution. Or Guy had had a small accident – even with the house converted as well as it was for a disabled person you couldn't rule out that happening from time to time. But there was Guy, slumped uncomfortably to one side in his wheelchair, his face screwed up in what looked like infinite misery but not pain. And there was his mother standing awkwardly behind him, alternately putting a self-conscious comforting arm on his shoulder and standing with her hands clasped in front of her. She was intently watching something that was moving along the path in front of her, obscured from Eva's view by the tall hedge that divided Guy's mother's house from the neighbouring property.

A man walking backwards with his hands raised horizontally in front of him came into view. Then a stretcher, with a red blanket spread across it. Eva knew that the whole of the rest of her life, and her sanity, were going to depend on what she saw in the next second. She knew who it was. She could just about cope with that; something had always been bound to happen sooner or later. But, she begged a God she had not spoken to for so long, the blanket had to be folded back, away from the still breathing face.

The ambulanceman stopped, checked his footing and took another step back.

Jill called David on his phone, though she sat only a few feet away, and in the cold business tone she reserved for phone conversations, told him that Simon would like a word straight away.

David got slowly to his feet. He wondered momentarily whether he was about to be made redundant, but discounted the idea. He didn't doubt that it was possible in the near future, once the new owners had managed to do an inventory of their new acquisition, but he couldn't believe that they would want to do it on the same day that the purchase was announced.

A few people watched him with heightened interest as he politely smiled and nodded at Jill, who told him to go straight through. Few of his colleagues were showing any inclination to return to their desks and resume normal Monday-morning activities, and the majority were still hungry for any item of further information. David could feel their jealous looks on the back of his neck, as though they thought he was about to be taken into the management's confidence while they remained excluded.

Simon, typically, was on the phone. He motioned towards the chair on the other side of his desk and gave a thumbs-up sign when David mimed closing the door behind him. David turned and met the stares of the people outside, whose curiosity was only intensified as he took hold of the handle and pushed the glass into its place.

He sat down to wait and noted that, whereas he himself had automatically replaced his tie at the end of the staff meeting, Simon was still open-necked. His jacket, hanging over the back of his chair, also appeared to be sporting a new badge in the buttonhole.

Simon punched the desk, said "Thanks for the heads-up" into the receiver and rang off. "Bob Krasnitsky," he told David by way of an unnecessary explanation. "SVP in HR out of Boston."

David nodded.

Simon leaned back with his hands behind his head. There was a satisfied smile on his face. "So," he asked, "what do you think?"

David was surprised by the question. "What do *I* think?" he replied. "Well, I haven't really had time to think about it. I suppose it's nice to be locally-owned and independent; on the other hand..."

"It's great news," Simon pronounced definitively. "Globe Two is a large international company, with global reach and offices in fifty countries. That's a fantastic network to tap into. We couldn't have done that before. Without this, where do you think TLO was going to be in five years, David?"

David suspected there was a right and a wrong answer to this one as well. "Well, with more and more market consolidations," he ventured, "I suppose growth was going to be difficult, unless we bought someone ourselves."

"Toast!" Simon declared. "There's simply no room any more for a boutique play in our business space."

"How long have you known?" David asked, thinking aloud.

Simon's smile faded and his eyes narrowed; he appeared to consider whether his influence and seniority within the company were being called into question. "A month or two," he replied defensively. "I had to know because of the due diligence that Globe Two were performing. I knew it was definitely 'go' on Friday. I had to attend a lot of meetings here and take stacks of calls on Saturday and Sunday." He shook his head slowly. "Ruined my weekend!" The satisfied expression returned to his face; David suspected that Simon's weekend had been anything but ruined.

"Do we all get to wear the badge?" David asked jokily, nodding towards Simon's lapel.

"Yes," Simon replied seriously, "everyone gets the Globe Two pin." He turned and pulled the badge on his jacket as far as it would come towards him and squinted at it. "Though I think this particular one is reserved for SVPs and above. Yours may be a slightly different design."

"I look forward to receiving it," David said quietly.

Simon's expression suggested he had heard the irony, was disappointed by it, but wasn't going to bother to respond directly. "Some friendly advice, David," he replied, "since we're now in an entirely new ball game, individually and corporately. Tad says he likes to think of Globe Two as a 'family company'. Which means these guys like their employees to be steady family types. I don't mean they don't have any divorcees, but they don't like anything out of left field going on in people's private lives. There have been some rumours in this office about you and some girl for a while, and now I'm told it's the one who turned up at the Charity Day. Frankly I'm surprised: I would have thought you'd set your sights a bit higher than that. Ignoring the way she behaved towards Mr Tweddle – and I'm not sure I'm entirely inclined to - she's obviously completely unsuitable, David, and I hardly need to tell you why – I think you know that already. In this game we're expected to be people with good judgment – it's the essence of our business relationships, and our business relationships are the essence of the business."

David said nothing.

"Now," Simon continued, "most of the business TLO has is not from the US, which is why we're such a good strategic fit, but personally most of yours is. You're not stupid, so you don't need me to tell you that you could overlap a lot with the accounts Globe Two already has domestically. Commonsense says they're going to be looking for added value in this office, and if they don't get it they could always pull the plug. Which is not to say you couldn't be redeployed if they move your current business back to the States, but for Globe Two to want to do that you have to have a face that fits, you have to buy into their culture. From today it's our culture. Do you get me?"

Fuck you, David thought. Fuck you and your fucking corporate culture and your smug superiority and let me show you where you can put your shiny new badge. I am an independent person. I sell my labour for a certain number of hours a week, no more, no less. I am not the property of the company.

Simon appeared to be waiting for an answer.

"Yes," David said meekly. "I get it. But there was actually very little going on with me and … And now there is nothing."

"Excellent," Simon smiled his approval. "Let's keep it that way. And what was it about she's now moved in with Guy or something? Did I hear that correctly?"

David wondered what Simon, and Globe Two, would make of Taz. "Yes, I believe so," he said quietly.

"Very odd."

"Maybe he's lonely," David suggested.

Simon reflected. "Could be. OK, thanks. Close the door behind you would you – I have some more calls to make."

Chapter Forty-One

Eva was sitting alone in a hospital corridor on an ancient, grey, stained plastic seat which had a triangular lump missing at the front, leaving a jagged edge. It cut into her skin and she had to part her legs uncomfortably to avoid it. She supposed she could stand up, but there was no way of knowing how long she was likely to be here. She would rather sit on the floor, but she suspected the staff wouldn't let her, and this wasn't the time to get into an argument.

She had had to pretend to be Taz's sister in order to be allowed to get into the ambulance with her. Guy had been too distraught to say anything, but his mother had cottoned on quickly and played along. Eva thought about the explaining she would have to do if Taz started talking. She had to hope it did come to that, because the alternative... Perhaps she'd blame the 'foreign accent syndrome' she'd seen something about recently on the TV. They'd be able to laugh about that afterwards; she'd look forward to that.

Nurses kept walking past and smiling at her, and at first she had thought that the smiles maybe denoted positive news, that they knew something hopeful about Taz's condition. But Eva soon realised that they gave the same practised, blank smile to everyone, from the husbands of women in labour to people coming to say their farewells to dying relatives. In their position she supposed she would do the same.

She noticed that, without paying any conscious attention to it, she had torn into small strips the polystyrene cup which had previously held the weak, tepid coffee she had been drinking for no better reason than that it occupied her mind for a few seconds. It reminded her of Taz tearing pieces off her copies of *Homeless Truths* when she got bored at the station. It seemed

371

very endearing now. She looked around for a bin and, when she couldn't see one, collected the pieces together and deposited them carefully on the lino under her chair.

The same one- or two-year-old child (she couldn't tell whether it was a boy or a girl) had come skittering along the corridor four or five times now, and although it smiled delightedly at the discovery of space and motion and Eva had made encouraging, sympathetic noises each time it passed, she was beginning to wish its mother, deep in conversation with two nurses under a notice-board further along the corridor, would pay it some attention and come and collect it.

Every thirty minutes she had to get up and go outside to call Guy, having had to promise to do that in order to prevent him from coming to the hospital. The most important thing – the second most important thing – was to prevent Social Services from becoming involved, which was far more likely to happen if a lot of people turned up with conflicting stories of who Taz was, where she lived and who she was related to. On the other hand, Eva really didn't want to be alone; it was strangely comforting to hear Guy's voice every half hour, even though he sounded frantic with worry and she kept having to tell him to calm down. He wanted to explain why he thought this was his fault, which she refused to listen to because, as she told him, it wasn't helpful at present. She knew there had been some sort of argument; in a twisted way that was comforting, because it meant Eva herself couldn't be entirely to blame.

She was surprised to find that the person she most wanted to talk to was David. Should she contact him? Why should he care? No, that was unfair; he would care. She tried to contact him after she had spoken to Guy for the fifth time, but both his office phone and his mobile went to voicemail. She felt an unreasoning anger towards David for not being available when she needed him.

The worst thing was that all that Eva could see was a pair of swing doors. She knew that behind them were Taz and a doctor and at least two nurses, but beyond that she knew nothing. The medics had been in there this time for about twenty minutes, and Eva had no way of knowing what they were doing, when they would come out or what they would say when they did.

She had decided that it was best not to call Amy, not only because, as far as Eva was aware, neither of Amy's parents was aware that she was still in touch with Taz – Sonia certainly wouldn't be, though it wasn't impossible that David was turning a blind eye to it – but also because the last thing Eva wanted to deal with now was a freaked-out teenager.

Until something happened or someone came out of the room, then, Eva was stuck alone in this corridor with its shiny cream walls, clumsily exposed piping, stark strip lighting and cloying smell of polish and disinfectant. And piss. All hospitals smelt of piss. It was the smell of the loss of dignity, of imminent death. But not in the present case, she was sure. Death had no business here. Taz had such a life force, though people who didn't know her properly didn't always see it. She *was* a life force; Taz had probably never been aware how crucial she had been to Eva's survival, especially in the early days. Well, as soon as she got the chance, Eva was going to tell her.

'Self-harmed' was what the nurse had written down on admission, which seemed like an odd way of putting it. Perhaps they thought that 'attempted suicide' constituted some sort of judgment. Perhaps it did – who knew what Taz had been trying to do? She had cut the arteries in her wrists, that much was clear. But – and this was the other reason that what had happened was Eva's fault – Taz had been cutting herself for years and Eva had just pretended it wasn't happening. She'd never actually seen her do it, but Taz was careful never to show her bare arms, which was a pretty blatant clue to anyone who wasn't trying to ignore it. Once or twice, from a distance, when

Taz didn't know she could be seen, Eva had caught sight of a set of deep scars running along the girl's forearms towards the wrists, as well as bruising higher up. She had taken comfort from the fact that the scars appeared faded – they had nothing of the livid quality of recent damage - and she had told herself that they probably represented a closed phase from Taz's past. Though there had also been the bloody towel she had discovered in the hostel two or three days after Taz had had her encounter with the Creep. She'd tried to convince herself that the blood came from the beating, but she'd known all along that it looked too fresh, so really it had been a complete cop-out on her part. But it just didn't seem possible that someone who had been through Taz's ordeal should then want to cause herself further pain; Eva didn't get it. Had Guy seen the scars? What had he made of them? Perhaps the doctor would explain everything when he eventually came out. Not that Eva really cared for any psychological theorising. Right now she just wanted to see Taz; to hug her; and then to pick her up and take her home.

Terry was leaning back with his feet on the desk and a pen in his mouth. He'd had two bits of news today, and they were both troubling him. For starters TLO had been taken over by Globe Two and it was the first inkling he had had of it. Colleagues were now telling him that they'd been hearing rumours for months, which was probably bullshit; but if it wasn't, how come T.R. hadn't known? Was he losing his touch? Worse, the sort of business Terry had been feeding to TLO through the arrangement with David Kelsey Globe Two had coming out of their arses. They'd almost certainly cancel, and Terry would have to find a new home for the business, but where? Kelsey would be out on his ear within the week, but even that wasn't good news: the point of Terry's recent activities was not simply that the traitorous shit should be destroyed, but that T.R. should be clearly responsible for his destruction. And on that subject, Charlie had come over to him very excitedly in Abbington's at lunchtime to tell him that the pikey girl had suddenly upped and left. If he'd expected a large tip he'd been disappointed; now that the slag had gone, what use was a greasy loser of a waiter going to be in future?

Terry sat and rattled his pen between his teeth. People were staring, but he didn't care. Business was about quick decisions: strategy and tactics. Strategy could wait till later in the week – there were bound to be other homes for his business. As for tactics, there was only one thing to do straight away: the pikey girl's bloke needed to be given a nudge and told to get his tartan arse down to London sharpish.

Eva thought it was odd how people could look so much more beautiful asleep than awake. Young children particularly. It was said sometimes about the dead, but Eva could never see that. She had not seen many dead people, but those she had seen had always seemed to her troubled, or in pain or bewildered, or simply…lifeless. The beauty was in the life.

Taz was sleeping now. In her normal life, when she was awake, she hid behind a mask of aggression or attitude or sometimes simple surliness; it took some time to get behind it, and some people never did, didn't try hard enough. Right at this moment though Taz looked so vulnerable and childlike and innocent. Well, maybe that was another mask because, although you couldn't blame her for it, whatever else Taz might be she wasn't innocent. Eva smiled to herself at the idea. And yet, in another sense, maybe innocence was exactly the quality that Taz had.

And would continue to have because she wasn't going to die. The doctor had told Eva that. Doctors usually tried to put the most optimistic gloss on things, but in this case Eva was sure that the man was right. Not least because he didn't have a sympathetic manner. Far from it: without actually saying so, he had given Eva to understand that he and his colleagues had quite enough to do already, treating people who fell sick as a result of diseases and other natural causes, without their workload being increased by people deliberately harming themselves. If it wasn't Taz's own fault, then it must be her family's and, of course, Eva reminded herself, today she was Taz's sister.

In which capacity there were going to be questions to answer, and things would get difficult. The no-nonsense West-Indian nurse had already made some reference to drug-taking in an accusing manner and Eva had managed to stare back blankly at her; but now that Taz's arms were uncovered the evidence was undeniable: you could see the needle marks on her skin. Eva hoped that they weren't recent. She had never seen Taz inject anything, she really hadn't. They had shared more than a few spliffs in their time, but Eva felt no guilt over that: it was absolutely clear that the experience wasn't new to Taz the first time they shared one, and it wasn't really dangerous anyway. But maybe she had known all along what Taz was up to: sometimes the girl appeared dazed; her skin looked bloodless and sickly; there were black marks under eyes that appeared hidden behind watery coverings; she got confused by her surroundings and she got violent, suddenly. So of course Eva could have put two and two together if she had wanted to. She hadn't wanted to.

She looked at Taz again and then bent forward in her seat and stared at her own feet on the shiny floor. She wanted to feel less alone.

Guy couldn't understand why his fucking mother couldn't drive this shit heap of a car any fucking faster. He looked at her face, in profile, as she drove. Calm, businesslike, carefully processing the data that her eyes and ears were providing to her brain on the state of the traffic, getting her limbs to react accordingly. Just slightly put out because once again she was being used as a taxi service by her grown-up son. But mostly because all this fuss was about that little...

"Is there any way, mother," Guy asked, trying but failing to keep the testiness out of his voice, "that we could go a little faster?"

His mother kept her eyes on the road but blinked two or three times in succession and coughed quietly, usually a sign that she was angry but concealing it.

"I'm going as fast as I can, darling," she replied in a patronising tone. "There's a lot of traffic as you can see for yourself. And there are speed limits. I don't want to kill us. You of all..." She realised what she had said, and her words tailed off in embarrassment.

Guy needed a punchbag for the moment. His mother was available. "I of all people should what?" he asked angrily.

"Nothing."

"I of all people should know the dangers of driving too fast, is that it?"

Guy's mother only sighed. Her face adopted the resigned, martyred look of someone who felt that she was doing her best but simply couldn't win. It was an expression she increasingly wore these days.

Guy knew he should stop now. But there was an undirected rage inside him, a feeling that had been building since long before today. "Is that it?" he shouted in her ear. He saw some of his spittle fly towards her; his upbringing reasserted itself and he hoped she hadn't noticed.

Guy's mother shook her head. "Oh really, Guy. If it makes you happy: yes, I did mean that. Satisfied now?"

Guy said nothing. They were negotiating a large roundabout. They must be half way to the hospital now; another ten minutes or so. It wasn't long to wait, but it seemed like an eternity after the hours he had spent on the phone trying to convince Eva that he should be with Taz, conversations that had ended with him losing his temper with her and shouting that he was coming in whether she liked it or not. The way things were going none of his few remaining friends in the world would want to know him by the end of the day. And if anything happened to Taz…He couldn't think about it. He welled up, he started to choke. He closed his eyes; momentarily he prayed for a second, fatal impact.

He opened his eyes again and looked up. His mother's face still showed the same determined, stoic expression. In a way he admired her: she had managed to cope with both the death of her husband and the permanent crippling of her only child, in whom she had invested so many of her hopes. So that now she had nothing left to look forward to, except years of looking after her son for a second time, having already been through the trials of the first. Presumably before the accident she had been expecting to be able to devote more time to herself until the time might come, late in life, when her son would have to look after her, as was the proper way of things. The fact that she didn't give up was truly admirable, but at the same time it was frustrating that she would never really show her emotions; you simply couldn't begin to read what was going on in her head. Even after she'd discovered Taz today she had been totally practical. She said it was a generational thing. Maybe it was, but you weren't obliged blindly to follow the example of your contemporaries, were you?

"I suppose you're hoping she'll die," Guy heard himself say.

His mother turned to look at him, although they were still in heavy traffic. "That's a wicked thing to say," she protested. "I'm wishing for no such thing."

"You hate her."

"I do not."

"You don't talk to her."

"Well... she doesn't talk to me either. What do you expect us to talk about? What on earth do we have in common?"

"I don't know. Me?"

"You want us to talk about you all the time? Even behind your back, when you're not there?"

"No..."

"So there you are."

"She thinks you resent her."

Guy's mother sighed. "I don't resent *her*, Guy." She was silent for a few seconds. "I resent our life. I resent the last few months. It isn't what I ever expected. Sometimes it makes me very angry."

"With me?"

"No, of course not."

"Are you sure?"

Another sigh. "Well maybe sometimes; I can't help it. But mostly with God: I really have problems with him these days. But I have no anger at all towards Taz. Why would I? Everything had gone wrong before she came along. I mean, she wasn't what I had in mind as daughter-in-law material a couple of years ago, but that's not her fault. I don't think we can even begin to imagine what her life has been like."

"She's good for me, mother. We help each other." Guy said gently.

"I know, dear," his mother replied with quiet sadness. "But don't bank on, I mean, you know she's not going to be around forever." She saw the anguished look on her son's face out of the corner of her eye. "I mean," she added hastily, "once she's better, some day she's going to want to move on. She's young."

Guy scowled at his mother but said nothing. He wanted to shout at her, to scream that he hated her, that she was jealous of his relationship with Taz. But he knew that she was only telling him what he, in his clumsy way, had tried to tell Taz. And that had left her lying on a hospital bed with her wrists slashed, fighting for her life.

Only one thing was now clear to Guy: if Taz died then he would not be able to go on. There would simply be nothing at all left to live for. Less than a year ago he had been a successful young man in the City, with a career that was really going places, money, a hectic business-related social life. Admittedly not much more than the occasional casual sexual encounter as far as women went, but that had been frankly all that he had wanted: he hadn't felt that he had yet reached the stage of his career where a wife and family were essential. But now Taz was essential to his life: he lived with the girl, told her everything, shared every thought and had no physical secrets from her.

Offered the choice, though, he would give anything to return to his previous life of shallow, self-centred ignorance with money, acquaintances he thought were friends and two legs that worked just like almost everyone else's. If the Devil wanted Taz's life in return was he prepared to give it? Or that of his mother, who was driving grimly on, unaware of her son's thoughts? It was a childish question and he dismissed it.

They drove into the hospital car park and went through the tiresome process of trying to find a space. Then they got out of the car in their now well practised, efficient manner and Guy's heart rate increased as his mother wordlessly wheeled him up the ramp into the seething chaos of the Accident and Emergency department. He realised that he must have made this journey a few months ago, in the back of an ambulance, but he had no recollection of it. The smell of the wards, as soon as he encountered it, was only too familiar though: it was the scent of many sleepless nights with no company except the occasional groans of his fellow patients, nights spent thinking about what life would have been if he had just made one small decision differently. It was the smell of fear, emptiness, desolation and despair.

Now Guy could see Eva. She was standing talking to a nurse and she wasn't crying. Taz must be only a few feet away and she was going to be OK; Guy was sure of it. He impatiently used all the remaining strength of both arms to leave his mother behind and accelerate along the corridor.

David was more than ever convinced that there was an inverse connection between the length of business meetings and their usefulness. And he suspected that another variable in the equation was the size of the company in question, with efficiency decreasing in direct proportion to expansion. If the last hour was anything to go by, he was going to be correct on both counts. Simon had started by giving what even by his standards was a particularly long-winded speech on the glories of the Globe Two takeover, without a trace of irony in his voice. Which was strange, because in the past Simon had thought Globe Two were naïve, unfocussed, too US-centric to compete effectively in the world market, inflexible and lightweight. He had said so, in so many words. And yet now they were everything that was most dynamic and exciting in the financial firmament: it was a great coup for TLO that it now found itself a member of the Globe Two family; it was a terrific strategic fit; synergies were obvious and the opportunities for staff almost boundless, both geographically and in terms of personal career development. It was a great day for everyone in this building, the headquarters of an organisation that they should all now think of as Globe Two UK.

David's attention waned and wandered. He thought about Eva. He would have to stop doing that; it was only going to make him miserable. If their brief acquaintance had made one thing clear to him, it was that he didn't want to be alone any longer, but there were other ways round that. Perhaps he could try online dating. It was the future: loads of people did it now.

Simon continued to talk, but most of the odd snatches of his speech that David heard seemed to be very similar to the words of Tad Crocker earlier in the day. Without, David noticed, any attempt to anglicise words that were not the same on both sides of the Atlantic: Simon wanted to check boxes rather than tick them, 'do the math' and have everything in place by 'January 1'. His accent had become a curiously nasal hybrid too.

David watched the faces of his colleagues and tried to gauge their reactions to what they were being told. He expected to find a lot of weary cynicism, at least on the part of those who had known Simon's previous views on Globe Two, but instead he encountered only serious, anxious expressions and rapt attention to Simon's every word. Because what the people here, departmental foot soldiers, wanted to know of course was whether they would still have a job in the new set-up; whether next month they would be able to make their usual mortgage payment; and, in some of the more fortunate - or overstretched - cases, whether they would still be able to afford school fees. David was no different: with his particular personal circumstances he needed the monthly salary payment as much as any person in the room. So why wasn't he paying attention like everyone else? The transfer of his job to India could have just been announced and he would have been completely unaware of it.

Simon seemed to be talking now of the need proactively to establish working relations with counterparts in other Globe Two offices, something that in his view would be an excellent way of demonstrating initiative from London within the Group, rather than waiting for the approach to come from the other side. And he wanted everyone to talk to all their major clients within twenty-four hours to explain the good news and ensure that none of them were picked off by predatory competitors, who, he warned, would not be slow in trying to exploit any perceived uncertainty. But everyone, he said, should be looking to pick up business as a result of the acquisition rather than lose it – aggressive targets were going to be set by senior management and closely monitored.

So, David smiled to himself, Oceania was allied with Eurasia and always had been.

A much more alarming thought came suddenly into his head: if everyone had to speak to their largest production sources, he would have to call Terry some time today.

Eva really hated David now for not being there when she needed him. She knew she wasn't being reasonable, but she didn't care. And yet she still found herself desperately hoping that any minute now he would answer his phone or, better still, by some miracle walk through the swing doors into the ward. She had now left a message on his mobile voicemail, something which she had been reluctant to do before; no specifics, but animated and forceful enough so that, she hoped, he would return the call as soon as he got the message. She needed support now, and no-one was giving it to her. Quite the reverse: other people seemed to be leaning on her because they thought she was strong. They were right: she was; but there was a limit.

Taz was still sleeping. Her condition was being described as stable, which was good. But now there was a danger that the medical staff were going to start asking all the wrong questions. Guy had turned up, despite Eva's best efforts to keep him away. A young man in a wheelchair - remembered by some of the staff - who had refused to reply to questions regarding his relationship to the patient, but had instead kept aggressively asking to see her.

Guy's mother had walked off on the pretext of fetching a cup of coffee; she had been gone for a very long time, though Eva had explained to her very clearly where the machine was. Eva guessed that she simply didn't want to be here. Perhaps it might be possible to play on that when she came back, and persuade her that there was nothing more to be done tonight and that she should return home. But convincing Guy that he should go with her, before their combined presence attracted the unwanted attention of an army of social workers, was going to be a much bigger undertaking altogether.

Guy's mood seemed to be constantly changing. To keep him quiet the nurses had allowed him briefly to see Taz, and his immediate reaction had been one of shock at her pallid appearance and the array of tubes coming out of her. He had sobbed loudly, but as he had then heard Taz breathing softly and seen that she appeared to be in no imminent danger he had wiped his eyes and appeared to calm down. But now outside the room he was quickly returning to an emotional state, one in which he wanted to blame himself for everything that had happened and didn't seem to care who was in earshot. Eva first tried the understanding approach. She put her arm round Guy's shoulder and told him that it was all going to be OK and that he wasn't responsible: Taz was lovely but you could never predict what she might do next.

Guy shook his head and looked up at her through glazed, reddened eyes. "It *is* my fault," he insisted, rather too loudly for Eva's liking. She looked around, but it appeared for the moment that no-one else had heard.

"Shoosh," Eva admonished him sympathetically but firmly, as though she were talking to a three year old. "You don't want everyone to hear you."

"It *is* my fault," Guy repeated, though more quietly this time. "Eva," he looked into her eyes imploringly, "I told her that I might not always be around for her."

Eva didn't know how to respond to this news. You didn't need to know Taz for very long to understand that if she had formed any sort of attachment to you then that would be a very stupid thing to say to her. And now the two people she was closest to had both said it to her in the course of a few days. Eva hadn't told Guy she was intending to leave, and she wasn't going to now. It required explanations she wasn't prepared to give. On the other hand, it would be the most contemptible hypocrisy to sit here letting Guy continue to think he was solely responsible. But what could she do?

"Well," Eva said finally, "we all know that nothing is forever. I'm sure that Taz does too. You know, maybe this was coming for a long time and there was nothing that any of us could have done to prevent it."

Guy shook his head again. "She got really angry," he went on, as though Eva had not spoken, "then she pushed my chair over, though really slowly as though she didn't want to hurt me." The recollection of this brought fresh tears to his eyes. "And then she ran off. And it was about an hour and I had no idea where she was or what she was doing and then my mother came home and saw me, and went in the bathroom and found..."

"Yeah, I know," Eva replied simply.

"I mean, she didn't even scream, when she..."

No, Eva thought; she probably wouldn't.

Guy sniffed and snorted the mucus that was accumulating in his nose and throat as a result of his tears, and began to pound at the armrests of his chair.

It alarmed Eva that people were beginning to stare. She decided that sympathy wasn't going to work.

"Will you just fucking stop?" she said in a half-whisper directly into Guy's ear. "People are looking."

"Let them."

"And then what? You know what will happen. If Social Services get involved we'll lose her anyway."

"She's all I've got, Eva!"

"Taz doesn't belong to... any of us, Guy," Eva answered sharply.

Guy looked round and the haunted expression on his face made Eva involuntarily shudder. She bit her lip. She needed to think practically. There was now no question of her going away any time soon, and if she pushed her luck too far with Guy she would have nowhere to sleep tonight. Why the fuck wasn't David ringing her back?

Guy said nothing. He slowly began to propel himself forward, then picked up speed and turned sharply left, causing Eva to retract her legs in a reflex action, though the wheel was at least two feet away.

Eva watched the back of the chair disappear swiftly along the corridor. She sat swinging her legs and gazing vacantly at the oversized numerals on the face of the large silver clock affixed to the opposite wall.

The red light was illuminated on David's office phone, denoting messages that he had not picked up. They could wait. It was probably more people from the market who had heard about the acquisition of TLO by Globe Two and wanted more information from the horse's mouth as it were; it might be the same ones that had called his mobile. There would possibly be one or two who would be genuinely concerned to know whether David still had a job; but more, he suspected, would be driven either by idle curiosity or by the desire to be first in the market with exciting news. Plus, there would be clients wondering whether their existing business relationship was going to continue, and competitors trying to work out whether the new situation gave them opportunities to muscle in on TLO's business (Simon was right about that).

Maybe Terry was one of those who had called; maybe he was the only one – the phone didn't tell you how many messages you had until you dialled the voicemail number - but David doubted it. He suspected, given the total breakdown in his relationship with Terry, that in future his former 'friend' was going to be communicating with TLO/Globe Two mainly via Simon, despite the latter's unconcealed contempt for him. Normally that would have been fine by David, but things had suddenly changed: Simon might try to delegate the work on the account to someone other than David, who now needed the agreement with Terry's company more than ever in order to justify his own existence. So, like it or not, David was going to have to ensure that he continued as account manager for Terry's business, unless he was prepared to risk the chill wind of redundancy at the age of forty.

He had picked up the phone to ring Terry three or four times already and had replaced it a few seconds later as the timed-out tone was emitted by the receiver. Everyone around him was on the phone, all having the same conversations with their clients. What struck David was how many individual conversations some of his colleagues seemed to be having. Just how many clients did some of these people have? Chris seemed to be on his fifth or sixth call. David knew that his own position had deteriorated, that he had begun to lose some ground at work, mostly since his divorce, but he had not previously realised that it had come to this.

He picked up the receiver once more and this time dialled Terry's direct number; it was still on speed-dial, a relic of better times.

"Ransome," Terry's voice answered quickly and abruptly. David was briefly thrown by this unexpected response and said nothing. "Hello," Terry filled the gap irascibly, "is there anybody there?"

David took a deep breath. "Terry," he said in what was intended to be a business-like voice, "it's David Kelsey."

"Oh, right," Terry replied coldly.

David found that he was almost relieved that Terry was apparently no more prepared to put on a show of friendliness than he himself was.

"Still got a job, then?" Terry asked.

"As far as I know. You've heard, then?"

"Of course. It's been a rumour in the market for weeks and, as you know, I keep my ear very close to the ground. Heard it was definite last night. When did you find out? This morning?"

David decided to ignore the taunt. He doubted that in truth Terry had known anything before the announcement. "Anyway," he continued, "we're calling our major business partners to assure them that it's business as usual and that the merger with Globe Two should, if anything, enhance the service that we are able to provide." David realised that he sounded like someone in a call-centre reading a pre-prepared speech, but he didn't mind that; whatever he said wasn't going to sound sincere. He wanted to get the call over as soon as possible.

"Business as usual from whose perspective?" Terry asked aggressively.

David cleared his throat. "Both parties."

"Really? You need to read your contract, Mr Kelsey. Despite my being screwed on most of the terms by you and your boss, the final document still gives both of us the right to cancel if the other one is taken over."

David put his forehead in his hand and closed his eyes as he listened. He knew that Terry was correct. The only salvation was that it was probably not in Terry's personal interest to cancel the contract straight away – he would need to have another partner lined up to take it over immediately or he would lose a large amount of commission – and, even if there was another interested party, someone at a higher level in Terry's company, taking a more strategic view, might be inclined to stop him. To ensure that happened, though, David would probably have to enlist the aid of Simon to have conversations at the right level, once more exhibiting David's own current weakness in the market.

"You have the right," David agreed calmly. "Doesn't mean you have to exercise it."

Terry snorted contemptuously. "Why wouldn't I?"

"Well, why would you?" David was aware that nothing that he could say was going to influence Terry's attitude - since that no longer had anything to do with business considerations - but he was angry now and wanted to hear himself make the argument and win it. He wasn't an idiot; he did understand his business. "It's a good deal for both parties, despite what you say, and I think you know that," he continued. "And the cancellation provision is there in case a change of ownership leads to a conflict of interest that wasn't there before, or to a reduction in financial strength. I can't see what the first might be in this situation, and as for the second, quite the reverse is the case: we're now much stronger financially with Globe Two's backing."

"We've had issues with Globe Two in the past," Terry said unconvincingly. "We're not entirely comfortable with them."

"Such as?"

"The point is, I don't think we will be in a position to continue this business relationship. We would prefer a new partner."

"I see."

"Business is business."

The smug self-assurance in Terry's voice told David everything he needed to know, and yet it seemed that, in spite of himself, Terry couldn't leave it there: he had to be absolutely sure that David was aware of his victory.

"I'm a very good friend, David, and a very bad enemy," he said triumphantly.

"Meaning?"

"I've said all I'm going to."

"Oh, go to hell, Terry," David replied in a weary half-whisper. He watched his colleagues, whose calls seemed to be ending in smiles and promises of lunch dates. Terry still seemed to be at the other end of the line, but he wasn't saying anything.

"Appreciate your support," David said loudly enough for his colleagues to be able to hear. Then he hung up.

Terry sat for a few moments savouring his triumph. It was slightly annoying that Kelsey had put the phone down just as Terry himself had been about to, but that was of no real consequence. If he knew Kelsey well, and he was sure he did, the guy would have a terrible stress-filled day and then be unable to sleep tonight, and maybe for the rest of the week. It really was possible, if Terry played his cards right, that he could get Kelsey sacked. Destroying his personal life would then be just a little extra entertainment.

Terry hadn't felt this good for ages. How best to celebrate? He daydreamed of a young girl with pouting lips and a little nose and great big eyes. The Alpha Male needed to assert his dominance; the instinct couldn't be repressed for ever.

David sat quietly at his desk for a couple of minutes before Jill came past with a matey smile on her face and said: "A penny for them". Why, he wondered, did people keep saying that? He smiled back ruefully but did not reply. He had not been thinking, at least not in ideas or concepts that you could explain to another person, so much as experiencing a feeling: a cold, lonely, vulnerable sensation, one that made him hate the solitude his life had recently degenerated into. He found that he was shaking slightly, partly from a frustrated hatred of Terry – how could he possibly have been so friendly with this guy for so long; just how bad a judge of character was he? – but also because he was not certain that he would be able to support himself, or Amy, in the future. He desperately needed at this moment to share his fear with someone, whether or not they were in any position to help. He wanted to talk to Eva right now. He wanted to ask her how she had coped when her fears turned into reality. He felt more respect for her now than ever before. He looked at the clock on his computer; Eva should have finished work by now. He would call her at Guy's as soon as he had picked up his voicemails, starting with the mobile.

It turned out that the first message was from Eva.

David left the office without offering any explanation. His colleagues stared as, in his haste to get to the door, he knocked some papers off his desk, leaving them lying fanned out across the carpet.

Chapter Forty-Two

Taz was in a nice place. It was so warm and comfortable; you could roll over and sink into its whiteness. It smelt clean, like flowers and sunlight. It was a field on a hill that stretched into the distance, as far as you could see, and there were trees at the edges, and a small breeze that ruffled the long green grass. And horses, lots of them but not too many, and they came up to where Taz was lying looking up at the sky and bent down and gently ate grass out of her hand. And she found some sugar in her pocket, lots of it, and fed that to them as well. Guy was there too, though still in his wheelchair, which was a bit sad for him, but it was OK. Taz could hear his voice, and Eva's as well - though so far she hadn't seen Eva - but she couldn't make out what they were saying. Now she saw Eva. She had been lying next to Taz all along, and she turned towards her and smiled.

There was something not right about her smile though.

Blood came pouring out of Eva's mouth, and her teeth fell out one by one, and Taz wanted to shield her face, but something was attached to her left arm and she felt a shaft of pain as she tried to move it. And her other arm was heavy and throbbing, and she was just too weary to lift it. Her whole body ached as though she had been lying in the same position for days. And now Guy was sobbing and choking and he looked as if he was about to have a fit; he shrank and shrivelled and disappeared into his chair, which was covered in mildew and rust. And the horses had gone, and it was dark and it was cold, and there was no moon and there were no stars, and nothing except Taz herself, trapped and unable to move. And right in front of her the face of the Creep, with his sweaty, beery smell, leering down at her. Now she wanted to cry because the foster woman had been right: Taz must have been really bad, and there was nothing she could do about it now.

Eva experienced a huge surge of relief as she saw David's thin figure emerge through the swing doors into the ward. All the emotions she had been trying to suppress came to the surface, most powerfully a shockwave of anger. Why had be taken so long? Why was he still stopping to hold the door open for strangers? What was there to look so fucking calm about? When he came up to her and smiled it took all her presence of mind not to slap him. She wanted him to hug her, but was sure she would push him away if he tried.

Instead he just stood with his legs slightly apart, and a worried and embarrassed expression on his face, waiting for her to speak.

The rotund nurse had caught sight of them in the corridor and interrupted before Eva could get a word out. "Good news," she said. A sweaty strand of her hair had broken loose and fallen across her ear; she paused to brush it away. "She's regained consciousness." She watched Eva and David's faces to gauge their reactions, and then adopted a matching look of hope and relief on her own.

"That's great," Eva replied. "Can we talk to her?"

"You're her sister, right?"

"Yes."

"And this is?"

"My...husband."

"And the parents?"

"Out of the country," Eva replied quickly. "She lives with us. Can we see her please?"

"Of course," the nurse smiled pleasantly. "I'll take you in as soon as the doctors come out."

"Thanks," David added with a friendly smile of his own. "That's great."

The nurse shuffled away. Eva appeared to be about to say something, but then changed her mind. David was going to ask her why he was suddenly married to her when he heard a wheelchair approaching behind him and instinctively made to get out of the way.

"What's going on?" Guy asked with the peevishness of a schoolboy who has been left out of a secret that the rest of the class knows. David turned, and he and Guy looked at each other for a couple of seconds without exchanging a greeting. Both expected Eva to answer, but Eva said nothing.

"Taz has come round," David said to break the silence.

"Weren't you going to tell me?" Guy asked. There was undisguised anger in his voice.

Eva still said nothing.

"Of course we were going to tell you," David replied in exasperation. "I've just arrived and they've literally only just given us the news."

"I'm entitled to know," Guy shouted. "I'm as close to her as anyone." The last part seemed to be aimed in Eva's direction. She did not react but sat down on a chair and folded her arms.

David understood that something must have happened between Eva and Guy before he arrived, but he had no interest for the moment in finding out what it was, still less in getting personally involved. He was as sure as he could be of anything, though, that if forced to choose between Eva and Guy, Taz would stick by her old friend. Even without today's events, which as yet no-one had fully explained to him.

"I can only repeat what I've just said," David said with a tone of forbearance that was intended to imply that his patience wouldn't last much longer. "They told us first because we were nearest, and we told you as soon as you arrived."

Guy blinked rapidly and looked around the corridor. "What did she say? I want to talk to her."

"You can," David replied in a businesslike tone. "We all can, when the doctors come out. You'll need to invent some sort of family relationship, though. Eva is supposed to be Taz's sister, and I'm supposed to be Eva's husband. Who do you want to be?"

"I wouldn't say before."

David didn't know what that meant. "Well, think of something quickly," he replied.

They waited for several more minutes. The doctors were taking longer than expected to finish whatever it was they were doing with Taz. Eva got up and began to pace up and down rubbing her fingers, while Guy fretted aloud over the possible complications that might have led to a relapse. Eva came over to David and whispered into his ear that she thought it would be best if, at least initially, she went in to see Taz alone, in case Guy's presence, after today's events, upset her again. David found that he had no stamina for the argument that would ensue, and answered without conviction that he thought it would be fine if they all went in together.

Finally the doctors, an older man and a younger woman, came out. The man spoke to the nurse, who pointed at and then beckoned Eva. The doctors spoke to her earnestly for a couple of minutes out of earshot of David and Guy. As subtly as he could, David physically obstructed Guy's wheelchair to prevent him trying to join in.

The doctors walked away down the corridor and Eva then came back with the nurse, who motioned them to follow her into Taz's room.

As they entered David felt the sudden embarrassment of intruding into someone else's intimate moment. Taz was lying still but her wide-open eyes followed Eva across the room, for one brief second fixing on David instead when she realised that other people were present. She saw Guy too, but her gaze registered no emotion and she quickly returned to scanning the comforting face of her friend.

Eva bent down, put her arms around Taz's torso and her head against the girl's cheek and tried to cradle her. Taz attempted to reciprocate but had only one free arm, with which she ended up touching Eva's ear and stroking her hair. Eva was shedding small, slow tears, and they made Taz's face glisten under the stark, artificial lighting.

Guy had parked himself a couple of feet away from the bed, on the opposite side from Eva, and was looking on anxiously but saying nothing.

David sat on a chair by the window, gingerly peeled back the curtains and looked out through the glass. He could make out the ugly silhouette of square, brick hospital buildings and the headlights of cars moving in the distance. A man walked past, carrying what appeared to be a load of grey sacks and flattened cardboard boxes. David found himself wondering how you ended up with a job like that.

The nurse excused herself and left, and Eva found herself a chair and wiped her face with her arm as she sat down. She pretended to give Taz a playful punch for all the trouble she had caused, and Taz smiled in response. David was struck by how young Taz looked, now that unaccustomed physical weakness had swept away the tough façade she normally offered to the world. Her face was grey, her eye sockets sunken. Her shock of brightly coloured hair somehow looked endearingly incongruous splayed out on a hospital pillow. It was easy to believe that she wasn't that much older than Amy.

Taz now looked directly at David and smiled, something she had never done before as far as he could remember. Eva looked surprised too: she broke off in mid-sentence, having become aware that Taz was no longer listening to her, and looked round at David as if to say that the next move was his.

David stole an awkward glance at Guy. Guy stared back. David picked up his chair and moved it next to Eva's. As he did so Taz unexpectedly reached out her hand to him and, after looking at Eva as though he needed her permission and getting no reaction, he gingerly took it. Touching the small, warm fingers brought back a memory.

"Hey, I've had a great idea," he said with the feigned jocularity appropriate to a hospital visit. "How about another go at the arm-wrestling? I quite fancy my chances this time. Let's say a fiver a go?"

Taz let out a short, tired laugh and squeezed David's hand a little tighter, as though she wanted to show that she could still take him on, but in fact there was now hardly any strength in her grip. David felt sorry for her in a way that he never had before.

"Give her a week to recover, and I expect you'll be regretting that," Eva said with a smile.

Taz nodded slowly, and David thought there was some renewed pride, and a hint of the old determination, in the way she tried to thrust out her chin.

David looked round at Guy to encourage him into the conversation. Eva noticed and bent down and gently ruffled Taz's hair. "Sweetheart, we don't want to upset you," she whispered, so that only David and Taz could hear her, "but Guy is here. Are you going to say hello to him?"

Taz's body squirmed under the sheets.

"It's up to you, love," Eva said in a soothing voice, leaning forward to stroke the girl's cheek.

"Does he hate me?" Taz asked almost inaudibly. She closed her eyes.

"Of course he doesn't," David interjected clumsily.

"Ask him yourself," said Eva, turning towards Guy.

Without warning Taz unceremoniously dropped David's hand so that she could wipe her eyes and then her nose with her fingers. David found himself in turn surprised and then amused and then disgusted. Eva tried not to laugh as David withdrew slightly, scraping the legs of his chair against the lino, in an attempt to put himself out of range should Taz decide to offer her hand once more.

Guy wheeled himself forward. "What was that?" he asked. Taz still wasn't looking at him and didn't reply.

"She's worried that you hate her," Eva said quietly.

"Of course I don't!" Guy protested. "How could I?"

Taz didn't react.

"But you, do you hate me?" Guy asked Taz. "I'm so sorry for what I said. I didn't mean…I'm not going to go away and, you know…"

Taz was now looking directly at Guy and there was the smallest hint of a smile on her face.

"Well," Eva said, making eye contact with David to indicate that she wanted his support, "why don't you two have a quick chat together? But C-G and I will be right outside if you need us."

David nodded in eager confirmation, and then he and Eva stood up to go.

"Guy's supposed to be your brother, by the way," Eva told Taz with a wry grin that she also directed at Guy. "I am your sister and C-G, David, is my husband."

"So we all have to talk with a Scottish accent," David said in his attempt at one.

"Don't confuse the girl," Eva admonished. "And what was that? – it sounded more like Bangalore!"

They all laughed. David gave Guy a friendly pat on the shoulder as he walked past him, towards the door.

Eva bent down to give Taz a parting kiss.

"Is Amy coming?" Taz asked very quietly.

Eva held her finger to her lips and slowly nodded.

Guy came out of the room about ten minutes later. A nurse had arrived to do some sort of test on Taz, the purpose of which she hadn't felt it necessary to explain, and Guy had been asked to leave. David thought he looked calmer, but no happier. He was cold and distant and David felt uncomfortable in his company. Eva had by now filled David in on what had apparently happened between Guy and Taz, and though that information didn't make David think any worse of Guy, it hung in the air like an unacknowledged secret. While he tried to make strained conversation with Guy, David kept looking down the corridor in the hope that Eva, who had gone to make a phone call, would be on her way back.

It was no less awkward when Eva did return. She looked slightly flustered and, when she did not volunteer the name of the person she had been talking to, David decided it was better not to ask. When the nurse came out, and reported that Taz was now sleeping, David suddenly felt the weariness of the day and suggested they all go home for the evening and return in the morning.

Guy shook his head vigorously. "You two can do what you like," he said airily, "but I'm not abandoning Taz, not now." He then wheeled himself away down the corridor before Eva could reply, leaving her to glower at his back as he retreated into the distance.

"He's upset, Eva," David offered by way of an excuse.

"We're all upset," Eva countered. "If he thinks…"

"It's not a competition."

"I know."

"And if it was you'd win it."

Eva looked up at David quizzically, and then put her hand on his arm. "Thank you," she said simply.

"She's his purpose now," David explained solemnly.

Eva withdrew her hand. "I know," she said with indignation. "I do get it. I'm not completely insensitive."

"Sorry." David smiled despite himself. "Anyway," he asked tentatively, "do you want to go? I can't see there's much more we can do here tonight."

Eva screwed up her face. "I'm not sure about leaving her with Guy. It kind of freaks me out at the minute."

David nodded. "I can understand that. But there are a lot of staff here. And Guy will probably go after we do, as soon as he thinks he's made his point."

"You think so?" Eva asked more brightly.

"Absolutely," David lied; it seemed to him far more likely that Guy would stay the whole night if they would let him, especially as the hospital was fully equipped with disabled facilities.

"OK," Eva agreed hesitantly. "It's only that I'm not sure I want to go back there. After what happened. Just me, him and his mother."

"He won't be there."

"You just said he would be."

"So I did."

Eva looked accusingly at David but then decided not to press the point.

There was an awkward silence, which became more uncomfortable with each moment that passed.

"How about you come round to mine?" David felt his heartbeat increase in the second that he waited for the answer. He had a dull memory of a conversation with Simon earlier in the day, but decided to ignore it.

"OK," Eva said quietly. "Thanks."

David waited while Eva quickly went to spend a few moments watching Taz's sleeping form in the darkened room. He debated whether to tell Guy that they were leaving, but when a cursory glance up and down the corridor failed to locate him David did not feel inclined to make any further effort.

"She looks really peaceful," Eva told David as she rejoined him and they began to make their way towards the exit.

"Good," David replied. "Now I can tell you about the rest of my day."

Eva looked slightly offended. "Does it matter?" she asked bluntly.

David's face was suddenly more serious. "Not compared with this. Any other day, though... TLO was taken over this morning by an American company and I might be out of a job."

"Seriously?"

David nodded. "Seemed like a big deal at the time."

Eva exhaled sharply and said nothing further.

Chapter Forty-Three

They arrived at the flat around twelve after a difficult
journey involving three trains, the last of which had become
becalmed for twenty minutes without explanation in a stretch of
forlorn Victorian suburbia only two stops from David's station.
The halt had seemed much longer than it actually was: one end
of the carriage had been taken over by eight youths of about
sixteen who had climbed on the seats, sprayed lager cans at one
another and exchanged random animal noises and aggressive
laughter. The other passengers behaved as though they hadn't
even noticed the group, retreating behind their newspapers or
into their phone and I-Pod worlds. The exception were two or
three people caught in the crossfire of lager, who calmly and
silently picked themselves and their belongings up and walked
back to the adjoining carriage.

David wondered what he was going to do if he and Eva
attracted the boys' attention. He wanted to suggest to Eva that
they too should move to the next carriage, but was worried that
she might think less of him if he did. Eva for her part was
watching the boys inattentively, as though there was nothing
about their behaviour that was unusual, nothing that she
couldn't cope with if she had to.

Eva looked more uneasy once they had got off at David's
station. She scanned her surroundings cautiously as they walked
to the flat as though she was expecting someone to emerge from
the shadows at any moment. David walked as close to her side
as he could, trying to appear protective and hoping that she had
not seen him shiver in the cold night air.

As soon as they entered the flat David excused himself and
went to the bathroom. When he came out Eva had made them
both a cup of coffee and installed herself on the sofa that had

generally been Taz's home during the week of her stay. Eva's familiarity with the place rekindled feelings of guilt in David's head. His mug was waiting for him by the chair he habitually sat in.

"Should we call, do you think?" Eva asked.

"They said they'd call us if..."

"Do you believe that?"

"Well, I wouldn't bet on it, but she looks fine now – there's nothing to worry about."

Eva didn't look reassured. She took out her phone, looked at it, then put it back in her pocket. "Maybe you're right," she said without conviction.

"I'm sure I am," David said positively. He told himself that Taz was young and strong, and she'd been given blood to make up for the quantity she'd lost. She was conscious and talking, so she was going to be fine.

"So, are you really going to be out of work?" Eva asked.

David shrugged. "It's possible. Some people will go, and there are definite overlaps with what I do. And I'm quite junior for my age."

"So you're not that expensive then? That should help."

David laughed. "I hadn't thought of it that way. I suppose that might help, except that a younger person doing the same thing would probably be even cheaper."

"Are you really that bad at your job?" Eva asked. "You always talk as if you are. Maybe you should do something else."

David was quiet for a moment. He knew what he wanted to say, but wasn't sure he wanted to say it to Eva. Was there any part of him that still wanted to impress her and, if there was, how pathetic and ridiculous was that?

"Sometimes," he began hesitantly, "I manage to convince myself that technically I *am* good at my job, but the problem is that my heart isn't in it any more and I just can't be bothered with all the politics and mutual backstabbing."

"And the rest of the time?"

David smiled nervously. "The rest of the time, I think that I'm simply not cut out for it. Unfortunately by the time I realised that I had responsibilities, including a daughter and a mortgage. And I couldn't go into something new at anything like the same money. Even if I knew what that something new was, which I didn't."

"You could move company."

"I could," David agreed, "if anyone else wanted me, but they're all pretty much clones of each other these days; it's the business itself I don't really like."

"Bummer."

David sat up straight. "Well, no… you did ask. Look, I wasn't asking for sympathy. I do understand that there are a lot of people in worse positions." He paused. "Much worse, obviously," he added in embarrassment.

They sat in silence for a few seconds.

"Do you think Guy has gone home?" Eva asked.

"I would think so," David replied. "If he was still there he'd have texted one of us. Just to make the point."

Eva took her phone out again and looked at the screen. "Nothing," she reported. "He was really pissing me off before you arrived."

David nodded. "Maybe you should text Guy's mother and tell her you're not going back there tonight."

"Really?" Eva leaned forward in surprise. "Why? Why would she care?"

David realised that his coffee was getting cold and quickly drank half of it. "Well," he said as he wiped a dribble of liquid from his chin, "I expect she likes having you around: the absolute nightmare scenario for her is where you leave and she is left with the two of them! And the poor woman had a terrible shock today: perhaps someone should check she's OK."

Eva looked David directly in the eye. "Maybe you're right," she replied. "David, there's something that I... "

David waited a couple of seconds for her to continue, but she looked embarrassed and he decided not to press the point. "I'll get some biscuits," he said.

When he returned from the kitchen with the biscuit-barrel Eva was staring into space. It appeared that she hadn't moved in David's absence. He proffered the barrel to her.

Eva thanked him distractedly as she took two biscuits but did not look up. "What happens to Taz now?" she asked. She brushed some crumbs off the arm of the sofa onto the carpet. "And what am I supposed to do about it?"

"You're not on your own," David assured her.

"Yes, but I *am*," Eva replied with a mixture of passion and despondency. She looked searchingly at David's face. "Really," she insisted. "I mean, I think she's going to be all right, physically. This time anyway. But I can't see how she can go back to that place with...with...him. If Social Services try to interfere she'll just run and end up fuck knows where. I keep saying I'm not her mother, and I'm *not*, but..."

"There's another possibility," David suggested diffidently. He was clear that he wanted Eva to move in with him again. Screw what Simon thought: the company didn't get to decide on his private life. Eva could bring Taz as well, if that was what she wanted, though it would complicate matters with Sonia and Amy. The biggest problem, which now occurred to David for the first time, was what Guy might do if he felt he had lost everything. David didn't want that on his conscience.

"It's not that simple, David," Eva replied earnestly.

"I see."

Eva shook her head slowly. "No, you don't. You don't understand."

The words sounded to David like a statement of fact, not a rebuff or rejection. "Then tell me, so I *can* understand," he pleaded.

Eva sat looking down at the floor and saying nothing. Her hair obscured her face and David could not make out what she was doing; whether trying to comfort her would be the best or the worst thing to do. Finally she looked up. Her eyes were red. Wordlessly she stood up and left the room.

Eva had been in the bathroom for more than ten minutes. David thought of busying himself by making more coffee, but decided that his body, exhausted though it now was, could not bear any more caffeine. He thought alcohol was inappropriate at the moment for either of them: it might make Eva say something she would otherwise want to keep to herself, and he did not want subsequently to be accused of tricking her. For his own part he wanted to be sure that he didn't say anything fatally stupid in response to whatever she might be about to tell him.

He tried to respect Eva's privacy, but there was no sound in the flat and little if any noise from outside. He could not hear her crying, but it was difficult to find another way to account for the amount of time that had elapsed since she had left the room. He thought of turning on the television, but that seemed somehow inappropriate and uncaring, even if he turned it off again the moment Eva reappeared.

The bathroom door could finally be heard opening after a quarter of an hour. David's heartbeat increased. He sat back in the chair and tried to appear relaxed.

Eva was now standing just inside the door but did not appear to want to move back to the sofa. She was trying to smile, but it was obvious that she *had* been crying: her cheeks were moist, her hair matted where it touched her face, and her eyes were still red. She brushed a tear away as she glanced at David.

David got to his feet and did what he now knew he should have done earlier: he walked across the room and put his arms tightly around Eva and rested his cheek against hers. She did not resist. He had no idea how long he stood hugging her, swaying from side to side and telling her that everything was going to be OK, just as he had soothed Amy when she had been a little girl. He felt contented, and at the same time ashamed of his selfish contentment. Eva was trying to tell him something, but it was coming out unintelligibly in fits and starts. And then, without entirely understanding what he was doing, but with a vague feeling that if he was wrong; if what he was about to do was inappropriate; if he had miscalculated her likely reaction his whole relationship with Eva was going to end right now, David slowly released her, turned her face gently with his hands so that it was directly opposite his own and planted a small kiss onto her wet lips.

Eva looked surprised, then uncertain. She had stopped crying. She brought her right hand up and David feared she was going to wipe her lip, but instead she flicked away another tear under her eye.

"It's OK," she said softly, as if sensing that David needed reassurance. But then, when David thought they might kiss again, Eva backed off and sat down, gesturing at him that he should do the same.

"OK," she said with renewed self-possession, producing a tissue from her sleeve and wiping her eyes and face, "you've always asked about me and now I'm finally going to tell you." She blew her nose, more loudly than she had apparently expected. "Well, I guess that's killed the moment, anyway," she laughed through the tissue and David laughed too, genuine laughter; he could feel the tension beginning to break. They could talk to each other, as they always had.

"OK," Eva said again, aiming the tissue at the wicker wastepaper basket, missing and stretching across to pick it up and deposit it directly. "Right, where to start? Shit, I'm really doing this! Last chance to back out. No, here goes. Well… I haven't told you much about myself, but I haven't lied to you. I mean, for example, my name *is* Eva and I *am* twenty-nine years old."

David leaned forward in his chair and nodded encouragingly.

"I had a boyfriend," Eva continued. "We were together since school. He used to be reckoned quite a cool guy. He was in the school football team, played for the district – there was talk that he might get a trial with a professional team, though for some reason, I can't remember now, nothing ever came of that. He liked all the right music too, had the right haircut, wore the right clothes. People either liked him or were jealous of him, and even then they respected him. You know how it is when you're fourteen or fifteen: you live in your own little world revolving around peer approval."

"I think Amy's at that stage at the moment," David agreed.

"Exactly. Anyway, a lot of the girls in our group fancied Alastair – that's his name - and some of them really had their noses put out of joint when it turned out that he had a bit of a thing for me. Because, well, I wasn't a geek or anything, I was sort of in with 'the crowd', but no-one thought I was one of the better-looking girls: there were a couple of real stunners; real bitches as well."

David smiled. "Way of the world."

"Anyway," Eva went on with a wave of her hand, "Alastair asked me out, and we got on fine, and I lost my virginity to him on my sixteenth birthday, because I said I wouldn't do it until it was legal. I think it was his first time too, though he said it wasn't. Too much information?"

David made an open-palmed gesture, which was intended to convey that Eva should continue.

Eva smiled and nodded. "OK. So after that we stayed together because we were having a good time. And I was really in love with him, as you are at that age, or think you are. But with love, if you think you are, you are, aren't you? What else is there? And one summer evening we sat and had a picnic on the beach together, just the two of us, and I made him promise that we would always be together, and I said that God was our witness. Seventeen we were!

"But the following year Alastair went to university and I didn't, and at first it was OK, just a novelty, and I went to visit him and he came home from time to time, but it was soon obvious that we had less and less to talk about and eventually it just stopped. I'm not even sure who ended it, if anyone did.

"Anyway, I got a job, had a good social life, went out with other guys. But never anyone I really wanted to... and I'm not sure I was even conscious of it, but Alastair was still there at the back of my mind.

"He'd gone off travelling after uni, and we'd completely lost touch, but then about four years ago we bumped into each other in the street. A bit awkward and embarrassing at first, but he looked good, really fit, and it turned out neither of us was seeing anyone so we had a drink together."

"He was kind of like he'd been before except a bit more serious and mature – which you'd expect – but I did notice from some of the things he said that he'd got a bit religious. I mean not just like everyone else at home - going to church is normal where I come from, not like down here – but this was a bit different. He'd met some people when he was travelling in the US, and they'd made him think, he said."

Eva broke off uncertainly. "You're not religious, are you? We've never discussed that, I don't think."

David shook his head. "Not at all," he replied. "I...some other time," he smiled.

409

"You know," Eva smiled back, "when you first came along, at the station, I did think you might be some sort of weird religious type trying to save me. You get some of those."

David tried to look offended. "I thought you thought I was a coffee poisoner."

Eva laughed. "That was my second idea. Anyway, going back to Alastair, it was a subtle sort of thing. It was more his language than his behaviour that started to change. God seemed to be directly involved in the smallest details of life. Do you know what I mean?"

David nodded. "I think so. It's like a religious Tourette's: if you take the words about God out of what they are saying it doesn't make any difference to the basic meaning."

"Exactly. Anyway, Alastair was still mostly good company and I still had this thing about him from way back in my head, so I put my doubts to one side and we got back together."

"But as time went on, gradually things started to change in his attitude to me. Or maybe they didn't. Maybe they had already changed by the time we met the second time and I was deliberately ignoring the signs. Alastair became less fun and more and more serious and controlling, wanted to know everything I had done or was going to do, who I had spoken to, where I was going."

"I can't imagine you putting up with that," David interrupted.

"No, well you didn't know me then. And it was all cloaked in the notion of him wanting what was best for me, and knowing what that was because God had told him."

"Did he hit you?"

"No. Never."

"Couldn't you have just...?"

"Ended it? It sounds easy enough when you are just telling the story but at the time I felt - I knew - I couldn't. I felt trapped and frightened and isolated, and part of me still loved part of him."

"But eventually you did? Or we wouldn't be having this conversation."

Eva shuffled uneasily on her chair. "Do you mind if I have a cigarette?" she asked shamefacedly. "I know you do normally, but I'm desperate for one. You know, after everything today and now this."

David got to his feet, walked across the room, parted the curtains and gently pushed the window open. The air was cold and smelt slightly damp. There was a crescent moon in the sky, but few stars. He fleetingly thought about Taz and Guy, wondered whether they were awake. "I'll find something to use as an ashtray," he told Eva as he turned back to face her, but she had already lit a cigarette and was drawing deeply and gratefully on it as she shook the match to extinguish it.

David walked towards the kitchen, picking up both mugs on the way and depositing them in the sink. He rooted around in a drawer until he found a small tin which had originally contained cough pastilles and was now full of rubber bands. He emptied it and then returned to the living room and offered it to Eva only a few seconds before the dead ash from her cigarette, which she was inhaling with all the pleasure of someone eating a really good meal, was going to fall into her outstretched hand.

"I never smoked at all in those days," Eva told him as he sat down. "Absolutely hated it. Do you not have any vices, David?"

David was aware that this question was not a compliment; it was often people's weaknesses that made them interesting. "Caffeine and alcohol?" he suggested with a slightly nervous laugh.

Eva did not respond. She inhaled sharply and looked up towards the ceiling again. "You were wanting to know how come I finally left."

"Yes."

"I fell pregnant."

David found himself automatically looking at Eva's stomach. He said nothing. Eva looked round the room in embarrassment.

"What did Alastair..?" David finally began to ask.

"He said we would get married straight away."

"And you didn't want to."

Eva shook her head forcefully. "It would have meant my last escape route was cut off. In a remote town with a child and a man who rules your life. There are hundreds of women like that where I come from, David, just the same as their mothers and grandmothers and generations before them, trapped and hopeless, resigned and defeated. I just couldn't face that."

"And your parents?"

Eva paused. The memory appeared to be a bitter one. "My wonderful, supportive parents were furious with me for bringing shame on the family, and insisted I had to marry him." She inhaled deeply again. The expression of contempt that played around her mouth didn't hide the hurt in her eyes.

David nodded. "And then?" he asked softly.

Eva realised that her cigarette had burned itself almost down to the filter. She leaned forward and stubbed it out in the tin.

"Then," she said quietly, "I sort of panicked and ran away. I had never even been to London before, but it seemed the natural choice and I just got on a train and came here. And I knew that I'd need to get a job, but I couldn't do that if I had a baby. And I knew I didn't want the baby, his baby, anyway. I started to see it as some sort of malignant growth inside me, or a monster that was about to burst out of my body, and I began to lose the plot completely. And before my sanity finally collapsed I went to see a doctor, and I told her it was killing me, and I hoped she'd tell me what I had to do.

"But she didn't; she said it had to be my decision. I so wanted the responsibility taken off me, but in the end I had to do it, and I did. I arranged to have an abortion, David. And it happened, and it was so clinical and unemotional that at first I thought I was going to be OK. But then I started to have these terrible fits of depression and guilt, I mean guilt like you cannot imagine, because all my life I had been brought up to believe that abortion was sinful, it was murder, and anyone who had one was going to hell. I mean, that was with my parents, long before I had anything to do with Alastair and the ideas he got in the US.

"I just couldn't find a way to work through it and forgive myself. I got some temp jobs, but I could never concentrate, and I either didn't do enough work or didn't do it properly, and in the end the agency took me off their books. Then I ran out of money, and suddenly almost without noticing that it had happened - which sounds ridiculous, I know - I was living on the streets, even more depressed, heading downwards without the slightest fucking idea of how to sort myself out, or even if I wanted to. And I got to a state where I really didn't care any more and I ended up doing anything, I mean anything, David, just to get food or sometimes just to get alcohol or drugs so that for a few hours the world would go away."

"But you dug yourself out. You overcame it."

Eva shook her head. "I don't think so. I'd still be there now, unless I'd ended up dead, if I'd had to do it all on my own."

"Someone helped you?"

Eva looked at David as though he was very slow on the uptake. "Taz helped me. The little spiky-haired monster came along. Suddenly there were two of us against the world, and she knew all the tricks of living that life, and you don't know how much better that made me feel. I wouldn't have survived without her, David. But where was I today when she needed me?"

"She's going to be all right," David told Eva reassuringly, sensing the unvoiced question. "You can't be with her all the time. You've never let her down."

"I keep thinking God is punishing her for being my friend, because of…"

David got up, walked across to Eva and put his arms round her once more. He kissed her cheek. "Taz is going to be fine," he whispered, "and so are you."

Eva embraced David unexpectedly tightly. "You don't know that," she protested.

"I do. I'm telling you."

"You don't!" Eva screamed. She pushed David away. "You haven't let me finish the story. He's found me, David. Alastair. He's found me!"

"How?" David asked incredulously. "When?"

Eva shook her head. "Last week. I don't know how. But I have to go away, somewhere less obvious."

David felt nauseous. The last few hours had taught him that he was deluding himself if he pretended that he didn't want – didn't need - Eva in his life, and now it looked as though he could be about to lose her after all. "You don't have to go," he pleaded. "What about Taz? What about," he hesitated, "…her.?"

"I know. But..."

"Then stay! What's he going to do? If he so much as…"

"It's not like that... I just can't bear to see him."

David put his hands on top of Eva's. She let them rest there but did not attempt to grasp them. "Then let me sort him out," he said with passion. "I'll tell him to his face."

Eva shook her head wearily. "It's not that simple. He wouldn't go away. Or if he did, he wouldn't stay away."

David thought for a second. "Then we go to the police. You're entitled to a life, Eva. Sooner or later someone has to make this guy understand that whatever happened before is history and he can't have you."

"You aren't quite getting it, David. It isn't just me he wants."

David tried to say something, but all that came out was an incoherent jumble of syllables.

Eva breathed deeply, folded her arms and looked down at the floor. "He says he wants to see his child," she said quietly. "He says he has a right to that."

She fleetingly looked up to watch David's reaction and there was an infinite sadness imprinted upon her face. David understood that no words of his were going to do any good. He had been unforgivably slow, but belatedly he had got it: it wasn't Alastair that Eva was most afraid of.

David put his hands around Eva's face, clasped her towards him and gently kissed her hair.

Chapter Forty-Four

Guy disliked himself for it, but the fact was that he was always consumed with jealousy whenever he saw anyone else with Taz: whoever they were, whatever their motives, and whether or not they represented any sort of threat to his own position. Amy was a nice enough kid as teenagers went, but Guy resented the fact that she had reached Taz's bedside earlier in the morning than he himself had been able to, and he was having trouble hiding it. It seemed to him that by her presence she was saying that she cared more or that he did not care enough, and he couldn't put up with that. He'd wanted to have it out with her as soon as he wheeled himself into the room and saw her stroking Taz's hair, but luckily he'd had enough presence of mind to control himself and not make a scene.

It wasn't his fault that he wasn't the first visitor of the day. Everyone knew that he had wanted to stay all night with Taz, but the hospital authorities wouldn't let him, so he had had to call his mother around midnight, waking her up, and then endure the humiliation of having to ask her to come and get him. They had driven back to the house in frosty silence for the most part; his mother, having grudgingly, it seemed, enquired after Taz's condition, had then asked if he knew where Eva was. Guy had replied that she'd "gone off with David Kelsey" in a tone that was supposed to convey the message that he was glad of it. His mother had looked surprised but hadn't pursued the matter any further. Then, on the way back to the hospital this morning - a journey she had refused to undertake until the rush hour was over, though she knew how desperate Guy was to get back there - his mother had again brought up the fact that Eva was not around and hadn't been in contact, as though he was supposed to care.

So David Kelsey's daughter had got there first; and now she was smiling awkwardly at Guy, which made things worse because it suggested that someone, maybe Taz herself, had told her what had happened between Taz and himself the previous day. Now, from her teenage perspective, she was judging him.

Guy smiled back. Amy came over and kissed him on both cheeks. She did that every time she came to the house and usually he didn't mind. She smelled of fresh soap.

"Hi," she was saying with exaggerated friendliness and concern. "How are you?"

"OK," Guy replied sombrely. "In the circumstances."

"Yeah, obviously." Amy's smile momentarily left her face. "Hey," she called across to Taz, "you're going to be fine, aren't you?"

Taz nodded slightly and tried to smile back. Guy wanted to take a better look at her and see for himself. He began to wheel himself forward and then, without asking or being asked, Amy started pushing the back of his chair. He hated it when people did that; he was perfectly capable of moving himself.

The chair came to a stop to one side of the bed. Because of the cabinet and various bits of equipment, tubes and wires, most of which didn't seem to be connected to anything, Guy couldn't get as close as he wanted to. Taz wouldn't be able to see him unless someone propped her up, and she didn't look ready for that yet. Amy sat on the end of the bed.

"Thanks for coming in," Guy said to Amy. "We both appreciate the thought," he added, before lowering his voice to a half-conspiratorial whisper, "but shouldn't you be at school?"

"Not this week," Amy told him as if he was some sort of imbecile who ought to know these things. She turned and mouthed something to Taz that made them both smile, and Guy was sure it must have been at his expense.

"Excellent," Guy replied amiably. "So how did you know that, you know...?"

"Eva called me."

Guy nodded. "Sorry, I suppose I should have. I guess I just couldn't think about anything except whether Taz was going to be all right. I haven't seen Eva. You don't know where she was when she called?"

"Here."

"Here?"

"Last night."

"Last night? You must have wanted to come straight away."

Amy looked uncomfortable. "Yeah, well I couldn't, could I. Mum doesn't... Eva said not to worry, it wasn't that serious."

"Did she?"

"Yeah."

Guy was aware that he was losing Amy's attention. She was replying to his questions but her gaze was fixed on Taz.

"And you haven't heard from her since?"

"A text this morning."

"Really. Do you know where she was?"

"Round at Dad's."

"I see."

"It's cool."

"Suppose they turn up here together?" Guy asked in a concerned tone.

Amy shook her head. "Dad has to work. He won't be here till the evening. Eva's coming in this morning. I don't know if she's working later."

"I suppose it all depends on your priorities."

Amy turned her face to one side and grinned at Taz.

"Still," Guy continued breezily after Amy and Taz had exchanged some words that he could not decipher, "your dad and Eva. What's that about?"

"It's great if it happens," Amy replied calmly. "I mean," she told Taz, who continued to look up at her, "from Eva's side I'm like yuk, how could she possibly want to, it's my dad? But she's great, and she'd be good for him too."

"C-G's cool," Taz said quietly but clearly.

"There you go," Amy told Guy triumphantly.

"Really?" Guy replied, unable this time to stop himself, though he knew the last thing he could afford to do now was to argue with Taz again. "Not cool enough to let you two be friends."

Amy shrugged. "He doesn't ask; I think maybe he knows. It's difficult with Mum and all."

"C-G's cool," Taz repeated.

Amy laughed. "I'd love to call him that; it really winds him up, you know!"

Taz nodded at her and her face seemed for a moment to have regained a little of its colour. It wore a weak hint of the old mischievous smile that Guy hadn't seen for ages, at least not aimed in his direction.

Without explanation Guy wheeled himself round to the other side of the bed and, by doing so, managed to get Taz's full attention: her eyes followed him and continued to watch as he came closer and closer. There were fewer obstructions now and he was able to reach across and touch Taz's arm through the sheets. He realised for the first time how tired she still looked: there was a green tinge about her cheeks, black marks under her eyes and a certain forlornness and bewilderment in her expression, though Guy was relieved to find no hostility.

"Hey, guess what?" he told her brightly. "You know that photo album mother told you about and you always wanted to see?"

Taz gazed back blankly.

"You know," Guy cajoled her, "the one of me growing up and all that, how I was before the… you know…happened, which was why I didn't want to look at it any more?"

Taz nodded weakly. Guy noticed out of the corner of his eye that Amy was eyeing him strangely.

"Well," he persisted, removing the outer plastic bag from the parcel that had lain unexplained across his lap since his arrival, "I've changed my mind and brought it with me. So now," he added jocularly, hearing some of the desperation in his own voice and hoping Taz couldn't, "you can have a good laugh at me as a kid and a teenager, with dodgy haircuts and spots and terrible clothes!"

Taz hardly seemed to react at all. Guy thought that perhaps he could make out a small smile of encouragement on her lips. Or was he deluding himself? He decided to plug on, because…, because he simply didn't have an alternative plan to fall back on. He hadn't been able to buy Taz something he knew she would like in the way that almost every other person in the country would have been able to do with no problem, without even giving it a thought (and God knew she wasn't fussy: if you just bought her a large bar of chocolate or something, she could be almost embarrassingly delighted, depending on her mood) because in his own case it would have involved having to plead with his mother to take him to the shop, and that would just be too humiliating at the moment. Turning up empty-handed at the hospital when everyone knew all visitors were expected to bring something and everyone else probably would have brought something, was almost as miserable a prospect. Amy, he saw, had brought in an I-Pod, which was lying on the cabinet next to the bed. He wasn't sure whether it was a gift or a loan, but either way he was sure Taz was going to love it. He'd thought about buying her one before, but had decided not to for entirely selfish reasons: he had figured that she would probably wear the thing the whole time, and then he would have no-one to talk to. But now he saw it differently: he hoped Amy's machine was a loan, or, if it was a gift, that he would be able to buy Taz a more modern one. And they could sit at the computer together and manage the music library, and that would be great too, because it would finally get Taz to show an interest in the PC, which up to now had seemed to bore her to death. There were a lot of computer skills Guy would be able to teach Taz, and that would be something he would feel was really worthwhile rather than just a way of killing time. It would also make a change from the reading and writing stuff; it had been a great moment the first time that Taz had written both their names, and Guy had experienced a feeling of elation that he wouldn't have been able even to begin to comprehend a year ago, but since then Taz had started to lose interest, as if she couldn't really see the point.

Guy realised that he had been silently staring into space for the last few seconds, lost in his own reverie. Taz was looking at him oddly and Amy's face wore an embarrassed grin. The album, the thing that had seemed such a good idea, that had lifted his spirits back at the house when he had thought to bring it to the hospital, was sitting awkwardly, pathetically on his knee. He almost wished he had never mentioned it. But Taz had definitely shown an interest in seeing it in the past, even telling him once that she was going to find it whether he liked it or not; though if she had looked for it she hadn't left any trace of her search, and, now he thought about it, it really wasn't all that difficult to find. Maybe Taz had just been being polite. Except that Taz didn't do polite.

No matter. Guy carefully laid the album across Taz's stomach, finding a strange awkwardness in touching her, even through sheets and blankets, that couldn't fully be explained by Amy's presence.

"Can I have a look too?" Amy sounded interested, or maybe she just felt sorry for the crippled man and thought if she showed some curiosity Taz might join in.

"It's chronological," Guy told both girls and then, as Taz stared back uncomprehendingly, he explained: "It starts at the beginning and I get gradually older as you turn the pages. Now these you are going to love," he continued with exaggerated jolliness, "they are just *so* embarrassing! Look, I'm almost a baby in that one; it might even be a dummy I've got there, it's a bit fuzzy. Can you imagine that: me with a dummy?!"

Amy seemed almost too keen to see Guy with a dummy, while Taz, the person he was hoping to cheer up and make laugh, still looked blankly back at him, smiling only when she looked at Amy and saw her do the same.

"Can you see properly?" Guy asked Taz, who once more looked at Amy. Guy felt rising frustration, but managed to contain it.

"I don't think she can," Amy answered. "Perhaps if we…is it all right to sit you up a bit?"

Guy felt his physical powerlessness the most at moments like this. Twelve months ago he would have had no difficulty in moving someone as slight as Taz. Now he had to sit and watch while a fourteen-year-old girl did what he couldn't. And Taz gazed compliantly up at Amy while the teenager moved the pillows against the headboard and gently pulled her friend into a more upright position, looking to ensure that the tubes were not dislodged from Taz's arm. Once or twice she directed a guilty glance towards the door and satisfied herself that a nurse was not about to enter.

"There you go," she announced proudly, giving the pillow one last pat, "you can see now." She winked at Guy as though she was asking him to agree, and he smiled weakly back and nodded. He tried to reach across to move the album into an upright position, but only managed to drop it onto the floor. Amy immediately scurried across to pick it up. Guy closed his eyes, and had another of the moments that kept coming back to him every time his body failed him, the moment in which he didn't get into his car after all but for some reason turned round and went back home, and then everything was OK. He could hear Amy crawling around on the floor in front of him and had a strong urge, which he knew was unfair and hated himself for, to roll forward and trap her against the bed.

Now he had his eyes open once more, and Amy was on her feet, her face red from the blood that had run into it as she bent down to pick up the photos that had come loose. Taz was looking at Guy, and for the first time since yesterday's 'incident' (he couldn't bring himself to call it anything else inside his head) there was the normal familiarity in her gaze. He was surprised that she hadn't laughed: normally Taz laughed whenever she found something funny, without any regard to the social context or the offence she might give, and what could be funnier than Guy dropping all his photos on the floor?

"There's a few that I don't know where they came from I'm afraid," Amy told Guy apologetically as she held the album out towards him. "I've put them all together at the back."

"Thanks," he replied softly. "Sorry about that."

"Nothing to apologise for."

"Well, anyway. Look," he sighed, "I think if I have it I'm just going to drop it again. Can you keep it and hold it up in front of Taz, and I'll talk you through it."

"Sure," Amy replied uncertainly, looking across the bed as she did so. "Well, we'll need to both be on the same side otherwise you can't see what I'm showing her. Hang on, I'll come round."

She dragged her chair across the floor and then there was a moment's confusion as Guy manoeuvred himself out of her way so that she could sit at the head of the bed.

Amy sat down, arranged her hair and opened the album. She began showing Guy one page at a time to allow him to give a brief overall description before she presented the whole thing upright to Taz.

"Let's see," she said briskly a couple of pages into the album. "We've done that one. Turn over. What's this?"

Guy looked at the proffered book. "That's mostly primary school. There's the one with the cricket bat. Looks too big for me. See the trophy? We'd just won the district cup."

"Who's that with your mother?" Amy asked.

"My dad," Guy answered, hearing an awkwardness in his own voice that he couldn't really account for.

"Of course," Amy replied, embarrassed in turn. "Who else would it be? That's Guy's dad, bottom left," she told Taz as she held the album out in front of her. "See?"

"Yes," Taz said hoarsely.

Guy tried to move closer, but was blocked by the leg of the bed.

"Looks nice," Amy chipped in.

Guy wanted to be able to confirm it, but didn't feel able to with any conviction. It wasn't that his father had been a bad man, but he had simply been someone who found his work more interesting than his wife and son. He hadn't neglected them financially by any means, and there had been occasions when he would make an uncharacteristic effort (like turning up for a school sports day) or, more usually, by some sort of unexpected purchase. Guy didn't exactly blame his father, and he wasn't blind enough to his own character not to know that he had inherited much the same attitude to career advancement, which had stood him in good stead before the accident. But candidly he was never going to remember his father with any great feeling of warmth, or love.

"I can't really remember," Guy said finally, sensing that an answer was expected of him. "He died when I was eleven."

Amy appeared to be about to say something, but then changed her mind. "Right," she said brightly, "and what's next?"

Guy looked at the next page as Amy pushed the book over in an arc towards him. "Skip that," he suggested, "it's the same as the last one really."

HUMAN CAPITAL

Amy readily complied. "And this one?" she asked.

"That one? Oh yeah, I'm about fourteen there. There's the under-sixteens rugby first fifteen. See if you can guess which one's me. As a hint, I had a lot of hair in those days."

Amy obediently presented the open album for Taz's inspection. Guy didn't care whether Taz got the right answer so much as that she appeared to be interested in the puzzle. And she did. The quiet intelligence that Guy had always thought he had been able to identify in Taz showed in her eyes, which moved in lively concentration across the page.

Taz said something that Guy was unable to hear.

"What was that?" he asked keenly.

"Second. At the back," Taz repeated, now sounding weary as though the effort of raising her voice was sapping her energy.

Guy could no longer remember where he was in the picture. "Let me see," he said eagerly.

Amy lifted the album across to him once more, this time as though the weight of the thing was beginning to tell on her. Guy examined it carefully. "Well done," he told Taz enthusiastically. "That's exactly right. I'm really impressed; a lot of people have got that wrong."

"I wouldn't have got it," Amy added.

Taz seemed to enjoy the praise. She blinked a couple of times, and there was a small smile of satisfaction around her lips. Guy was keen to continue, but with the terrible timing that now dogged his life he was suddenly aware that he needed to go to the toilet. And unfortunately it wasn't something that could be delayed: since the accident he got much less warning.

"Just a sec," he said apologetically. "I'm just going to pop to the gents' for a second if you don't mind." He smiled broadly at Taz. "Won't be a minute."

Amy looked worried. "Are you OK," she asked uncomfortably. "I mean, do you need any…"

"I'm fine," Guy replied abruptly as he started to reverse the chair away from the bed. He looked at both girls. "Thanks all the same."

Amy and Taz looked at each other quizzically for a couple of seconds after Guy had left and then both burst into a fit of giggles. Taz subsided first because laughter seemed to be causing her physical pain, and Amy finally controlled herself by putting a hand over her mouth.

"Do you think he heard us?" Amy asked as she took her hand away.

"Dunno," Taz sniggered.

"Have you *ever* seen anything *so* boring?"

Taz wiped the end of her nose with her hand but did not reply.

"You feeling any better now?" Amy asked.

"Dunno. A bit."

Amy gazed thoughtfully down at Taz and suddenly felt the urge to cry. She'd always thought that Taz was as tough as she was cool. And how cool was it to have been living without either of your parents, with no teachers to piss you off, no-one telling you what you were and weren't allowed to do with your own face and hair, for as long as you could remember? Even Hayley Stubbs and her crowd at school couldn't compete with that: they were bigging themselves up if they'd stolen a random magazine from the newsagents, whereas Taz had stories about breaking into houses and stealing jewellery and stuff. Amy loved telling people that and seeing the shock on their faces. The fact that Charlotte and Becky, neither of whom Amy now went round with, told everyone that Taz was a psycho only made her cooler and them more lame.

But now Amy looked at Taz and saw that she looked really sad, and small, and vulnerable. She wanted to ask her what she had been trying to do yesterday, whether she had really wanted to...but she couldn't find the right words, or the right moment.

This was all too heavy; she hadn't been in this position before; she was all on her own; why wasn't *anyone* here to help her? Eva? Even her dad?

"Hey," she said brightly, "let's laugh at more of these photos of Guy and his boring mates." She began to flick with nervous rapidity through the pages of Guy's album. "Boring, boring. God, isn't that the worst acne you've ever seen? No, not Guy, his mate, I mean how gross is that? That guy should be wearing a bag over his head. That's even worse than Siobhan Lewis. She tries covering it up with *this much* make-up," Amy indicated a distance of two centimetres or so between her thumb and forefinger, "and thinks she gets away with it, but she doesn't: no-one talks to her."

"Gross hair," Taz said without interest.

"Looks like my dad in my parents' wedding photos," Amy agreed. "I was like 'didn't you have mirrors in those days?'!"

"Really stupid," Taz said wearily.

"Really stupid, yeah. Boring, boring, boring." Amy continued to turn the pages. "Oh look, here is one with my dad. Not that you don't know what he looks like already. Oh no, why does he always have to have that grin in photos? It looks like he's had his brain taken out. It's *so* embarrassing."

But Taz wasn't looking at the picture of Amy's dad; her focus was fixed on another photo on the adjoining page, and her eyes were growing wider and her face whiter. Then she closed her eyes, turned her head and started to squirm in the bed, as if she wanted to get away, but was being held back. Amy in her surprise remained motionless until Taz suddenly screamed in frustration and lashed out with her free hand, punching the book to the floor and catching Amy a glancing blow on the side of the face.

"For fuck's sake, Taz!" Amy cried out, holding her stinging cheek and giving Taz an angry, reproachful sideways glance in the expectation of an apology that never came. Taz was staring ahead with a look that Amy had never in her life seen on anyone's face before, a look of uncontrolled, mad, violent hatred.

"What's the matter, Taz?" Amy asked fearfully, quickly moving back out of range. "I only showed you some photos. They're not even mine. What is it?"

But Taz was no longer recognisable as her friend. Despite her weakened condition the look of ferocious distrust and hostility on her face was unmistakable. Amy wanted to leave. Someone was going to get hurt here, whether it was Amy or Guy or a nurse or Taz herself. Amy didn't want to be around to see it. She got up and started to back away towards the door.

Taz seemed to realise at the last moment what was happening. "It's the Creep," she said simply.

Amy stopped in the doorway. "What?"

"It's the Creep. In the photo."

"Taz, it can't be," Amy reasoned from a safe distance. "There are, I don't know, like x million men in London. What's the chance that the Creep is someone that Guy knows?"

"It's him."

The look in Taz's eyes was so resolute that Amy was instantly convinced that, although the girl couldn't possibly be right, she genuinely believed that she was, whether as a result of drug-induced delirium or simply because she had made a mistake.

"OK," Amy said, making her way warily back towards the bed. "Show me. But you have to promise to keep calm or I'm going to freak out and leave. OK?"

Taz nodded and Amy carefully retrieved the album from the floor for a second time, continuing to watch Taz out of the corner of her eye as she did so. This time, to her relief, her friend remained completely impassive.

"Right," Amy said, pushing back the hair that had got into her face and cautiously opening the album and placing it in front of Taz. "I think this is the page. Which one?"

Taz stared intently at the photo. She wiped her eyes quickly with the back of her hand. "Him," she said, pointing with her index finger.

Amy leaned across. "Him?" She looked up from the page in astonishment. "It can't be him, Taz. I mean, when I was a kid…"

Taz put her hand around a clump of her own hair and appeared to be about to start pulling some of it out. "I'm not lying," she tried to shout.

"No-one's accusing you of lying, Taz," Amy replied soothingly. "It's just that it can't be. So many of these middle-aged guys look exactly the same."

"I'm not lying!" Taz was becoming increasingly agitated, and Amy had to intervene quickly to steady the drip tube before it became detached.

"The only thing is," Amy conceded, thinking aloud in an attempt to calm Taz down, "there was something recently. I told you about it at the time? With this guy's wife?"

Taz was still now and staring up at Amy as if she expected her to go on. Amy didn't know what to say. She didn't want to believe it. She didn't believe it; it was too much of a coincidence. But she wasn't sure. Not any more. "I know," she said with sudden inspiration. "I remember he has an area of really white skin where he burnt himself or something when he was a kid. Where is it?"

Taz seemed to see something in her mind's eye. "His right hand," she said without hesitating. "And he had a long red thing on his neck."

Amy had forgotten that, but now remembered. A mark on a neck below a friendly face on a body sunbathing on a childhood holiday. "Oh shit," she said involuntarily. "Shit, shit."

"You promised," Taz said firmly, staring at Amy so intensely that the other girl looked away.

"Yes," Amy stammered, "but that was…"

"You promised," Taz interrupted. Her voice had lost its earlier feebleness. "You said Eva would never do it," she reminded her unwilling listener, "but you would. You said that."

"Taz," Amy pleaded, "it was just something you say, a bit like…"

Taz's large eyes stared directly back at Amy. "You and me are going to kill the Creep. You promised."

Chapter Forty-Five

David woke up and in the first instant of consciousness knew that something was better in his life than it had been since... since longer than he could remember. No, he could remember: since the first few months with Sonia. It was the same feeling, but in this instance unqualified by later memories.

Eva was still sleeping. David leant across and breathed in the scent of her hair. He caught her perfume on his own arm too and lay back for a moment to enjoy it. How long was it now since he had smelt of anyone but himself? It was the scent of liberation from solitude.

Making love with Eva for the first time had not been the big deal he had imagined it to be. Neither of them had suggested it in words; it had just seemed the obvious thing to do at the right moment when there was no longer anything further to say. To David's relief there had been none of the awkwardness that he knew could occur when someone has been a friend too long before becoming a lover, the strangeness of the newly revealed and unfamiliar body of a familiar person. And Eva had not held back like someone just using sex as a means to procure whatever else, material or otherwise, that she might need. That possibility had inhibited him in the past in his relationship with Eva, he now realised.

According to the bedside clock it was a quarter to seven. The alarm would be sounding in five minutes if he didn't turn it off. He had had only four hours sleep after an exhausting day, and yet he felt more refreshed than he had in a long time. He had fallen asleep without difficulty and slept without interruption; he could not remember when that had last happened. He had been troubled by no bad dreams and no periods of mental

431

confusion. He could not imagine being more at peace with himself.

But wasn't his feeling unforgivably selfish? He imagined Taz in her hospital bed. He saw the misery and fear on Eva's face as she told her story. He couldn't bear the thought that he was going to lose Eva as soon as he finally had her. Surely she understood that she wasn't facing things on her own any more and didn't need to go away. Didn't sleeping with him mean that? Or was it just a farewell gift? He closed his eyes again.

The alarm sounded, a disembodied emotionless whine that David quickly reached across to cancel. Eva seemed to stir for a few seconds but then settled back down and the previous rhythm of her breathing soon resumed.

The absurd thing was that now David was expected to get up and go to work. He could not for the moment think of anything that could conceivably be more trivial than his job: the deals, the clients, the money. Who could possibly care, what difference did it make?

And yet for the moment there was no way to fight the Simons or Juniors or Tad Crockers of this world. Reality involved things like maintenance, rent and food, all unavoidable and requiring money, which - in the absence of any saleable talent he was aware of - David could get only by continuing with his current employment, wretched though that prospect now seemed.

He got up and walked softly around the bed so that he could see Eva in the half light. Her face seemed disappointingly troubled, her features drawn together, her brow tense and lined. Although David wanted to let her rest, Eva seemed to sense his presence and opened her eyes. She looked up at David for a couple of seconds as she struggled to focus. She did not smile at the memory of the night, but, to David's relief, she did not recoil from him.

"How's Taz?" she asked.

"No news," David told her reassuringly. "They haven't called."

Eva sat up. "Have you checked voice messages?" she asked anxiously. "We might have slept through it."

"You gave them your number."

Eva switched on the bedside light, picked up her phone from the bedside cabinet and examined it. "Nothing," she said. "We should call them. What's the number?"

"They said they'd call us if...I'm sure everything is fine."

Eva looked at David reproachfully. "How do you know?" she snapped. "They're big places, they lose things. Or something happens, they can't find the number, they're too busy with some other emergency."

She found the number and called it. She impatiently redialled twice before the call was answered and she was put through to the appropriate ward. Then there was a further long wait which had Eva nervously banging her hand against the bedside cabinet and rolling her eyes.

"Yes," she said quickly as soon as she heard a voice at the other end. "I was w...what surname?" An awkward pause before she continued. "McKechnie, that's right. She's fine? Great. Tell her I'll be in later. Eva. Her sister, that's right. Thanks a lot."

She hung up and looked over at David again. "She's OK."

"Great," David replied. "I knew she would be. She's a tough little thing."

Eva blinked a couple of times and appeared to be irritated by David's words. He had intended them to be reassuring but knew that they might have sounded complacent at best, uncaring at worst.

"Are you OK?" he asked hesitantly. He braced himself for what Eva might have to say about the previous night.

Eva sighed: "I'm sorry, ignore me." She lay back and looked at the ceiling for a moment and then sprang into a sitting position. "I need to get down the hospital as soon as possible, just so I can see for myself. I'm worried about her with strangers."

"I can come with you if you like."

"You need to get to work," Eva replied quickly.

"I can call in sick."

Eva shook her head. "You said yourself: the company's just been taken over, they're gonna be getting rid of people and you need to be visible."

David tried to find a way to avoid the logic of what she was saying and couldn't. But he was disappointed that she wasn't making the opposite argument.

"Need the money, David," Eva reasoned with a smile when it looked as though David might be wavering.

David slowly nodded. "Yeah," he said softly, "you're probably right. But I'll keep my phone on this time. Meetings, whatever. So if you need anything at all, for whatever reason, whenever, just…"

Eva was getting out of bed, draping herself in the duvet and reaching for her clothes.

"OK," she said. "It's a deal."

David stopped in the doorway. "And you promise you won't, you know…, at least until we've had another chance to…"

"I promise."

David sat on the train and for once the petty antisocial behaviour of his fellow commuters didn't annoy him: if they wanted to share their music and germs with the rest of the carriage, let them. The fact that his sensation of wellbeing and relief of tension was probably to a great extent chemically and hormonally induced by sex with Eva – he deliberately hadn't calculated how long it was since he had last slept with a woman – did not bother him.

He wondered if, or when, he should tell Eva his own story. Last night had definitely not been the right time: I'll show you mine if you show me yours might be OK for the primary school playground, but it wasn't the stuff of which mature adult relationships were made. But he did want to tell someone, and soon. It was funny that no-one ever asked about anything pre-Sonia, or thought to enquire why he wasn't in touch with his parents. One day he would tell Eva about Cambridge, about Alex, about Isabella, about his own (deliberately?) incompetent suicide attempt, the unsympathetic hospital staff and the even less sympathetic authorities at Beauchamps College, who had made it plain he should leave (not that he had ever thought he could go back). He had always agreed with Eva when she told him that he couldn't possibly understand what it was like to be homeless: how would she react when she discovered that wasn't quite true? The problem with the story though, and why he had never told Sonia, was that he could not think of a way of telling it that allowed him to emerge with any credit. Until he could, perhaps it was best to keep it to himself.

David entered what the new signage already clearly marked out as the Globe Two building and made his way silently up in the lift. In the office people were running around and making animated phone calls; there was a buzz about the place that suggested that David was the last to arrive by an even greater margin than usual.

His heart sank as Jill told him yet again that Simon wanted to see him. Actually what she said was "Simon was looking for you", which had the effect of drawing attention to his starting time in a disapproving way. Usually David would have asked how long ago, but today he figured that he didn't want to know. He hung up his coat and made his way reluctantly towards Simon's office.

As soon as David came into his line of sight Simon beckoned him in with an impatient hand gesture. There was someone David did not recognise sitting at the other side of the desk.

"Trouble with the trains?" Simon asked testily, but David was saved the necessity of replying by the visitor, who stood up and offered his hand. He was in his late thirties, tall and broad with short, neatly parted hair and the beginnings of a double chin. His suit looked expensive and the tie, whether or not by the wearer's design, was displaying its *Salvatore Ferragamo* label. His handshake was firm and his smile friendly but without depth.

"Hi," he said, "I'm Jim Caramole, Globe Two International Markets." David noticed that a small badge in his lapel, set out in the corporate colours, said exactly that.

"David Kelsey," David replied. He saw that Jim was squinting at his jacket.

"No pin?" Jim asked David before turning for clarification to Simon, whose own badge was once again on display.

"Next day or so," Simon said simply.

"You gotta wear the pin," Jim told David before punching him gently on the upper arm and adding: "hey, just kidding. If you don't got 'em you can't wear 'em. Right?"

"Right," David agreed.

"Right. You gotta get these guys the pin, Si."

Simon smiled weakly. "I'm on the case," he assured Jim.

"Hey," Jim asked David, advancing across the room towards him and causing him involuntarily to retreat, "didn't we meet before?"

"I don't think so," David replied weakly, aware that his inability to remember anyone until he had met them at least three times had caused offence more than once in his past business dealings. "I'm not sure…"

"Sure we did. At the conference, in Chicago wasn't it? When was that?"

"Three years ago," David replied.

"Or was it in Denver the following year?"

David shook his head. "No, I haven't been since Chicago."

"Really?" Jim appeared nonplussed. "Why not?"

David shrugged. "I was getting less and less out of it every year. Same people, same speeches."

The look on Simon's face suggested that this was the wrong answer.

"Screw the speeches!" Jim shouted. "Networking is the name of the game at conference. Don't you want to meet your clients?"

"Well, yes," David conceded, though in truth he increasingly didn't care whether he did or he didn't.

"Sure you do. And not just your current clients. You gotta work the hotel bars and the lobbies as well. That's what I do. That's what Globe Two does. And guess what? We're the most successful company in the market. Go figure!"

David nodded and smiled politely. He had never thought that Globe Two was the most successful company in the market: the brashest maybe, but not one he particularly respected. He remembered a time, not so long ago, when Simon thought the same.

"Anyway the thing is," Jim continued, "I thought you were a pretty smart guy in Chicago and I like smart guys. I could be wrong, but I'm telling ya Jim Caramole is right eighty-five percent of the time, maybe ninety. Tad says what about the other ten, I tell him I'm working on it. So what do you say you come and work for me at GTIM?"

David looked at Simon, who gazed dispassionately back at him.

"Where?" David stuttered. "I mean, in Atlanta?"

"Sure in Atlanta," Jim replied, dismissing what he clearly regarded as an unintelligent question. "That's where our office is!"

"What about here?" David asked Simon. He felt a rising sense of panic and anxiously tried to compose himself so that he didn't say the wrong thing.

Simon slowly shrugged. "It's a new landscape," he said. "You're Globe Two: why do you want to do US business out of London when you have operations all over the US that can access it more easily and more cheaply?"

"You a family man, David?" Jim interjected.

David hesitated momentarily. "Yes...," he replied.

"Divorced," Simon added to David's immediate intense irritation. "One daughter."

"That's great," Jim grinned. "I have two myself. How old is she?"

"Fourteen."

"That's some age, isn't it?" Jim said in a comradely way. "She live with you?"

"With her mother." David squirmed uncomfortably. "Most of the time. But I like to be around."

"Sure you do," Jim nodded sympathetically. "Say, how often do you see her now?"

"Normally one weekend in three." David's discomfort was causing his voice to drop towards inaudibility.

"Excuse me?"

"One weekend in three. Normally. But I'm not far away if..."

"OK…" Jim appeared to be thinking for a second. "Well I'm a 'can do' sort of guy, so let's say as part of your compensation we give you one return flight a month to the UK. We can do that. Coach, but hey you can't have everything. You get to see your girl almost as much as you do now and, guess what, she has the coolest dad in the class because she can fly out and spend her vacations with him in Atlanta!"

"It's a good offer, David," Simon said seriously.

David knew that in career terms it definitely was: it was a job that would attract a lot of high-powered applicants if it was ever advertised. Yet here it was, being offered to him on a plate simply because Globe Two now owned TLO.

"Can I sleep on it?" he asked, knowing that it was a cowardly request, that he was deferring his decision for a day while perfectly aware that nothing was going to happen in the meantime to change his instinctive response.

"Sure," Jim replied. "Call me on my cell." He took out his wallet, produced a business card and handed it over. He smiled at David, then at Simon and stood up from his seat. "Oh," he said, "I guess the most important part, right? Based on what Simon tells me you're making here, you'd be looking at a forty percent raise."

He offered his hand and David took it. The expression on the American's face suggested complete confidence that it was a done deal.

Simon leaned across the desk to shake hands as well. "Great to see you," he told the visitor. "Take care."

Jim left the office, and although David knew that the conversation was supposed to be at an end – Simon was putting his jacket on to go to another meeting – he wanted to linger, though he didn't quite know how to phrase what he wanted to ask.

"It's a no-brainer, David," Simon said in a forceful tone, as if he could read his subordinate's thoughts. "You've got to take it."

"What's the alternative?" David enquired diffidently.

Simon leaned against the door for a moment and looked coldly at David. "As the man says, you're a bright guy: you work it out. Things have moved even more quickly than I had envisaged yesterday. We aren't going to be doing US business in London any more and we're fully staffed on the international side which, in any case, isn't something you have much recent experience of. Bluntly, it's the perfect opportunity to move to a new location and put your career back on track. You've got it in you, we all know that. It's just whether you want to apply it."

There were so many things David wanted to say that none of them arrived coherently on his tongue. "Thanks," was all that would come out. "I'll come back to you in the morning."

David sat at his desk staring into space for so long that even Chris eventually noticed and asked him whether he had had some bad news.

"No," David shook his head. "Potentially very good news actually."

Chris smiled and winked at David before picking up the phone for the umpteenth time in half an hour. "Well I just hope I don't look like that when I get very good news," he replied.

David wanted to run his job offer past someone, someone who had no interest in the matter, and though he was sure that Chris would tell him that he had to go for it, he thought it would help just to hear himself describe the situation aloud. He waited patiently for Chris to come off the phone, becoming increasingly exasperated as five minutes became ten and ten fifteen. He needed something to do to pass the time, but everything that he had been working on now seemed pointless if it was going to be transferred to the US. He looked at some papers on his desk but failed to concentrate on any of them.

He wanted to talk to Eva, but that wasn't possible either. She would probably tell him to go, but he would be upset if he thought she meant it, and she might feel completely betrayed that he could even think of doing it.

Chris was still leaning back in his chair, enjoying reminiscing about a day he had spent at the races with whichever client he was now speaking to, when David decided that no-one was going to miss him if he went out. He picked up his coat and hurriedly left the building.

He wasn't sure initially where he was heading, and felt only a vague, undefined need for space. It was a cold day, but there was only a gentle breeze and he had sufficient layers of clothing to withstand the elements without discomfort. He found himself drawn towards Tower Hill which, with its likely crowds of tourists, seemed to offer precisely the mixture of company and isolation that he was looking for.

There was a man standing on a box dressed in a now shabby but originally expensive brown overcoat, undone to reveal a mustard-yellow waistcoat, white shirt and red tie. He had a trilby hat perched precariously on his head and was announcing the forthcoming end of the world. He seemed remarkably calm in the circumstances, except when he was interrupted by a passing heckler - usually someone in a group keen to impress their companions; then he would raise his voice to threaten all that hell had to offer to unrepentant sinners.

David bought a can of cola from a vendor in a wooden kiosk and sat down on the end of a wrought-iron bench. A mother and pre-teen daughter conversing in some sort of Eastern European tongue moved up to accommodate him. He smiled at them; the mother nodded politely but the daughter, half hidden behind an oversized ice-cream in a way that reminded David of Amy not so many years previously, stared blankly back.

David watched the white walls of the Tower, shining in the winter sunshine. London looked at its best today. He would miss it if he went abroad. Or would he really? It wasn't often like this, and even if it was, he couldn't honestly say that he usually noticed it very much, except at moments such as this when he was artificially nostalgic.

The job offer had a lot in its favour. It was a chance to start again. He hadn't been happy with his life for a long time. This morning things had seemed different, but was that feeling any more than an extended afterglow? Was there really any objective basis to support the view that his life in England was going to get better? The Atlanta job was still in the same business, something that in itself he felt pretty jaded about, but perhaps in a new environment his enthusiasm would return. And if he didn't take the offer, and they made him redundant (or maybe they could just dismiss him if he refused to move – he needed to check his contract) then what was he going to do? He had unavoidable expenditure and no savings. No kidding: he really could end up on the streets at forty.

He hated the fact that he had so completely lost control of his own life that he was forced into this position. Maybe he had never had control; how many people did? Without control of your life he didn't think it was possible ever to be truly happy. But maybe you had to settle for less than that.

He sat up, inhaled deeply and then took a long draught of the ice-cold cola. So he had to take the job. Sonia wouldn't mind, so long as the cheques for Amy's maintenance still arrived regularly; she might actually prefer it. As for Amy: his relationship with her, he thought, had started to blossom a little over the last few weeks and months as the young woman started to emerge from the teenage chrysalis; but even so it would be naïve of him to imagine that with the rest of her life developing in the way that it was bound to do - university, career, relationships - she would miss him as much as he would miss her.

It all came down to Eva. If they had made him this offer a couple of months, even a week ago, it would have been so much easier to say yes. Then, for all that David had already become aware of his embryonic feelings for her, Eva's reluctance to respond and to share anything of herself would have made it possible for him to conclude that he should move on. Now in twenty four hours the whole game had changed. How could he move to Atlanta and abandon Eva to a life spent running away from her ex-boyfriend?

Why couldn't she go with him? It sounded ideal: to start a new life, all but anonymously, together. He couldn't believe that Alastair would track Eva to Atlanta. So that was the solution! David's spirits immediately soared and sank again as quickly as he saw the glaring flaw in the plan: Eva wouldn't leave Taz. At least not now she wouldn't, but maybe when everything had settled down again? Or Taz could go as well! It was a nice idea for a moment but completely unworkable: the US immigration authorities weren't going to admit a whole menagerie of unrelated people, particularly if one of them didn't seem to know and probably couldn't prove her legal name or age. And, if she could, might well have a criminal record.

He needed to be brutally practical, because the bottom line, as Simon would say, was that if he didn't go to Atlanta he had nothing to live on. The Machiavellian approach would be to ask Eva to go with him, and then if (when) she declined, the burden of the decision would be hers. He would look after her financially until she was on her feet; with a higher wage and lower living costs he would easily be able to afford it.

The only problem with this plan was that, inconvenient though it might be and try as he might to fight against it, he had begun to fall in love with the woman. It was no good telling himself that it was chemical and hormonal, that he should have outgrown it at his age, and that in time it would fade. It was akin to the sensation he had felt when he had first met Sonia, but all the stronger because, with the benefit of greater maturity, its origin was less physical. And it was not infatuation: he didn't idolise Eva; he could list a number of things about her he didn't always like. But he was falling in love with her nonetheless.

A pigeon scavenging amongst the dropped food wrappers came pecking almost up to David's foot. He watched it for a while, wondering how old it was and how much longer it would be able to survive before the elements or a predator or a malevolent human managed to destroy it. After a minute or two the pigeon tired of the crumbs from a ripped sandwich bag and waddled nonchalantly away. But it came too close to the Eastern European woman, who instinctively raised her leg, causing the frightened bird to flutter into the air and graze David's shoulder with a frantic wing as it passed by.

Chapter Forty-Six

Eva was impatient to get to Taz's room because, however reassuring hospital staff might be on the phone, there was always that feeling of trepidation until you could see the person for yourself. And, anyway, she missed her. When she had checked in at the nurses' station a few moments ago they had said that it was definitely OK to visit, so Eva was surprised as she rounded the corner to see that the door to Taz's room was closed. She put her head against the wood and listened for sounds of conversation but heard nothing. A young nurse was coming past and Eva asked brightly whether it was OK to go in. The young girl seemed perplexed by the question; she looked at the closed door, consulted a list on a clipboard that she was carrying, listened as Eva had done, then knocked slightly gingerly on the wood. When there was no response she slowly opened the door and put her head into the room. She stopped suddenly and Eva, who had been intending to follow her, collided with her back.

The door was now fully open. Eva could see that the bed was empty, the sheets disarranged. Some equipment had fallen over; tubes hung loose. Some photos were scattered on the floor. The window was open.

The nurse's face had gone white. "She was here when I last looked," she started to stammer, "with a couple of visitors."

"What visitors? A guy in a wheelchair?"

"Yes, and another one. Girl of about fourteen."

Eva's heart sank.

"Please stay here," the nurse instructed, trying to sound calm and in control even while she struggled to compose herself. "I need to raise the alarm. We may need you to assist the police."

The nurse ran off. Eva went quickly into the room and looked through the open window in the forlorn hope of seeing two girls trying to hide from view. But there was nothing to be seen except the red brick walls of other buildings and two large grey refuse containers.

"Taz!" she shouted forlornly. "Amy! You there? You can come back. It's fine!"

Nothing. Eva put her face in her hands. How could Taz have got out in her current state? Amy must have helped her, but why the fuck would she do that? And if Guy wasn't anything to do with it, where the hell was he? Another thought occurred to Eva; she looked at the space between the bed and the window, and then out through the window onto the ground, and was relieved that she couldn't see any blood.

Noises behind her now. Voices. Urgent voices.

The nurse had said police. No, she couldn't do that.

Eva turned and ran. Out of the room, past the young nurse, the ward sister and a fresh-faced doctor with a stethoscope round her neck, all of whom looked too startled to stop her. Into the corridor, but when she turned right towards the main entrance there was Guy, a matter of yards away, advancing slowly towards her in his chair with a calm, unassuming expression on his face. She made eye contact with him for a split second, enough to alert him that something wasn't right, then looked guiltily away.

Was she panicking or doing the right thing? Eva didn't know. She turned around and ran in the opposite direction, past several more wards and finally through the swing doors into the car park. She crossed it rapidly, grazing her hip against the door mirror of a car that was parked too close to its neighbour, then turned left into a covered alleyway and stopped.

She listened for a few seconds and could hear only her own breathing and her own heartbeat. She was as certain as she could be that no-one was following her and felt an instant rush of relief, immediately tempered by the knowledge that the hospital was completely infested with CCTV cameras and that they would have her fleeing image on at least half a dozen.

She started walking again. She needed to think rationally and sensibly. There was a problem but it could still be contained, put back in its box, if it was sorted out quickly. But could it? In what scenario could you get from here to Taz being back in hospital, where she needed to be, without involving police and Social Services? And in what alternative world did David not find out that his daughter had been exposed to a serious threat to her personal safety, and whose fault ultimately that was?

Eva breathed deeply, got out her phone and dialled.

Chapter Forty-Seven

Amy was beginning to think this was a really bad idea. She wanted to talk to someone but her friends were no use, her mum would go mental, and John didn't really count, though he thought that he did. She wanted to call her dad, but she'd been lying to him for months about Taz. Well, not exactly lying since she had never told him that she wasn't seeing her (and he hadn't asked); it was just that she had never said that she was. That left Eva - and if you thought about it, this was sort of her fault in a way - but Taz kept saying that Eva mustn't know where they were or what they were doing. And Taz was turning kind of weird.

It had been kind of fun in the hospital. They had planned it really well. They had to wait until the doctor had been and disconnected Taz from whatever the thing was that they had her hooked up to. He hadn't been very nice, and actually he'd been a bit rough with her as well, as if somehow it was all her own fault, which it was in one way. But that wasn't really fair. After that Taz could move about, but she still seemed a bit weak and Amy whispered into her ear (because Guy was now back in the room) that maybe tomorrow would be better and Taz upset her by saying that Amy was bottling it, which she wasn't. Then Guy said that it wasn't fair that they whispered things that he couldn't hear and they both smiled at him together and Amy said that it was just girlie talk.

Amy still thought that Taz probably would wait until tomorrow because she could see in the mirror they found that she still looked like shit, and she almost fell over when she tried to walk round the room. But then the fat nurse came in and said that the lady from Social Services was coming round in a minute and Taz sort of lost it and said she wasn't having that, and the nurse just snorted, said it was no big deal, just a few questions and stuff, but Taz said, right out loud, that this bitch should go and fuck herself, which was really funny at the time because the nurse looked really cross and Guy didn't know where to look. The nurse tutted and went off but then Taz just sat there like a statue and wouldn't reply to anything either Guy or Amy said. Then Guy said he needed another slash, and wheeled himself off, and suddenly Taz came back to life, got out of bed again by leaning against Amy's arm and said they had to go right now. She put Amy's coat on without asking and then tiptoed off towards the door. But to Amy's relief she soon came back and said there were too many people about, and Amy quickly agreed. But then Taz looked at the window that had been left slightly open and said that was how they were going to get out. She got up unsteadily on a chair and half threw herself at the opening, half fell into it. Now was the bit that Amy kept playing back in her head, because Taz didn't have the strength to get out on her own, so she started asking Amy to help her. Amy hesitated for as long as she could, probably only a few seconds but it seemed much longer, until finally, when Taz was getting really impatient and there no longer seemed to be any hope that someone was going to come into the room and stop her, Amy went and gave her friend a small shove until she tumbled through the aperture onto the grass outside.

For a second Taz didn't move, and Amy thought that she had killed her, but then the small body started rolling around, and Amy, after a last look towards the door (and telling herself that Taz would never speak to her again if she went for help) got onto the chair and climbed through after her.

It was a bit of a blur after that. Somehow they got to the taxi rank without being stopped and there was a line of cars and no-one waiting. One or two of the drivers gave them odd looks, but luckily the guy at the front hardly spoke any English and didn't seem to care who they were so long as they could pay the fare, which Amy showed him they could. They still bundled themselves into the car as soon as they could, though, and thankfully it moved off straight away. Amy was going to stick her tongue out at the other drivers through the back window, but in the end she didn't.

"Where to?" the driver asked, but he had a really funny accent and Amy couldn't understand him the first time. He repeated it, only clearer, and this time he sounded like he was going to get annoyed, and Amy was worried he might stop the car and throw them out. She looked to see what Taz thought, but Taz seemed pretty much out of it: her face looked green and her eyes were rolling then suddenly blinking and opening scarily wide. She wasn't going to say anything.

Amy gave her home address. She didn't know where else to go. She felt sick. She was crying a little bit. It should be OK, she thought, at least for a few hours: her mum always went out on a Tuesday, and John would be at work.

It seemed to take forever, but eventually, with Taz shivering and rocking from side to side, they arrived at the house. There were no cars outside – not Amy's mum's or John's or her dad's or the police – and none of the neighbours appeared to be about, though some of them were so nosey that you could never be sure that they weren't spying through their net curtains.

Taz found enough strength to get out of the car with a little assistance and stood on the pavement looking up at the house while Amy got ripped off by the cabbie, who pretended that he didn't have change or that he couldn't understand that she wanted any, and drove off with almost all the money that Amy had access to.

Amy liked using her own key, though she'd made out it was no big thing when her mum had told her she could have one. She quickly opened the door and put her arm round Taz and dragged her inside with her.

In Amy's room Taz fell on the bed without taking Amy's coat off and then found the remote and turned the TV on. There was some sort of cooking shit on, but the expression on Taz's face suggested that she was going to be content to just lie there and watch it for the rest of the day.

Amy pulled up a chair and sat silently staring at the screen for a couple of minutes. There were so many emotions welling up inside her now: fear, more like terror, of what she was getting into; guilt, for the trouble she was causing, and in case something happened to Taz and it was her fault. And an increasingly intense anger against Taz herself, who had got her into this situation and was now lying on Amy's bed as if she didn't have a care in the world. Amy was going to explode if she didn't say something.

"Taz!" she screamed, waving her arm in front of the other girl's passive face in a despairing attempt to get her attention. "What do we fucking do now?"

"Oh, shit. You're kidding me," David said wearily. "Well, she can't have got far on her own."

There was a pause at the other end of the line and then an intake of breath. "The thing is," Eva said hesitantly, "she's not on her own."

"Who's she with?"

A short pause. "I think she's with Amy."

There was a rushing sound in David's ears, and the people around him suddenly seemed further away. "My Amy?" was all he could find to say. He tried to compose himself. "How does she come into it? I mean, what the...Did you ...?"

"Look," Eva interrupted, "you can be as angry as you like after this is all over, and you're entitled to be, but it's a waste of precious time now. Where do you think Amy would have taken her?"

A little girl in a pink skirt held onto her mother with one hand and a balloon with the other and smiled innocently at David, who stared back blankly.

"I'm more worried about where Taz might take Amy," David told Eva bluntly. "But if it is the other way round, then I don't think she'd go anywhere except home. There'd be no-one else there during the day. I'll try her mobile."

"I've already done that," Eva admitted awkwardly. "Goes to voicemail every time."

"Have you?" David replied shortly. "How about Taz's?"

"I tried that as well. Just rings. I think it's still at the house actually."

"OK." David closed his eyes and tried to think rationally. "I'll try Amy. She'll probably pick up messages even if she deliberately isn't answering."

"Good idea," Eva agreed. "Just a minute." A police Astra came into her line of vision several hundred yards away; it appeared to be driving towards the front entrance of the hospital. Eva started walking again, putting more distance between herself and the ward buildings. "Sorry about that," she told David. "It's nothing."

"Oh," David said without interest. "I'll go to the house and see if she's there."

The singular pronoun jarred with Eva, but she knew that now was not the time to complain about it. "I'll go round some of the places Taz knows," she offered briskly. "Let me know as soon as you have anything. Sounds noisy there – are you in the office?"

"Down by the Tower of London. Doesn't matter." David stood up and simultaneously ended the call.

Amy was wondering how much trouble she was in, and how to stop it before it got out of hand. She hoped that Taz would fall asleep and then maybe it would be possible to ring her mum and get her to sort it out, get the police round or something. Mum wouldn't be happy, but there was a chance that she would be so relieved that she'd forget to be angry. The problem was that right now Amy was really scared of Taz. It wasn't likely in her present state that the girl could even hold a knife, but Amy didn't want to find out, and she also didn't want to be on the receiving end of whatever else Taz's currently confused brain might be capable of. As instructed, Amy hadn't been answering her mobile, but even picking up a message from Eva and relaying its contents – basically just to get in touch and not do anything silly - seemed to have really pissed Taz off. She refused to listen to the message herself, which was a pity because there was something in Eva's tone rather than her actual words that Amy thought might help to get Taz to see sense.

Amy jumped as the phone rang while she was looking at it.

Taz turned round slowly. "Who is it?"

"I don't know," Amy replied defensively before deciding that lying was not a good idea and that anyway she was not very good at it. "Oh no, I think it's my dad."

"Don't answer it!" Taz said aggressively.

"I wasn't going to," Amy protested. "Thing is, he never calls me during the day. So someone must have told him."

Taz, apparently unconcerned, was once again staring at the TV screen. "Listen to the message, you'll find out," she yawned almost inaudibly.

Amy did as she was told. She waited until the phone stopped ringing and the message was left, then called voicemail. "Dad knows you're out of the hospital," she relayed, "and that we're together. He's probably on his way round, but even if he isn't, he'll probably tell Mum, and even if he doesn't, she and John will be back in a few hours." Amy stopped abruptly, aware as the pitch of her voice rose that she was beginning to sound hysterical and that calmness was what was needed at the moment. Calmness, together with some sense of urgency.

"We can't just sit here forever, Taz," she pleaded. She was trying not to sound too pushy, but at the same time she didn't want to let Taz know that she was scared of her.

"Chill," was all Taz would say in reply. She seemed interested only in seeing whether the couple on the screen were going to finish converting their barn somewhere in rural France into a restaurant in time for the tourist season and before their money ran out. "Why don't the programme people just give them the money?" she asked after a pause. "Then everyone would be happy."

Amy didn't know whether to laugh or scream. "Because…," she began, "well, it would just ruin it, wouldn't it?"

Taz looked round as though she expected Amy to explain further, but Amy had other things to communicate now that she had Taz's attention.

"Taz, we have to leave," she said firmly and loudly, but then she hesitated. She had no idea where else there was to go; she had never had to find out. Maybe they could find somewhere for Taz, and she herself could come back and sleep at home. She wasn't sure that this was the moment to suggest that though; she didn't want to experience Taz's reaction if she thought that another person was letting her down.

"We're gonna kill the Creep, yeah?" Taz looked searchingly into Amy's eyes. Her gaze was surprisingly penetrating, even in her current torpid state, and Amy felt herself begin to blush.

"Well, Taz…," she managed to splutter before she got a grip on herself. If agreeing was what was needed to get Taz out of her house, she decided, then she was going to go along with it. "Yeah, sure," she continued more confidently, "like we said."

Taz sat up and swung her legs over the edge of the bed. She inadvertently put weight on her bandaged arm and winced at the pain. "How are we going to find him, then?" she asked bluntly.

Amy was acutely aware that Taz didn't fully trust her. "I don't know," she began, pretending to think hard. "Perhaps if we went to the station…"

"Your mum must have his address," Taz interrupted. "She have a book with addresses or something?"

"I don't know," Amy replied truthfully. "She sends out Christmas cards and stuff, so I guess she does. I don't know where she keeps it though."

Taz was on her feet and half way through the door. "Great," she said, "we'll find it."

She led the way unsteadily down the stairs and Amy followed. Amy thought she did know where the address book would be, if there was one, but she wasn't sure that she wanted it found.

Taz began pulling at drawers in the kitchen and scattering the contents as if she were burgling the place.

"Careful!" Amy said in what was intended to be a friendly tone. "This is my house."

Taz turned and looked at her suspiciously. "It's you and me together now, right?"

"Yes, but…"

"And you said you hated your mum."

"Only sometimes when she pisses me off. Most of the…"

"And John. He gave you that pervy look once, you said."

Amy breathed in deeply. She couldn't be certain where this was going. She thought somehow she was being tricked, but she couldn't see how. It occurred to her for the first time that Taz might actually be smarter than her. She wanted this to end and she wanted Taz out of her house, and there seemed to be only one way to achieve that.

"I've remembered," she said soothingly. "I think she keeps it in the desk in the study. Stay there."

To Amy's relief, Taz did not follow her. Amy did not like the idea of leaving Taz alone in the kitchen either; once in the study she rifled impatiently through the desk and quickly found what she was looking for.

"Tah tah!" she said with exaggerated delight, holding the address book above her head as she re-entered the kitchen. From a cursory glance around the room it did not appear that Taz had touched anything in her absence.

"Where does he live?" Taz asked directly.

"Somewhere in Kent," Amy replied, putting the open book down on the table. Taz peered at it guardedly. Amy couldn't tell whether Taz was able to read it and wasn't about to ask; in any event her mother's handwriting wasn't the clearest in the world.

"Is that a long way?" Taz wanted to know.

"It is," Amy answered emphatically, hoping that the distance might put Taz off. "I don't know how we'd get there." She saw Taz looking at her suspiciously again. "Trains, hitchhiking, whatever, I suppose," Amy continued, trailing off at the end and smiling in embarrassment.

Taz appeared to be deep in thought. "What about where he works?" she asked.

Amy shook her head and bent down to look at the book again. "I don't think so." She saw something and wished that she could be absolutely certain that Taz still couldn't read. Otherwise she daren't take the risk of lying. "Oh, well," she said quietly, "there's a phone number. Might be years out of date, though, Taz."

Taz only shrugged. "Try it," she ordered.

Amy found the landline phone and began to dial. Then she hung up, dialled the code to withhold her own number and punched in the digits from the address book. "Suppose he answers?" she whispered to Taz, who was now standing right next to her attempting to listen through the earpiece.

There was no time for her reply because a businesslike woman's voice quickly answered. Amy nervously gave the name.

"I'll put you through."

"No...Hello!" Amy shouted in panic, preparing to hang up quickly if the call was connected, but to her relief the woman was still at the other end of the line. "I just," she cleared her throat and tried to make her voice sound deeper and posher, like an adult, "I just wished to confirm that he works for you. I have a parcel for him. Could I have your address please?"

Amy scurried across the kitchen with the phone cradled under her chin, rooting frantically around in the dishevelled drawers until she found a pen and paper. She quickly wrote something down, mumbled thanks and hung up. Then she read the address out to Taz. "It's in the City, near to where Dad works, I think," she added.

Taz nodded. "It's OK round there," she said approvingly. "Rich people. Some of them are nice. Sometimes they just give you money and don't even want to do anything."

Arriving at last in front of the house, David didn't know what to do. He stood for a few seconds looking up at the windows and trying to regain his breath. The train had arrived almost twenty minutes later than scheduled, without explanation – not that he cared what the reason might be – and he had become increasingly frustrated as the carriage lurched slowly forward a few yards each time before coming to a halt again. He had tried to employ the time usefully, repeatedly calling Amy's mobile, but it had immediately gone to voicemail each time, which suggested it was now switched off. Why was that? Would Amy do that? Why would someone else want to? David had realised that his stress was showing because he had begun to get strange looks from the sprinkling of passengers around him, and one middle-aged woman had shuffled uncomfortably in her seat as though she wanted to move away from him but daren't. Too bad; he couldn't worry about them.

He had run some of the way from the station to the house and walked so quickly for the remainder that the muscles at the back of his legs had started to hurt. But he was here now. What to do? He thought there was a light on upstairs, visible through the window of the front bedroom and coming either from the hallway or from Amy's room, but he couldn't be certain. If the girls were there and he rang the doorbell he would tip them off, which might allow them to escape. He could let himself in assuming that Sonia, or more likely John, had not had the locks changed, since he did still have his old key. There wasn't a burglar alarm, unless that was newly installed as well.

He brought the key fob out of his pocket and started to move towards the front door. He halted. The problem with surprise was what Taz might do if she felt threatened. Suppose she had access to a knife? He didn't think she would stab him if she knew it was him, but he couldn't be absolutely sure. He thought of Amy, how she might be feeling now, and desperately wanted to hug her. And he understood at that moment that as her father he had no option but to take the risk, whatever might happen to him.

The key fitted the lock and turned it. David pushed the door gently and it slowly began to open, but then it would go no further: someone had put the chain into its socket. David momentarily lost his temper and tried to force the door open. It juddered and there was the sound of splintering wood, but the chain held. And now David could hear raised voices and confused irregular footsteps, and what sounded like Amy's voice coming closer. Then it seemed as though she had stopped, or maybe she was being held back, and he was sure there was some sort of altercation going on.

"Amy?" David shouted. "It's Dad. Are you OK? It's all right. You're not in trouble."

There was no reply, but more high-pitched voices. It sounded as if Amy might be crying. She clearly wasn't the one in control.

"Taz?" David said as calmly as he could. "It's David. C-G. Everyone's worried about you. We don't think you're well enough to be out of hospital yet. You've had a horrible time and lost a lot of blood."

David listened but now there was only silence. He tried again. "It's not just me, Taz: Eva thinks so too. Perhaps you should call her? And Guy as well..." David trailed off; he wasn't sure what, if anything, to say about Guy.

No reply came.

"Amy *please*," David shouted in desperation, and when there was still no response he made a second attempt to force the door. It would not yield and left him winded and with a searing sensation in his right shoulder. He crouched down to recover and heard the sound of a key being turned and doors being opened at the back of the house. Still holding his shoulder he hobbled along the path to the side gate, arriving in time to see both Amy and Taz climbing over the back fence. David called out to Amy and for a fleeting moment made eye contact with her as she sat astride the fence panel offering a hand-up to Taz, who clearly was not in possession of her normal strength and agility. He thought he saw an imploring look in his daughter's eyes before Taz clumsily joined her and they both fell out of view.

David knew where the path led to: it was a dead end in one direction, which meant that the girls would have to come out round the corner by the school. He hurried there as quickly as he could, but the route Amy and Taz were taking was much more direct, and by the time David arrived he saw only their backs as they ran into the distance. He called after them, but they were now so far ahead of him that he could not even be sure that they had heard.

Eva felt a strange sense of relief when David's call came. He sounded pretty upset, but she thought she had been able to console him a little: where the girls were, she told him, was a pretty nice area, so they weren't in any immediate danger. Maybe they'd come back of their own accord and, if they didn't, there was still time to find them. She'd go up and join him and they would look together. He agreed without argument. Eva hung up, closed her eyes and breathed in deeply.

She had spent two hours trying to locate Taz in places that she knew were familiar to her: mainly parks and stations as well as some out-of-the-way alleys and walkways in the sprawling South Bank complex. It had been bringing back bad memories. She had never understood how Taz seemed to feel at home in these areas. Eva could associate them only with a pitiless, eviscerating solitude. She didn't know what was harder: seeing new people in places where she had expected to see familiar faces or seeing the familiar faces themselves, only so many months and years more weather-beaten and London-battered, and that much more out of it on whatever drink or drugs they were managing to lay their hands on.

An old bag lady called Crow in a staircase by the Hayward Gallery recognised Eva and told her she looked well. Eva quickly looked down at herself and supposed, comparatively, that she did. She responded coldly by simply asking whether Taz had been there, and walked rapidly away when the answer was no, afraid that a request for help might be coming next. She put the same question to a lot of others, people that her experience had taught her to find, but who had managed to make themselves completely invisible to the commuters and patrons of museums and theatres going about their business only a few feet and yards away. After the first new face shook his head at her question about the previous occupant of his spot, in a way that indicated that he actually did know the answer, Eva learned to keep her curiosity to herself.

Amy was thinking this might be cool after all. She cringed at the memory of what a wuss she had been only an hour or so ago. The look on Dad's face as she and Taz had made their escape over the back fence had been quite something, and then him puffing round the corner like an old man as they disappeared into the distance! Amy had been feeling a real buzz ever since. The two of them had gone into two or three small Indian shops where Amy had looked at the magazines and tried to look innocent - she was a sort of decoy - while Taz stole enough food and drink for both of them without anyone suspecting anything. At first Amy had felt really embarrassed, but she didn't now.

They sat on a bench in the park and ate pasties and crisps and shared a bottle of cola and then a can of beer that Taz had produced from somewhere. Amy told Taz that she was really great but Taz shook her head and said that normally when her arm didn't hurt she could have nicked all that lot from one shop, no problem.

Amy felt a bit light-headed after the beer. She laughed at Taz wearing clothes that were too big for her in all directions (Amy's own, borrowed at the house to replace the hospital pyjamas) though actually Taz could carry it off and didn't look that stupid. But now she saw them on someone else, Amy thought the clothes, particularly the pink top, were a bit immature. She looked down at herself and hoped she didn't give the same impression. The alcohol was really flowing into her brain now and it suddenly seemed a really good idea to tell a couple of old biddies who happened to be passing at the time to fuck off. She laughed at their reaction and turned to look at Taz, but the smile was quickly wiped off her face when she saw that her friend didn't seem to approve.

"We want to be invisible," was all Taz would say, and Amy just nodded and decided not to question her further.

The sudden frostiness from Taz momentarily burst the bubble of Amy's elation; for a few seconds reality returned and she wondered what would happen when she eventually went back home, what trouble she would be in. Mum would be furious, though hopefully she would blame Dad. Dad would try to be angry, but he just wasn't very good at it, bless him. She remembered them arguing over the famous mobile-snatching incident; it had been enjoyable to set them against each other – she'd done something similar a few times and it could be fun as well as usually ending with her being bought some sort of treat – but now that neither of them was around and she missed them, though only a bit, she felt a small twinge of guilt.

Once Taz became friendly again, which didn't take long, Amy thought very little about her parents, though she held onto the vague notion that the longer she was away the more relieved they would be to see her, and so the chance that she would be in trouble of any sort would diminish with time. And maybe she wouldn't be going home at all, ever. This was an exciting life: drinking beer in the sunshine in the park, keeping an eye out in case they were spotted and had to make a run for it. It was a bit cold now, and getting colder as the sun started to set, but whatever. Amy pictured Charlotte and Becky, sitting at home right at this moment, probably doing their homework for next term already, though they pretended that they didn't. How sad were they?

Most of the time it was just Taz and Amy, which was great. Taz didn't say much, but then she didn't really need to: she just *was* cool and Amy liked to watch her and copy her. A couple of times Amy was a bit worried for a moment that Taz still wasn't well: she had stumbled once or twice, as if she was a bit faint or something, and had closed her eyes for a while on the bench in the park. But mostly she seemed fine.

The sun had now completely disappeared. Taz suddenly decided that it was time to get on a train to the City and Amy meekly trotted along behind her to the station. They got in through a hole in the fence and had to cross over the line a few yards beyond the station to get onto the platform they needed, and although a few people had seen them do that Amy noticed that they looked away as soon as Taz made eye contact with them. Amy tried it as well and it worked for her too, though not as well. On the train they had a six-seat area to themselves, and kept everyone else away by putting their feet on the seats opposite, and again no-one said anything, even though some of the boring middle-aged people had to stand up. At the station in the City Taz showed Amy how to get through the barrier by tailgating someone with a ticket. When Amy tried it she stood on the heels of the woman she was following and instinctively apologised before she had time to realise that Taz could hear her.

Amy didn't think that she had been to the City since her parents had split up. Before then her mum had brought her on a couple of occasions to meet her dad before going off to see a show or whatever, but the station seemed much larger today, and the artificial lighting in the street appeared starker and brasher stripped of the warmth of her memories.

She really wasn't sure now what the plan was. It was early evening so she hoped that Taz didn't intend to do anything tonight. The idea brought a sense of relief. She didn't believe that Taz was actually going to kill anyone, despite what she said, but the more time passed, Amy felt, the more the likelihood of her friend doing something stupid would reduce.

Taz still wasn't saying much, at least not to Amy. She seemed to be comfortable in and around the station and had met a couple of people that she apparently knew.

One was a young guy with shabby hair and bad teeth who sat outside Tesco's asking people for change as they went in and out. His name was Fly or something – maybe it wasn't: Amy hadn't heard it clearly and didn't want to ask for it to be repeated – and he smiled when he recognised Taz, who seemed to understand what he was saying, though it was slurred and almost entirely incomprehensible to Amy. She also noticed that his arms and upper body were gently shaking as he gave a cigarette to Taz, and then the two of them smoked and chatted for a while without seeming even to notice that Amy was there. At home Amy was totally against smoking – John couldn't disappear off to the garden for one without earning a stern shake of the head from her when he came back into the house – but now she wanted to try it, and resented the idea that she was being treated as a child. Should she ask? What if she tried it and didn't like it? Or, worse, what if she started coughing and they laughed at her?

Suddenly Taz and Fly seemed to fall out about something. He kicked out at her and missed. She called him a cunt and he told her, three or four times, to go and fuck herself. Taz stood up and stomped off down the road and Amy, realising that she was staring at Fly, whose enraged, mottled face clearly showed that he did not like the attention, got up from her own uncomfortable squatting position – it was too dirty to sit down – and ran as fast as she could. She quickly caught Taz up and asked her what the problem was, and then repeated the question in case Taz hadn't heard it, but she did not receive a reply.

The second person Taz stopped to talk to was a middle-aged woman who reminded Amy a bit of Mrs McGovern at school, except that this woman's face was rounder and yellow-tinged, with evidence of a few recent cuts and bruises, whereas Mrs McGovern had a flawless white complexion considering she was probably over forty. This woman's eyes were more prominent and red as well; she looked bewildered and sort of lost and she was staring suspiciously at Amy, who now felt awkward about the comparative smartness of her own appearance, the newness of her clothes and the tidiness of her hair.

The woman sat by a wall at the foot of the stairs to the main station concourse with a shopping trolley bulging with plastic supermarket bags. Taz sat down next to her. Amy didn't mind too much when she wasn't invited to join them because the area next to the wall looked very dirty, as though people had been pissing on it or worse. The woman put her dirty gnarled hands on Taz's face at one point, but Taz seemed perfectly happy to let her do it, and sat there with her for a few minutes before getting up and walking back towards Amy, who by now had moved some way away, and was standing by the entrance to a newsagent's shop.

"She's a good girl," the woman shouted out in a husky voice, the words apparently for Amy's benefit. Amy smiled and nodded back at her in embarrassment.

Taz also smiled for a moment and then her expression was serious once more. "She says Eva has been round looking for us," she told Amy.

Amy found herself oddly excited by the news. "Why don't we call her?" she suggested quickly. "I mean," she added nervously when Taz narrowed her eyes, "we don't have to tell her where we are, just that we're OK."

Taz looked at Amy without blinking for a few seconds then shrugged, produced from her coat a mobile that she had somehow managed to acquire during the afternoon and, with her eyes fixed on the screen, quietly asked Amy for the number.

Eva's body was still shaking with rage. She'd wanted to call Taz a fucking stupid, selfish little bitch as soon as she had heard her voice at the other end of the line, but she'd had to contain herself because she was frightened that Taz would hang up if she started having a go at her. She had tried to keep Taz talking in order to win her trust so that the girl might agree to come back to David's place voluntarily. Win her trust? How was it possible, after all they had been through together, that she didn't already have it? And yet she couldn't deny that when that plan had failed she had tried to get information from Taz that would give away her whereabouts; and when that had also proved unsuccessful she had tried a third strategy, which was to try to make Taz feel guilty about involving Amy. She should have known better, because Taz simply wouldn't get why fourteen was too young to be looking after yourself, or that Amy's protected upbringing paradoxically made her that much more vulnerable. Taz had sounded calm but slightly confused and her speech was quieter than usual and abnormally slow. She had ignored requests to put Amy on the line and kept making barely coherent threats to kill the Creep. Eva had ignored these and tried to make her understand that she wasn't currently strong enough to be out on the streets on a cold night. Taz had just sounded as though she was getting bored with the conversation. All that Eva had managed to extract from her before she rang off was a promise that she would call again.

With a heavy heart Eva began to dial David's number and then changed her mind. She wasn't far from his station now; it would be better to tell him face to face.

Chapter Forty-Eight

Guy didn't like the attitude of the WPC who seemed to be questioning him as though he were a suspect in regard to some unnamed crime. She had been all sympathy to begin with, which he had ascribed to his disability – it happened a lot and he hated it – but as she delved more deeply into the circumstances of the disappearance, complicated by the fact that David Kelsey's daughter was involved and was a minor, she seemed to want to concentrate more and more on his own relationship with Taz. He hadn't tried to perpetuate the ridiculous fiction that David and Eva had given to the hospital staff, that they were all somehow related. David and Eva could answer for that when their turn came to talk to the police.

"So," the WPC said, pushing one side of her hair back for the umpteenth time, though it was short and hung like a pelmet, and immediately returned to its previous position, "you're telling me that you live with this girl, 'Taz' –is that right?"

Guy nodded. "She lives with us. My mother and me."

"But you can't tell me what her full name is, or her date of birth?"

Guy said nothing; an answer did not seem to be expected.

"Or even," the WPC looked up, "her age?"

"Not exactly," Guy agreed. "Seventeen or eighteen I would imagine."

"You would imagine?"

"I'm pretty sure."

"But she might be younger?"

The stare was hostile and penetrating; Guy needed a couple of seconds to formulate a reply.

"She might, but I don't think so. Anything is possible. I might be twenty-one."

"And how old are you?"

"Twenty-seven. I already gave you my date of birth."

"That's quite a lot older. Who else lives with you, Guy?"

"My mother, as I said," Guy replied coldly, finding that he resented this young woman addressing him by his first name. "I had my own place before the accident, but had to move back in with her because of, you know..."

"Of course. Just the three of you, then?"

"Yes. Well, no."

"Yes or no?" the WPC asked impatiently.

"There's a woman called Eva who was a friend of Taz and so I took them both in."

"And how old is she?"

"About thirty."

"Couple of years older than you. And she lives with you as well?"

"Yes. Though I expect she's about to move out."

"Why?"

Guy shrugged. "She's become very close to Amy's father."

The WPC sat up. "The plot thickens. Do you think she might be involved with this?"

Guy scratched his head. "It's possible. She was here earlier. I have her mobile number if you think..."

The policewoman looked down at her notes as though something was clear for the first time. "This Eva is the one who ran away from the hospital before we arrived?"

"Yes."

"Any idea why she would have done that?"

"You'd have to ask her."

"Hopefully we will. OK. And the other girl..." The policewoman looked back at her notes. "...Amy Kelsey. Do you know her?"

Guy shook his head. "Well, very slightly. She's the daughter of David Kelsey, who I used to work with."

"And she met Taz through you?"

"No, through him," Guy replied firmly. "He formed some sort of relationship with Eva, who I think was selling *Homeless Truths* at his station. Taz was her friend and Amy was his daughter, so they met like that."

"And you?"

"Me?" Guy noted nervously that the policewoman was now writing down his answers word for word.

"How do you fit into this curious little group, Guy?"

"Oh, well, David invited me round to his flat one weekend, and they were all there then."

"Really? And you said *Homeless Truths*. This Eva was homeless?"

"They both were," Guy confirmed. "Well, in a hostel, then briefly staying at David's until I took them in."

"That was good of you."

The reply sounded both sarcastic and suspicious to Guy's ears. He resolved to remain calm. "David threw them out one day because of some childish incident," he replied patiently, "and it was a cold night and they had nowhere to go."

"But he and Eva are back together again now?"

"I think so."

"Clearly she's the forgiving type. And did you like having Taz and Eva at your house?"

"How do you mean?"

"Was it a pleasant experience? For you?"

"Well, yes, I mean it was company. It got a bit lonely with me like this and just my mother to talk to."

"They were just company, then?" the WPC asked brusquely. "No more?"

Guy took a sip from the glass in front of him to give himself time to work out what he was being accused of. What could he be accused of? Was this woman trying to trap him into saying the wrong thing?

He cleared his throat. "Well," he conceded, "Taz helped to look after me sometimes – only if she wanted to – and Eva was living there, well, really just because Taz wanted her to. She had stopped selling the magazines and got some sort of job in a kitchen or something, doing the washing-up, I think."

"You're not Eva's biggest fan?"

"She's OK."

The WPC stared at Guy for a few moments as though she expected him to continue. "And was she involved in the incident that led to Taz's admission to A & E?" she asked finally.

Guy shook his head slowly. "No."

"So what did happen?"

Guy took another sip of water and looked towards the door. "Taz couldn't read or write, and I've been trying to teach her." Guy could feel a catch in his throat and stopped.

The policewoman smiled at him without warmth. "Good for you, and then what?"

"So sometimes she's a bit reluctant, and yesterday I was trying to convince her it was for her own good. I told her she would need to be able to read and write in the future because I might not always be there, and she, well, you can see, she got really upset."

Guy began spontaneously to cry. He hadn't planned it; he didn't like the sight of men crying.

The policewoman remained unmoved. "OK," she said, flicking back the pages of her notebook so that the cover showed once more. "Well the first thing to do is to find these girls. We'll need Eva's number, Amy's father's number and address and any information you can give us as to where you think they may have gone. Places Taz talked about, maybe from the time she was homeless. We can check hostels and stations and other likely haunts, and should be able to get Amy's home address on the database even if we can't get hold of her father."

Guy wiped his eyes with the back of his hand and nodded. "Thank you," he said softly. "I'll give you all the help I possibly can, obviously. I just want her found safe and sound. Both of them."

The policewoman looked past Guy into the distance as though weighing up whether or not to tell him something else.

"OK," she said again. "Our only priority now is to get these girls back safely. I should warn you though that when we do, and we have more information about Taz, depending on what that tells us we may want to ask you some more questions to satisfy ourselves as to the nature of your relationship with her and what contact, if any, you made with Social Services. Do you understand what I'm telling you?"

"Absolutely," Guy replied compliantly. "Whatever you like once we've got them back."

The policewoman nodded and put her notebook into her jacket. Without offering a handshake she got up and began to speak into her radio, then turned and walked through the door, leaving Guy sitting alone.

Chapter Forty-Nine

David and Eva travelled back into the City in silence. To Eva's mind they had wasted two hours looking for the girls close to Amy's house, because the more she thought about Taz's likely behaviour, and the more she reanalysed in her head the earlier phone conversation and the bustling background sounds, the more she was convinced that Taz would have taken Amy to somewhere she knew in central London. The question was whether she was bright enough, or devious enough, deliberately to choose somewhere that Eva didn't know.

David was ashen-faced and staring directly in front of him, and Eva didn't know whether or not it would be helpful to put a comforting arm round him; in the end she decided not to. She had also chosen to stay out of the way when he had had to go and tell his ex-wife what was going on. He hadn't tried to persuade her to do otherwise, and she had felt doubly sure that she had made the right decision when, observing from a safe distance, she had seen the police car draw up outside the house. She had made a few circuits of the area to keep warm as she waited for David to come out. It seemed like the sort of quiet, genteel, slightly dull sort of place that her parents lived in. She couldn't picture David living here, though, despite the fact that she knew he had. The house was too modern, too large, suggestive of success, and David just didn't have that air, whatever other qualities he might possess. Basically he was a loser. She didn't mean that unkindly; it was just the simple truth. She herself was too, so was Guy, so was Taz. That was the only thing they all had in common. It didn't matter how each of them had got there, through character flaw or circumstance. They would maybe win a few battles along the way, but Eva was sure they were all destined to lose the war.

When he emerged from the house David didn't need to tell Eva that Sonia blamed him for everything: she could read it deeply etched onto his sad, weary face. He had aged in a day. She wanted to tell him that Sonia had never deserved him in the first place, but it could wait for another time.

David said hardly a word after that. He hadn't once reproached Eva for keeping Amy and Taz in contact with each other. Maybe he was just so transfixed with fear at the thought of what might have happened to his daughter that nothing else mattered. Maybe he'd always known and blamed himself for doing nothing. If he did accuse her later, Eva had decided that she wasn't going to try to defend herself, beyond saying that at the time she had thought that she was doing the right thing. That would have to do.

The train was pulling into the London terminal. David was already on his feet. Eva felt butterflies in her stomach and noticed that she was perspiring, although it wasn't hot. It was just after nine and London looked familiar: cold and dark, impersonal and menacing; whoever you were, it didn't care whether you lived or died. The eerily lit empty office buildings served only to amplify the memory that was growing inside Eva: the debilitating terror of solitude. She knew it too well; she didn't want to experience it again.

As everyone slowly left the carriage as though this were just another normal evening, Eva remarked how David, despite his agitated state, instinctively stood aside to let her out ahead of him.

Chapter Fifty

Terry was really pissed off. The internet service on his computer at home had gone up the pictures, and when he'd tried to ring them to tell them to sort it out pronto he'd ended up with a connection to Poppadom City or wherever talking to some Pakistani who hardly spoke English, at least not with any accent that Terry could understand, and who seemed to think sounding subservient made up for it. After a minute or so Terry had had quite enough of that; he'd told the computer wallah to shove an onion bhaji up his arse and rung off. He'd tell Serena to sort it out tomorrow; there was a chance that during the day they'd have English people on the phones, and if they didn't Serena seemed to have far more patience with foreigners than Terry could ever muster. But then she didn't have a stressful job to do, unless you called sitting around at home spending his money stressful. If she didn't have any better luck it might be time to move service provider anyway: Terry had seen a couple of TV reports about people being jailed for looking at the sort of thing that helped him wind down after a difficult day, and he thought the longer he had the same connection the easier it would be for some police-state snooper to track what he was looking at. So much for privacy, free speech and human rights!

Serena wasn't in at the moment. She'd gone off in a huff earlier, taking her precious whiny kids with her, but she'd be back. It wasn't a serious argument, only some hysterical bollocks about him having been too aggressive again in bed the night before. He'd explained as patiently as he could – perhaps too patiently as it transpired – that not for the first time she didn't know what she was on about. At the altar, he'd reminded her, she'd said "I will" not "I might, every now and then, if I feel like it" and his conjugal rights were just that. He hadn't even hit her for fuck's sake, just used his weight and the strength of his arms, once they were already in bed, to get what he was entitled to. He couldn't see that it was any different from countless earlier occasions; maybe her head was being turned by her coven of friends or by the programmes she watched on daytime TV while he was slaving away to earn a crust. He suspected she still saw Sonia Kelsey, though she denied it; now there was an obvious man-hater who would turn any woman against her husband given half a chance. He almost pitied Kelsey that he had ever been married to her, except that you couldn't pity a Judas.

Disappointingly there was no word of Kelsey being made redundant after the Globe Two takeover, and in fact it wasn't going to be easy for Terry to pull his own contract, despite what he had told Kelsey on the phone: he had no immediate alternative business partner to turn to and his own bosses (half of them still in nappies) seemed to think that Globe Two's takeover of TLO actually increased its financial strength. There was even a horrible rumour running in the market that Kelsey might be one of the people Globe Two was intending to redeploy to plum jobs in the States.

His mistake, Terry now realised, was to have accompanied Kelsey himself to the *Inferno Club*. If he'd sent Mac it would have been possible to circulate pictures of Kelsey with the Asian tart around the market without his own good name becoming in any way associated with it. If it had ruined Mac, the cocky shit, as well, so much the better. Terry took the photos the *Inferno* people had kindly let him have out of his drawer and, smiling, looked through them once again. Actually there was nothing going on – Kelsey was so out of it that even when the slitty-eyed slapper had his member in her mouth it was as flaccid as you like – but the pictures would have been enough to do for him.

Too bad. In business you had to look forward, not back. Proactive. Now there was a word that Terry usually hated, but it was perfect now. If you wanted something to happen then you had to make it happen yourself. Tomorrow morning, discreetly of course, he would be taking a few minutes out of his crowded schedule to meet a certain gentleman who would be arriving by train from Scotland. Ever keen to help, Terry would give him any information he required, make a few suggestions of his own, then wind him up and set him off.

If everything turned out the way Terry expected then pretty soon it would be party-time. A few drinks to celebrate and then a few more. Then Serena would find out what rough was.

Chapter Fifty-One

Amy wanted to tell Taz that she was cold but Taz seemed to be asleep and Amy didn't dare wake her. Part of what was cool about Taz was that she could be a bit scary, but now that it was dark it didn't seem such a good thing after all. Amy didn't feel that she really knew the girl she was with tonight, or had been with all day, and she didn't think that was entirely or even mainly due to Taz's state of health, though that didn't help: Taz had drifted a lot mentally in the past few hours and her facial skin now looked almost ghostly in the stark fluorescent lighting of the underpass.

Amy's mother had tried to keep her away from Taz and Amy had rebelled against what she had thought was ignorant prejudice and an overbearing parental attempt to continue to control her life too far into her teens; but the truth was, Amy now reflected, trying to shake off the tears that threatened to form in her eyes, that she had nothing in common with Taz and really never had had. Taz clearly both felt and looked at home sitting on the concrete piss-stain-streaked floor of a grey, cold station underpass at the dead of night, using bits of a cardboard box, stuffed with newspaper, as mattress and duvet. She hadn't spoken for hours except to tell her companion what they were both going to do next, and then she didn't listen to any of Amy's suggestions, which were intended to be helpful. Amy had pointed out the CCTV camera in the underpass when they had first arrived there and said that it might be safer to sit under that because people probably wouldn't attack them if they knew they were being filmed, but Taz had simply shaken her head as if this was an idea that was so stupid that it wasn't worth replying to, and gone and sat further along.

Amy wondered why Taz had brought her along at all. She knew that Eva always said that if you were a woman on the streets you didn't want to be alone, that two were ten times safer than one, but Amy couldn't see that she would be able to do very much, if it came to it, to protect Taz: her own upbringing had been too comfortable and easy, involving her in no violence that she could remember, beyond the odd hair-pulling incident at school. She realised as well, with growing unease, that she was so naïve that she probably wouldn't realise anything was happening to her until it was too late. The thing was whether Taz would protect her. To be fair to her, she probably would, or would at least try to, assuming she woke up in time, but she wouldn't have her usual freakish animal strength. Before she fell asleep, Taz had been eyeing the few passers-by with a sort of puzzled indifference, however close they came, and some, all men, had been coming closer than they needed to, given the width of the underpass. Amy didn't look at them but she shuddered anyway.

Amy regularly looked across at Taz to ensure that she was only asleep, was still breathing; it was some comfort to see the vital signs, but what would she do if they suddenly stopped, or the breathing started to sound strange? They had done first aid at school, but nothing like this. Amy felt even more alone, even more frightened.

There was a really scary moment when a whole group of lads about four years older than Amy came down the steps making strange animal shouts, singing loudly and drinking from beer cans, and then hung about in the underpass for what seemed like an age, showing no sign of moving on. Two of them went back up the stairs as though they had lost someone and then came back down a couple of minutes later. Then the group drifted slowly along the passageway, though at any particular moment individuals could be moving in any direction, and they started small fights between themselves and threw beer in each other's faces, and that made the others laugh and applaud. Amy wanted the police to appear, but she didn't think there was any chance that they would, so she tried to make herself as small and inconspicuous as possible, pressed low against the wall, avoiding all eye contact with the young men. And eventually they did all pass by, and it was as though they hadn't noticed Amy and Taz at all. Maybe they really hadn't. Taz hadn't noticed them either: she had slept through the whole thing.

Almost immediately a man in his early thirties in an expensive-looking suit, with an open-necked shirt and the first signs of stubble on a face framed by dark hair just long enough to be fashionable rather than unkempt, came across gesturing with his head towards the departing group of lads.

"Pretty unsavoury looking bunch," he said with a smile in an educated accent, and Amy immediately felt that he was someone from her world, someone that she could trust and who would be able to help her.

"Boys!" Amy smiled back. "All noise. Probably harmless."

The man nodded then squatted down by her side. "Rough night to be without a bed," he said sympathetically. "Can't be easy at your age. How old are you?"

Amy was about to tell him when something made her hesitate. "Guess," she said, strangely elated at having someone at last to talk to.

"About fourteen, I'd say," the man replied with a more serious look in his eyes.

"I'm older than that," Amy told him, but she was a bad liar and she felt herself blush.

"You could be fourteen," the man said, looking Amy up and down in a way she wasn't entirely comfortable with.

"I could be anything you like!" Amy heard herself giggle with embarrassment.

The man nodded slowly and then smiled again. He started to rummage in his pocket, and then produced a large black leather wallet. "Be fourteen for me, then," he said, looking directly into Amy's eyes and holding out three notes. "That's thirty. Without a condom."

Amy continued to smile at the man for the couple of seconds it took her to take in what he was proposing. Then she suddenly felt sick and wanted to cry. But she had a stronger instinct telling her to get out of danger first.

She stood up quickly, which gave her a physical advantage over the still crouching man. She could kick him so that he lost balance, or go directly for the groin, but she hesitated too long and he was able to push himself out of range then get to his feet. The movements woke Taz, who opened her eyes and looked crossly at the scene before her.

The man had quickly recovered his composure and the smile had returned. "Suit yourself," he said calmly. "But you won't get a better offer. I'm quick and I'm pretty gentle."

"Fuck off," Taz ordered dismissively, showing the middle finger.

The man turned to look at her and a sneer developed on his face but he kept his distance. "Fuck you as well," he said. "Look at the state of you. You're so fucked with drugs you'll be lucky to last the night. For you I wouldn't pay thirty *pence*!"

Taz didn't reply and the man turned his back and walked slowly down the passageway as though he had been doing nothing more than passing the time of day.

Taz sat up slightly. "How much did he offer you?" she asked matter-of-factly, with no sense that this might be a painful subject for Amy. "Thirty?"

Amy nodded sheepishly and began to cry.

"With or without?"

Amy didn't want to answer, but Taz repeated the question. "Without," Amy answered almost inaudibly through her tears.

"Fucking cheapskate." Taz looked genuinely offended. "And you're a virgin too. That's serious extra."

Amy did not respond, though she felt sick at the prospect of what Taz might expect her to do once they ran out of money. And she *was* a virgin, though she'd never told Taz that. Among her friends at school they all pretended that they weren't, but she thought that almost all of them were lying.

"I'm not doing...*that* for anyone for any price," Amy screamed. "That's just so... gross and disgusting."

She was halted by the expression on Taz's face, which seemed to express all of the gulf between them. Amy suddenly felt like a spoilt, rich brat. She wanted to qualify what she had said, with something that showed she understood that Taz had had to do all sorts of things to survive, but her instincts instantly told her that this would only make matters far worse, highlight the fact that she, Amy, had two parents who fell over themselves and each other to ensure that she lived in comfort and that she got just about everything she wanted with no effort required on her part. God, how she missed them both now.

Taz suddenly blinked then turned away. She took up her sleeping position again and closed her eyes.

David wasn't going to allow himself the luxury of feeling tired. It was six o'clock in the morning and he had been searching for Amy all night. She was his daughter, and he didn't have any others – not that he seriously imagined that parental love was diluted by being distributed – so he was going to find her and ensure that she was safe. There had been some moments since his split with Sonia when, as a result of particular aspects of his daughter's behaviour, he had tried to persuade himself that he no longer felt the old unconditional love for her, but it was all bullshit. Teenagers could be crueller than any other age group, to each other as well as to their families, and Amy was no exception, but none of that was important. David didn't know whether what he felt was genetically programmed, or whether it mattered if it was. The urge to preserve Amy's life was a stronger emotion than anything he had ever experienced before, stronger even than being in love: that could, and did, pass, but this wouldn't.

Eva was still by his side, as she had been all night. He had been so wrapped up in his own thoughts that he had hardly spoken to her, he now realised. She had just plugged on in her indomitable way, taking him round all the homeless hangouts that she knew and where she thought there was a chance that Taz might have taken Amy. They had been to stations and bus depots, underpasses, narrow alleyways that smelt of rubbish and piss, shop doorways, sheltered car parks, former markets that had been converted into parades of upmarket shops and wine bars, anywhere that, according to Eva, offered the chance of a few feet of unoverlooked space in which to sleep. At David's insistence they had even been to a couple of hostels despite Eva's firmly expressed view that doing so was a waste of precious time.

Eva talked to a lot of homeless people. David was struck by how many of them there were and by the fact that he hadn't previously noticed them. Normally he would have felt sorry for this army of outcasts in overcoats and woollen hats, with the same grey faces and drug- or drink-induced catatonic expressions, but today he didn't have time. It was all he could do not to kick the ones who just grinned when Eva asked whether they had seen Taz, and he was hardly any more tolerant of the ones who simply stared back uncomprehendingly. They *ought* to know where his daughter was. And when the smelly guy with the unkempt beard and leathery face trying to get at food in a huge bin behind a posh hotel seemed to hint that he would know something if it was made worth his while, Eva literally had to restrain David and walk him a few yards away where she calmly explained that the man, who was still looking suspiciously on, was an army combat veteran and, even in his current incapacitated state, both willing and capable of beating the shit out of any City worker. David then wasted thirty pounds, ten at a time, before it became clear that the man in fact knew nothing, and then Eva just pulled on David's arm and he meekly followed her.

He hated all these people and their squalid world. He didn't care how unlucky they had been in life. They were all equally responsible for anything that might happen to Amy. David hated Taz, hated himself for ever having let her within a hundred miles of his daughter. It was all his own fault. Why could he not have passed Eva by, as thousands of other commuters had every day, and even if, like a few, he had felt some sort of need to buy her magazine, what on earth had possessed him to start talking to her and offering her coffee? He wanted to rewind so that none of it had happened. Amy would then be safely asleep at home. David looked at Eva, who was walking briskly towards the next place on her mental list, black marks under her eyes and frown-lines etched on a face that looked like it was suddenly being expected to bear all the troubles of the world. David knew it would be so much easier if he could hate her as well. But the hatred wouldn't come.

Eva suddenly darted into a small newsagent's shop, which was just opening for the day, and came out a minute later with two bottles of water. Until he saw them it had not occurred to David how thirsty he was. He drank the whole litre in less than a minute while Eva silently and dispassionately looked around and collected her thoughts. The water seemed to release the fatigue in David's whole body and for the first time he was aware of the pain in his feet. He wanted to cry, but momentary eye contact with Eva told him that they did not have time for weakness, either physical or mental. He looked at her again just because it seemed to give him comfort. He gave up trying to hate her once and for all.

David looked at his phone. It had rung several times during the night, Sonia each time, desperate for news that he didn't have, but at least with no bad news of her own to pass on. The recrimination in her voice had been restrained but unmistakable. There would be a verbal flaying later on, once Amy was found safe and sound, but he could put up with that; it was such a small price to pay.

David and Eva were now in a non-descript grey-concrete shopping area of a largely Asian part of North London. A desultory group of men, young and old, was starting to unlock doors and peel back shutters, making preparations for the day's trading. The tower of a church along the street was picturesquely silhouetted in the last of the moonlight.

"God has a funny sense of humour," David told Eva bitterly.

Eva said nothing, took another swig from her bottle of water and continued to look around her while she thought through what she - what they - should do next. "Come on," she said abruptly. "There's two stations still to do."

Guy was relieved that the police had stopped asking unpleasant questions about his relationship with Taz – though he wasn't stupid enough to imagine that they were finished with him on that score – and that instead they were involving him in the investigation as though he were some sort of star witness, or at least the best they had for the moment.

Over the past few months he had become used to being no longer of any use or interest to anyone, unless you counted his mother, who was acting mostly out of a sense of duty, and Taz. And now suddenly other people were paying attention to him again, however temporarily, and Guy was having to keep reminding himself that he shouldn't be getting a buzz out of it. He could almost understand the weirdos who confessed to crimes that they had never committed just to get noticed, for the notoriety that it would bring them. He himself wasn't that sad yet – hopefully he never would be – but the rush he was feeling at this instant, even given the miserable circumstances, was so much preferable to the empty nothingness his everyday life was likely to become if Taz didn't return and it was just him and his mother again. Everything and anything was better than that.

He couldn't remember the last time he had been up all night. He had become more emotional during the early hours, had wanted to cry over Taz, over not only what might have happened to her, but the fact that she apparently no longer…it was difficult to put it into words: he'd never thought that she loved him exactly, she was too complicated for that, but there had been some sort of connection between them before, and he couldn't see how that was ever going to be restored now. He remembered the relief at finding that she wasn't hostile to him in hospital, before the terrible realisation that she was looking at him as though he were a stranger. Perhaps he had imagined it. Or maybe it had been because she was weak and tired; maybe things could be the way they were before, once she was found and made well again.

Except he knew that if he really believed that he wouldn't be helping the police: he would be giving whatever assistance he could to David and Eva.

None of the scenarios that involved the police was at all attractive. If they located Taz she would try to run; and if they cornered her, even in her weakened state, she would turn violent. Guy hoped she hadn't managed to acquire a knife. On the other hand, if she was caught, there was going to be all sorts of shit with Social Services. If she *was* under eighteen – and he genuinely didn't know how old she was – then they'd try to contain her in some sort of institution, Guy imagined; and if they succeeded for any length of time sooner or later she'd have another go at slashing her wrists, only this time she might do a better job.

Two days ago seemed like years. And yet as the sun was coming up and a few rays of light were beginning to penetrate the gloom through the undersized windows of the nineteen-sixties concrete bunker in which the police station was situated, Guy found that, as had so often happened to him since the accident, daybreak made emotion give way to reason, and that brought greater clarity in its wake. Now it seemed to him that Taz was so inherently self-destructive that if it hadn't been himself and his unfortunate remark it would soon enough have been someone and something else. The question was, when it happened again, whether she would take anyone else down with her. Did he want to be that person next time round? Maybe it wouldn't be such a terrible thing.

The young policewoman was now coming towards Guy with a friendly smile on her face and two steaming styrofoam cups in her hand, one of which she handed to him. Evidently, Guy reflected, she imagined that he had no short-term memory: a few hours previously she had been all but accusing him of child rape; now she was pretending to be his friend. Well, she wouldn't be the first person in recent months to assume that he was mentally as well as physically disabled.

"Good news," she told him. "Amy switched her phone on. We couldn't get a signal last night, but we've been able to get some idea of the area she's in again this morning. It's a bit confused because it's central London and very built up, but we've got her to within a few hundred yards, and we can make some educated guesses about the most likely places. Why don't you get your mother to come and get you? We'll keep you informed of progress." A more senior male officer beckoned to her from the open doorway. "Looks like we're off now," she told Guy as she put her cup down on an empty table.

"You'll need me," Guy protested. "She'll listen to me."

The woman folded her arms and eyed Guy with suspicion.

"I'm the only one," Guy continued breathlessly. "Really. Otherwise she'll run or lash out and someone will get hurt."

The policewoman turned to look at her boss so that Guy could no longer see her face. After a pause the senior officer simply shrugged and left the room.

There was early and there was fucking early, and this was the latter. Terry could remember when if you got to the office at eight you had the place to yourself for at least half an hour, and a lot of the guys pitched up at exactly nine thirty, if not after. Not any more; now all the kids were falling over themselves to be the first one in: seven thirty, seven, six forty-five even. They lived in daily dread of arriving after their boss, or of leaving before him.

Not that getting up early was ever a problem for Terry. Certainly leaving the house early wasn't. He had no desire to be around when Serena was walking around in a miserable daze as though she didn't know what fucking day it was. And Christ, was she a mess to look at in the mornings these days. By the time he got home she had usually managed to make herself reasonably presentable, but he suspected it took longer and longer, and it was less and less convincing from close quarters. Maybe it was time to trade her in; there was no shortage of fit skirt interested in a bloke as successful as Terry Ransome. Only trouble was that Serena would take the shirt off his back in the divorce court, and he hadn't worked as hard as he had over the years to end up in a bedsit on his tod. He had to be a bit careful.

Serena had come home eventually last night but said that she wasn't talking to him, like it was some sort of punishment. The stupid cow. As if silence wasn't exactly what any man was after from a woman! Most of the time, if it wasn't Serena on the gripe it was the kids caterwauling. Christ, it never stopped, any of it.

No, getting up early was never a problem for TR, unless he had a particularly vicious hangover, but he was too much in control to suffer from many of those. Maybe when he had been younger and greener, but not any more. Control was what you needed; control was everything.

Work was where Terry was most himself, so why wouldn't he get there as soon as he could? Some frigid tart in the office had once told him that there was no way to distinguish him as a person from what he did for a living, as if that was some sort of criticism or something. He'd taken it as a compliment: Terry was about business, and deals, and bargains driven hard; he wasn't a fucking nursemaid or some sort of limp-wristed social worker.

If the people on this train were typical of the sort you got on the six thirty, then Terry doubted that he would be catching it much in the near future. Ignoring the annoying issue that he should be travelling first class anyway but this service (as they laughably called it) didn't have a first-class compartment, the characters in the carriage were a particularly unsightly bunch. There were the crop of sharp-suited, gel-haired youngsters permanently on mobiles, one of whom reminded Terry of Guy from TLO prior to his accident. Some of the others didn't look like they were shaving yet. The remainder, in a variety of tatty, washed-out shirts and jeans, had to be maintenance staff or cleaners or something, going in to open up the offices before the real workers arrived. Hardly any women; no real surprise there, seeing that hard work was involved.

Terry had it figured that, assuming that the train ran on time (and it was a big assumption with the useless fuckers that now ran the railway companies - they were a disgrace to the free market) that he would have plenty of time to wind up the little jockstrap and set him off and still get to the office by eight. If everything went perfectly, there was a good chance that stories of what Rob Roy had been up to would reach Terry via the normal market grapevine by the end of the day. If not, it would only take a day or so more. Terry could be patient that long, though not much longer.

Across the aisle some herbert had just put his trainers on the seat opposite. Terry glared at him: he wondered when good manners had been outlawed. Best not to get him started on that.

He checked his inside pocket for the photos. All there, safe and sound, if a little sweaty. He smiled to himself. What was the phrase from that film: 'cry havoc and let slip the dogs of war'? Yeah, something like that.

Amy was confident that she wasn't going to cry any more. At first she'd been too scared of the way Taz might react if she woke up, and so had kept it bottled up, but Taz had slept for hours, almost without moving, and Amy had found herself constantly listening to her quick, irregular breaths to satisfy herself that her companion was still alive. There had been the odd moment when she had found herself thinking that maybe it would be easier if Taz died, except that the dark had scared Amy since she was a baby, and to find herself alone next to a corpse, in the pitch black, in a confined space, with no means of escape, was going to send her completely out of her head. In any case she didn't hate Taz; not really. She just knew now that Taz's life really wasn't cool and, impossible as it would be to admit it to anyone but herself, that Amy Kelsey belonged more in the comfortable, middle-class world of her parents and schoolfriends than in Taz's screwed-up universe. A lot about Taz now frightened her, not because Taz had actually changed or previously hidden anything, but only because Amy hadn't looked at Taz properly before, hadn't wanted to. She found that for the first time she felt sorry for the sleeping girl, wanted to help her rather than be her. And she also knew that as soon as it was light and the underpass was unlocked she was going to leave, alone, and go back home.

Amy hadn't slept at all. Once or twice she had walked up and down for a few yards when her backside started to hurt or she began to get cramp in her legs, but she had never strayed too far from Taz. She knew that she was doing this out of a desire for self-preservation rather than from any wish to protect the other girl, and she also now understood that this was nothing to be ashamed of.

There probably wasn't any immediate physical danger. Amy didn't think that anyone could get in any more than she could get out - the underpass had been locked at both ends by a tired looking African guy in some sort of blue uniform, who had clearly seen the two girls but not been surprised by their presence - but she couldn't be sure, and she wasn't going to chance being on her own.

She'd taken her mobile out a few times. She'd looked through a few old texts until she realised that they were only making her more homesick rather than comforting her. But the glow from the screen was good, even though it lit little more than the fingers she was holding the handset in. Each time she switched it on she wondered how much longer the battery would last. She dreaded the prospect of hours in total darkness.

Amy was getting hungry, which wasn't really a big deal; but she also wanted to go to the toilet, which was annoying because she never normally needed to in the middle of the night, and it was getting more urgent as time passed. She tried thinking about other things to take her mind off it. She thought about her mum and her friends, and her dad, and sometimes about John, and about the pet rabbit she'd had as a young girl. They all seemed like such warm memories now, and sad because of it, because they were all things that she wanted right at this minute and couldn't have. She thought of Eva too. She liked Eva, a lot; she thought Eva would be out there trying to make everything OK, though she couldn't quite see how. She hoped Eva wouldn't get the blame for all this from her dad; she could picture the two of them together and she liked the image.

Maybe there was a corner of the underpass where she could have a pee. From the smell of the place, she wasn't going to be the first. The idea seemed horrible, though. How could you do it, even if there was any light which there obviously now wasn't, without getting all your clothes messed up? Amy looked through the darkness towards the figure of Taz, still sleeping soundly, and realised the girl must have peed in places like this hundreds of times.

Amy wasn't sure if she dared, but after a lot of hesitation she finally leant across and shone the light from her phone a few centimetres above Taz's face. The little freak looked strangely happy and almost innocent now. No, not even almost: really. Whatever she was dreaming about, and there was movement behind her eyelids, wasn't troubling her.

Amy wasn't going to be able to contain herself much longer. She'd have to pee somewhere. In the morning it'd be really obvious it was her, which would be so embarrassing, and she had decided that she would stand by the entrance and duck out as soon as the shutter was lifted. It couldn't be long now.

She fumbled her way across, sat down awkwardly by the opposite wall and started to take down her jeans. But there was a slope, which meant that if she went here the wee would run towards where Taz was lying. For some reason, despite everything else she was feeling, the idea and the picture of it she had in her head - her squatting down and then a stream of her pee waking up a confused Taz - seemed really funny to Amy. She laughed spontaneously before she could stop herself, and she heard the dead echo of her voice reverberate from the stone wall. She wondered if she had gone mad already.

But now it seemed there was a God after all, because Amy could hear a grinding at the far end of the underpass as the shutter screeched and reluctantly lifted; and then a different man, in the same pale blue uniform as the one who had locked them in, peered indifferently along the tunnel, saw nothing he hadn't seen many times before and retreated.

Amy quickly re-hoisted her jeans and hoped that the man had not seen her. She wanted to run to the station toilets now, but she wondered what would happen if Taz woke up and found her gone. Maybe she wouldn't, except that people could be seen in the distance, coming in through the newly-opened entrance, and even Taz wouldn't sleep for long with a lot of people in such proximity. Amy quickly went over to Taz and, finding that she was scared to touch her, shouted into her ear until she finally woke up.

"They're opening up," she told Taz's puzzled face, "I need a pee. I'll be back in a minute." Amy ran off along the passageway, only slightly troubled by the knowledge that her last words had been a complete lie. At the entrance she stopped momentarily, looked back and gave Taz a small smile.

Taz watched her go impassively. She tried to sit up but it took two attempts. She didn't feel well. She couldn't work out why that was until she saw her wrist and instantly remembered. Her body seemed weak, and her brain didn't seem to be doing what it normally did either. She was shaking slightly too, though so far as she could tell she wasn't cold.

She watched the people going by, and couldn't even be bothered to beg. Very few of them were willing to make eye contact and, if they accidentally did, most of them immediately looked away. A small number, as ever, would hold her gaze, as if they wanted to tell her that it was her own fault that she was sitting there. Fuck them. If they...

Then in an instant everything changed and all those small thoughts evaporated as though they had never existed. Taz saw him. She was immediately certain it was him. He was a fairly nondescript overweight middle-aged man, a face in a swarm of early-morning commuters in an underpass just like hundreds of others in London stations. But Taz recognised him, could have picked him out of the crowd of an entire sports stadium. For a moment she forgot that Amy wasn't there and went to call out to her. No use. The girl had gone and wouldn't be coming back. In Taz's life people left her; that was what they did.

The man saw Taz. He looked at her with what she was sure was fleeting half-recognition, but he seemed totally focussed on something else, checked the inside pocket of his jacket and moved on without even a moment's hesitation.

Taz closed her eyes and pictured a horse in a field. It was a bright summer's day and the sunshine felt warm on her face. She reopened her eyes and felt in her pocket for Amy's mother's kitchen knife. It was still there, hard and cold. Taz used up her last ounce of strength to get to her feet. Patterns danced before her eyes and she breathed in deeply to make them disperse. Now at last she could see, but the middle-aged man had gone. Moving as quickly as she could, her legs heavy and unstable, Taz followed the crowd up the stairs and onto the concourse.

"Oh, Christ," Eva said, using her arm to bar David's progress, "what the fuck is *he* doing here?"

"Who?" David asked, continuing to concentrate on putting the money that he had just withdrawn from a cash machine into his wallet, having spent almost everything he had started the night with on taxis. Eva was now gripping his sleeve in her hand and physically pulling him back.

"Guy!" she replied in an urgent whisper.

"Where?"

"Down there on the concourse. Don't look."

But it was too late. David had looked over the edge of the walkway just as Guy had glanced upwards, and he didn't think there was any doubt that he had caught his eye.

"He saw me."

"Shit."

"It might be good. It might mean we're in the right place."

"Good? With the half of Scotland Yard Guy will have brought with him?"

"Eva," David replied testily, "I don't care if he's brought the whole of the SAS. I hope he has. I want my daughter back." David could hear the emotion in his voice, the fatigue of a night without sleep, the shame and terror at his proven inability to protect his own daughter. He was too tired to conceal it any longer.

Eva let go of his arm and nodded slowly. "You go and talk to him," she said simply.

David's phone rang. It was Guy, frostily telling him that there was no point trying to pretend he hadn't seen him.

"I wasn't going to," David replied equally coldly. "I'll be right down." He ended the call and looked at Eva. He had grown to need her so much during the night that he found he didn't want to be without her now.

"Go," she said. "I'll keep looking. Call you in a few minutes."

David nodded. He wanted to kiss her, but it seemed so inappropriate. He scanned the walkway to work out the most direct way to get to the concourse, saw some stairs a few yards away and made his way towards them, impatiently pushed his way through a crowd that was coming in the opposite direction. He ran down the steps, slowing down only when he reached the concourse and figured that Guy would be able to see him. He walked impassively up to the wheelchair-bound figure sitting by a French bakery kiosk, next to a sign announcing that this was platform ten. "Hi," he began wearily, "what's the news?"

Guy started to speak. He sounded as tired as David felt but he was in better control of his emotions. He said that the police were sure the girls were somewhere in the vicinity. David thought about his wasted night and wondered how long Guy had known this, and why the fuck he hadn't called to pass on what he knew. But he didn't have the luxury of losing his temper, not until Amy was safe. Wordlessly he left Guy and went to speak to a young policewoman standing a couple of yards away.

Terry looked at his watch for the tenth time. He didn't like being kept waiting, particularly by some arsehole of a kilt-wearer who should have been here ten minutes ago. All the Jock needed to do was turn up; Terry had spoon-fed him everything else. What more was he supposed to do? Fucking gift-wrap the photos?

To save time he was now standing on the platform where the train he now figured Braveheart would be on was due to arrive. For the past few minutes he had been aware of the presence of a young girl sitting on a bench at the end of the platform. He was sure that she was the same one he had noticed in the underpass on the way into the station. The bright pink top stood out, not only because of its colour but because it looked too smart for a street kid. So did her jeans and coat, but they also seemed too big for her, so they were probably a charity handout. Her hair was wild and her face pale and druggy. Terry thought he might have seen her somewhere before, but a lot of them looked very similar. He wondered what she might be prepared to do, or have done to her, for drug money. What better way for the Alpha Male to celebrate his forthcoming final victory! The only thing was the kid had sat down as if her legs were going to buckle under her, and since then she had remained motionless with her head in her hands as if she was trying to get the blood back into her brain. She wouldn't be any use if she couldn't walk.

Terry looked along the platform. He thought he could make out the lights of a train in the far distance, though he couldn't be sure, and there was always the possibility that the points would transfer it across to a different platform at the last minute.

He looked around again and saw that the street kid was now on her feet and walking unsteadily towards him. Her face was white and shiny and there were black circles around her eyes. A slight tremor was running through her body. She needed her fix, Terry thought, and she needed it bad; that opened up all sorts of possibilities. She was opening her mouth as if to say something, but her voice was so weak that he couldn't quite make it out. She was pointing at herself and at him.

With a shudder Terry now remembered where he had seen her before, and he stepped back and looked around for an escape route. But the kid was coming closer, shaking her head, trying to smile and saying it was OK, she didn't mind: if he wanted to do it again it was OK but this time it was going to cost him fifty because she needed it, couldn't do it for less. Now she was trying to take his hand, drag him along, but she didn't have enough strength and her skin was cold and clammy. He couldn't quite loosen her grip, though, even when he saw the livid scar on her wrist and tried with his free hand to press against it as hard as he could. The girl howled like a wounded animal, her face became contorted with pain, but she would not let go.

Terry looked around again to make sure that no-one he knew was watching this embarrassing inconvenience, and one of the last thoughts he ever had was that somehow, in a way that he would never be able to understand, David Kelsey had turned the tables, outmanoeuvred and totally defeated him. Because Kelsey was right there, only a few feet away, along with the cripple. And they weren't alone: there were police uniforms all around them, though Terry never got the opportunity to count how many. And here he was in broad daylight, in a public place, in full view of all these people, holding the hand of a young homeless girl he'd previously enjoyed beating to within an inch of her worthless life. It had to be a set up. Yet what didn't make sense was that Kelsey looked as amazed as he was; there wasn't even a hint of triumphalism on his face.

Terry used his full body weight to push against the girl, who lost her balance and, at the same time, her grip on his hand. She fell and now lay squirming on the ground. Terry looked from one police face to the next to see whether they would buy the idea that he was a respectable businessman being harassed by a beggar, but their expressions gave nothing away. Everyone was advancing towards him now, but it was as though everything was in slow motion with no soundtrack. Kelsey and the cripple were shouting at the girl, as if calling a name, and she was still on the ground but now she was looking up at Terry. She was taking something out of her pocket, and as she tried to get up, Terry saw something that looked like the glint of a blade. He instinctively kicked the kid in the face as hard as he could and knocked her senseless onto the concrete.

Now Terry was confident he could talk his way out of this, because the kid was clearly deranged; was carrying a knife; had been trying to rob him. But suddenly there was something a lot more pressing to deal with: a wheelchair was being driven straight at Terry, occupied by a young man whose hauntingly calm expression suggested that he knew and accepted that this moment would forever define him; that he at last understood what the previous twenty-seven years had been for.

For a split second Terry was distracted by the incipient air-rush of something behind him, and he failed to take evasive action. When the wheelchair hit him full on he lost his balance; along with the wheelchair and its occupant he was carried backwards over the edge of the platform and down onto the track, just as the train carrying the man he had made such careful plans to meet was slowing down before the buffers.

Postscript

"And two more beers."

The Indian waiter nodded slightly, picked up a tray that now contained only a few crumbs of poppadom and moved away. The young man who had given the order began to take off his tie in preparation for the arrival of the food; he noticed that his companion had merely tucked his own inside his shirt but he found the resulting look faintly comical, like something you might do at school; it wasn't an image that for his own part he wanted to project in a restaurant that was full of market people. Not really top people - it wasn't expensive enough for that - but mostly people of their own generation, guys around thirty, starting to make it.

"Well, thanks, Hugo," the other young man was saying. "I appreciate it." He raised his bottle of beer in salute to his companion, who reached across and half-heartedly clinked his own against it. "Here's to the continuation for another year of the relationship between RN&R and Carson's, and..."

Hugo waved the toast away with the same small, impatient movement of the hand that he had used when the waiter had been trying to get him to choose side orders, and the cynical smile on his face told his fellow diner that he hadn't been invited out today to exchange pleasantries.

"Yeah, yeah, yeah," Hugo said, "never mind all of that, Adam. What was it like?"

"What?"

"What do you think?"

"The funeral?"

"Ten out of ten. You're obviously management material."

Adam sighed and looked round the restaurant. If he had known that Hugo only wanted to talk about Guy's funeral he would probably have pretended to have another appointment, particularly as it never looked good to be available for lunch at only a couple of days' notice. But he supposed he should have guessed: no-one at the moment seemed to want to talk to him

501

about anything else. Interest in the whole saga, which had immediately gripped the market with rumour and counter-rumour like nothing else he could remember in his eight years in the City, appeared to be showing no sign of waning. Quite the opposite: there seemed to be an almost insatiable appetite for any snippet of new information, only increased by the fact that the funerals had now taken place.

Adam scratched his head and tried to look bored. "What's to say?" he asked laconically.

Hugo smiled in a way that suggested he was prepared to humour his companion for the moment. "Who was there?" he suggested. "Who wasn't there? How many people? Who said what, on or off the record?"

Adam rubbed his eyes for a moment. "OK," he said as if rehearsing an answer he had given several times before, which indeed he had. "I suppose there were about twenty people there."

"From the market?"

"A few from TLO."

"Globe Two UK."

"Yeah, well you know what I mean."

"Stevens?"

Adam shook his head. "There was a girl someone said was Simon's secretary who seemed to be in tears, particularly when the curtains closed. But none of the top people were there. Go figure: it's a very big embarrassment for them. I mean, in the circumstances, they could probably have coped with the suicide side of it, but you know the fact that he, well, you know…"

"Murdered one of their business producers?"

Adam emitted a short nervous laugh; it was odd to hear it stated so bluntly. "Yes, well, if it was. I mean, to be fair, as far as I know, the police haven't actually said it was deliberate, I mean either to kill himself or Terry Ransome."

Hugo smiled knowingly again. "Go figure," he said softly, mimicking his companion.

A different waiter turned up with some samosas, kebabs, chicken wings and naans as well as two tall beer bottles. He pushed plates around on the table until everything fitted. Hugo and Adam stopped talking while he was there but otherwise made no effort to acknowledge his presence.

"No-one else from the rest of the market?" Hugo asked once the waiter had gone, taking a bite from a samosa as he spoke.

"Not that I recognised," Adam replied, trying at the same time to prevent the juice from a chicken wing running down his chin.

"David Kelsey wasn't there?"

"I don't know what he looks like, apart from the picture that appeared in the papers, and I'm told that was quite old. But I think a couple of the TLO/ Globe Two people were saying that he wasn't. They weren't clear whether it was his choice or Guy's mother or something to do with the investigation."

Hugo nodded. "So Guy's mother invited you, then?" he asked casually, reaching for a bowl of chutney, as if the answer didn't particularly interest him.

Adam pretended to have a mouth too full to allow him to talk while he tried to work out what Hugo's agenda was, what he knew already, and how best to respond. The question was whether Hugo was simply annoyed that he had not been invited to the funeral - he had undoubtedly been closer to Guy than had Adam during Guy's time at TLO, though neither of them had seen him since the accident - or whether he knew that Guy had been texting Adam at the time of his crash, and was either trying to get Adam to admit it or was just enjoying watching him squirm. Frankly Adam couldn't see how it could reflect badly on him: it wasn't as though he hadn't forced Guy to text him while he was driving; he hadn't even been aware of it at the time. But it was a notoriety he judged he could do without at

503

this stage of his career. He had done what he thought was the honourable thing by turning up and offering his condolences to the bereaved mother in person without actually introducing himself. If anyone asked him, and a few had, he said that Guy's mother seemed to cope pretty well: she didn't break down, she greeted everyone very courteously and thanked them for coming; but when you got up close to her she looked weary, sad and very, very lonely.

"She did," Adam finally replied to Hugo's question. "He didn't have any other family as far as I'm aware. I mean, not close family. I think there may have been some cousins and uncles etcetera at the service."

Hugo nodded slowly. He briefly made eye contact with his companion but his gaze was no longer probing. He licked his fingers then wiped them on a serviette. "No sign of any runaway kids and bag ladies then?" he asked as an impish grin spread across his face.

Adam was relieved that the questioning no longer directly concerned himself. "Not that I noticed," he laughed, "and I imagine I would have."

"It's a bizarre story, though, isn't it?" Hugo went on. "I've heard so many versions of the story, ignoring on the news, I mean just around the market."

"I know," Adam agreed, pausing to take a large swig of Indian beer. "Rumour now is that the kid had had a row with Guy and ended up in hospital."

"He'd never struck me as the violent type."

"Yeah, but being like that I guess you must get depressed and it's easy to see how you could go off your head a bit."

"Granted," Hugo nodded. "But how do you beat someone up if you're in a wheelchair?"

Adam shrugged. "Maybe he used some sort of implement, sort of when she wasn't looking."

"Pretty rough on a kid."

"The police said she was eighteen. In the paper."

"Well, whatever. Either way you can't condone him a) shagging her and b) knocking her about."

"Well, no, I wasn't," Adam replied hurriedly, wondering whether he was being manoeuvred into saying something that he didn't mean so that it could be reported round the market this afternoon. "What I don't understand is what his mother was doing while all this was going on. I mean, she must have known."

"I don't know. Maybe anything to keep her son happy and out of her hair."

"Takes some believing, though, doesn't it?"

"Maybe."

"And what I also don't understand is exactly where David Kelsey and Terry Ransome fit into it."

Hugo looked slightly discomfited that he was now being expected to answer questions rather than ask them. "I don't know," he said with an open gesture of his hands, "other than the fact that they knew each other, used to be quite close friends apparently, and both knew Guy. Maybe the kid was just trying to find a way to get away from Guy."

"What, by contacting *his* friends? That doesn't make any sense. No-one in their right mind would have gone to Terry Ransome for sympathy."

Hugo snorted derisively. "Well, she wouldn't know that, would she, poor little cow. Why else is Terry there and why does Guy attack him?"

Adam looked mystified. "I agree it doesn't make sense. No, but there's more to it. I've heard from a number of sources now that Kelsey was shagging the kid's mate, the bag lady, and she was also living with Guy at one point."

Hugo wiped his mouth on the large white cloth napkin then put it down and raised his hands. "Then I've no idea. I give up."

"Someone told me Globe Two were shipping Kelsey out to Atlanta," Adam ventured.

Hugo shook his head slowly and deliberately. "That was before all this. All bets are off now: he's on indefinite leave, but no-one thinks he's coming back. I mean, can you imagine, with Globe Two's carefully polished image, chairman's charitable foundation and all that shit? Apparently Steve Allen had the job of telling Tad Crocker what had happened and the dude went absolutely ape, was gonna fire just about everyone in the London office. Someone was trying to tell me yesterday that Kelsey and the bag lady had started a decorating business, but that's probably a pinch-of-salt job. I mean, who the fuck would hire them?"

"Well," Adam commented ruefully. "At least David Kelsey is still alive. More than Terry can say."

"True," Hugo agreed with an ironic grin. "Difficult to say anything at all if you're dead! I heard his wife was very upset at his funeral. Wanted to throw herself on top of the coffin. Was shouting about Guy rotting in hell and threatening to dig him up apparently."

"Oh, well," Adam smiled cynically, "I'm sure at least she'll have some financial compensation to take away the pain."

"Ah, now that's the other thing," Hugo said brightly, as though he finally had something original that he wanted to pass on. "According to Mac, who I bumped into last night in *Kimono's,* she might be in for a nasty shock there."

"Would you trust anything that weaselly little shit told you?"

"Not normally: I mean, I'd count my fingers if I ever inadvertently shook hands with him. But I can't see what he'd gain by lying about this."

"So what's he saying?"

"Basically that Terry was drowning in debt. Tried to have the lifestyle that he thought he ought to have, but couldn't do the deals to deliver it. Big house, flashy cars, private school fees to keep the wife happy and impress friends and neighbours, but by the end he had hardly any business except one big deal with Kelsey at TLO, and even then he'd screwed up the negotiations over the commission rate. And Globe Two probably wouldn't have renewed it."

"Why's Mac so pleased about that?"

Hugo shrugged. "Mac hated the way Terry tried to treat him as his boy. He's about our age, has his own deals, same as we all do. Terry was last year's news as much as David Kelsey was."

"Perhaps Terry killed himself," Adam suggested, unable to prevent himself thinking aloud.

Hugo threw back his head and laughed. He checked to see that he hadn't inadvertently spat some food onto the table. "Right," he said sarcastically. "He knew that Guy was going to drive a wheelchair at him at high speed as he was standing on a platform as a train came in. Or maybe Guy was in fact trying to save him and it all went tragically wrong. Or maybe they had made a secret pact between them because they thought the future of the market was klutzes like you and they just couldn't bear it any more!"

Adam smiled back good-naturedly. His attention was now focussed on the sizzling dishes of food, preceded by a delicious smell of hot spices, which were heading in his direction. The small part of his brain that was not at this moment devoted to curry resolved not to be available for lunch the next time Hugo called.

The gardener didn't see it as part of his job to interfere. For a start they didn't pay him enough to risk getting himself injured, or worse, and secondly the people he would be defending were dead already; so whatever happened to them, or to their graves, wasn't going to make much difference to them now. Maybe that wasn't a very Christian thing to think, but despite - or perhaps because of - his job he had never been especially religious.

He was accustomed to finding empty bottles on the graves in the mornings, where groups of lads had been, or couples, and sometimes he found condoms too. It was disrespectful, but it was nothing new; people had got up to the same when he had been young himself except that in those days they often hadn't had the condom and had lived to regret it. The syringes were more recent, but that was another story.

So usually his policy was to live and let live. Generally people didn't bother him and he didn't bother them. If someone was up to something, the sight of him was normally enough to make them scarper. There were really bad things, like actual vandalism of headstones and the like, but thankfully that tended to take place at night, when he was miles away at home. It wasn't nice to see the expression on the relations' faces when they saw the damage, and it created extra work for him to boot, but such was the way of the world.

Generally during the day, though, he kept himself to himself and just quietly worked round the grieving relatives who came to pay their respects to the departed. There were some, mainly elderly ladies, who visited every day, and others who turned up at the same time each week. And then there were some who came a lot when the grave was fresh but whose visits soon tailed off. And again there were some plots that never received any visits at all, and although the gardener did not regard himself as a sentimental man (quite the opposite in fact, for much the same reasons that he was not religious), he did sometimes make a point of tidying around those graves a little better than the others because he knew that no-one else was going to. He figured that if there was a God after all, then these little acts couldn't do him any harm.

At this precise moment, though, he was feeling a little uneasy. He was continuing to work, raking some leaves which had blown in yet again from the overgrown weeping willows in an adjacent garden. At the same time, out of the corner of his eye, he was monitoring the activities of a small teenage girl in an oversized grey hoodie, who was standing motionless in front of one of the newer graves, a position she had maintained for almost ten minutes now. The gardener had not seen her before; the only previous visitor to this plot had been a lady of advanced middle age, probably the mother, who came with fresh flowers about once every four weeks, and usually trimmed around the stone in a business-like manner with the shears she brought in a striped plastic carrier bag. She never stayed very long. The gardener had never spoken to her, but he had the impression that she wasn't the sort who wanted to stand and reflect.

There had been some story around the time of the funeral that the son might have killed himself by throwing himself under a train, another that it had been an accident. For a short time people had pointed out the gravestone to one another. Someone had said that it had made the papers and the local TV news. Well, if it had, the gardener hadn't seen it; the news was usually depressing, and after a day's work he wanted to look at something more cheerful.

If it wasn't for the fact that the teenage girl had been standing stock still for so long, the gardener would have been sure that she was up to no good. There was something hard and determined about her features, and also what you might call a defensive aggressiveness about the way that she carried herself. More troubling was the fact that she seemed to have a male companion: a much larger unkempt, long-haired, unshaven type in his mid-twenties, who was pacing up and down in the bushes a few yards behind the girl, smoking one cigarette after another - which wasn't allowed: there were large signs that you couldn't miss - and stubbing them out on the grass, which was a serious fire risk. Yet for all his obvious impatience, it was clear that the young man wasn't about to disturb the girl.

The gardener relaxed; he couldn't see that there was any real mischief that the two of them could be getting up to. Maybe the girl was the dead boy's sister, except that there was no way she could be related to the mother. Well, he didn't know, and he never would know, and he didn't care; he had more than enough work to be getting on with.

But now suddenly the girl had run across to the next grave along and she was taking flowers from a vase; and now she was going onto the next plot and doing the same again, except that this time she had knocked the vase flying and didn't seem to be about to set it upright again. She was moving on once more, literally leaping from grave to grave, collecting more and more flowers as she went, until she had amassed a chaotic multi-coloured bundle that she peered through and held tightly clasped closely to her chest, with blooms and stalks pointing in all directions.

Still carrying his rake the gardener moved reluctantly and gingerly towards the girl. When he was still two graves away from her she suddenly noticed his presence, turned and looked directly at him, tensed and bristled. The gardener saw her stance and the raw determination written across her hard little face, and the little courage that he had found instantly left him.

He instinctively backed away, but the girl now seemed in two minds as to whether or not to confront him. She stared angrily at him for several seconds. Then the anger seemed to fade and she looked down at the flowers she held as though they were precious jewels and stooped to pick up a couple that had slipped through her small fingers. The gardener breathed out and felt the tension ease in his muscles. But it seemed that he had relaxed too soon because now the boyfriend was coming over, and things seemed about to get nasty. The gardener tightened his grip, with both hands, around the handle of his rake; he hoped that would be enough to make the other man think twice.

But the girl was no longer concerned by anyone else's presence. She ran across to the grave she had spent so much time looking at and gently dropped all the flowers on top of the stone. She stood motionless once more, for what seemed an age. The gardener's eyes were drawn to her; at the same time he remained nervously aware of the presence of the unkempt young man, who had halted some ten feet away, and whose stale scent carried in the wind.

The girl was looking towards them both, and you could see from her eyes and her cheeks that she had shed some tears. Watching the gardener, she started warily to move away; then, when she perceived it was safe to do so, she turned her back and broke into a run. The boyfriend held a lit cigarette out between his fingers in the gardener's direction and gave him a final menacing look. Then he too turned on his heels and ran after the girl.

The gardener leaned against his rake and watched them go, followed them with his eyes as they ran along the inside of the brick perimeter wall, past the chapel, towards and then through the exit gate. He saw them meet up outside and slow to a walking pace. The wall partially obscured the view, but he continued to observe them until they were lost in the shadow of the trees beyond. He breathed out and felt his body relax.

It didn't take too long, with a little guesswork, to restore the purloined flowers to their rightful owners. But the blooms that the young man's mother had brought three weeks previously had died off and become brown, dry and brittle, so that at the last moment the gardener changed his mind. Looking round to ensure that he wasn't observed, and with the image of the proud, determined young girl in his mind's eye, he left one small red carnation on the stone where she had laid it.